# Uncommon Justice

by

Roe

PublishAmerica
Baltimore

First printing

ISBN: 1-59129-368-5
PUBLISHED BY PUBLISHAMERICA, LLLP
www.publishamerica.com
Baltimore

Printed in the United States of America

*To Caira, Lora, Roman and Ella*

# Prologue

## Part 1

"Do it again, Daddy, do it again."

The man smiled broadly at his son.

"Here it comes, Kenny." He put the old limber glove up in front of his face and held the frayed ball in place with one hand. His blue eyes peered out over the tips of the grass-stained leather fingers. Quickly he looked to the left, then to the right, then behind, acting like he would throw the ball if he had to.

The little boy started giggling. "Come on, Daddy," he said. "Throw the ball! Throw the ball! Throw the ball!"

"Got to check the bases for runners, son; they might steal."

"Daddy, come on, they ain't gonna steal," the boy said. "I already told 'em not to."

Daddy smiled. "Oh, I'm glad you told me, son—don't have to worry about 'em now."

The boy smiled and nodded his head.

Daddy assumed an animated pitching stance, sticking his rear out and burying his face in the glove. The little boy took a couple of swings, slicing the hot summer air with his Louisville Slugger. Then he tapped it once or twice on home plate, which was an old piece of canvas from a trailer tarp.

"I'm ready, Daddy," he said. And he waited patiently, looking at him intently, wondering when the ball would come.

Daddy went into a wild exaggerated wind up; his right arm whirled around like a windmill out of control, then he whirled it back the other way and finally released the ball. His light underhanded pitch drifted slowly toward the boy. The little boy concentrated on the white speck as it came toward him. He squinted in the late afternoon sun.

*Swoooooosh.*

The little boy nearly fell down after his bat cut through the air. The ball lumbered on by and thudded into the ground behind him and rolled into the garden.

*Awwwwee.* His face folded in defeat; the little boy stared at the hard-packed ground around home plate, his eyes full of disappointment. "I missed it," he said quietly, thinking his daddy hadn't noticed.

"Wow," Daddy said. "You almost knocked one right out of the park."

The little boy looked up surprised. "I did?"

"You did," Daddy said.

"Yahooo…yahooo…didi didi do." The little boy danced in a triumphant jig around home plate, his arms raised, pushing the bat up in the air, clutching it with his little thin hands.

"Hehe, haha, wooode wooode weee, I'll knock the ball out of the park and into the trees."

The little boy skipped back to the garden and sang his song over and over, proud his Daddy almost saw him hit the big one. He grabbed the ball laying in between cornrows and ran out as fast he could. The scarecrow, with his black patch eyes and corncob nose stared down at him. He thought he heard the scarecrow tell him to get out. But, he could have been wrong about that.

He threw the ball hard as he could back to Daddy. It went about eight feet before it slapped into the freshly cut green grass.

"Good throw, Kenny boy, good throw," Daddy said. He jogged up near home plate and plucked the ball from the ground.

At the same time, the spring on the screen door creaked from the back porch and a small woman in a faded floral dress appeared, an apron tied to her slim waist.

"You two gonna have time for fried chicken or are ya gonna play baseball all evenin'," she said. A grin spread over her face.

The little boy looked up at his momma. "Me do! Me do! Me do!" he cried. He threw the bat down and skipped part-way to the house and then spurred into a gallop like an unbroken Shetland pony.

Daddy tucked the glove up under his arm and gathered the bat and ball. He walked toward the little white farmhouse smiling, a large oak tree devouring his shadow as he passed underneath.

"Good game, Kenny," he said. He tapped the boy gently on the top of the head with his old glove.

"Good game, Daddy, good game," the little boy said.

"You should've seen me, Momma, you should've seen me. I hit a big one!"

# Prologue

## Part 2

"Get yer ass inta dat house boy." He stood and looked at him, his eyes bearing down in a cruel stare. "By Gawd if I have ta tell ya ont more time...get ya lazy ass in dat house!"

The tall thin man stared at him, pointing his finger toward the house. "Get yer ass a goin' boy, or by Gawd so help me I'm gonna learn you'in a lesson. I'm gonna a learn you'in a lesson good."

The boy trembled before the towering man, not knowing whether to go in the house and take it, as he had on so many other occasions, or run. He stood for a time thinking about what he would do.

Finally, he said, "I ain't gonna...I ain't gonna take another one of your whoopins, ain't gonna, Daddy Jerry."

The man's face compressed to stone. His brows furrowed. His hands clinched tightly, one wrapped firmly around a lineless fishing pole.

The boy began backing away, one foot carefully and slowly placed behind the other, knowing if he slipped, Daddy Jerry would be on top of him.

"Gawddamn you, Jimmy...gawddamn you, boy. Come ta me right now!"

"Ain't gonna do it...ain't gonna go in that house no more...only bad things happen in that house."

The man inched his feet forward, trying to make the movement unnoticeable to the boy. But the boy did notice, and would slip one foot behind the other, when Daddy Jerry moved his. He kept his front to him, afraid to show him his back. Their eyes were locked in a dead stare, neither blinking, as the sweat rolled from their brow. It was a duel that went on for nearly twenty minutes in the cruel hot afternoon sun.

Finally, the man eased a bit and didn't move. It made the boy nervous.

"Boy, I'm gonna give you'in a chance ta do what's right by me."

The boy stared at him for a moment then shook his head *no*.

The man gave him a wily grin. "My granddaddy always said if ya get a horse that won't take ta the bridle, then all ya got left ta do is ta beat the horse about ta head," he said. "You can write it down, you little shit, I'm gonna beat ya about the head with dis here rod. I'm gonna put a bridle right ta yer mouth boy, right ta yer mouth."

The boy was scared, and started moving back quickly now, but not wanting to turn his back on him. Daddy Jerry was lean, with long legs. Legs that were made for running, and for chasing, and with them, he had a good chance of running the boy down.

When the boy ran from him, usually the he would catch him. But sometimes, if he made it to the woods, he would get away. For the times he didn't, well, he prayed to God he would help him and come and save him. But God never did. He would take a beating that not even God could watch, he thought. That's why he didn't come; he was sure of it. The shame of man so great he had to turn away.

"All right, ya little shit, I warned ya, now yer gonna pay, yer gonna pay me in skin."

Suddenly, the man lunged at him, grabbing a clump of sweat soaked cotton t-shirt with one horn nailed hand. The boy jerked and turned and twisted and began to run. Off balance, the man fell forward; his body clapped on the hard-packed earth. The boy bucked stoutly away from him, pulling from his outstretched grasp; his shirt tore away.

He ran as hard as he could, nearly falling down at first, but gained his footing. Daddy Jerry, pushed himself up by his arms and jumped to his feet. A package of Pall Mall cigarettes worked out of the pocket of his sweat-drenched cowboy shirt and tumbled to the ground.

He ignored them and ran behind the boy, his long legs making up the distance in the open crop field, until he was near behind him. He whipped the fishing pole back and then forward as he ran, trying to strike the boy. The rod ripped through the air, but caught nothing, only slicing the powdery loose soil, the dust rising up around the cut it made in the earth.

The boy's feet slapped into the soft soil of the field, his heels kicking up clumps of dirt. He ran toward the woods, knowing his chances were better there. Daddy Jerry watched as he started to lose distance, his lungs heaving moist warm air into them, his legs more sluggish and weary, sweat streaking down his face.

The man let his legs come gently to a stop, as he watched the boy disappear into the woods. He crumpled over, his hands leaning on his knees, his eyes pulsating; the boy was gone.

He raised a fist above his head and shook it. His breath now eased a bit. "Gawddamn ya boy…gawddamn ya! You'll come out of those woods sooner or later. Tonight…tomorrow, it don't matter, cuz I'll be waitin on ya, boy…waitin!"

The man stared a long time at the woods, sweat running off his nose in a trickle from his brow. After a while, he shook his head, turned, and walked slowly back across the crop field, defeated.

# Chapter 1

He was the kind of man you wanted to stare at for a long time, to examine every inch of his features, to wonder how he arrived at such a misfortune in life.

The old man definitely inspired curiosity, much the same way as a two-headed baby might in a freak show. It left one to wonder what sick demented specimens of nature were guilty of producing such a perverse monster. But perhaps the old man was the guilty one. No one would probably ever know, at least that's the way Kent saw it.

His long salt and pepper hair clung together in greasy strings bouncing about his beard. It was thick and carried the evidence of the morning's forage for food in the local garbage cans. His grizzly-darkened hands, nails dirt packed and fingers only showing flesh tone in the cracks of his skin gripped possessively the shopping cart he pushed. The left wheel flopped wildly back and forth as he crossed the street slowly.

*God in heaven, what an animal*, Kent thought.

Gray tape held his worn wing-tip dress shoes together; one heel flopped about with each step. He looked as if he wore several sweatshirts under a worn and faded denim jacket, his elbows exposed through the frayed holes in the fabric. The jacket contrasted greatly with the old blue Dickie pants that were way too short for him, exposing his dirty sockless ankles. The buttocks and knees were nearly worn white.

He thought about the passage in the Bible that said, "If your eye offends you, pluck it out." Well he damn sure wasn't going to do that, but this old man did his best to offend his eye.

He didn't want the old man to catch him looking. What if their eyes met? Then the old man might recognize the look of contempt on his face. His curiosity might be betrayed. He probably saw those same eyes, full of the same contempt a hundred times a day, by those who might be misfortunate enough to pass by him. *His eyes*, he thought, *they would give him away.*

But yet there was something familiar about him and he couldn't look away, something in his mannerisms that he knew. He watched him intently with great fascination from the safety of his car, trying not to look directly at him, but not away from him either. He was cautious, and sure the old man didn't suspect his examining eyes. As he passed by him, he leaned forward in his seat trying to make out his features through the forest of thick unruly hair. It sickened him.

Inspecting him closer he felt sure he had seen him before, that he was a memory somewhere lost inside him, but couldn't place it. It was a connection not yet known and it bothered him. Was it possible he knew him at sometime, somewhere? *God, he hoped he wasn't adopted and this was his real father. What a shitter that would be.* He grinned to himself.

The light turned green and he waited for the old man to clear the street. He watched him, his hunched back now turned to him; he figured it was safe to stare. He did it egregiously.

Then abruptly the old man turned toward him and delivered a thinly veiled smile.

*He knew.*

His eyes were penetrating, his stare unyielding, his mouth grizzly.

*But what did he know?*

Kent quickly turned away. His heart galloped wildly in his chest like it would leap from his drumming throat at any moment. *Did he know him?* he wondered. *Who the hell was he?* Something hidden behind those eyes made him scared to look at him again; they were ominous, and his planned smile creepy. He watched in the rearview mirror, horrified that the old man never let the car leave his sight. He continued to watch him until the distance swallowed him up in the rearview mirror. His breath was tense and uneasy; his hands tightly clutched the steering wheel, until it caused him jabbing pain. He ransacked his mind trying to remember the old man, but the memory was too deep and hidden and wouldn't show itself; all his head could produce was uninformed thoughts.

The wind picked up and soon the rain began to fall in heavy blankets: the droplets like pebbles falling in thin air, pelting his windshield. Suddenly, without warning, a distant memory slowly came to him, horrid, troubling, and blinding in cruelty; it violently surfaced from his youth. The hideous recollection sent a chill through him and he felt a cold tickle in his heart.

He forced the putrid thought from his head, only to have it stubbornly return again, this time worse. He winced at it with shame and disgust. He closed his eyes momentarily and held his breath, forcing the memory away. He hoped to God he would never think of it again; that it would stay buried like it had for all these years. And he hoped, in his selfish heart, the old man would crawl off somewhere and die.

# Chapter 2

Jagged arcs splintered across the inky clouds. An orange tinge bathed the contents of the late evening in a soft glow. Little dark tails dipped from the low hanging clouds, dancing about and then disappearing from where they came.

The truck shook as sudden gusts of wind swept across the road. The fog swallowed up its windshield and the rain pelted it unmercifully. Through it he watched the black tails begin to droop down lower from the clouds again. It sent little tingles of fear up the back of his spine and stung his neck. The storm promised to be unforgiving, which is quite typical of Oklahoma storms.

Kent Jackson was coming down off his beer buzz and drifting somewhere between drowsiness and a headache. The road was a blur of black asphalt, bright yellow lines and shimmering sheets of rain bouncing off both. He could barely see three yards in front of him. After that there was nothing but the gray hue of rain.

He thought he might pull over at one point, but dismissed the idea. He thought about the old man he had seen in the city, with the shopping cart and his glassy stare and nefarious grin. He didn't want to stop anywhere, on any road after seeing him. *He was the type you would take for a ride*, he thought, *the kind of ride you don't come back from*. No, he wasn't stopping.

He was tired and wanted to get home. If he had known it was going to start a downpour, he would have never left the bar. The sun was just out twenty minutes ago. But here he was, the rain, the road and him; but he would make the best of it and suffer through the worst the storm could offer.

A long ash dropped from the cigarette he was holding and fell onto his lap. He sat up abruptly and brushed vigorously at his crotch and legs, looking down to see exactly where the ashes went. He heard a muffled thud and looked up just in time to see his truck halfway on to the shoulder and heading into the grass. He couldn't see well out the passenger side window, it was covered in a cloudy film, as was the lower half of the front windshield. He jerked the steering wheel abruptly to the left, not knowing how far he had drifted.

The mud grabbed his tires and the Toyota 4Runner began to fishtail. He turned the wheels hard to the right, and then quickly back to the left trying to correct the out-of-control vehicle. His left front tire caught the asphalt, launching his truck onto the road again and across the center medium. He jerked his wheels to the right, putting the truck into the left lane; his tires gripped the blacktop and he accelerated on down the road.

After driving a ways, he was curious as to what the sound was he heard while on the shoulder of the road. *Perhaps he kicked up a rock and it had hit the undercarriage of the truck*, he thought, *or maybe a deer had broad-sided him*. He didn't know, but it felt soft and the sound was muffled.

He looked in the rearview mirror to see if he hit something, to see if maybe there was a deer lying back on the side of the road. Slowing the truck down, he stared intently in the mirror, carefully examining the road behind him. It was hard to see against the thick rain, but then a flash of lightning splintered through the sky, illuminating the road behind him. "Goddamn, what is that?" he said quietly to himself. He pressed his foot lightly on the brake and the Toyota rolled to a stop.

The rain lightened a little and he strained his eyes through it, hoping to see what it was, but sure he saw something there. Maybe forty yards back, maybe more, but something was lying on the shoulder of the road. For a moment he thought about driving on, not sure of what to do. He didn't want to go back, *God knows I don't*. He didn't want to see what was there. About a minute passed by before he talked himself into it.

He dropped the Toyota into gear and reversed back slowly. A knot the size of a plum formed in the lower front of his throat. His hair stood erect on his neck. A light mist covered the back windshield. He strained hard to see through the glass. His pulse raced. Something was wrong, very wrong and he knew it.

He drove closer to the brightly-colored object laying on the side of the road. At twenty yards away, a white flash of lightning highlighted its features. He accelerated faster toward it, clearly worried now, worried about what it might be. At ten yards away, it began taking on a different form. A rush of adrenaline flooded his body as he looked at it, surging through every inch of nerves, burning to their ends. The familiarity of it took his breath away. His hands gripped the steering wheel, arms tightened; he took a long deep breath and closed his eyes. He thought that if he kept them closed long enough, whatever it was would go away. But when he opened them it was still there. He knew what it was now, but he refused to believe. But by God he had to believe, this was real, this was now, he had to act!

He pulled over to the shoulder and threw open the car door with one leg, no longer denying it. He ran around the back of the Toyota, pivoting slightly on its wet surface with his left hand. He slipped on the oily blacktop and careened sideways down the back of the truck, his feet sliding out from beneath his body and laying him out on the road in a heap.

It was then that he saw what it was; the image poured and burned into his mind like hot molten lava. He looked at it not wanting to believe, but he had to believe. *My God, it's a woman!*

He lay there mesmerized for a moment, looking at her body, and then rolled briefly onto his back and glanced up at the darkly grayed sky. It told him it was becoming every bit the darker side of twilight. As he lay there, he felt deep down in his aching soul he was about to see a darkness blacker than any night, he was about to fall headlong into a horrid abyss, from which he would never recover.

He got up on his knees and crawled to her. His mouth gaped open, trying to breathe; his eyes open wide. He reached out a hand and touched her, but she didn't move. He noticed her leg was bent somewhere at the mid-thigh upwards parallel to her torso. *Goddamn, her leg!* The sight of it panicked him and he looked over his shoulder down the street and then past his truck. There was no one but them on the road.

He shook her body gently, like you do when you wake someone up from a deep sleep.

"Can you hear me?" he whispered.

He waited and listened, but she didn't respond.

Another surge of panic rifled through him, as he looked at her, not knowing what to do. It was an unfamiliar role for him. He reached for her hand; it was cold. He let it go and his face folded into a tight grimace.

"Are you all right?" he asked. He raised his voice. "Can you move?" He shook her again. She didn't move and she didn't say anything.

The fear rose in him, swelling like a hot boil on the verge of bursting. His heart began pounding in his chest. *I've got to get hold of myself,* he thought. He breathed deeply and then again. "All right, just turn her over, turn her over and perform CPR and everything will be all right," he said to himself.

He rolled her onto her back; her hair was pasted to her face with mud and blood.

*You can do it...come on.*

He cupped her head in his hand and lifted her up. *Everything will be—*

He was about to reassure himself, but then he felt it, something warm and wet, seeping between his fingers and onto his leg. He didn't have to look; he knew what it was. He put her neck in the crook of his arm. Her head slumped toward his body and a trickle of blood leaked from the side of her mouth. She moaned and coughed for a moment. Her hair fell away. He saw her face clearly, her features were familiar and at that moment he realized who she was.

"Oh my God!" he screamed.

He felt all the blood drain from his head. The wretched talons of panic firmly ripped into his spine; he knew her. It was Tina Hall, his neighbor. She and her husband Jim live down the street, not but a block away.

He looked down at her bloody face; she was gasping for air. Fear bolted through his body again. But suddenly, all he could think about were the consequences if she died. He had been drinking. The evidence was on his breath. It probably wouldn't go over well with the higher-paid help at the firm, if he had a felony on his record, let alone, God forbid, a prison sentence and financial compensation to the grieving spouse. *Goddamn it!* He was in deep shit to his head and he knew it.

He leaned over her and put his ear on her chest. He strained to hear it, the heartbeat, but he couldn't. He gripped her wrist to check for a pulse and after a moment finally felt one. No matter how hard he willed it in those next few minutes, he couldn't make her well again. He looked at her for a moment, thinking about what to do, thinking hard, as she lay dying.

He laid her gently back down on the rain-soaked earth. He stood up and stared at her still thinking, thinking of the consequences, and how his life might be altered, destroyed even, because of this unfortunate accident. *But no one else would see it that way*, he thought—*no*. He would be just another drunk in a car that killed a mother of two and left a husband to raise them by himself. He clenched his fist and looked down the road and then back up—*nothing…no one*.

Her eyes began to flutter and finally they opened. Her mouth moved but she didn't say anything. Her fingers twitched and finally moved. She was conscious.

He fumbled in his pocket for his cell phone, and looked at her as she tried to speak. He thought about how many drinks he had that night; was it four whiskey sours or was it five—he couldn't remember. He knew the consequences; they hit his brain like a ball-pin hammer. *First-degree manslaughter at least*, he thought, *or vehicular homicide*. How many times had he read of similar accidents in the newspaper, people going to jail for the exact same thing. He always thought it was just plain bad luck. Now he was the one out of luck and other people would read about his poor misfortune. Perhaps he could plea down to third-degree manslaughter and do his jail time and probation. *But shit, this is not the way his life is supposed to go, goddamn it! His life would be ruined.*

The horrid thoughts raced through his mind as he watched her for a moment, groaning, laying there dying on the ground. If she lives, she hadn't seen him, he thought. If she dies, there was little anyone could have done, and no one around to point an accusing finger his way. He put the cell phone back in his pocket and right then decided there was nothing he could do for her, that she would probably die anyway. He walked around for a moment thinking, looking around, up and down the road. But no one was there, just them.

He watched the rain droplets gather on the crevices of her face and form dark spots on her fuchsia jogging suit. He knelt beside her one last time, as if to reassure himself that this was what he wanted to do and maybe to see up close that she was going to die anyway. He picked up her hand to find a pulse on her wrist, and unexpectedly she squeezed his hand tightly. It frightened him and he dropped her hand in the mud.

He knew the decision to leave her in God's hands would have deep consequences for her family and loved ones. He felt she was a victim of circumstances and he could not really be blamed. If he called the police now and she died, he would be prosecuted and her blood would publicly taint him the rest of his life. He could imagine himself losing his job, his family reduced to poverty; they would live in shame for what he had done. He couldn't accept that. *No, this is best,* he thought.

Too much time had passed. She would probably die anyway. *To live with this would be a small price to pay for freedom,* he thought. Kent stood up. His decision was made. *If Tina lives, well all the better, the police will never know who did it anyway. If she dies, they still won't know,* he thought.

Having made up his mind he quickly turned from her. A little part of him felt she was staring at him with his back turned, pleading with him not to go, to call for help. The thought sickened him and the knot in his throat became tighter. He felt sorry for what had happened, but nothing could be done to reverse course...not now. He took a couple of steps forward, then turned and looked at her one last time, and then turned back and walked quickly to the driver's side of his truck, his feet splattering water on the asphalt as he did.

He looked up and down the road again, but saw no one. Kent climbed into his truck and sat down in the seat, slammed the door and pulled the gearshift out of park and down into drive and accelerated quickly onto the blacktop from the shoulder of the road.

As he drove, he tried to convince himself what he did was right. Right for himself and for his family, given the circumstances. He knew his rationalization would be considered sadistic by others if ever found out. Even to him it was troubling. But what alternatives did he have that were acceptable. *None*, he thought. *There was nothing anyone could do to bring her back...even if she were to receive the best medical attention right now, she would probably be no more than a vegetable at the least, and a burden and financial drain on her family.* "Yes, everyone needs to think of what is best," he said quietly to himself. "This is for the best…there is nothing I can do about it now."

As he turned off Coventry Road onto Freemont Avenue, he began to wonder what she was doing jogging. He thought about it for a moment and realized she had been caught out in the sudden downpour and was probably trying to get back home. She probably didn't even see or hear him coming. *She was trying to get out of the rain...that's all, before you came by and killed her—you asshole! How could she be laying back there dying... it didn't seem real.* He had just seen her with Jim, not but two or three days ago at the supermarket. But now he is responsible for her dying. *Goddamn it*, the thought of it made him sick.

How would he live with such a horrible thing eating at his conscience? But he had lived with other things before—bad things he had done and he would do it again now. Each time, it became a little harder to keep the lies down and the guilt from coming up. It sometimes stuck in his chest and throat like a bad case of indigestion. The worst of the guilt would churn in him at night, silently creeping into his dreams and murdering his sleep.

*This will add to the fire heap*, he told himself. *This will be a little more difficult to keep down. This will greet you at every waking moment like a bad case of heartburn. You will see her face, her agony, her horror, as she lay dying, every time you close your eyes*, he told himself. *Every time you do, you will see her...as she lay dying.*

But, Kent Jackson would soon discover what is best is not always right and justice sometimes comes in the form of an unyielding double-edged sword. It cutting both ways, one way one time, then wielding back, severing the vulnerable part of a man's fleshy soul, until he is bitterly broken, ravaged and subdued and unmercifully weakened, leaving him surprised and unbelieving when utterly destroyed.

# Chapter 3

Lisa Jackson looked at her husband across the table. He wasn't eating. He stared at his plate.

"What's wrong?"

"Nothing…why?"

"You're quiet tonight."

"It's been a long day."

"Aren't they always."

"Don't start." He looked at her, his brows furrowing, his eyes dim, a hint of anger beginning to burn in them.

"Well, you're not acting like yourself."

He didn't say anything. He returned to picking at his plate.

"Then again, maybe you are acting like yourself," she said. The words darted off her tongue, intending to spear a soft spot in him.

He looked up at her again. He didn't need this tonight.

"Is this what going out with the guys after work and having drinks does to you, or is there something else going on?" The question was meant to let him know she was probing.

"No…look, I'm sorry, I'm just beat. I don't mean to be so distant. I've just had a tough day…and I don't feel very well."

The demeanor of her face changed. Rarely did she ever hear Kent complain about being sick. She laid down her fork and a look of concern spread over her face.

"Where are you feeling bad?"

"My stomach hurts…it has hurt all day."

"Why didn't you come straight home after work? Instead of—"

"Come on, Lisa, you know and I know, I have to meet with clients to stay ahead of the game; that's just the way business is done."

He didn't like to lie to her, not because it morally offended him, but because he had to keep track of all the lies he told and he told too many. After awhile it was hard to keep his stories straight. He only lied when he absolutely had to. Like when he would screw one of his more shapely coworkers during lunch at the local fleabag hotel and Lisa would call while he was out. *Yeah, he definitely had to lie about stuff like that.*

But what he said about being sick wasn't that far from the truth. His stomach rolled as he looked at the spaghetti and meatballs on his plate. It reminded him of the gruesome scene he had just witnessed an hour before; it reminded him of Tina Hall. He could still feel the warm blood flowing through his fingers.

"I thought you looked a little pale tonight. You were so quiet I just didn't know."

"Maybe it's a stomach flu or something," he said.

"It's going around," she said. "Why don't you go on upstairs and take a nice hot shower and then get into bed."

"Yeah…maybe I will…it might make me feel better." This was exactly what he wanted her to say; now he could be alone and have time to think—to gather his thoughts. Think about alibis, about possible explanations, what he had forgotten—if anything. He didn't want to sit around the family dinner table chitchatting about work or what the kids did in school. *No…not after he had just run down the next door neighbor, the mother of two, in his Toyota. No, he didn't want to do that.*

He shoved his chair back and stumbled away from the table and made the long hard climb to the top of the stairs.

"Call me if you need anything," she hollered. Her voice rising up after him. "I can bring—"

"Yeah…okay, I will," and then he closed the door to the bathroom behind him, drowning out the last part of what she said.

The hot streams of water felt good on his body and he tried to keep his mind free of the accident. He focused instead on retracing the events after he got home. *Had he taken care of everything?* he wondered. He didn't know. He had never done anything like this before. He shut his eyes and let his mind drift over the course of the evening.

*Okay, the car, it was a little fucked up, some minor scratches, a small dent, he would take care of it later.* His clothes and shoes were a mess. It looked like he had killed half a dozen people in them and crawled through a jungle to do it. They were rain-soaked, muddied and had large patches of bloodstains scattered over them. His shoes were mud-caked and splattered with blood. He would have to get rid of them too, he told himself.

When he came home, he had taken all of his clothes off down to his boxers in the garage, watching the door closely as he did, hoping to God his wife wouldn't get curious and open the door and ask why he wasn't coming in. Or better yet, why he was standing in his underwear out in the garage? He had tossed his dress coat in a storage cabinet, along with the clothes and shoes, and shoved them down underneath a pair of old coveralls and oily rags and a cardboard box.

He had slipped in the back door from the garage. His wife was warming his dinner in the kitchen. The kids were watching an old rerun of *Perry Mason* in the living room. Wearing nothing but horseshoe boxers, he had snuck past them without saying a word and climbed the stairs. After locking himself into the bathroom, he had retrieved a can of Comet and a scrub brush from the cabinet sink. He had turned on the hot water and let it run through his hands. He worked them together until the dried blood washed into the basin, turning it red. He had sprinkled the Comet on his hands and scrubbed them vigorously with the brush, until he felt the abrasive begin to tear at his skin and the granules embed into his fingernails. The skin on his hands was swollen and reddened. He remembered that no matter how hard he had scrubbed, he hadn't felt clean. *It was the dirt inside*, he thought, *that's what he couldn't get rid of.*

He had reassured himself all the blood was gone, until he looked down at his leg. On his left thigh was a dried red patch, where Tina's head had been. He took the scrub brush and scoured his thigh until his skin was raised and nearly all the hair removed. For good measure, he had poured alcohol all over his hands and on his leg, but he didn't know what good it would do if the police examined his body for evidence. It felt cool and then quickly evaporated.

He remembered looking up at the mirror; his reflection had disappeared under the fog that had spread over it. It was just as well; he didn't necessarily want to look at himself.

He had put some jeans and a tee shirt on just before his wife started jiggling the door handle.

"Kent, are you okay? What are you doing in there?"

Lisa's voice had reminded him of his mom's voice, standing outside the bathroom door at twelve o'clock on a Saturday night. "Kenny...are you all okay? Are you okay? What are you doing in there?"

*Yeah, Mom, just wonderful, let me finish heaving up the rest of my guts and I'll be right out for some good old-fashioned, cold fried chicken. And by the way, thanks a fuckin' million for jiggling the door while I'm gripping the old porcelain steering wheel here and trying to concentrate on the task at hand.*

The showerhead spewed out hot streams of water on to his neck and shoulders. *The clothes, the coat, the shoes and the dent in the car, all of it would have to disappear*, he thought. He leaned against the wall of the shower and recalled all those Sundays his mom and dad made him go to church and Sunday school when he was little. He figured it hadn't paid off too well. *Thou shall not kill*, he thought. He pondered the words. *Had he killed? Is that what he had done...when he left her to die?* He shook his head as the water streamed over his eyes.

He knew that he was beginning to wrestle with his own conscience...what he had done was wrong...*but wrong, sometimes could be right*, he thought. Down in his heart, he knew he would have to go to his grave with this...that is, if he wanted to preserve his family's integrity, his way of life and his freedom.

Perhaps he was caught already. He didn't know if anyone had seen him there, though he knew that the road wasn't well traveled. He couldn't take his mind off the fact that she was probably still laying there, cold and alone, on a God-forsaken patch of rain-soaked earth on the side of Coventry Road. A beautiful mother of two lay dead because of him. *God, how would he live with that?* He didn't know how, but he knew he had to.

He tried not to think about it anymore; it made him panicky. He didn't like to feel eaten up with guilt...it was like being out of control, as if your body and mind had no boundaries to contain it. He gripped the porcelain handle and shut off the stream of water. A sudden chill came upon him as he opened the shower curtain, shaking and depleted.

He nearly tripped getting out of the shower. He stumbled to the counter opposite the other side of the room. He put one hand ungracefully on the vanity top and he took the other and wiped the bathroom mirror to remove the fog. The wake of his hand left trails of beaded water and he strained hard to get a good look at himself.

He wanted to make sure or perhaps reassure himself that he looked the same, or that he did not see any telltale signs of guilt on his face. His light brown hair and blue eyes revealed nothing—just lack of sleep. But the worry lines were deep in his face and he thought he looked older than his age of thirty-nine.

For the most part he looked like the same person he was yesterday. But he knew that he would never be the same after this. He touched his finger to the mirror where his forehead was, and wondered what lay there in his brain. What sick organism was devouring it and clouding his judgment? He shook his head and closed his eyes, and then opened them. He was still there.

# Chapter 4

He frantically walked up and down Winding Creek Drive and the adjoining blocks for nearly an hour looking for his wife who was now overdue. Once or twice he stopped at a couple of doors and knocked, asking neighbors he knew if they had seen her. They had not. *Thank God he had not knocked on this door*, Kent thought. He would have probably confessed right then, laid it all out on the table so to speak, coughed up his guts about the whole thing. The pure terror he saw Jim going through nauseated him and sent a trickle of shame into his soul.

He kept his radio on the local NPR station to pick up any news of the accident, but none was broadcast. He had a sick feeling that any moment the police would come and arrest him in front of his family. Drag him out like a howling dog and take him back to some county jail where the inmates would rape him all night and beat him for being a woman killer, until he was dead. He thought of how he would be the shame of the community, his family and his father, if he was even accused of killing Tina.

His eyes fluttered at the proposition and a shiver curled around his spine. He took a long deep breath and told himself that everything would be all right, that people get away with a lot worse. And after a moment of thinking he thought that he was pretty good at getting away with things himself. His life was certainly littered with examples.

He stared down the street from the upstairs window, as a police car pulled into the Halls' driveway. He had been watching the house for about a half hour, knowing that they would eventually come.

He was sweaty, and warm prickly waves of heat turned his arms into a rash of goose bumps. His nerves festered in his skin. The hair on the back of his neck turned into porcupine quills as fear set in.

The sight of the policeman nauseated him. His black uniform conjured up nefarious images of the Nazi SS, inhumane torture and long stints in labor camps where the ultimate end was a gas oven for each inmate. Jim tried to shake the paranoia, as he watched the policeman walk around in front of his car and onto the Halls' front lawn where Jim was. He had been there for nearly twenty minutes or so, with a cell phone in his hand, staring down Winding Creek Drive, hoping he could catch a glimpse of his wife coming home. But Kent knew she wouldn't be, and the pain that would cause Jim and his children made him even sicker. *Jim would soon know his wife would not be coming home tonight*, he thought, *not tonight and not ever*.

Kent ran to the bathroom and barked several times over the porcelain pool of water. Finally he vomited, heaving yellow spew from somewhere inside him. Straining with each lurch of his stomach, his ribs clutched his sides in digging pain. At each pitch forward, all he could see in his pulsating eyeballs was the face and body of Tina Hall gazing up at him, sheets of rain falling hard on her body, the sound of it rippling off her jogging suit and turning it dark, her face smeared in mud and blood, the rain streaking through it; she lay motionless, gasping sporadically, she lay dying alone, and he stood towering over her knowing it.

Jim slowly returned to his viewing perch at the bedroom window, his face pasty white, his forehead and hands clammy. He watched through the dwindling light of the cloudy evening as the police officer gripped Jim's arm. It was obvious Jim was distraught; at one point Kent thought Jim's knees would buckle as he stood swaying in the yard.

He kept expecting Jim Hall at any moment to point his finger up at him through the window and mouth the words *he did it*. But that was just his paranoia beginning to have a little fun inside his head. He assured himself that no one knew and no one would know, if he kept his mouth shut. But it was hard forcing back the guilt.

*Is this how I had been raised as a boy?* he thought. As he watched, his conscious now bellowed at him, taunting him. The voice was familiar, it was faint and haunting, it pursued his moral judgment, questioning it. The voice was his father's, he pushed it far from him and away. He was afraid to hear what his voice might say.

"Goddamn it, pull yourself together." He said the words softly to himself and they floated on the air.

"Honey, did you say something?" Lisa stood outside the doorway of the bedroom and looked at him as he stood gawking out the window, talking to himself, like a fool, he thought.

"Uhhhhh...nothing Lisa, just talking to myself...about nothing."

"Are you feeling better?"

"No, I don't think so."

“What are you looking at out there?” she said. She walked over to where he was standing.

Kent tried to shut the blind in time, but fumbled the twirl rod, inadvertently making them wider.

“What are the police doing at the Halls’ house?”

“I don’t know.” The words came out flat, when what he really wanted to say was, *how the hell should I know, do I look like a fucking mind reader!*

“I wonder what could ever be the matter. Do you think we should call them and ask if everything is all right?” she said.

Kent studied her intently, wondering if she was *just dumb or fucking dumb*. He couldn’t decide right then, but assured himself he would have plenty of time in the evening to find out.

“Probably nothing, just lost the dog I bet, no need to call,” Kent said, his voice sounding remote and dry.

Another car pulled up in front of the Halls’; it was dark blue with no markings and had plain hubcap coverings, *which could only belong to an investigative unit*, he thought. Seeing it sparked another surge of fear in him, and his clinched hands became moist; beads of sweat began to form on his forehead.

“I wonder what’s happening. I’m starting to get worried. I think I’m going to call,” Lisa said. She looked at Kent.

Kent looked back at her, clearly irritated now, wishing it had been her that he ran down on Coventry Road.

“No…no, I don’t think we better get involved.”

“Get involved…in what?” She looked puzzled.

“Well, Lisa, God knows what. Who knows what those people do.”

“Those people…what are you talking about…they are our neighbors…they’ve lived there for nearly ten years. What are you saying?”

“I’m not saying anything…I just think we shouldn’t get involved until we know what’s going on. You have to be subtle about these things. We don’t want an over zealous police officer thinking we are somehow involved.”

“Kent, I don’t know what you are talking about…involved in what? You sound as if they are in the Mafia or something. I am going to call Joan next door and ask her if she knows anything.”

There was nothing he could do. She was hell bent to find out what was going on. *If she only knew*, he thought. Half of him wanted to tell her, but he knew he couldn’t. He never would.

She walked down the stairs to the kitchen. He waited for a moment and then followed behind her. He stopped at the top of the stairs and then crept quietly down to the bottom. The kids were in their rooms. He carefully watched the top of the stairway landing for them at the same time he strained to hear Lisa's conversation.

"Oh, no…no…I can't believe it," Lisa said. Her voice was trembling. Jim knew that high-pitched voice well; she only used it when she was really upset. "That's terrible. I just saw her this morning at Dillards. We talked about having a stamping party next Thursday evening." She paused and started to sob through her words. "Poor Tina, my poor friend." Her voice whimpered as she said goodbye. After she hung the phone up she wept in the kitchen.

Kent swallowed, trying to remove the lump lying deep in his throat. He pleaded with her in his mind to stop crying. He didn't think they were that close. He prayed she would not tell him any of the details that Joan might have known about the accident. He knew that he would have to relive the memories over and over again as it was. What he really wanted to know was what the police knew…if anything.

He heard Lisa leaving the kitchen, coming toward the stairs. He turned abruptly, about to climb the stairs, not wanting to be caught by his wife and having to explain why he was listening to her phone conversation, when he saw his daughter Samantha staring down at him from the top of the stairs.

"What are you doing, Dad?"

"Uh…I'm just standing here…uhh…I have to get something downstairs and, uh…and, I started to go back up and get something." He sounded like a dumb shit and he knew it, standing there struggling for an explanation of why he was rubbernecking around the corner of the stairs eavesdropping on her mother's telephone conversation in the kitchen. He immediately thought of a small metaphorical animal struggling in a snare, looking for an appropriate response to its predicament. Lisa walked around to the foot of the stairs and stood surprised seeing them both standing their gawking at each other.

"Well what are you two doing?" Lisa said. She looked at them while they stared at her, a quizzical look spread on her face. His daughter didn't say anything; she just turned and blew out a long breath, like *whatever* and rolled her eyes as she passed by her nine-year-old brother in the hall. Their son David came around the stairwell and looked down at them.

"Mom…Dad, can I go over to Ronnie's house tonight? He's just got that new video game, Star Hunt, and I—" Lisa didn't let him finish.

"No…it's a school night and I don't want you going out tonight. Maybe this weekend." Kent walked up the stairs, past David and winked at him. "Sorry, squirt," he said. He took his hand and roughed up his hair.

Suddenly they heard a knock at the door. Kent stuck his head back around the stairwell and looked at Lisa.

"Who is that?" Kent asked.

She looked at him, eyes red rimmed. "I don't know, Kent, let me look into my crystal ball and tell you who it is. In fact let me get the door while I'm at it too." The words were biting, but he thought she was just distressed over Tina's death.

Kent hesitated for a moment, as she walked toward the front door, not sure what to do. *What if it's the police…what if they found out? Shut up! Shut up! Do you hear me and get a grip on yourself goddamn it!*

"Maybe we shouldn't—" But it was too late; she opened the door before he could get all the words out of his mouth. The rest of them hung in his throat like a chicken bone.

The look on Lisa's face was full of surprise when she saw the police officer standing there bathed in the glow of the bright yellow porch light.

Kent felt his heart starting to gallop in his chest at the sight of him. *Well this is it. Somehow they found out it was me that killed her*, he thought.

Lisa didn't say anything; she just stared at the police officer and then back at Kent. Kent stared back at her and then to the police officer.

"Good evening, Ma'am, does a Mr. Kent Jackson live here?" The police officer's voice was deep and full of all business. It filled the silent house, and seemed to echo around the walls, as he waited for an answer.

"Well uhhhh, yes he does," Lisa finally said. I…I will get him." Her voice sounded suddenly sluggish and tired. Jim now heard and saw everything in slow motion. It had a certain amount of surreal quality.

Lisa walked from the foyer to the edge of the stairs. When their eyes met she had a worried look buried deep in them and Kent shot a look back at her that said for all purposes, *I'm guilty*.

Lisa whispered a string of jumbled up words rapidly under her breath as he passed, "Is there…is there something wrong? Do you know…what he wants? Is there someth—"

Kent interrupted her as he tore away from the grip she had on his arm and whispered quietly, "I don't know."

The words "I don't know" stunned Lisa. *Why did he say that?* she thought. *Was there something wrong?*

Kent walked to the door that was ajar, took a deep breath and tried to choke down the panic. He opened it slowly.

"Officer," he said. They both nodded at each other. "May I help you?"

"Sir, my name is Officer Brady. Sorry to bother you this evening, but I would like to ask you a few questions."

"That's fine...what is this about?"

"Sir, this evening one of your neighbors, Tina Hall, was killed in an accident."

He tried to look shocked and even gasped in front of the officer when he heard it. "How did it happen?" Kent didn't want to ask the question. Hell, he knew damn well how it happened. But he thought the question was expected.

"She was killed in a hit and run accident."

"That's awful...do you know who did it?" Another expected question, but he hoped the officer wouldn't say, *Yeah you did, you fucking moron, now get you hands behind your back.*

"No sir, not yet, but we're still working the case."

Kent nodded his head, like he was glad that Lakewood City's finest were on the job.

"We've asked a few people in the neighborhood if they saw Mrs. Hall go on her run tonight, to try to get a better time frame of the accident."

"Well I can't help you there, I didn't get home till late, so I wouldn't have been here to see her."

"Oh," the officer said. "And what time was that?" It was just the way he said it that Kent didn't like. It caught him cold, as if the officer had just discovered something by accident. Kent felt like he had just waded out into a marsh of sucking mud and sand and would be lucky to get back.

"Well it was about 6:30 tonight." Kent hedged the time about thirty minutes hoping that would in some way exonerate him, though it had really been seven.

"That's fine then, can you tell me what route you took from work this evening and what time of day it was?"

Kent cringed at the question...he almost wanted to run into the yard and down the street. He felt panicky. His finger and thumb found the backside of his thigh and he pinched it as hard he could. *Goddamn it, grab a hold of yourself,* he thought.

"Mr. Jackson, could you tell me what streets you came home on?"

Kent began to get uneasy about what the officer was asking. He thought about the question for a moment. It sounded fully loaded, but he didn't want to hesitate with his answer. "I always go south on State Route 4 and cut across on Apple Gate Avenue to Fairmont, and then to here, Winding Creek Drive." He wondered why the officer had not asked him what street he took tonight, instead of asking a general question of what street he usually takes.

"I see," said Officer Brady. He looked intently into Kent's eyes and put a hand up to his chin to rest on. "That's a little bit of a detour isn't it? Do you ever take Coventry Road from 4? One of your neighbors we talked to tonight, Mrs. Joan Van Ark, said that you usually get home pretty late and might have seen something, maybe even a drunk driver or could have even seen Tina jogging." The officer let his voice die away with the last words and there was silence, as his eyes locked with Kent's. Jim just stood, not saying a word, not knowing what to say. *Damn that fucking bitch Joan Van Ark*, he thought.

Kent smiled at the officer, and said as cool as a cucumber, "No, she's mistaken, I rarely take that road." The words came out through a tight smile, his hands tightly clinched, fingernails digging into his palms as he said it. "I usually go that way because I can pick things up from the market on Apple Gate," he added. "It's more convenient." His lips formed an even larger smile.

"Oh, well that's fine," said Mr. Jackson, "I just want to make sure I talk to anyone who may have come home that way tonight or may have seen her. But you didn't?"

For a moment, he thought the officer was first agreeing with him that he didn't take Coventry Road, but then as he processed the words slowly realized he was asking him the question again. There was an undeniable pause in Kent's answer. He thought carefully about what he might say. He could change his answer right now and probably be all right...tomorrow though would be too late. He thought about the gas he had purchased with a credit card off State Route 4, right before Coventry Road. That was far south of Apple Gate—no way he would be able to really explain that away later.

"No...no I didn't," Kent finally said. The words slipped from his lips like drops of honey, easy to pour out, but impossible to clean up without causing a smear. Kent's face slightly grimaced.

"Good enough, sir," Officer Brady said. He faintly smiled at him. "I want to thank you for your time this evening, you have a good night now."

Officer Brady turned and walked back down the driveway and onto the sidewalk and back toward the Halls'.

"Uhhh, yes, you too. This is a real tragedy you know." He made his voice intentionally louder, hoping to come across genuinely concerned. The officer didn't turn around; he kept walking down the sidewalk.

"I'll call you guys if I hear anything," Kent called after him. Officer Brady turned for a brief moment and waved half-heartedly and kept walking. Kent thought he probably didn't hear what he said.

*Okay, time to shut up, you're over doing it. Just keep your piehole shut. Am I safe now? Did I pass the sniff test…was it over? I guess the true answer will come in time*, he thought. That bothered him; it would be a tough wait.

He put his arm on the side of the doorframe and propped himself up, staring at particularly nothing, thinking about that bitch, *Joan*. Kent heard the whine of a car engine and glanced up the street. His eyes honed in on the same dark blue car he saw earlier, the one he had assumed belonged to the police. The car accelerated up the street toward him. As it approached he noticed the dome light on inside.

He followed the car with his eyes as it passed by. Horrified, he saw Jim Hall in the back seat staring out the window. For a moment Jim looked up and their eyes met. Kent pulled his arm out of his pocket and up halfway from his body transforming the motion into an impotent wave. But he thought that perhaps it was inappropriate and so he aborted the gesture half as quick in mid-air, and his hand quickly disappeared back into his pocket.

*What a hypocrite you are, Kent, you're a real good for nothing*, he told himself. He sifted through his jaded mind for something that would bring him comfort from his guilt and acidic anxiety, but nothing came. His remorse over the accident became entangled with worry over the prospects of being caught. He gently closed the door and slipped back into shadows of the house, fully knowing its walls, windows and doors were a false sense of security.

# Chapter 5

Watching the clock tick off the minutes he fell deeper into the eager waiting grips of panic. He told himself she was okay; she was just a little late. But part of him didn't believe this.

Images flashed from his imagination and then disappeared, horrible images. His wife, trying to scream under a thin tight layer of tape, covering her mouth. Bound and naked, silently sobbing between each scream, lying inside the hot trunk of an old Chevrolet Monte Carlo, driving south down Highway 35 to God knows where. Or her body lying sprawled out and broiled from a lightning strike, blackened and charred, beside a nearby road.

His eyes widened, his hands trembled, fear spread over him, plunging him into a tight spiral of trepidation. He looked at his watch, making sure the clock above the mantle was correct. It was. It read 7:30 p.m. *She should have been home by now*, he thought.

He tried to reason the times in his head, but couldn't. He expected her home from her jog early given the sudden downpour of rain. Maybe she was safe, tucked away somewhere waiting out the storm at a friend's house. *But why didn't she call? Why wasn't she already home?* The rain had tapered off a little while ago. She would have had time to get back by now; it didn't make sense.

Thirty minutes passed and still there was no sign of her. Jim stood in the front yard of his house, looking down Winding Creek Drive toward Freemont hoping to catch a glimpse of her running towards him like a graceful impala, her blonde hair bouncing above her slim figure. But she wasn't there.

Usually her run would take no more than an hour and if this was a normal run she would have been back around seven o'clock. That would make her thirty minutes late. *But this was no normal run*, he thought. There had been a heavy downpour around 6:30. He expected her to be home earlier. She was never late.

He took a few steps toward the house, thinking he would call the police. He stopped and told himself he was being irrational. Did he really expect them to call out the National Guard because his wife was a little late from her evening jog?

He turned around and walked a few blocks up Winding Creek, knocking occasionally on a neighbor's door, asking if they might have seen her. He would leave each time disappointed, falling further into a state of apprehension about what to do.

He walked to Freemont and looked down both sides of the street, but he didn't see her. He felt a sudden panicky urge to run down Freemont and scream her name, thinking, if he ran fast enough he might quickly find her. The impulse pounded at his brain like a sledgehammer, but he resisted it. He told himself he was probably just overreacting.

Slowly he walked back toward his house, looking over his shoulder once or twice hoping he would see her, but he never did. Each time a bucket of ice cold fear drenched his body. He stared at his house, it seemed far in the distance. He felt faint, his feet heavy, his heart beating rapidly, a chest-stabbing surge of panic squeezing him tightly, putting its claw-like hands firmly around his heart.

He gave over to it, the anxiety, and the fear. Standing in his front yard, he turned around and looked back at Freemont again, it verily visible in the distance, hoping to see her. Night was now falling fast. He looked back down at his watch; it was a quarter past eight. He stood now in near darkness, convinced something was wrong. He felt a sudden gush of dread spread over his body, as a cool wind began to blow gently through his hair.

It was then that he saw the police car in the distance, bathed under the glow of street lamps. He knew immediately why it was coming. He watched it lumber down the street towards him, the lights blinding his eyes, as it pulled to a stop in the driveway. He stood there dazed, staring at the officer getting out of his car. He knew, at that moment, he was alone.

# Chapter 6

The officer approached slowly, apprehension in his steps. Jim's eyes followed him. His face freckled; thin light reddish-blonde hair decorated the top of his head. He knew what the police officer would say before he said it. He knew he would remember this moment for the rest of his life.

The officer smiled. "Good evening, is this the residence of Mrs. Tina Marie Hall?" the officer asked.

Jim didn't answer. He only looked at the messenger of death softly, trying to remain in the world where he had a living wife. But he knew the policeman wasn't going to let that happen. His voice, his words, would shatter his life like a crystal ball falling on a marble slab.

"Sir, do you know a Tina Marie Hall?"

After a moment the word "yes" slipped unconsciously from his tongue and then "she is my wife," followed.

"Are you Mr. Hall?"

"Yes."

There was a short silence. Jim could see the officer trying to figure out how best to say it. He searched his eyes, still hoping he wouldn't say words that would change his and his children's life. A lump grew to the size of a plum in his throat as he waited.

"Sir, there has been an accident...your wife died from injuries sustained in an accident. I'm sorry for your loss."

Jim's legs weakened. He felt as if he might collapse from his own weight. His body wavered slightly, and gentle cool wind blew through his coal black hair. His face wrinkled, his mouth tightened, large tears swelled in his eyes and trickled down his face. The policeman looked like a blur as he stared at him through tear-filled eyes. His throat made a whine as his lips began to quiver.

He wept uncontrollably; his hands continuously wiped at his face.

Then he staggered, almost falling on the ground. Officer Brady caught him by the arm, supporting Jim's weight.

After a moment, Jim struggled for words, but couldn't make them form from his bone-dry lips. Finally he whispered in a small hoarse voice.

"What happened to her?"

"Mr. Hall, two detectives will be by shortly with a lot more details than I have."

"Can't you tell me anything?" he asked. His fingers trembled as he combed them through his hair and looked up toward the star-filled sky, trying to damn up the uncontrollable flow of tears streaming down his cheeks.

Officer Brady looked at him for a moment, not wanting to give him the details, wanting to leave that job to the detectives. He was already in bad shape. But he knew he had the right to know what he knew.

"Your wife was running westbound on Coventry Road and was struck from behind by a vehicle. She was alive when police arrived on the scene, but died en route to the hospital."

"How do you know it's my wife?" The words of denial almost shocked him, but it wasn't just that, it was a sense that maybe this was just a horrible mistake.

"Mr. Hall, your wife was wearing a black fanny-pack today. She had an Oklahoma driver's license in it. Also there was a library card and a Texaco charge card. Clipped to her belt was a yellow CD player. On her left hand there was a gold wedding band and above it, on her wrist was a sports watch. She wore a gold necklace with a..."

"It's her," Jim said, interrupting the rest of his sentence. After a long pause he slipped the words under his breath. "I just thought there might be a—"

"Mr. Hall, you don't have to explain anything to me. You have a right to ask any question you want and as a public servant I have an obligation to answer. This is a tough time, I know it is, and I'm very sorry you have to go through it."

Jim nodded a little with his head, and said in a trembling voice, "I appreciate that."

"There's something though, something—I just can't help feeling responsible. If I—" His face swelled up with guilt. He felt sure if he had found her in time, she would still be alive. His face reflected the blame.

"Don't blame yourself," Officer Brady said. "It's not your fault."

The officer's words were kind, but they didn't make him feel any better. He watched, as another car approached and pulled up next to the yard. It was a dark blue Crown Victoria, and two men were sitting in front.

"Here are the detectives now," Officer Brady said. The two men stepped out of the car. The officer went over and spoke with them a moment and then walked back with the detectives. "Mr. Hall, this is Detective Randy Trower and Roger Flint. They will give talk to you about the accident and answer any questions that you may have. In the meantime, I'm going to ask a few of your neighbors if they saw your wife on their way home from work or were out during the time of your wife's accident. Maybe somebody saw something."

"What do you mean?" His voice sounded puzzled. "Saw something? Saw what?"

"You haven't told him yet?" Flint asked.

"Told me what?"

Officer Brady shook his head no.

Flint looked at Jim. "Mr. Hall, your wife was killed tonight by a hit and run driver."

"Oh my God." Kent put his hand to his mouth in disbelief.

"Right now, we're trying to pinpoint exactly when she left and if there are any witnesses," Flint said. "Do you know when your wife left this evening?"

"Yes it was just a little before six, she usually leaves around that time to go on her run."

"We thought that's what she was doing…it looks like she got caught out in that nasty storm we had tonight," Trower said.

"Yes, I was worried, I wanted to call—"

"We understand," Flint said.

"But, if I would—"

"This is not your fault," Trower said. He patted Jim's arm. "She was found around seven. By the time you would have found her—" Trower shook his head.

"Do you have any idea who it is?" Jim asked.

"No," Flint said.

"Time is crucial though," Trower said. "If we get on this right away we have a good chance of finding out who it is. But, probably whoever hit her was more than likely intoxicated or had a warrant and knew they would go to jail for a long time."

"It could have even been done maliciously," Flint added, "but we doubt that."

"Why…why do you doubt it?" Jim asked. He looked at them intently, searching their eyes, wanting to know.

"Well, there are several things that led us to believe that…it's just—"

"I have a suggestion," Trower interrupted, not wanting not to upset Jim anymore than he already was. "If you would like we can answer the rest of your questions at a later time...when you feel you might be more up to it."

"Where is she now?" Jim asked bluntly.

"Mr. Hall, your wife was transported to Lakewood City Hospital," Trower said. "Now she's waiting to be identified at the Lakewood City Morgue. If you want, we can drive you now or someone else to identify her. And, if it's more convenient we can arrange for it in the morning. It's a formality, even though she had ID at the time of her death, next of kin is required to verify who they are in a case involving homicide."

"No, I want to see her now."

"Okay then, and perhaps on the way, we can answer a few more of your questions."

"Before we go I need to go in and make arrangements for my children and make phone calls; it may take a little while."

"You go right ahead and take your time; Officer Brady is going to ask your neighbors some questions and we'll be out in the car."

"Thank you," Jim said. He looked at Officer Brady and stuck out his hand and shook it. Brady smiled and shook it and told him to take care.

Jim walked slowly to the house, not knowing how or if he could tell his children. He paused briefly on the porch, and then slowly opened the door and disappeared.

* * *

He held his nine-year-old son and thirteen-year-old daughter in his arms. He wondered how one tells a child that their mother is dead. For some reason they already knew. They had been crying in their rooms when he found them.

They now stood in the living room, locked in each other's arms, never wanting to let go. He was afraid of losing them, they were afraid of losing him. When their grief reached a silence, Jim whispered hoarsely to them. "Janie...Kevin...I want you to know, I love you and I'm sorry."

They held their father tight, not ever wanting to let go, afraid to. They clung to his arms, weeping; their faces buried in his chest, his hands stroking them gently on their backs. He would whisper something occasionally to them, reassuring them and they would sometimes shake their heads, as if understanding. It was an unbridled grief giving off a heavy aroma of sorrow that permeated the room.

They held each other tightly, mourning the loss of mother and wife. On the coffee table in front of them lay an open magazine to a page that Tina Hall had been reading. Her glasses were nudged in the crack of the thin binding. There was a lipstick smudge on a cup nearby; her fingernail file lay across a large hair clip she had used that day, strands of her blonde hair still in it.

They all noticed those things almost at the same time, and each seem to sense the other, wondering how something this tragic could have touched their lives.

Their father told them that he would be gone for a while, and that he would call Aunt Mae, and she would probably be over to stay with them while he was gone. They both loved Aunt Mae and Jim thought she would be good for them right now. Quietly Janie and Kevin settled together on the couch and stared at their mother's things.

Jim had two phone calls to make: one to Aunt Mae and the other to Tina's parents. He didn't want to make the last one; it would take every bit of his strength to do it. But he knew he had to.

After making the phone call to Aunt Mae, who was now on her way over, Jim picked up the phone again and then placed it back on the receiver. He took a long breath, and thought for a moment, and then picked it up and dialed Tina's parents.

"Martha, this is Jim."

"Jim, how are you?"

He knew that Martha would be suspicious; he never called them. It was Tina who always called them. It's not that he didn't like them, they just weren't his parents. For that matter, he didn't know what he would say to parents anyway, if he had any.

"I'm fine, Martha," he said.

"Are the kids okay," she asked.

"Yes, the kids are okay too," he said.

"Is Tina okay?" she asked.

"Martha, I've got something to tell you and Herb. Could you tell him to get on the phone please?"

"What...what is it, Jim, is there something wrong with Tina?"

"Martha please, would you have Herb get on the other phone."

There was a pause for a moment. Jim swallowed hard wondering how he would get through the next couple of minutes. He thought about just telling them to fly in from Colorado, that he had something to tell them. But he thought that would probably make it worse. There just wasn't any good way to tell them that their little girl was dead.

"Hey, Jim, what do you know?"

"Uhhh, nothing Herb, hey listen, I…I've…I have something to tell you both and I don't really know how to say it."

"Jim, you're scaring us a little now. What's wrong?"

Jim could hear Martha breathing heavy on the phone, that hard short breath indicated she was worried. He didn't know how to tell them, whether to blurt it out all at once or let them guess until they got it right. He chose the first one.

"Tina was involved in an accident this evening and she didn't make it…she's…she's gone." His voice started to crackle with the last couple of words. The reality of saying it made it all too real. It was then he knew from the sound of his own voice that his wife was actually dead.

He heard what sounded like a phone drop on the other end of the line. And then heard Martha cry out loud. Her voice sounded distant and muffled.

"Oh no, Lord…no please, Lord…don't take my baby…please don't take my baby, Lord…please don't take my baby from me …"

Jim wanted to put the phone down. He didn't want to listen to it. His pain, his children's pain, had been enough. Finally, her voice broke down into uncontrollable sobs. He could hear Herb trying to comfort her in the background. But how can you comfort a mother that has just lost a child? *You can't.*

Herb got back on the phone. He tried to compose himself. Jim knew this would be hard on him. Tina was a Daddy's girl and always had been. Herb finally spoke with a quivering voice.

"Jim…Jim how did this happen? Are you sure she's dead?"

He recognized the voice. It was the voice of Herb's in the clutch, the way he talked before he retired over six years ago. The questions came in rapid fire and seemed endless, as if Herb did not believe him. It made Jim feel he didn't trust him to get the situation right—that Herb was trying to ask a question that would prove this was all just a misunderstanding and nothing had really happened at all. Jim understood though.

Herb was a man of reason, a former oil executive from Tulsa. He wasn't prone to panic. He was used to being Johnny on the spot with questions and answers. But there was no reasoning to this. It was quite insane. He was trying to use all the power he could muster from the end of a telephone over seven hours away, to make Tina alive. It was heartbreaking.

"Herb, it was a hit and run accident."

"Are you sure that it's her? Did anyone see it happen?" he asked.

"Yes, I'm sure. She had her ID and I'm going down to identify her tonight."

*Goddamn, this conversation can't be real,* he thought.

"Do you know how it happened?"

"No, not all of it, not yet."

Finally there was a long silence and Jim heard muffled cries through the phone. *Herb now accepted it,* he thought. He always knew him to be a man of little emotions. He sounded like a wounded animal on the other end of the line. He found himself flinching at each grotesque sound of grief he made. It bothered him listening to another man cry. It seemed unnatural. Finally, he heard a sniffling broken and badly crackling voice on the other end.

"Did my little girl suffer?" Herb quietly asked.

Jim thought about the answer before he gave it. "No, Herb, she died instantly. There was nothing anyone could have done." Jim struggled over the words, nearly choking on them, partly feeling guilty he had not found her first and partly because he was not telling Herb the truth. But, he didn't want to inflict anymore hurt on him or Martha. It was their baby girl and she was gone.

"We will fly in soon," Herb said, the life now removed from his voice. "We'll pack and be out there by tomorrow."

"Okay, Herb, let me know when. I'll pick you up at the airport."

"Don't worry about that, Jim, take care of the kids. Do what you can for them. You've got enough on your plate. We'll catch a cab."

"Okay, I'll see you tomorrow."

"Okay, Jim, I know it's probably just as hard losing a wife as it is losing a daughter."

"Yes," Jim whispered.

There was a long silence.

"She was my baby girl, Jimmy…I'm going to miss her." His voice was trembling.

"I know, Herb…I am too."

Jim waited for the click on the other end before he put down the receiver, just in case Herb had something else to say. There was nothing though. There was a click and then he waited in silence. He thought Herb might pick it up again. He didn't. The connection went dead and then he put the phone gently on the receiver.

* * *

After a few minutes there was a knock on the door and he saw Aunt Mae holding her hand up over her eyes shielding them from the bright porch light, peeking through the screen door. "Is anyone home," she cooed, her voice bathed in sweetness. She knew quite well they were. But she needed her introduction, not wanting to rush in on a private moment. *Good old Aunt Mae, she was an eccentric old lady, but sweet as peaches and cream.*

"Come in, Aunt Mae," Jim said.

He opened the door for her. She gave Jim a hug and gave him a wet kiss on the cheek. She walked across the room and met the kids half way and hugged them as they lapsed back into tears. "Oh my loves," she said, "I know, I know."

Aunt Mae was nearly a surrogate grandmother to the kids; she lived close by and saw the kids often. Actually she was their great aunt, sister to Jim's mother-in-law. She had an estranged relationship with her sister, but it was one she seemed to relish in her old age.

She was a woman in her mid-sixties, frosted silver-fox hair—the best tint that could be bought in a bottle at Wal-Mart. Her fingers were adorned with long fake pearl-colored nails and a variety of silver and turquoise rings that went well with her leather tan complexion.

She was a talkative, caring woman, busy as a bee when she came in usually, mostly running her mouth a hundred miles a minute, nobody knowing a goddamn thing she ever talked about. But it didn't matter; she was pleasant.

This time she was quiet though, only like a woman can be. She turned her full attention to the children, carefully coddling their emotional state. Jim thought that this had to be hard on her too, losing a niece. But she didn't let it show. She was truly one of a kind and he felt a lot better about things after she was there.

Jim took her aside for moment and spoke quietly. "Now I'll try not to be gone long, Aunt Mae."

"Don't you worry about it, Jimmy," Aunt Mae said.

He had always liked it when she called him Jimmy; it gave him a feeling he belonged in the family. Not as if he was just a temporary member of the family as Martha often did. It made him feel like a son; and he had never been a son before.

"You know, you don't need to worry about a thing, I'm here as long as you need me," she whispered. "I love 'em to death. Whatever you need, Jimmy. You take care of yourself now...you got other things to worry about, you leave this to me...okay?"

Jim nodded. Aunt Mae's words were reassuring. He felt better about leaving them. *She knew what to do in this situation*, he thought. She had two kids of her own; but both had died as young adults—one in the Army and another in an automobile accident. So she had her fare share of run-ins with death.

Jim thanked her before he opened the door to go. She pressed a finger to her lips and blew a "shhhhhh" and reached up and gave him a hug and patted his back. "You take care, Jimmy, we'll be right here when you get back."

"I will, Aunt Mae," he said.

# Chapter 7

Jim crawled in the back seat of the Crown Victoria, and watched as light mists of rain formed on the windshield as it pulled into the road. There was silent awkwardness in the car. The only sound was the faint hum of the engine and the monotonous whine of the windshield wipers. Nothing was really appropriate to say, so no one said a word as they drove up the winding street under the strange pale blue tint of street lamps.

He glanced out the window and saw his neighbor Kent Jackson staring back at him from his front door. He thought for a moment he had waved, but wasn't sure. He glanced away thinking Kent hadn't recognized him because he was in the detectives' car. His mind turned to other important things as they took a curve in the street, slowed for a dip and turned onto Freemont Avenue and disappeared.

Detective Trower looked in the rearview mirror a few times as he drove. Each time his eyes would meet Jim's and he could see the questions beginning to form.

"Detective, what else do you know about the accident?" Jim asked.

"Well," Trower said hesitantly, "let me first ask if Mrs. Hall had any enemies, anyone that was angry with her?"

"No…no one. Everyone got along fine with Tina. She wasn't the type to have confrontations."

"Well, we didn't think anything like that happened anyway, I just had to ask. However, there is something you should know." Trower's eyes grew tight and dark staring at him, as Jim looked back bewildered and frightened at what he might hear.

"From what we have determined from the crime scene," Trower continued, "it was an accident, a hit and run of course, but that—"

Trower looked at Flint pausing. Flint nodded.

"But we think you should know, we believe Tina was left intentionally to die. Whoever was driving that car, didn't just hit her and drive on. Whoever it was, got out of his car, probably to see how badly hurt she was and then left her.

Jim's eyes grew large in the rearview mirror, and his hand brushed through his short black hair. He stared out the window, not quite believing what he was hearing.

"Why? What makes you think that?"

"For one," Flint said, "there were two reoccurring tire tracks in the mud next to your wife's body.

"And…so what does that mean?" Jim asked.

"What it means," Flint said, "is that the first time the perpetrator's car left the road was when he hit your wife. The second time was when he went back."

"Back?" Jim asked puzzled. "So whoever this person was just drove his car back and looked at her?"

"No, it was little more than that," Trower interjected.

"What do you mean?"

"We don't think the perpetrator noticed he hit her until he was further down the road," Flint said. "For some reason he must have noticed her and—"

Trower looked back at Jim, and interrupted, "It was raining pretty heavy this evening, I know visibility wasn't good…Christ, I nearly had a wreck myself. So he may not have seen her."

"The perpetrator backed the car to where the body was," Flint continued to say, "onto the shoulder of the road. We think he got out of his car and walked over to where Tina was lying. We have a couple of shoe prints and what appears to be some knee smudges in the mud beside her."

"Oh God," Jim gasped under his breath.

"Mr. Hall, perhaps this wouldn't be a good time to go into it," Trower said.

"No, I want to know now," Kent said. "Please?" His voice was flat and sharp.

Flint nodded to Trower, and he continued.

"There is clear indication that the perpetrator picked up Tina's body, perhaps to see if she was still alive. There is evidence on the ground her upper torso was moved given what we've seen."

"What?" Kent asked, his voice now grim.

"Are you sure, Mr. Hall, you want to hear?"

Jim nodded.

"There were two distinct blood pools from a wound in the back of her head. Her hair was matted on both sides, which indicates she had been moved and her head rested in two positions, one where she fell after being struck by the vehicle and the second after he laid her back down in the mud. Also, there were some faded blood trails left on both sides of her face the rain didn't wash away. They were distinctly different; indicating her head had been turned at different times. But the big thing is that we could make out two sets of body prints of the upper torso in the soft mud, especially the elbows."

Jim sat there stunned. He wanted to cry. What they described was a woman who had died an awful death, not the woman he was in love with, who in his mind was still very much alive. *Surely these weren't the same women*, he thought. But they were.

What bothered him was that someone had touched his wife, no, not just touched her, but defiled her as she lay dying. But his cloudy head wouldn't let him understand the importance of what they were trying to tell him. But there was something there, important, he just couldn't put his finger on it.

"Why did this person do those things...go back and move my wife?"

Flint took a long pause and then answered, "It wasn't that he wanted to move her; he wanted to know if she was dead or alive, and if alive, how hurt she was. We are just speculating now, but with our combined experience," Flint nodded to Trower, "it was probably someone that had been drinking...couldn't see all that well due to the rain, hit her and didn't even notice until he was down the road a bit. He backed up, tried to see if she was okay. When he saw that she was badly hurt, he probably got scared and...and he had to make a choice...either try to get her help, take the chances on her dying, or run. Either way he knew he was in trouble."

"Vehicular homicide," Trower said. "There ain't a jury in Oklahoma that wouldn't convict a drunk driver for killing the mother of two, and there ain't a judge that wouldn't send down the maximum sentence."

"So, Mr. Hall," Flint said, "what we're left with is an individual that made a choice to walk away and leave her and hope that no one saw."

"He might as well put a bullet in her head," Trower said. "The law, a jury, they'll look at it the same way."

Jim didn't say anything. His eyes were fixed, staring out the window, into the darkness. The detectives looked at each other, thinking they had said too much. The car was silent, except for the low hum of the motor and the whine of the windshield wipers.

They pulled down an inconspicuous service ramp, and followed it around a bend, then along a short strip of pavement that emptied into a small parking lot beside the hospital. In front of them hung two orange double doors; the word "ENTRANCE" glowed above them in large red letters, and a sign displaying the words: "Lakewood Coroner's Office" set off to the right of the doors.

It began to rain heavy as Jim stood up from the car. Right away, his attention was drawn to the doors. There was a thick black bumper attached to each one that showed signs of tremendous wear. He realized somewhere in the back of his mind the wear came from stretchers being bumped against them, as bodies passed in and out of the building, day and night.

He was surprised the doors swung open so easily, given how large they were. As they entered through them, they came to a second set of double doors identical to the first and they walked through them and down a hallway, and then stopped in front of a lighted counter. Below the counter, taped to the cinder-block wall, was a homemade sign that read: "Sign In." Behind the counter, a plump woman with frosted white hair, chubby cheeks and a double chin, decorated with a large discolored mole, sat looking blankly back at them. Detective Trower stepped to the counter.

"What can I do ya for tonight, hun?" she asked.

"Here to ID," Trower said.

"Sign in here," she said blandly. She handed him a dark brown clipboard, with papers attached. Trower filled in the spaces for a moment and then turned and looked at Jim.

"Ready?" he said.

"Okay," Jim said, nodding.

Trower handed the clipboard back to the woman and she tore a carbon copy from the bottom and handed it to him.

They made a number of winding turns, passing office doors, some with etched opaque glass, all with handles tarnished dull with age. Homemade signs randomly hung in the halls. One said: "Don't Leave Stretchers Unattended," another: "Please Clean Up All Spills." Jim found the place dank and musty. A pungent aroma erupted in his nose as they turned abruptly and walked through a set of double doors similar to the ones at the entrance of the building; a sign over the doors written in bold white letters on a red plastic plate of glass read: "Room C."

He felt queasy when they walked into the room, and his head began to feel light; he thought at any moment he might fall forward on his face, but was determined to keep his balance, and so continued to walk forward, toward an uncertain site. He was nervous, his hands moist, not knowing what to expect, but expecting the worse. His nostrils were filled with the smell of disinfectants and other unidentifiable odors. They irritated his nose and constantly reminded him of where he was.

There was a single metal table almost in the middle of the room with the shape of a body on it protruding underneath. A single large light dangled from the ceiling above, saturating the sheet with an artificial brightness, causing a bluish-white hue.

Other metal tables were pushed to the sides of the back wall waiting to be receptors for other bodies. A stack of blue sheets was folded neatly on one of them. He knew Tina was probably under the blue sheet, on the lone table. They walked closer. He felt himself disappear in a tunnel, where only he existed. His eyes never left the table as he walked forward, in heavy feet.

He felt pangs in his stomach as they approached. She now was no more than fifteen feet away. He didn't notice the detectives had stopped walking with him until he was several feet in front of them. Flint turned to an orderly that stood nearby. He showed him a paper, and then Flint pointed at the drawers seated into the wall at the left of the room. The orderly shook his head and pointed to the table, where Jim already knew she was.

The orderly, dressed in a long knee-length white coat, with some sort of silver instrument stuffed into his left breast pocket, walked to the side of the table. Flint motioned for Jim to go ahead.

He walked slowly, his legs were rubbery; he felt them give a little, and his body swayed for moment. But he kept walking, carefully placing one foot in front of the other, until he came to the table. The orderly began to lift the sheet off her face, but Jim stopped him with a gentle hand and motioned him away.

He brushed his fingers along the sheet, and then abruptly withdrew them for a moment, surprised at how coarse it was. *She deserved better*, he thought. He slowly pulled the sheet back from her, and there lay what he had asked God not to be.

He held out a single finger and slid it along the contours of her cheek. Her skin was cold, and pasty, and foreign to his touch; he broke down and wept uncontrollably beside her, his head lying on her shoulder.

He thought it unbelievable that just six hours ago he watched her laughing with the children at home. He had kissed this same cheek, touched these same hands, and now she was gone. He squeezed her hand and brushed the hair back from her face; he bent down and kissed her gently on the forehead. "I love you," he whispered. Softly, he pressed his face against her cold cheek, tears bulging, then falling from his eyes onto the sheet below. He prayed to God that she would wake up, that he would feel her warm breath on his face. He stood there for a long time, but the warm breath never came.

Finally he relinquished all hope. He raised a little, and surrounded her hand with his and held it tightly for a moment, and then wiped the tears from his eyes. He took the sheet carefully in his hands and gently laid it back over her face. He stepped back for a moment, not wanting to leave her, looking at her one last time. Finally, he walked away.

Flint said nothing, just handed him the clipboard and pen, and showed him where to sign. Jim signed it and handed it back and walked hurriedly through the double doors, through a series of turns and out of the building to the car.

He slumped down into the back seat; his mind turned to his children and memories of the past. He watched Trower and Flint walk out of the building and get into the car. They didn't say a word and he didn't speak to them. He just sat silently in the back seat, staring at the little beads of rain that gathered on the window, and then following them with his eyes as they tumbled down to the seal.

The ride back to Jim's house was an eerie feeling, the detectives recalled, as if somehow they had left Jim Hall behind in the morgue. What they took home that night, perhaps, was only a remnant of the man he used to be, a man that had nothing now, but his children and his demons.

# Chapter 8

The drive back was a long one, longer than the trip there it seemed. He said not a single word, just looked out the window at nothing, memories flooding his head. Every once in awhile from the rearview mirror Detective Trower would catch a tear or two rolling down Jim's cheeks and then he would turn away, leaving him to his lament.

He had met Tina at the University of Tulsa in Oklahoma. Jim was a senior and Tina a sophomore. A mutual friend introduced them, and soon after, they fell in love, and their lives entwined and they were inseparable.

They made a good-looking couple and everyone told them so, everybody except Tina's parents. It wasn't that Herb and Martha didn't like Jim…they were just unsure of him: his raising, or lack thereof, and the meager prospects of what he could eventually offer her in terms of a comfortable future, were plaguing questions. Prudes, no—realists, yes.

Class and tradition summed up the noticeable difference between the two. Tina belonged to a well-to-do upper middle-class family. Traditional in every sense of the word and protective. Her parents were uncompromising when it came to external challenges to the family, especially those challenges that threatened to give their daughter a life of mediocrity. But there was nothing they could really do. Lose a daughter or gain a son: the choice was simple enough.

But there still remained concerns and worry that Herb and Martha entertained often, especially when they began to find out more about Jim. Tina had never known what it was to do without: to do without parents, to do without clothes and sometimes without food. She had never known what it was like to be on her own, truly on her own. Nor did she know what it was like to want for things that she knew she would never have. She didn't know what it was like to fear, to hate and to be mistreated. However, Jim knew about these things; he knew about each one in cruel detail.

He was orphaned when he was three. His mother had been a slut teenager, pregnant at sixteen, just a child herself. She was killed in an accident soon after having Jimmy. Born out of wedlock, he never knew his father, perhaps his mother didn't either. It didn't matter. He had long since given up the fantasy of having a blood relative.

He was passed from foster home to foster home. More often than not, these were not homes, but merely houses—places to stay—and most of the time they only provided the mere necessities to sustain life. He never knew a stable environment of love and support, only the horror of a less than adequate foster family that had little interest in him and more in the subsidy the state and federal government provided to support him. Rarely did he see any benefit from it.

More than once he was taken out of a home for physical abuse, neglect or worse. These were painful, searing memories that often haunted him with the faces of his tormentors at night.

Jim graduated high school and received a scholarship to the University of Tulsa. He avoided the pitfalls that usually sideline and penalize children of similar background. He worked hard in school determined to become more than statistics said he should be. He was straight as an arrow and held stubbornly to the moral high ground, when those more fortunate faltered. He read the Bible from front to back when he was thirteen, even though at the time he was not living in such a God-fearing home. He learned early about the difference between right and wrong, and more importantly came to know that the boundary between the two were grayed and invisible. And with this learning, he came to understand the rewards and consequences of both.

Many would say that Jim Hall pulled himself up by his own bootstraps. It was a hard climb, but he had done it. No matter how many times Tina would listen to the stories of Jim's life, she would never truly know how he had suffered. The dark times he knew well as a child were untranslatable to words.

Their perspectives were from two completely different worlds. But, those worlds had emerged to complement one another very carefully. She was proud of Jim, and all he had accomplished, especially given where he had to start, and she knew that wasn't much.

Life had taught him to measure success in different ways. To him, it mattered what kind of man he was, what kind of father he made to his children and what kind of husband he was to his wife. Not how much money he made and how many things he could provide for them. He thought differently than most men, and it was this quality that Tina so greatly loved about Jim.

While her girlfriends complained of getting no attention from their husbands at all, Tina was always bathed in it. Unlike Jim, their husbands were barely noticeable when it came time for school projects, family outings and marshalling the kids. Jim was always there. He may not have made a ton of dough, but he was the best at providing for, and giving his love to his family.

Was it her father's idea of success? No. Nor did he understand Jim and how he thought about life. Their two perspectives were different, but their backgrounds were too. However, Herb did appreciate the fact his daughter was still very happy and that most of his friends' children weren't. They were either divorced, living back at home, or in the torrent throws of an abusive relationship. He was very grateful for the harmony and stability Jim provided for his daughter and grandchildren. He respected Jim. He often thought Tina could have married much worse.

He woke from his thoughts as the Crown Victoria made its way up Winding Creek Drive. He looked at his watch; it was after 1:00 a.m. All the houses lay in darkness, the edge of their front yards bathed in the glow of streetlights. As they made the final curve in the road, he noticed a light on at the Jacksons' house. Jim wondered what they were doing up; it was late. *Kent was probably burning the midnight oil on some project*, he thought. As the car approached the Jacksons' house, he strained to see in but the parted vents in the window blind shut abruptly and the light in the house extinguished abruptly.

The television flickered sporadically, casting shadows and bright lights onto the picture window, as they pulled into the driveway of his house.

"Here we are, Mr. Hall," Trower said. "We'll be in touch in the next couple of days. If we find out anything beforehand, I'll let you know. Call in the meantime if you have a question."

"We're sorry for your loss," Flint said. Trower nodded.

Jim shook hands with the detectives over the back seat and thanked them for all they had done.

"Goodnight, Mr. Hall," Flint said.

"Goodnight," Jim said.

The headlights from the car cast a shadow of him on the house. He looked like a big dark monster with short legs and dangling long arms; his head was the size of a watermelon as he crossed the front lawn. As the car drove away, the freakish shadow disappeared and Jim walked slowly towards the house. A full orange moon peaked between black clouds outlined in gray, and beamed down onto his face, painting it with a light glow. He let his legs come to a stop and looked up at it hanging there in the sky; he wished for a moment he was standing on its surface, far removed from where he was now. He dreaded entering the house; he knew it held a special kind of misery for him.

The steps to the porch felt insurmountable as he climbed them. Each one was a mountain all to itself. To help, he put a hand on top of each knee to push himself up the brick incline that lead to the porch.

It was cooler than usual that night and the front door was open; only the screen door remained closed. Jim could see Aunt Mae sleeping on the large recliner as he passed by the picture window. Inside the house he could hear her snoring violently, the sound of it loud enough to wake the dead. He paused for a moment at the window, and watched her puff out her onion lips with each breath. He smiled.

Jim knocked gently, but she didn't regain her consciousness. He tried again, this time louder, and then louder still, and finally he called out to her in a resonating whisper: "Aunt Mae...Aunt Mae...it's Jimmy."

"Wha—What?" She looked around for a moment, bewildered. Finally, her head cleared and she said, "Jimmy, is that you?"

"It's me, Aunt Mae."

"Just a minute. Let me unlock the door."

Aunt Mae got up awkwardly from the recliner, showing every bit her age and walked over and flicked the switch of the lock and opened the door.

"Oh, Jimmy, you look awful...let me get you some coffee or something..."

"No...I'm too tired. Are the kids okay?"

"Well they're good as expected, Jimmy." Her eyes glanced at her long fingernails while she tapped them against the dark leather skin of her forearm. "Poor Janie cried herself to sleep tonight, Jim...she's hurtin' plenty bad. I feel sorry for the poor thing."

"What about Kevin...how's he holding up?"

"About the same as Janie. He took a picture off the wall of Tina, the one with the thick wood frame, taken at her birthday last year and stared at if for hours. I think he went to sleep with it.

"I tried to feed them, Jimmy, but they weren't much hungry. I guess the stress and all."

"What about you, Jimmy, let me get you somethin'."

"Nah, I don't feel like eating too much myself."

"Are you sure?"

"Yeah."

"Why don't you stay here tonight, Aunt Mae." He looked at his watch. "It's nearly 1:30; too late to be going home."

"I've already called Harry and told him I would. He's going to drop by some things tomorrow...I'm here as long as you need me, Jimmy."

Jim put his arms around her and gave her a hug. "I really appreciate—"

She pouted out her lips and crossed them with her finger and gave him her trademark, "Shhhhhh." It was something she always did, when she didn't want to hear what you had to say. As if the idea you were thinking and about to say was completely ludicrous, and she knew that before you said it.

"Do you need me to get anything for you; and, you know where the spare bedroom is."

"I know where everything is; I am fine. If you need something during the night just come and get me—okay?"

"Okay, I will. Thanks Aunt Mae."

"Goodnight, Jimmy." She reached up and gave him a hug and a kiss.

"Goodnight."

Jim watched Aunt Mae walk slowly down the hall to the spare bedroom. She passed by Janie's and Kevin's bedrooms and stopped briefly and looked in each one and then disappeared into the darkness of the hall.

For the first time, a random thought asked the question of how hard it would be to raise his kids by himself. The thought frightened him. The difficulties of being a single parent he knew would be daunting, and silently he doubted how affective he might be. But, after a moment, he realized he would be as good as he had to be.

He reached down and picked up the television remote off the endtable. After several tries he finally found the off switch. The television made a *swooosh* sound and the blackness swallowed up the white on the screen.

He leaned straight-armed against the recliner. His head hung at the crotch between them. His brain folded the day's events over and over again in his mind. He pictured Tina smiling at him, like she had yesterday morning, before he went to work. She was in her purple terrycloth robe, her dishwater blonde hair piled on her head pinned together with a large brown and yellow speckled banana clip, the kind he always kidded her about, because if all else failed, it was the next best thing to actually having to fix your hair.

He finally stood up and rubbed his forehead with his hands, trying to remove the pain that was slowly pulsating above his eyes. He walked to the kitchen table and sat down for a moment, trying to imagine living in the house without Tina. He couldn't. The thought of it ate away at his stomach, and he felt acid in his throat.

Abruptly, his thoughts were interrupted. He heard Kevin scream out from his bedroom. Jim stood up and sprinted down the hall, accidentally hitting his shoulder on a picture frame as he passed by it, sending it crashing to the floor. He couldn't make out what he was calling out in his sleep; the words were jumbled and unclear. He stood in his doorway, listening for a moment.

"Is-mo-com-hom?"

"Is-moa-conem-hom?"

"Is-mo-ma-coing-hom?"

When he reached his bed he finally understood. The words hit him like a ten-pound sledgehammer, crushing him whole.

"Is Momma coming home?"

"Is Momma coming home?"

Kevin opened his eyes and screamed: "Dad! DAD! Is Momma coming home?"

Keven was wide-awake now peering up at him in the darkness. The aquarium he had beside his bed made little white reflections on his perfect blue eyes. Jim grabbed and hugged him and held him tight.

"It's all right, Kevie, It's all right…everything is going to be okay."

After a moment his son pulled away and looked up at him, his eyes full of tears, his hand trembling in front of his mouth, as if there was something terrible he wanted to hold back, afraid it might escape.

Finally he said softly, "She's not coming home, is she, Daddy? Momma ain't never coming home again…is she?"

He looked at his boy for a moment, and finally shook his head. "No, Kevie, Mom isn't coming home." His voice crackled and pitched as he forced the words from his mouth. And once he heard them, he marveled at the reality of their truth. To the boy, it could not be his mother his father was talking about; it surely was somebody else's mother. But, he knew that it was his, and that denying it would not change the fact that she was no more

"I dreamed she died, Daddy…and it scared me. I dreamed she told me goodbye and that she wouldn't be able live here anymore."

Tears swelled up in Jim's tired eyes. He rubbed a finger over them, wiping the moisture away, not wanting Kevin to see them.

"Sometimes, Kevie, we have to say goodbye to people we don't want to say goodbye to. Those we love…those we care for, it makes it just that much harder. But sometimes we don't have a choice, and all we are left with is to just say goodbye."

After a moment, Keven said, "I don't think it's fair, Daddy, that she left me." Then he paused, looking at the pale blue wall and then spoke again. "I need her…need her stay with me." Tears rolled down his cheeks. His breath quickened, as he sobbed in his father's arms.

"I need her, Daddy," he said

"I know you do, son, we both do, and so does Janie."

Jim brushed Kevin's light brown hair with the palm of his hand hoping that he would soon fall asleep. Finally the little Kevin drooped down into his soft pillow, while Jim pulled the blanket up over him and tucked it around his body the way he liked.

"Sleep, Kevie, sleep," Jim whispered, and the little boy drifted away.

Jim sat on the big brown couch in the living room. The couch had a way of surrounding your whole body and sucking you down in it like quicksand. He hadn't cared for the way it felt before, but he liked it tonight. It was comforting in a strange sort of way. Odd to think about a piece of furniture as comforting, he supposed, but he did.

He laid his hands over his face, and stared at the wall through his fingers. Tears rolled from his eyes and down the sides of his stubble-covered cheeks. He heard nothing but a slight hum in his ears and the "tick" of the clock on the mantle. His eyes drifted about the room, falling and lifting from one picture to another, from one memory to the next, until they came to a blank space on the wall where a picture used to hang. The space of wall said more than all the pictures combined. His wife's picture used to hang there, now it was tucked away in the arms of her little boy.

He thought it bizarre that last night his wife had slept with him in their bed and tonight she lay under an ugly blue sheet a million miles away. He stared at the blank space again, his head faint from exhaustion and lack of sleep. *She was just thirty-seven*, he thought, *how unfair.*

Jim laid his head back on the couch, closed his eyes and drifted, trying to think of a better time, a time when Tina was alive.

He welcomed the sweet seduction of sleep. He succumbed to its persuasion; its potency seized him and he fell far into the depths of it.

* * *

*Jimmy…Jimmy…Jimmy.* He heard a soft voice weave its way to his ear, a woman's voice.

*Wha…who…who's calling…*

*I'm over here, Jimmy...*

*Where?*

*I...I'm over here by the road.*

He knew who it was, and he felt her warmth wrap around him, her breath was full of life in his ear. *Tina...Tina...I can't see you. I'm here...I'm here—I can't see you.*

*I'm over here, Jimmy. Hurry...hurry—before it's too late. I can see you, Jimmy...I'm waving my hands, can you see me?*

*Yes...Yes, Tina...I see you now...thank God you're alive...thank God...I knew you were alive!*

*Come, Jimmy...before it's too late.*

Jim stumbled across the meadow, his feet sinking into the soft mud as he trudged toward the road where he had seen Tina. He caught glimpses of her through the thick fog; he swiped at it as he ran to get a better look. She would fade in and out through it, but he still heard her cries clearly. They were just over the other side of something earthy. He stumbled as he ran up an embankment and fell. His hands clawed at the dirt, grass and rock as he pulled himself up to the road.

The road was hot and steamy, and he stood up from all fours, as if he had just accelerated a million years through evolution. He stood there—knees grass stained with mud smears, rain-soaked shoes and his shirt half untucked. His hands were covered with cuts and bruises—fingernails outlined in black, packed full of the earth he had just clawed through.

He was unbelieving, unable to accept what his eyes told him was true. Lisa stood in front of him, in her fuchsia jogging suit staring down at something in the road. The fog was thick and he couldn't see what it was. He walked closer.

*There...there, you see, Jimmy...he hit me with his car. Honey, I am worried he's not going to get me help. He's been drinking and...and he doesn't want to get in trouble, Jimmy.*

He looked down and saw his wife badly hurt, lying there unconscious—rain beating her blood-soaked face. There was a man kneeling over her. He was holding her head screaming something. Jim couldn't hear the words, though, couldn't even see his face, only the man's long tan dress coat and black hair—his back was too him. Carefully the man laid her head and body down on the ground and abruptly got up. He wiped his blood-stained hands on his clothes and turned away; his eyes were full of fear.

He looked around him, then walked back quickly to his car. Jim struggled to see his face. He did everything he could to see him, but the man turned the opposite way each time he got close. The man sat down in his car with one last glance up and down the road. Jim screamed at him: "*GODDAMN IT, JUST DON'T LEAVE HER HERE. Oh God no! You're...You're not going to do this...You're not going to just leave her here, are you? Are you?*"

Jim's voice trailed off as the man closed his car door and drove away. His rear tires spun through the reddish earth and splattered watery mud behind him. Jim looked at his wife lying there on the side of the road, observing this last humiliation done to her. Light brown splotches that looked like chocolate ice cream stains covered her jogging suit and the breast of her white t-shirt. The mud and blood commingled with Tina's hair, and painted her face in a frightening swirl of violent dimensional colors. Her appearance was the last indignity of a ruthless act, perpetuated by a man driven by self-preservation.

*Jimmy, what are we going to do?*

His eyes reverted from his wife laying on the ground, to Tina that was standing over herself. She was crying and frantic, pleading with him not to let her go.

*I want to see my children again, Jimmy...you can't let me die here...please...please.*

Jimmy tried to pick her body up in his arms, but he couldn't lift her. Tina weighed no more than a hundred and twenty pounds, but no matter how hard he tried he couldn't raise her body from the rain-soaked earth. Each time he tried, he failed.

*Come on, Tina! Come on!*

He fell down, again and again, in the reddish mud and rock, driving the slushy sharp ingredients it contained hard into his knees, each time breathing in cloudy baked air into his lungs that drifted from the asphalt nearby. He would glance up at Tina, she was crying, her hands on her lifeless body as he tried to extract her from the rain-soaked earth. He was weakened. He had no strength. He was beaten by this uncontrollable debilitation. He suffered under her gaze, in his failure to carry her to safety. Finally he fell to the ground defeated, knowing that he could not pluck her from the ground. He put his mud-stained hands over his face and cried into them, but then felt a warm hand on his shoulder.

*You can do it, Jimmy...you can do it, I know you can.*

He raised himself up, and pulled his fingers across his face, wiping the wet soil and rain from the corners of his eyes. He looked at her with strained determination. *(Tina...I'm going for help, okay, I love you, honey, I'll be back...I'll be back for you.)*

*Jimmy, your voice...it sounds far away. There's not much time, honey...hurry, please hurry.*

Her words were ringing in his ears as he ran as fast as he could down the road. His shoes slapped at the hard blacktop as he heaved air in and out of his lungs. He stared down at the bright yellow fluorescent line in the middle of the road, trying to ignore the pain in his side from a cramp. He closed his eyes as he ran—his arms numb—the soles of his feet stinging.

"Do you have a phone," he yelled. "My wife, my wife needs help...please she needs an ambulance!" The clerk at the Quick-n-Snack kept on talking with an old man in front of her. She had long brown hair and was starkly slender. On her red low-cut blouse was a tag that said in the upper part, *Hi my name is*, and there was a well-worn space in the middle with white raised letters on black tape that said: *Sherry*. Directly below it was, *how can I help you?*

"Now, Daryl, you know I ain't got no time to be flirtin' with ya...I got payin' customers here...you old fool."

"I am here to buy cigs, darlin', and ya know it. I'm just lookin' over my choices."

The little old man looked like he had been wearing his pants and shirt about a day too long. His odor permeated the air, and stung his nose. The crevices of his neck were entrenched with dirt—his face was skeleton like; the skin stretched tightly over his cheekbones.

"LADY...I NEED A PHONE...NOW!" Jim yelled.

The lady looked dead-on at the little old man. "Come on, Hun—make up yer mind."

"Jim jolted toward the lady and slammed his fist on the counter. "Goddamn it, listen to me...I need some help...NOW."

The woman was unflinching...she turned and reached for some cigarettes the old man had requested as if she had not heard him.

"Can't you not hear me? CAN'T YOU HEAR ME? WHAT'S WRONG WITH YOU ALL?"

His incessant attempts to get attention from her or anyone in the store produced no noticeable reaction. It was as if he wasn't there, as if he was caught in time as an observer, nothing more. Unable to change what needed changing, unable to do what needed to be done. They didn't even look at him; nor did *Hi my name is Sherry*. Frustrated, he stumbled back in disbelief, turned and flung open the door—jingling the gold bells tied to the red yarn attached to the top of it. The sound of the bells trailed behind him as he sprinted back down Coventry Road, where Tina lay dying.

Jim saw the flashing lights of vehicles in the distance. His heart was pounding in his chest, his eyes pulsating as he fixed them on the blue and red strobes in the distance. The harder he ran the further they seemed to be. He imagined the road as one large black treadmill working against him—under the hegemonic influence of the slick black death that was so cleverly trying to steal his wife away from him. He was determined to not let that happen.

*Faster…Faster…*he told himself.

*I'm so cold, Jimmy—so cold…*

Jimmy ran through the strangled traffic and around the police cars and emergency vehicles. Tina was standing over the two men in bright white shirts looking at what they were doing to her. The men wore thick black belts crammed with every imaginable item—flashlights, scissors, tape—a plethora of things shoved into the detachable pockets. One was pumping her chest with his hands and blowing air into her mouth with his—screaming, "Breathe damn it, breathe," between each action. The other man rubbed paddles together with clear jelly flinging from them and put them on Tina's bare chest and yelled, "CLEAR!" The sound of an electrical charge reverberated off her body with a *whooooomp*. Tina lurched upward from the ground as the electric shock passed through her body. The other man put his fingers to her neck and yelled, "I still ain't got a pulse—HIT HER AGAIN…HIT HER AGAIN!

*I'm leaving, Jimmy…I want to stop! I want to stop, Jimmy…my kids!*

"CLEAR!"

*…whooooomp…*

A moment elapsed.

"Nothing…NOTHING GODDAMN IT…I ain't got a pulse!" one of the men said. The other man tore into a plastic package. His arms raised in a flurry of movements; he pierced the soft end of the bottle with a syringe, and drew out the clear liquid solution from it. He flicked the syringe and tiny bubbles raised to the top of the needled end, and then squirted out a portion onto the ground, with methodical precision.

*Colder, Jimmy…I'm getting colder.*

*Hold on, honey…hold on—they're gonna fix this….*

The man in the white shirt slashed through the air with the syringe and penetrated her breast, sinking the needle deep into her soft heart. He squeezed the plunger with his thumb as the magic potion disappeared inside her body. The other took her pulse and then pressed the paddles on her chest again and yelled, "CLEAR."

*Whoooomp.*

"Come on," said one of the men, "LIVE."

Jim was concentrating hard on the men in the white shirts, his body straining uncontrollably as if he were willing them the strength to save her. Praying, praying to God…to Jesus…to anybody who would listen. *If they would just let this one go*, he thought*…just this time….*

Jimmy looked up for a moment, surprised to see Tina standing beside him now looking at him…not looking at herself anymore. Her eyes, they were telling him something, but it was something he didn't want to hear. She looked peaceful, like after those times when they made love late at night, and her face would lay quiet doused in soft moonlight. He feared though this might be an eternal sleep, more than a simple kiss could break.

*No, dammit…you're not going to leave! I need you…the kids need y—*

*Shhhhhhh…Jimmy, I don't have much time left.* She slipped her hand in to his. *I want you to listen. I'm going to leave you pretty soon—you and the kids. I don't want to, baby. I'm going to miss you, but I guess it's my time.*

Jim tried to reach up and touch her, but his arms felt like they were bonded to his sides—he pulled at them with his shoulders but they were hopelessly bound in ropes of paralysis; the only feeling was her hand tightly squeezing his.

*Tell the kids I'm always going to be their mommy and that I love them…and that I will be with them and watch over them; when they need me—I will be there.*

*Tina, no…no*, Jim whispered, standing there helpless, gazing at her. Tears dripped off his cheeks; his lips formed the silent words *I love you.*

*I'm proud of you, Jimmy; you're a good man. Raise our kids, honey, the best you can. I'll be with you, honey…I'll be with you. I have to go…he's taking me now. I love you, honey…I love you—always remember…I'll be with you.*

*NO! NO! TINA…TINA! Don't go…don't go…Tina…Tina…Tina.*

"That's it, let's transport her," one of the men said, "she's through." The other one nodded and grabbed a packaged yellow sheet from a bright red box. Jim watched as they covered her body unceremoniously: first throwing the debris of their life saving work between the lower parts of her legs. "Sort it out later," one of them said. They loaded Tina's body in the ambulance, unhurried, physically drained, and adding another uncensored morose memory to their already large collection.

Jim stood there as he watched the emergency vehicles pull away. The police hesitantly let the gaggle of cars through to their destinations: the people inside them, unaffected by the tragedy that had just occurred. They were just spectators, he thought, unmoved by the loss of one of their own.

Jim woke up in a lather of sweat, the kind that dampens your body and makes your clothes stick to your skin. He felt his heart beating fast and hard in his throat, his mind verily aware of what was real. He glanced around him, trying to get his bearings—hoping to see Tina still standing there in front of him. She was not. Nor was the road, the ambulance or the rain. It was just him, sitting in the living room listening to the unnerving tick of the grandfather clock nearby.

He pushed his legs out in front of him, stretching them and letting them drop to the floor. He stared for a moment out the large picture window that broke up the monotony of the living room wall. Life was going outside. He saw that; and he didn't understand how it could. There was a boy riding his bike on the sidewalk, with dog in tow, cars marching down the street off to work for another day that was just like the day before. Nothing had changed. Only that his wife had died. Sadly he thought her passing left no interruption in the busy, daily life of his fellow man.

He looked at the old clock as it belched out eight chimes from its hollow belly. *What was there to do today?* he thought. *Everything and yet nothing.* He wasn't quite sure what to do now, what purpose there was, if he did do it.

He heard Aunt Mae stirring in the bathroom, going through what sounded like an ungodly morning ritual of flatulence and gargling, sprinkled with intermittent rushes of water from the faucet. He began to think about what life would mean for him now...now that his wife was forever sleeping.

He remembered the dream and what she had said: "Raise our kids the best you can." The words haunted him. The meaning of the words had great responsibility attached to them. He tried to negotiate the gravity of his predicament. But nothing would comfort the responsibility that had now been placed in his hands.

He thought about Kevie and Janie. How unfair this had been to them. About what words he would use today, in trying to comfort them. But he knew that nothing on heaven and earth would bind the ugly head of sadness that would feed upon them for the days and years to come.

As he thought about it, despite all his best intentions, he couldn't stop feeling hate for the man that he had seen in the long tan dress coat, the one with black hair. This man was the one who had left his wife to die on a muddy patch of ground. His emotions mixed portions of grief and sadness with the lethality of others like hate and anger. He couldn't find forgiveness in his heart for him, though he knew that was what Tina would want him to do.

He heard his children stirring from their sleep. He braced himself for what lay ahead in the day and what he might say. His body was already tight with anguish in anticipation of them. *Damn the man who had delivered this dark hour*, he thought. But, he assumed this man was far away by now.

Little did he know that he lived only a few houses away.

# Chapter 9

"Well you are," she said.

She was adamant now, as she took the pot roast from the oven.

"You're going with me to take this dish over to the Halls'. It's not going to kill you to show some concern for someone else." Her tone was condescending and her face was wrought in deepening distress over her husband's apathy to the apparent suffering of others.

"It's not that I don't want to go, Lisa. I feel bad about what happened. I like those people. I just have…I have a lot of things to do today, a lot of important things." His excuses tried to cloak the *dirty hungry guilt* that lay hidden deep inside him. It was now devouring every conscious moment, trying to get out, scratching, clawing, and doing everything it possibly could to reveal itself. He prayed he could keep it imprisoned.

His words rang deafly on her ears. His acid tongue was morose to her and his excuses were childlike and not forthcoming: like sluggish words that slowly poured out lies from his mouth like thick molasses.

"Kent, I'm going to say this one time and I hope that you hear me. Are you listening?" She looked at him like *by God you better be*.

"Yeah, I'm listening." *Listening to that noise gushing out your pie hole*, he thought.

"I put up with a lot of your crap over the years, but today, so help me, if you don't do this one act of decency…I mean they were our friends for Pete's sake." She turned sternly looking at him, flowery oven mittens adorning each hand push passed her wrists, her hair perfectly shaped with all the artificial color her face could handle. A checkered apron hung from her neck, loosely tied at her waist, it being the last hope of circumventing any culinary mishap that might spoil the black knee-length dress of which they lay underneath.

Kent knew he would have to go. He was already running two hours late as it was. He had canceled his office appointments at nine and ten; it was now near eleven. He had dared not dismiss the issue and leave until it was resolved, but it wasn't going to be and she wasn't going to leave.

Lisa didn't give ultimatums very often, but for some reason today she was adamant. He didn't like when she used words that threatened him; the words contained precocious implications for their marriage. It reminded him of his dependents on her. He didn't want to ever lose her. *No, that would be too expensive, too messy.*

*Maybe this would not be such a bad thing after all,* he thought. *No one would suspect I ran my neighbor right the hell down with my truck and then showed up on her husband's doorstep offering my condolences the morning after. What kind of sick fuck would do that? It's just,* he told himself, *well, I feel...bad about it. Goddamn bad! And I don't want to feel bad. It's like I woke up this morning and something was slowly nibbling on me, piece by piece, and here it is almost eleven, and I feel it's eaten halfway through my fucking brain.*

*I'm afraid to go over there, I admit it,* he told himself. *Afraid the thing inside me, making me feel bad, might get restless, might start eating at me, eating holes right through me, might even start eating a hole up through my body, through my neck and out my mouth. Then the dirty hungry guilt would show its fucking ugly head to everyone, and that would be it. I'd spend the rest of my life being a cum receptacle in one of the fine correctional facilities we have here in Oklahoma. No, I can't let that happen. I've worked too hard and came too far to lose it all now. Not over someone that didn't have the good sense to keep her ass home when it looked like rain—fuck that!*

Kent reflected on his thoughts for a moment as he put on the dark red and hunter green-striped tie in the kitchen. He was appalled at his own propensity for unwholesome pragmatism. He thought that perhaps he had become so detached from his own feelings he couldn't feel another's pain other than his own. It was a darkness that troubled him, a malaise that had implications, but after awhile the thought was gone. The *dirty hungry guilt* had retreated; it had lost, at least for now. But, he was sure it would return.

He twirled the loops nervously around his fingers as he looked at Lisa. She was pissed as hell, preparing the food in rapid fashion with overtly loud concussions directed squarely in his general direction. He didn't like to see her this way, to use threatening words, to make a nasty fuss over something that wasn't a big deal, at least not to him. He would go because he needed to. He would go because there would be hell to pay if he didn't. After all, he could control that thing inside him, *couldn't he*? He would have to just slam the lid down on it and hold it down tight. *Tick-a-lock just like when you're a kid, and you take an imaginary key and pretend to lock up your lips and then throw it away.* It would be just like that. "*Tick-a-lock.*"

"Did you say something?" Lisa asked.

"Uh, no…just talking to myself."

"You know, Lisa, you're right. I don't know what I was thinking. I need to go over and give Jim Hall my condolences." He looked at his reflection in the dark microwave window, brushing a few hairs into place. "There's nothing more important than supporting Jim and his kids through this horrible time." He flicked his eyes toward her and then back, lips parting to bare brilliant white teeth to the makeshift mirror. "I'm sorry, honey, I have been a pain. I don't know what came over me." He turned and walked across the marble tiled floor, and gently put his hands around her arms at the lower biceps. "Sometimes me don't think so good." He flashed her a big dumb-looking smile, then kissed her firm red painted lips, then her cheek, then her neck.

"Come on, forgive me…please? You know what, I'll even take the rest of the week off. You'll have me for two whole days."

*Oh great…how lucky can one girl get,* she thought.

"All right, all right," she finally said, "you'll mess up my face." She pushed him away, still looking mildly irritated. She pressed her lips together smoothing her lipstick and shook her head as if to say…*probation, buddy, you're on probation.*

She was suspicious of his sudden overture to make peace. He had conceded too early. *He wants something, maybe?* she thought. She suspected her quick victory would be hollow, and come at a price.

"Help me carry these dishes out to the car," she said curtly.

"Yes, ma'am."

Kent picked up the hot dish forcing a smile. He could see a large browned piece of roast crowding the potatoes and carrots through the glass lid, some drowning in the warm thick broth. He carried the dish out to the van and laid it carefully down in the back of it. Lisa followed him with a hot blackberry cobbler and two purple towels slung over her shoulders.

"What are those for?" Kent asked.

"To put around the dishes so they don't spill." Her voice was still tense.

"Oh, I never would have thought of that."

"That's why you have me here, isn't it, to think about the things that you don't want to; to do the things you don't want to?"

The question was sharply pointed and he ignored it. *She just needs time to cool off,* he thought. He smiled at her nice like and then changed it to a patronizing smirk, throwing his eyes up toward the overcast sky, as she turned her back to him.

The distance to the Halls' was a short one, but it was a long drive for Kent. He was nervous about seeing Jim, but curious to see if he suspected him. Curious to see if he could tell what he was hiding, inside him. But Jim had no reason to believe he was hiding anything, no reason to suspect him. It's just that he felt it showed on his face. That's what he was curious about. Did it show on his face?

Kent was filled with anxiety as he stood at the Halls' front door with Lisa. Already he could feel the *dirty hungry guilt* trying to escape. *Maybe this wasn't such a good idea.* He breathed deeply, sighing each time he exhaled. He stretched his arms outward—exposing the pale white undersides of his wrists, which stayed hidden under his shirtsleeves for most of the year. He shifted his feet back and forth anxious like some kid on his first day at school in anticipation for what lay behind the door. He gave off the impression he was predominately bored, much to the displeasure of his watchful wife. But, he knew that the real reasons lay further inside, deep inside him.

"What's your problem?" she asked. Her eyes shifted with his body moving from side to side. His tie swung back and forth as if it were a pendulum whisking through the air at every nervous twitch.

"Nervous, I guess."

"Well stop it," she said under her breath. "Act like you're here for a reason and not to wear out your shoes."

The door opened and behind it stood a middle-aged man that neither one recognized. His hair was dusty blonde and he had it combed neatly to the side.

"Hi, won't you both come in."

Kent looked around. He recognized a few faces, but not many. Most he guessed were out-of-towners that rushed in after they heard the news. They stood there awkwardly, with overly warm dishes in their hands, gawking at people who gawked back. Searching their red-rimmed eyes, he could see the shock and devastation that Tina's death had brought to their eyes. Perhaps most of them would keep her memory ebbed in a secret place, far deep in their minds, not to get the memory of her out until they could better deal with the hideous cruelty of it at a later date.

Two old ladies appeared out of nowhere, greeted them and took their covered dishes and scurried back to the kitchen.

"I don't believe we've met. I'm Ted Vance, Tina's brother."

He flashed a smile and stuck out his hand.

Kent stood silent, motionless, and oblivious to the hand that jutted out toward him. He just stared at him with a slight whimsical grin, his mind back peddling at the sudden proposition of meeting Tina's brother. He felt like he would puke right there on the cream-colored carpet.

"And you are?" he said. Ted's hand was still extended; he looked intently into Kent's face.

*I killed your sister!* The words formed in Kent's head—the *dirty hungry guilt* now trying to get out.

Lisa looked up at her husband, puzzled. She grabbed Ted's hand and shook it with a smile, as she nudged Kent from behind with admonishment. "We're the Jacksons—Kent and Lisa—neighbors from down the street. We're so sorry to hear of your loss. Tina was a special person."

"Thank you. Yes, she was. We are all horribly devastated over this, especially Jim and the children. It was so sudden."

*Go ahead and tell him! TELL HIM NOW, YOU GODDAMN COWARD, tell him how you killed his sister and left her to die in the mud—you prick. What a nasty piss hole thing to do.*

Kent shook Ted's hand weakly, his eyes glazed over. He didn't say a word.

*What's a matter, Kent, Tina got your tongue?*

"I would like for Jim to know you're here, would you come with me? He's in the dining room with the kids."

"Uh...no, we better not bother him. We know he's been through a lot and probably just needs some peace and quiet." Lisa listened to her husband talk. It was as if someone had taken over his body and forced him to say overtly stupid things to a man that had just lost his sister. His voice droned through a flurry of excuses, each one greater than the last when objections were raised, almost to the point of being ridiculous. Finally Lisa had had enough.

"Yes, we would like to do that and offer our support and prayers to Jim and the family," Lisa said. She glared at Kent.

Kent stared blankly back at Lisa. His head slightly shook in disagreement, much to Lisa's embarrassment, but he said nothing; he just began walking with them, like a man going to the gallows. The *dirty hungry guilt* cackled out a hideous laugh inside his ear.

He didn't want to see Jim or his children; he didn't want to see anybody that had anything to do with Tina. For a moment the tinges of madness began to impale him. He wanted to run out of the house screaming that he'd killed her. He was terrified now, as each step took him closer to the husband of the wife he had killed. The *dirty hungry guilt* now curled up inside his throat; its furry thick tale tickled his vocal chords. It whispered to him, faintly, like a feather brushing over an eardrum. *Tell them...Tell them...Tell them what you've done.* He swallowed hard before it devoured him. His eyes were wide, face flushed with blood, and he felt it laying on him. His wife looked at him, her face folding in disappointment. He was scared, goddamn it, he was scared. *What if it tried to get out again?*

The three walked down a hallway into the dining room. It was painted cranberry and in the center stood a long cherry wood table, a potpourri of food covering it. On the wall hung brilliant colors painted on canvas by a woman who was now heavily mourned. Around the table were arranged a hodgepodge of mismatching chairs as well as the matching ones. In these seats sat the nucleus of the Hall and Vance families, who were now feeding at the trough of sorrow.

This was not what Kent wanted to see. This was not where he wanted to be. With them, wading up to his neck in the pitiful agony of death. The room reeked with the odor of fresh sorrow, it rising in heavy waves from their bodies. They sat there with incredulous looks on their faces, not wanting to give her up, a malady that hung thick in the air.

The food on the table went untouched, their stomachs already full from bitter grief. Their pain replaced food as their sustenance; their hunger abated by indulging in it. Their memories ambushed them in silent reflections, directed by some trigger from the past.

Kent was not happy. Fear and guilt mingled as he looked into Jim's dark sleep-deprived crevices. Jim got up immediately and Lisa stepped forward and gave him a hug, patting him on the back as she did and silently whispering, "We're going to pray for ya, Jimmy—whatever you need just let us know."

*You're no good, Kent, just an ugly monster running amuck. Why don't you get the hell out of here and go find yourself a nice knotted rope to slip around your neck and hang out in the garage for awhile. It would make you feel a lot better, and I could go away and bother somebody else.*

Kent felt a massing in his throat as Jim embraced him. Kent lightly put his arm around him and told him that "everything would be okay." He had no idea what he was saying at the time. He just said it. He thought it sounded good.

*You liar, you filthy liar, you killed his wife, and then tell him everything will be okay? How the fuck do you know? Tell them...tell them now...tell them before it's too late!*

"Kent, Lisa, I want you to meet Tina's parents," Ted said. "This is Herb Vance."

*I killed your daughter and left her to bleed to death beside a muddy road. (Shut up!)*

Herb stood up and leaned across the table and shook hands with Kent and then with Lisa. He was a big man, about six feet two and had giant hands. His shiny white hair shimmered as the light from the chandelier caught it just right. His face had a red tinge to it, like a man who had too many drinks over too many years.

*TELL THEM! TELL THEM...tell them now, you miserable fuck!*

Kent choked down the hard lump pressing in his throat. He couldn't breathe. He inconspicuously tugged at his collar, hoping for relief. He felt faint and noxious and he wondered if the guilt was displaying on his face. His eyes diverted away from Jim's. He didn't want him to see what was trying to claw its way out his throat.

"...and this is Martha," Ted said.

*I killed your baby girl and let her bleed on a muddy patch of earth beside a Godforsaken road! (Shut up! Shut up!)*

Kent looked at her, his heart racing; she neither looked at him nor looked away. She was lost to her own grief, *about to shake the hand of her daughter's killer.* He lifted his hand and she shook it coldly saying not a word. She looked up for a moment and locked her hollow eyes to his, as if she could see the deep darkness he was hiding. Kent quickly let go of her hand and her eyes drifted once more.

Kent glanced around the room, surveying the collection of faces, while Lisa converted a handshake with Martha to a maternal embrace. He strained to search each person's eyes, paranoid of the resonating voice inside of him, suspicious that someone might see the *dirty hungry guilt* pass over his face. He saw no one, but took careful note of Jim who was staring directly at him. *Did he see something in him?* He forced a smile at him and nodded his head, but one was not returned. He feigned glancing around the room, still aware of Jim in his peripheral vision watching him. He drew his eyes back to Jim and then noticed that someone was speaking to him, but Jim hadn't responded. They nudged him and he jerked for a moment and his fixed eyes broke from the trance that was either locked to the wall or Kent.

Kent was now wrapped in a shroud of self-induced fear, while Lisa made nervous chitchat. His tortured mind pleaded for her to just *shut up—to just shut her mouth* so they could leave. He felt as if he were going to vomit again, but realized how embarrassing the reality of that proposition might be.

He saw Jim's children, Janie and Kevin, seated together securely near their father. Their eyes were clearly tortured—red and puffy—filled with deep fallen despair. Their clothes wrinkled and hair lifeless, awoken from a beastly nightmare, alarmed that it was real. The girl, probably every bit of fourteen, had a white tissue in her pale hands, crumpled and soaked in sorrow. The end of her nose was red and tortured. Her lips trembled. The boy, perhaps nine, sat in silence, holding his father's hand. He saw how close they were and for a moment admired them, wishing that he was as close with his own son. The boy looked bewildered. Turmoil whirled around in his deep brown pools, grief etched upon his face, meekly subdued by a sadistic pain that would never leave him.

His thoughts ebbed as Lisa began her commentary of love, prayers and support and ended it with goodbye. *Thank God*, he thought. He was relieved when she said it. Some confidence returned to him, as he felt the *dirty hungry guilt* slide back down his throat. The coven it had made for itself in the base of his throat now felt empty and he could swallow without pain. But he was cautious. He knew it could return.

Lisa recounted the display of grief they had just witnessed. "It was savage," she said out loud as she undressed. "I have never seen lives so totally destroyed. I just hope—and I know it won't do any good now—but I just hope they catch the sick bastard who did this. He deserves all that they can throw at him."

Kent listened to her words, and wondered if she would feel the same if she knew it was he that had done it. If she knew that if he were to be found out, all this around them would flutter away, that their lives would be crushed. That he would go to prison, she and the children would be paupers. There would be no more big beautiful house and no more nice cars. If anyone found out about this, it would all come crashing down. He pondered the consequences for a moment. Then said, "Yes, I hope they get the bastard." The words slid off his tongue, the word *bastard* had slick and slippery feel. It was him.

He sat on the large king size bed and lay back with his feet touching the floor, staring at the cottage cheese ceiling. He began to think—hard—turning his attention to another matter, a matter that needed to be dealt with rather hastily. *Evidence.* He had to get rid of it…all of it…everything and anything that might implicate him.

He wasn't sure who might have seen him. He was entirely sure he could keep the *dirty hungry guilt* inside. Either way, he had to get rid of any and all evidence. He shuddered to think what a search warrant would turn up, let alone the dent and scratches on the right side of his Toyota. That was what he was really worried about. *That goddamn dent.*

He needed to concentrate, to come up with a clever plan that would get rid of it. A plan that involved less risks as possible and took into account all that might be probable. *Don't make a mistake*, he thought, *think, dammit, think.*

*Tina's funeral is Saturday—trash pick up Monday.* He would dump the clothes then. *And then there is the matter of the dent in the car.* Kent thought about that ugly fucking dent on the right truck fender, probably about the size of a woman's head. He wanted no written record that he had body work done on the car, until he could *what, do what? Have an accident? Yes, an accident*, he thought.

He would take the car out tomorrow and wreck it, damage it—in a collision with something. He thought hard about it. *Yes, that might work.*

He studied the days—Saturday morning was out. The funeral was at 9:00 a.m. and they already had dinner plans with Lisa's parents that evening. Sunday was mandatory church till noon, an appeasement to his wife, a trade off of sorts for his ill behavior he practiced during the week.

*Friday... Tomorrow...*

He would need an excuse to leave—*go to the store perhaps*—and the right place that others frequented less often. He thought about a large grocery store parking lot or discount store and concrete blocks that prevent people from knocking down lampposts. How convenient it would be to hit one of them by accident, right in the spot where he had hit Tina. But there would be people and he didn't want anyone to think he was doing it intentionally; he couldn't be that obvious.

He thought about telephone poles, but most stood some distance from the streets and roads.

*Guardrails... Guardrails...*

He pondered it. This introduced an element of accidental authenticity, but also a degree of elevated danger. Kent rubbed the top of his head, spurring his brain to think about the possibilities of what guardrails had to offer. Serious injuries ranked among some of his concerns. *Something might go wrong,* he thought.

Lisa walked around the bed glancing at Kent. "What are you thinking about?"

He didn't answer—he was momentarily lost in thought.

"You know it might have been just me, but you acted kind of strange over there at the Halls'. Is there something bothering you?"

Kent snapped out of his trance. His eyes began following her around the room. She was naked from the waist up, still in her pantyhose, her hair now pulled on top of her head.

"Nothing…nothing at all," he said, as he rolled on to his side, eyes fixed on her.

Lisa looked at him and sat down close on the bed. "This whole thing is so strange, you know…it's hard to deal with really. I mean, I just talked to Tina yesterday morning…we were talking about dinner plans, maybe next week…I…I just don't know." Tina put her middle and fourth finger between her brows gently and started to rub—attempting to relieve tension that had built up over the course of the day.

"Here, let me do that." Jim laid her down on the bed, and then kneeled beside her. He stroked her brows with his large soft thumbs until all resistance vanished from her face. She reached up after a time, and took his hand and placed a kiss in the middle of his smooth palm. He kissed her gently on the lips and held her in his arms—she kissed him back and all became forgotten. They melted into each other as day turned to evening, leaving the unsettling day behind.

# Chapter 10

The Toyota idled as it sat in front of the Quick-n-Snack. He sipped a cup of black coffee, watching patrons walk in and out of the store. He looked at his watch; it was 9:45 a.m. He sat the coffee down and gripped the steering wheel tightly, thinking about what he might do and how he might do it.

He flinched at the idea of intentionally ramming his car into something heavy and solid and made of metal or concrete. His body tightened as he considered how the impact might feel, the jarring of it, the forward lurch, the tearing of metal screaming in his ears, his head being slung forward in a pillow of air. The proposition made him queasy, and his throat grew dry and narrow thinking about it.

Perhaps he would attribute the wreck to inattentive driving. A ticket would probably be issued. A small price to pay for getting away with—*was it murder*? In his mind, *no*. Just an unfortunate accident he had been unlucky enough to find. It wasn't as if he set out to kill her intentionally. *No, it wasn't that at all; it was just an accident*, he told himself.

Kent guided the car up Freemont Avenue searching for the right opportunity at the right time. After nearly half an hour, the panic built in him; his fear of returning home empty handed with nothing to show for his effort, but the nasty head-size dent in his right fender. The dent that had been caused by the accident banged away at his head. But he saw nothing. There were either too many people or it was too dangerous.

The best spot he could think of was a nice set of guardrails located at a bend in the highway on State Route 4, south of the Belmont exit. *People crashed into them all the time. He could just plow right into them*, he thought, *slow down to about thirty-five and destroy that nasty little dent forever*. But if he went there now, how would he explain it to Lisa? He told her quite assuredly, he was going to Super Wal-Mart, and the closest one was up north on Apple Gate Street. He had no business on State Route 4. Besides, seventy-five miles per hour was the average speed on 4, and he might wind up a permanent part of the guardrail. *It's been known to happen*, he thought. An image of him with his head dangling out the shattered front windshield was a little more than he wanted to sign up for. He quickly dismissed guardrails and continued hunting for other lucrative targets.

Kent dodged a number of potholes worn into the asphalt as he made his fifth return trip up Freemont. If he wasn't back soon, Lisa was going to worry and when she worried, she began to ask questions that he had to stretch to get answers for. And he didn't feel up to rattling a laundry list of why he wasn't playing hide the sausage with whoever was at the top of her list right now.

He began to feel the slight fishhooks of panic needling into his skin. *He had to do something...drive off the road, smash his car into a bridge, smack a truck, anything now, anything.* In his paranoia, he could see a platoon of police waiting for him at his house, all pointing fingers at the dent in his fender. He could hear their voices. *There it is! He's the one; he's the little fucker we've been looking for. Take him to the pokie, take him now and shove him in with the big fella that likes nice tight white-collar men.*

His eyes strained, searching the road. Gripping the steering wheel tight, his body clinched into one giant cramp. Anxiety spread over his skin like red-hot hives. He waited for the right opportunity...watching...driving...waiting. And then he saw it. The world stopped. He heard nothing. He felt nothing. A moment caught in time hung helplessly in his vision. It waited there for him...wanting him to seize it. There before him was a 1974 pea green Chevy Impala, a sacrificial lamb sent from the golden gates of heaven. It lurched out onto the street in front of him. He wiped his mouth quickly with the back of his hand. He hesitated for a moment. He had enough lead time...probably 15 yards. He could miss it, swerve and miss it—miss it by a mile.

*Do it! Do it! Do it!* A voice cried inside of him. He listened to the voice; it was sweet and salty, licking at his ears, enticing him to do it. *"Hit the old car, goddamn it,"* the voice said, *"show it no mercy, no mercy by God, no mercy. Just do it! Do it now!"*

He accelerated hard, charging the Impala, until he was right upon the old clinker; he abruptly braked for show and then sheered right into it. The braking was just enough to appear as if he had tried to stop and miss it, in case there were witnesses.

He hit the Impala's midsection, catching it at an angle, raking it down the side with his bumper. The impact was not as bad as he might have expected; the air bags didn't even deploy. It felt more like one of those cheep carnival rides when you're a kid, a ride usually called the Octopus or Hell-Cat or something like that, whipping you around violently against the rigid sides of a small tin corrugated metal box. Hitting the old Impala felt the same, except the ride took seconds not minutes.

He lurched forward in his seat briefly, the belt digging into his gut, like dental floss in teeth. The breath was forced from his lungs. He wasn't really frightened; it all seemed to flow in slow motion, coordinated and surreal. His Toyota came to rest in the other lane. Looking up, his eyes widened as a gravel truck plowed screeching toward him. It fish-tailed sideways, braking hard. His body stiffened to brace for the impact; his mouth gaped open in shock at the enormous beast rapidly approaching.

It stopped just a foot short of the Toyota. Kent held his breath for about ten seconds, then finally let out a long breath and loosened his grip from the steering wheel, relaxing slightly. His heart pounded like a set of pistons thrashing back and forth from the inside of his chest. For a moment he had become part of his truck, stiffened and straight legged, foot jammed on the brake, pulling the car's steering wheel like an aircraft yoke, bracing for what he was sure would inevitably come. But it didn't and he was safe.

Kent slightly turned the ends of his lips upward, faintly smiling, silently complimenting himself on a job well done. *It couldn't have been executed any better*, he thought. He glanced over to the Impala; a Hispanic man and woman and their kids spilled out of the car. All looked shaken but unhurt. They spoke rapidly in Spanish, conversing back and forth. He supposed they were asking each other if they were okay.

The driver of the car turned and looked at him. Kent shrugged as if to say, *It was just one of those things.* The Hispanic man's face tightened violently and he strutted like a bull toward him, ready to charge at any moment. He had a buzz cut and wore a black shirt with ripped-out sleeves, jeans and brown sharp-towed cowboy boots. Black inked tattoos decorated his huge loaf-like arms. Kent noticed, on his left bicep was a skeleton laughing, riding a Harley-Davidson motorcycle. "Death Rider" was written in smart calligraphy below it. A pit bull with a sharp spiked collar sat center of his right elbow and wrist. "BRING IT ON" was penciled above its head.

He threateningly pointed at Kent, as he walked. His broken English spewed out obscenities and epithets. Kent shot him an appeasing smile. He took his hands and pushed them down repeatedly, as if to try to conjure up a calming effect, to tame the hideous behemoth coming full-steam toward him. As came closer, Kent feebly choked some words about not having time to stop and he tried to miss him. *Some excuses are just better than others*, he thought, as the man clinched his fist and said, "Yew gon-eh-pey yew god'am az'hole...gonna tomp eh mua-ole n'yew."

A police car approached, just when the driver Hispanic man drew back his giant brown fist. He wondered if the man would throw it. He stiffened his face waiting for the impact. The man looked at Kent, deciding what to do. He looked extremely irritated. He looked at the police car and then at Kent and slowly lowered his fist to the side of him. But it remained clinched. Kent felt a little relieved. The driver walked away, shaking his head, speaking in Spanish. Kent could only make out one of the words he said: "punta." He smiled; he knew what that one meant.

He watched him as he walked back to his family. The woman was crying, glancing and shaking her head at the car and pointing at it. Finally, she put her pinched face into her hands and wept. The two children clung to her dress, scared as their father omionously loomed near.

Several police cars later, all seemed to go well. He watched as a wrecker pulled the Toyota and Impala to the side of the road. He was questioned by police on how the accident happened, as were other witnesses. He gave them all the cliche answers and statements they were looking for: "he pulled right out in front of me—paying no attention at all...I tried to stop...I'm lucky he didn't kill me." He also threw in, "I was so scared, I stood on the horn for nearly a minute" for good measure. Although, he was scared he didn't honk the horn—it just sounded good. The police seemed satisfied with his side of the story and quickly dispelled any doubts that it was his fault. Kent was satisfied and congratulated himself on a good day's work.

The police wrote a ticket to the Hispanic man, while his children played on the grass-lined ditch beside the street. His wife now leaned against the bumper of the Impala, gawking at the traffic as it started to flow.

Kent walked around his truck and looked at the damage. He was pleased the ugly head-shaped dent had been transformed to a much larger one. Lines of green and black mingled with the champagne-colored fender and door. He felt somewhat pleased with the outcome, smiling to himself, relieved.

He stooped closer, examining the crushed front end of the truck and then his eyes were drawn to where the smaller dent had been just a few moments ago. And that is when he saw it. Embedded in the crevasses of the torn paint, between the swatches of pea green and champagne gold were microscopic school bus yellow slivers of something. He bent his head, sweat rolling off his brow, carefully inspecting them closer. He had not seen them until now, but they must have been there before; he wasn't sure.

He saw small jagged teeth of metal, almost invisible to the naked eye, protruding ever so slightly in the paint, most laced with even smaller yellow minute slivers. He took his fingers and brushed lightly over the jagged rips in the paint, feeling the little shavings lodged in the crevasses of the torn paint. Kent recoiled as a metal splinter bit his finger. A little bead of blood formed at the top of it and dripped into the palm of his hand and then onto the ground. He ignored it and went back meticulously examining the yellow shards nudged in the body of the Toyota.

Little tugs of fear now began to rip at his heart as he thought about what they were. He looked closer again and thought hard to himself, the unrelenting sun overhead bearing down on him, unforgiving.

*What could it be?*

He picked at one of the teeny metal jags with a fingernail, a hand cupped underneath. With finesse a little yellow sliver tumbled into his hand. He rolled it around in his hands, back and forth, one to the other. He poked at it, pressed his fingernail into it. *Hard*, he thought. He squinted intensely, studying the tiny yellow shard. *Plastic*, he thought, *this has to be plastic.*

*Hard...yellow...plastic.* He turned the words over and over again in his mind...*Hard...yellow...plastic...yellow plastic.* He looked at the Impala; it was solid pea green, except for the chrome bumper—nothing yellow at all. *It had to be tied to hitting Tina, but how?*

He thought back to two nights ago, trying to place it at the accident scene, but could not on his first attempt. Unconsciously though, he had seen it before...somewhere...that same color. He picked at the jags of metal and paint where the splinters of yellow plastic were lodged, but they would not come off easily. He thought they would go unnoticed, that no one would get curious about them, but he might be wrong; he wanted to leave nothing to chance.

*Hard...yellow plastic.*

He forced himself to remember the accident (as he liked to think of it), which he didn't want to do. Ever since that evening, ever since he had killed Tina, he had replayed it over and over, again and again in his mind. The memory lingered in him like the perfume of a woman. It haunted him, her pale face, her blank eyes, her body lying there distorted.

*What was there?*

He strained to place himself there with her on the side of that road, on that gruesome evening. He didn't want to. He didn't want to see those things that now haunted him, every moment, in every thought, things that were now beginning to feed in the night on his dreams. But there she was...sprawled in front of him...distorted...bleeding...dying; laying undeserving and undignified in the mud, gasping for air that wouldn't come.

The burning images rolled back to him. In his mind, he saw a white jogging shoe lay three feet away, beside her on the asphalt, a necklace with a cross meshed into a collage of gravel and red mud near her head. From the corner of his mind's eye, he now remembered it; he saw it clearly. He didn't want to, but there it was…far off in the grass beside the road, it lay there. A yellow box, headphones still attached, partially shattered like paint spilled and splattered on the ground.

*Goddamn it*, he knew what it was now.

He thought for a moment, his mind racing. How was he going to fix this? The police were just right there. He laid odds that they had orders to look for anyone with similar damage to their car. *If they looked closely, would they put two and two together?* he thought. The little bit of comfort and relief he had felt earlier now completely melted away.

He looked over the hood of his truck. He squinted as the sun glinted off the metallic champagne shine. He watched as a tow truck loaded the Impala, then over to the man he affectionately thought of as "Death Rider" who was still pleading his case with the police. His mind was swimming in the debris of the day. The heat and humidity were heavy on him like a wet blanket, intertwined with the guilt of killing Tina and the stress of trying to make it all go away. He felt sick to his stomach as if he might vomit at any moment, so dizzy he might fall straight away into it if they were to occur in order.

For a moment, he looked up into the hot Oklahoma sun. The warmth scoured his sweaty face. He felt faint and top heavy, as if he would fall down beside his truck, face down in the dirt. He looked away from the sun. His eyes were full of spots and he tried to blink them away, but they wouldn't go. They were like the memories that burned brightly in his head, dark and foreboding, and never fading.

He squinted his eyes at seeing his reflection in the windshield of his Toyota. He saw himself there, a man, and a boy, who was used to things going his way. But he felt that the times were changing, that he would not be able to just fix this, like he used to fix other things.

For a moment, he thought of simpler times, when he was able to manipulate the outcome, to make them work out his own way, to his advantage, to avoid trouble he had ultimately caused. He was calculated about it and careful, knowing fear stalked him, waiting for him to trip up. And if he ever did, the fear would be on him like a pack of wolves on a carcass, ravaging his body and never letting him up, until his flesh was eaten to the white of his bone. He thought there was a very serious possibility that not only had he tripped this time, but also he had fell right down into it. He was bathed in fear now, like a body bathed in sweat.

His mind rolled back to a time when he was eight. *God, if he were eight again. That's when you can get a way with anything.* He thought about the fire he started in the bathroom of his house when he was ten. His parents thought it was an accident, but he knew better. The house had a built-in gas heater in the wall of the bathroom. It had a knob where the flame could be adjusted for a desired temperature.

One day he took the pink floral curtain that hung in the bathroom down. He held them in front of the blue flames. They looked surreal as they danced in front of his eyes. He liked the way it looked. It didn't matter, his mom and dad had told him a million times not to mess with the gas heater.

The flames tempted him like a moth to come closer, to pull the cloth closer to the flame. He watched in horror as the darkness began to swallow the little flowers in the middle, until the darkness turned to flame and spread outward. The fire's seductive crackle laughed at him as it swallowed the curtain whole, burning it up to his fingers.

He almost screamed as he dropped the curtain. When they fell, all hell broke loose and they exploded into flames. He had a fearful desire to scream for his mom and dad, but he didn't, he held the terror inside as the flames began to lick at the rug of the bathroom eating it up like a grass fire prodded on by a strong wind at its back. He didn't yell for help or scream. He just walked away, out of the bathroom and down the hall to his bedroom, the words of his mom and dad to stay away from the gas heater, echoing in his head.

He stayed there hoping and praying his parents would smell the smoke before it burned down the house. He was determined that he would go up with it, to pay for what he had done. But he wouldn't tell on himself. If it were found at all, it would be an accident, and one not by his design.

Before long, he heard his mother scream and then his father battle the flames in the tiny bathroom. He came running out as if he knew nothing at all. Smoke and tiny black debris flew everywhere. His Dad had caught the fire in the nick of time. No one knew the wiser, except Kent. From then on he knew he had the gift, the gift to manipulate and deceive and to get by with what he had to. This was not the way he was raised; those things were a sin, but he was lured to them.

Sometimes he felt separated from the fine moral underlining his parents had sewn into the fabric of his soul. The hellfire and brimstone they warned him of did little to deter his ravenous appetite for unruly behavior. He often felt his own man, even as a child, but it was hidden deep within him. The only problem was the guilt of it would always come and feed on him, and try to eat him w hole. And each time he did something, something he knew to be wrong, that cauldron of inflamed emotion grew irritated, and the more crowded it became, the more uncomfortable it was; the voices of confession each one wanting to scream out of him, like a desperate child, angry and abused.

He had a knack for hiding his dirty little secrets, his darker deeds, behind a thin veil of self-righteousness, as he liked to think of them. But the memories followed, some more than others and they tormented him; and he understood early on there was a price for choices he made in life.

The pretty blue-eyed thin face of an old high school girlfriend always lingered with him, among many other faces. But hers came to visit the most. When he was a teenager he got her pregnant, but refused to accept the responsibility for it when she told him, nor accept the consequences. He thought about that and what he did afterwards. It turned his stomach: getting her drunk that night and giving his friend ten dollars to fuck her in the back of his old Pacer. He spread it around school the next day that he was breaking with her because "she was a whore that had cheated on him with one of his friends."

In her defense, she claimed the baby belonged to him, but he denied it. With her reputation ruined, her parents not believing her, she suddenly went quietly away for awhile. He thought about how that poor girl suffered feeling perhaps a bit of remorse. It was all hushed up by her parents, that she wasn't pregnant, that her grandmother was sick in Canton, Ohio or some such place, and that's why she had to go away. But come the next semester, she was back in school: no belly and no baby on the way. He pondered the implications of it. *Did it make him a murderer*? He didn't know. But sometimes at night, he would awake suddenly, thinking he heard a baby's cry and then there would be nothing at all. He took a long breath; a flood of memories trickled to a stop, like a water hose being pinched; he refused to think of them anymore.

"Kent…my God, are you all right? I saw you from my car as I was passing by. Are you hurt? Do you need a ride home?"

Kent turned and stood paralyzed for a moment, his eyes blank and glossy, looking as if he had just witnessed in his mind, something horrible, something grisly, not sure what to say. He couldn't move his throat at first; his brain would not engage his tongue to form words. A sudden new surge of sweat broke out over his body. Finally, he forced himself to speak the word thick in his mouth as he said, "Jim."

"I was coming back from the pharmacy. Martha, my mother-in-law is sick and needed a prescription filled."

"Uh…I'm sorry to hear that, you…you shouldn't have bothered, I am sure your mother-in-law needs you and you have been throu—"

Jim interrupted, "Hey…no, it's not a problem, I just wanted to see if you were all right and if you needed a ride home."

"Sure…no, I'm okay. The Impala over there turned out in front of me. I couldn't stop and I hit it."

Jim looked over at the damage of his car, staring at it intently. "Well you won't be driving that home, the fender is bent into the tire."

Kent looked in the general direction of it pretending to acknowledge Jim's assumption and said, "No, I guess not." He began to feel conscious of the tiny scratches in the paint and the infinitesimal metal jags, embedded with yellow plastic shards nudged in them, and the small sharp slither he nearly forgot in his hand. He felt it with his thumb and immediately let it fall freely through his fingers unnoticed to the ground. Unconsciously, he felt his body and legs wanting to move in front of the damaged car, to cover it up so Jim couldn't see it. His body tensed as Jim leaned over and lightly brushed the dent with his hand and made a whistling sound. Kent watched in horror, the *dirty hungry guilt* now screaming loudly in his ear: *Tell him! Tell him now! Before you can't live with it anymore!*

"Man, that Impala sure did a number on your truck. You want me to stick around and drive you home?"

"Uh…no…I…"

"Mr. Jackson," Kent turned to see a police officer approach, "would you please come with me for a moment, so you can get Mr. Hernandez's insurance information and we can explain a couple other things to you, while the other tow truck arrives."

Kent's heart pounded as he stared at the officer. He didn't want to leave Jim standing alone with the Toyota. What if he turned nosy and began to poke around and examine the dent and see the yellow plastic from his dead wife's CD player embedded in the body of his Toyota. *Now that would be a bitch, wouldn't it,* he told himself. His head began to pound now and his hair felt hot under the sun.

"Mr. Jackson, if you will just come with me for a moment." The officer said the words again as if he needed to remind him of what he had just said a couple of seconds ago.

"Oh…okay. Jim, don't think I will need a ride, I'm going to be too long here…you need to get back, I'm sure…you got a lot on your mind."

"Well…if you're sure, okay then. I mean this is not going to delay me in any way…there is nothing that urgent that won't keep for a while…I'd be happy to—" His eyes fell back down to the damage on the car.

"No, no, I don't need—" Kent caught his voice sounding too frantic. "I mean, Jim, I, I'm just going to be okay."

Jim paused for a moment looking at him queerly, and finally said, "Okay, whatever you say."

As Kent walked with the policeman to one of the squad cars, the little hairs on the back of his neck began to stand. Each footstep jarred his body, reverberating up through him. He watched Jim out of the corner of his twitching eye. His image lingered there, in his periphery, not budging from the spot. Kent began to sweat profusely now, shirt and pants sticking to his moist body, every inch of him worried and wanting to run over to his car and drive it off, smashed fender and all. He hoped Jim would just go the hell home and get away from his truck, before he saw something, something that would make Jim ask questions he couldn't answer.

Kent turned toward the officer as he spoke, leaning slightly on the police car as he glanced toward his Toyota, trying to act as if he was interested in what the police officer had to say. Jim was staring at something, looking at his car. He looked like a figure frozen in time. Kent saw Jim rub his hand against the dent a few times, gazing intently at the fender over the wheel. *What was he doing, didn't he hear me the first time…I don't need a goddamn ride!*

He felt his head spin out of control in terror as he saw Jim crouch behind the fender now; he could only see the top of his black hair from where he stood. A new wave of panic surged through him, electricity felt like it was bouncing hard off his bones and ricocheting to the ends of his limbs. His skin crawled and muscles tightened; his left eye began to jerk uncontrollably, as sweat poured into it from his brow. He blinked it away, rubbing it lightly. The salt burned, watering his eyes. He squinted, trying to get a clear image of Jim.

Another officer came and began talking to Kent, standing in front of him, speaking words, but Kent couldn't understand what he was saying; he was too distracted. He searched for Jim, struggling to see him, subtly looking around the officer, his eyes irritated from the sweat and the hot dry wind blowing into them and the twitch that now tortured his left one.

He strained his eyes looking for Jim, while trying to engage the officer with conversation about the accident. He squinted and held a hand over them now, shielding them from the glinting sun that hung near mid-sky, pounding the earth with blinding rays, reflecting from the cruiser's windshield and the officer's mirrored sunglasses. He thought deeply, urging himself to think to get a grip on his panic, on what he might do if Jim suspected him. There was nothing to do though; he was stuck in some sort of purgatory where time became irrelevant and unmoving and he was forced to accept the consequences of his actions at last.

The officer's mouth kept moving surreally. Jim stared at its ugly hole, as it vomited words incessantly. He thought Jim was probably still there by the Toyota, doing and thinking God knows what. His mind raced through a canyon of treacherous rocks, as the police officer just stood there, yapping, blocking his vision with his big flat brimmed hat that bounced around on his head every time he nodded. *It was all he could do not to tell the guy to move the fuck out of his way.*

But he didn't, he just nodded his head, and said "yes" to this, and "yes" to that, all the while feeling his throat growing tighter with each heartbeat, as droplets of sweat fell from his forehead, forming little splash stains on his light blue shirt. His mind began to surge in panic, racing forward and wondering if Jim had long enough to put two and two together. Uncertainty now pecked holes in what first appeared to be a very careful plan, within a certain complicated picture. He thought briefly, anxiety plagued, his mind flashed to his pregnant high school girlfriend (*this is your baby*) and back again. *Would it now be his turn to go away? Like she did?*

The police officer handed Kent a slip of paper with the big Hispanic man's insurance information, and asked Jim if he would like to have a ride home. Jim stood there listening, nodding his head, but searching desperately for Jim. He glanced around as the traffic moved by him and back and down the road. He saw him, the back of him at least opening the door to his car, glancing back at him for a moment, and him feeling awkward at him doing so. His face vaporized from the heat rising from the road and the cars. He expected him to wave, but he didn't. That worried him.

Kent stood there helpless, not knowing what Jim had seen, what secret he had found. It was one of those things that was going to bother him, the uncertainty of not knowing what Jim knew.

He ran his hands through his sweat-filled hair and let out a long breath, staring down at the ground. He reached for a crumpled package of cigarettes in his shirt pocket and fished one out, slightly bent and moist. Kent hung it in his mouth with a shaky hand and lit the white stick, drawing on the cigarette quickly and deeply. The tobacco and paper burst into a red fire and then it turned to dull gray ash. Maybe he was just looking, and that was all. *Looking at nothing?* he asked himself. Maybe he hadn't really seen him look at the fender. Maybe his eyes read too much into it. *Maybe I'm just being paranoid?* Maybe, maybe not.

# Chapter 11

Jim turned the motor off and took the key out of the ignition. He stared through the windshield, his hands still tightly gripping the steering wheel. Something bothered him, about Kent, but he wasn't quite sure what it was. Something wasn't right. Perhaps he was just stressed out, his imagination out of whack, but why shouldn't it be, he had just lost his wife.

Still he weighed the reality of his doubts. His mind returned to examine what he probably thought was mere suspicious paranoia. But, he remembered what Detective Trower had said about the CD player having traces of what he referred to as gold metallic paint. He thought about Kent's car, its color and the scratches in the paint and what appeared to be minute yellow slithers embedded in the body of Kent's truck. There was something lodged there, something that looked different when he ran his fingers along the grooves. He felt the rough composition beneath. Surely he was paranoid now, estranged from his senses to suspect such a thing, and from his neighbor.

But yet, there was no denying what he saw was out of place; perhaps it was a testament of something that had happened before. There was no continuity between it and the damage to the two vehicles. But what had sprung the pangs of his curiosity was the thought of his wife's little yellow CD player she enjoyed listening to on her runs, and Detective Trower saying there was some gold paint on the shattered box, that was probably from the car who had hit her. *So was he being paranoid? No*, he thought, perhaps just the thoughts of a man that was trying to find finality amidst an unforgivable tragedy; a man that had just lost the woman he loved. He was probably wrong. He had to be. *His neighbor wouldn't do such a thing. He has known him for years.* Suddenly he felt a brush of guilt for what he had been thinking, then dismissed the whole thing from his mind.

He laid his head back on the truck seat and let out a long breath. He let his mind wander back to her, back to Tina. He would struggle with himself not to think of her, but he would acquiesce, not able to resist her memory, and with the memory not able to prevent the pain of her death.

He had not been able to sleep in their bed since it had happened. But, he had tried. He would find himself searching for her warm body in the bed, but not finding her. Then waking up and remembering she was dead. Then he would replay the accident all over again in his head, and this would go on and on until dawn. He would fold the events, as they played out, intertwining the personalities, seeing her body lying under the blue sheet, bathed in the white light. He would then see her laying as she had in the dream, alongside Coventry Road, in the mud, gasping for breath, her standing there beside her dying body, pleading with him to get help. *Get help...get help...get help!*

The images would drive him from his sweat-soaked bed, chastising him that he had not done enough to save her. But now he began to think he would be lucky just to save him from himself. He would sit up for the rest of the night and he would not sleep. He dared not.

Since Tina's death he had asked himself the critical questions of *why? Why her? Why his wife? Why now? Why did this have to happen to him, after all he had been through in his life?* The questions hounded him and nibbled at his sanity, nudging doubts in his faith of God and mankind. Tina had been a barrier to those doubts that were usually spawned by the tragedies of his childhood and at odds with his life now. She had rejuvenated him every day with her warm love, constantly restoring his faith in other people and their faith in God.

But now she was gone and he had nothing to prevent the flood of horrid indecencies that would come and scream at him to remember them...to avenge them. He knew the memories well, they were cunning and shrewd, and would wait for just the right time to appear and reintroduce themselves. When he was vulnerable, when he was sick, when he was depressed, when he was whatever, there they were, ready to fill him with all the hate and vile he could hold. And sometimes they would taunt him for not wanting them, for not wanting to hold more. They would eat freely from him if he let them. And Tina wouldn't let them. Her voice was now silent. She could no longer make the memories go away.

Suddenly he thought of his young mother who died so young and tragic. Sometimes he found himself hating her in quiet moments for spreading her legs to the vile essence of life that she must have craved. Would she have kept them closed if she had known what kind of pain it had caused him? He wondered.

When he was a boy, he hungered for a family, a real family. But he quickly learned that all families were not the same. Sadly, his forgiving love only returned betrayal. Each time it did he lost a mother and a father all over again. His trust in people died with each loss. His disappointment he spread to all humanity and his cynicism dashed any hope he ever had in it. All that kept him from drowning was his faith that there might be a God that may deliver him from this someday.

He breathed deeply, the truck beginning to get hot inside, the air stuffy, but still he stayed. A memory persisted and he entertained it, knowing he shouldn't. His mind began to drift, his defenses lowered and he was swept away to a dark time.

There was Daddy Anderson, as he liked to call himself and his wife Momma Anita. *Mean Little Anita.* This was the first family he really remembered; he was about six. They held out so much promise for him, but in the end they left him emotionally devastated.

At first they were nice enough. They did all those things a young boy liked. He remembered the hot chocolate that Momma Anita would make special, laying the marshmallows thick on top just the way he liked it. She would tuck him in bed at night and read stories from Dr. Seuss. The words soothed him in their sing-song rhymes as he would drift off to sleep.

> Have no fear! said the cat. I will not let you fall.
> I will hold you up high, as I stand on a ball.
> With a book on one hand! And a cup on my hat!
> But that is not ALL I can do! said the cat...

Then she would kiss him on the head and Daddy Anderson would too.

Everything seemed to be going well before *Mean Little Anita* came to call. She would take over Momma Anita's body when she drank the enchanted potion, with the letters S-T-A-G printed on the side. When she did, she turned dark, cruel and mean. She didn't like little boys anymore when she drank it. She didn't like them to cry, to laugh or to do anything.

The first time it happened, he was laughing at cartoons on the television. He loved Bugs Bunny and Daffy Duck cartoons. He felt eyes on him at first, except they weren't her eyes. He smiled at her, and asked, "What's wrong, Momma Anita?"

"You...little...shit." She said the words slow as molasses, letting them drip from her tongue. Her eyes narrowed and her face wrinkled into a scowl. He didn't know what she meant, but he knew it must be bad. She wasn't smiling back. He didn't know what to do. He just lay there frozen until she came toward him with the tree limb in her hand.

"Yer gonna pay for what ya done," she said.

The little boy combed his mind, but he couldn't think of anything he had done. He was terrified, trying to smile at her and hold her hand. She slapped it away and asked him why he deserved to watch cartoons after the nasty little thing he had done.

"I love you, Momma Anita…I love you," he said. The words were pleading and his voice full of fear.

"You dirty little shit," she squealed. She held up a bed sheet in one hand, the other hand gripping a long leafless tree branch.

He didn't mean to pee on them, he just woke up and was doing it. He had forgotten all about it until now.

"Do you think that I could do that when I was little and get away with it? Hell no! And you're not either," she yelled. She gripped the tree branch in her hand. It had strips of bark missing, freshly ripped from the oak tree outside.

"I'm sick of it! I'm sick of it I tell ya! Ya little fucker…ya think you're just going to piss all over the bed? Ya fucker!"

Jim remembered the first lash. It struck him across the ribs and down his groin. The second across his head and the third across his feet as he withered in the floor. He curled up into a ball and cried, saying over and over, "I love ya, Momma, don't hurt me! I love ya, Momma, please, Momma Anita…don't hurt me."

He was always confused when she pulled him tight and hugged him afterwards. She would cry and tell him that she loved him and that *mean little Anita* wouldn't come out anymore. He always thought it was the S-T-A-G that made her do it. But when he was older he realized that *mean little Anita* was born long ago, as a little girl, raised by a drunken father who spent his better days in back alley bars. He had a penchant for French kissing her, especially when he was mad at her mom. He wanted her to make Daddy happy with her body when Momma wouldn't. He would tell her it was okay, through beer-soaked breath.

There was something hidden inside of her, something terrible and dark that only came out to play on certain days. He was afraid of it, afraid of her, afraid of *mean little Anita* who didn't ever get the chance to be a little girl.

These ghosts still haunted him; he supposed they always would. Perhaps there was a special place in hell for those that do such things, perhaps not. But strangely he often felt sorry for the woman he called Momma Anita, all those years ago. She was held hostage to her own terror, much the way he was now and perhaps always would be.

* * *

"Hi, Daddy, what are you doing out here in the hot car?"

Jim lurched forward in his seat. He turned and smiled at Janie, she was beautiful, standing in the early afternoon sun. She looked like her mother, he thought, her golden blonde hair and small-featured face with a pretty smile.

Jim let loose of the steering wheel, wondering how long he had been sitting there. "Are you doing all right, baby?" he asked. "I know you're not doing great, but…are you going to be okay?"

"I miss Mom, Dad. Everywhere I look, there she is." There was a long pause and then she asked, "Are you going to be okay, Daddy?"

"I don't know, honey, but I want you to be. Daddy will make out the best he can. Don't worry."

# Chapter 12

Music filled the background as those who came to pay their last respects filed into the First Methodist Church. There were two rows of slender pine pews the length of the long sanctuary. A podium rose in front of the church, covered in deep rich emerald green carpet. Mounted at the center was a lectern, and a giant gold cross hung on the wall behind it. A sea of flowers outlined the podium, thick with red, white and pink. A lone mahogany coffin rested on purple velvet-covered cloth just below it, its lid closed and covered with a wreath of flowers—on them the words: *We Will Always Love You.*

Jim sat on the front pew, Janie sitting close to him to his left, and Kevin a small space apart from his father to his right. Herb, Martha and Ted sat to the right of Kevin and to the right of them sat Aunt Mae. The rest of the family sat behind them, and friends of the family filled the pews further back and those pews on the left side of the sanctuary.

Jim held Janie close, her head leaning on his shoulder, tears dripping from her eyes forming dark ovals on his suit jacket. A dark blue dress adorned her slender frame, her mother's favorite gold pendent fastened to it. A tissue crumpled in her hand.

Kevin looked broken, slumped over in the pew, face full of despair, looking too mature for nine years old. His dark suit was rumpled, hanging gangly on him, his dress shirt a bit too big, ballooning mildly between his jacket, poking through to the outside. His eyes were red rimmed. His hair was still firm and damp from a wet comb.

Herb put on his best brave face to say goodbye to his baby girl. His brows knotted, his lips pressed together firmly. His hands gripped one another, as if needing to bind them; his nerves made them tremble as if they were out of control. He looked at Martha blankly and only for a moment, and then squeezed her lifeless hand. He had little doubt she would never recover from her daughter's loss. She died with Tina that day and Herb knew it.

Martha, beleaguered, eyes drawn to the floor, sat lost. Her hands cupped upward resting on her knees, as if pleading for God to answer her prayers. She was drawn in the face, grayish, her blue eyes now dim. Her black dress, with white silk piping, hung loosely around her body. She sat silent without a tear. There were no more to shed.

Dressed in a black suit, eyes baggy and bloodshot from a lack of sleep, Jim stared blankly at the pastor delivering the eulogy. His tie hung to the side, exposing a row of neatly-spaced yellow pearl-colored buttons buttressed against a white crisp starched shirt. He wanted to look his best; it would be the last time he would see her.

The reality of her death was now placed squarely in front of him. No longer did he deny it. Now he thought all possibilities were gone. Disappeared through an invisible window in time, they went, never to return. Kissing her gently, feeling her breath at night, listening to her voice, melodic, swaying, reading Hemingway and Faulkner, now all that was gone. She had disappeared into the flame.

Jim pulled his son close and gazed at him. He had tears flowing down his cheeks. His fingers shook as he wiped them away. He leaned over and kissed him on the forehead. "I love you," he whispered.

Kevin silently mouthed the words back. "I love you too."

Jim looked deeply within him, his face covered with grief. Jim now knew the depth of a mother-son relationship, he could have only guessed before not having a mother of his own.

He found it tragic that Janie and Kevin now had lost their mother, like he had before them. But at least they had the opportunity to know her, thank God. They could at least have her memory to comfort them during hard times, to call up an image of her face when needed. Jim had nothing but blanks.

When the pastor had finished the eulogy, a tall sinister-looking man in a dark suit seemingly appeared from nowhere. He walked across the emerald green carpet to the coffin and moved the flower arrangement out of the way. He slowly and reverently opened the lid to the coffin and then disappeared as mysteriously as he came. Mourners were led down the right side aisle, past the immediate family to the body.

Jim watched the parade of people through a stone-like stare. Some touched her hand, others kissed her, the majority silently walked by, staring at her as if Tina's body had put them into a hypnotic trance. Those close to the family hugged the kids and shook Jim's hand, patting him, lamenting, offering heartfelt condolences and wishing them well.

Through the blur of people, Jim focused on Tina, her face—the face he knew every inch of so well. Slowly, through her healing love, she had helped him restore his trust in people again, washing away over two decades of deep-seeded mistrust and hatred. The pain that once tormented him from his childhood memories had abated and Tina had been the medicine to provide the relief.

Yes, there had been other women, but none like Tina, none that had pledged their undying affection to him, that respected the gravity of his past. She saw something that the others hadn't been able to see. A beleaguered person callused and emotionally exiled, standing affectionately cold and starving behind a defensive wall he had constructed for himself. It was a deterrent for those inclined who thought they could love him, an excuse for those who couldn't.

But she did. She loved him, and took extra care too. She was his deep emotional refuge, life-giving sustenance and the only one who could have saved him from what he was destined to become, an albatross set emotionally adrift spawned by childhood circumstances beyond his control.

He remembered a weekend trip they had spent together. It wasn't much but all the world to them at the time and what he wouldn't give for it now. A Holiday Inn, with a pool, stranded in the middle of nowhere, off an exit on the side of the road, but all they would need. They became more than just lovers that weekend, they became deep close friends. Lying naked together, watching each other, eating plates of food from room service, searching each other's eyes each minute, taking nothing for granite.

But now those were memories just dancing in time, teasing him, taunting him, blaming him, accusing him of being naive. The hurt and pain were beginning all over again. He had finally believed in something other than what his childhood experiences had taught him. But perhaps his instincts had been right. What was taken from him was uncommon, an uncommon love that he could never replace.

Jim stood with Janie and Kevin and they made the long walk to her coffin. Jim put his hands on their shoulder as they both peered into the silk-laced box together. She was there, alone, and they were there, alone, wanting so much for her to come back.

Janie held her mother's hand. "I love you, Momma," she said. Then she broke down and cried, hands in her face. Jim pressed her face into his chest, hugging her tight.

Kevin looked at his mom, tears freely flowing now. He fished something out of his pocket. It was a rabbit's foot she had given him one time, after coming back from a trip to Texas to visit her aunt. Kevin put the foot in her hands and petted them. "I love you," he whispered.

After Janie and Kevin said their good-byes, Jim stood alone at the coffin. He ran his hand along her shoulder and arm, and tears fell onto her light lavender dress. He brushed her hair back like he had done a thousand times before. He bent over and kissed her and then moved his mouth close to her ear. "It wasn't supposed to be like this, honey," he whispered. "It was supposed to be forever...I love you." He reached for her hand one last time, and hushed a final goodbye, brushing her wedding ring with his fingers, and then tore himself away. She was gone forever.

* * *

It was another hot Oklahoma summer day. A dry warm wind blew from the southwest. It swept over everyone, drowning them in a thick stale searing air. It dehydrated you, as you stood there. You could feel it. Your lips cracking, giving in to the unrelenting licks of heated air.

It blew across the Little Mount Hope Cemetery, which was neither a mountain, nor did it hold out any promise of hope. It lay at the outskirts of a small town. A town that had long since quit living; a town that held people barely living in it. It lay there wasting and in it the people with simple lives wasting with it.

The limousines and an entourage of cars made their way up the short potholed gravel and black top lane. The lane and cemetery were flanked on both sides with ripened gold wheat. A rusted iron sign arched over two small stone pillars, announcing where you were at its entrance.

Kent had made the forty-five minute drive there, owing much to Lisa's insistence. He hadn't wanted to. The funeral had been more than too much for him. The memory of Jim with his kids beside Tina's coffin was enough to send him to counseling for several years, he thought. But who was he kidding; even if he actually needed it, he could never talk about it. His lips were sealed to a silent vow that if broken would incriminate him.

He stood in the hot glaring sun, the Hall and Vance families some distance in front of him, under a small tent that sheltered the coffin, held aloft over an opening in the earth. Lisa clung to his arm sobbing, daubing her nose and eyes with tissue intermittently. As the Pastor lay Tina to rest, the warm wind swayed the wheat around them like a giant golden sea. It crackled and snapped as it swayed, the sound of it eerie as it echoed across the dry air.

The *dirty hungry guilt* crawled up into his throat trying to get out once more, like it had done during the eulogy at the church. He choked it back down the best he could. His legs felt weakened by the hot wind passing around him. It stole his breath. He struggled for composure, his head dizzying, the guilt and his tie snug on his throat strangling him; he no longer heard words, just the cured crisp wheat lashing against itself under the cruel noon sun.

A prayer was said, and then Jim stood, walked over and touched the coffin. He laid a flower on it, as did Janie and Kevin, Herb also, Martha too weak, but Aunt Mae did as well and then Ted. And it was done.

Jim walked past Kent, his head bowed in thought, his children held in each arm. He glanced at him. Kent tried not to look, but it was too late. He nodded at Jim, hoping that he could read his eyes. There was nothing. Not a single sign. He thought he had nodded back, but maybe he hadn't, perhaps he was just walking over some uneven ground.

He watched him as he got into the car. He wanted to say something to him, but he didn't. He really wanted to say how sorry he was that this had happened. At that moment, he would trade his life for hers if it would bring her back. *Nothing would now, though,* he thought, as the limousine began to fade from view. He turned to Lisa, she staring at him; he put his arm around her and kissed her. "What was that for?" she asked.

"Nothing," he said.

They walked slowly to the car and then left, leaving behind the Little Mount Hope Cemetery. It now possessed Tina Marie Hall for all eternity. She would haunt Kent Jackson for the rest of his life.

# Chapter 13

He leaned against the hood of the van. His eyes were vacant as he stared at the garage wall, projecting images of the last several days through his head. It was late Sunday afternoon. He had really expected to see the police in his driveway before now. None were there. He now felt a surge of confidence he might get away with it. That it would be hard for anyone to poke an accusatory finger at him now. *It would seem too ludicrous to do so at this point,* he thought.

He convinced himself he had been too paranoid about Jim Hall the day of the wreck. Perhaps he wasn't the type of guy that could put two and two together. He faintly smiled. But, if he were wrong, nothing could be done about it anyway.

He thought about the bloody clothes he buried at the bottom of the storage closet. He had a strong urge to take them and throw them into a garbage can somewhere in the city and be done with it. But he worried about getting caught with them or somebody discovering them. *How would I explain that?* They were under his control now, and he didn't want to lose that control. *No,* he wouldn't allow himself to make any mistakes, not now. He wouldn't risk it. He wouldn't panic. He would leave things alone, at least until Sunday. *Trash pick up is on Monday,* he thought. He will get rid of them then.

Digging through the cabinet in the garage, full of work clothes and oily rags, he felt for them and then his hand recognized the feel of his tan camel hair coat.

Glancing around, he wiped the sweat from his forehead and pulled the crumpled coat up to the top. Fumbling the coat in his hands he ran it back and forth looking for what he knew was there. And then he saw it clear as day, the dark dried blood stains. There were three, one larger than the others, and two smallish one shaped in a peculiar sort of way.

He laid it to the side briefly and dove back down to the bottom again to retrieve the rest of the clothes. Within moments he brought up everything he wore the night of the accident. His clothes made that evening come alive again. From the reddish mud caked on his shoes, to his blood-soaked pants and socks it was real. *Goddamn it was real.*

The mixture of mildew, blood, the strong scent of sweat and mud nauseated him. The musty odor stung his nose. He associated the smell with death and it upset him. He thought of Tina and almost vomited but he held his nose, and breathed from his mouth until the queasy feeling past.

His hands were now sticky and moist with sweat. The clothes clung to them as he held them. He was nervous, as if some of Tina had not died and she lingered in them. Her final moments permeated in the material, haunting him as he held the soiled clothing tight.

He reverently folded them one by one, making sure the dull stains were hidden on the inside rather than showing out, just in case his wife came out to the garage. He put them on top of each other and carried them upstairs, laying them neatly on a short redwood bench next to the garage door.

Kent thought for a moment about what to do. He went into the house and retrieved a garbage bag he would put them into. Then he would slip it into the garbage can. And when it was late enough, he would wheel the cart down the driveway to be emptied and picked up early in the morning. He faintly smiled again. *This had been too simple.*

He stepped back out into the garage and walked toward the short redwood bench. He stooped down to pick up the clothes when he caught sight of Jim Hall walking up his drive. Kent's mouth went dry. He froze, paralyzed in front of him, staring and stooped over like an old man suffering from a bad case of bone-breaking osteoporosis. He quickly felt the surge of panic rising up inside him. His heart began to pound away faster and harder the closer he came. He wanted to scream, to tell him stop where he was and not come closer. But he didn't. He just stood there, statuesque in terror. Kent stood straight up, almost exaggerated, like a cartoon character caught doing something they're not supposed to.

He shifted his feet toward the neatly-stacked clothes on the bench, trying to turn fully toward Jim, at least to stand so he blocked some of his view, hoping and praying none of the blood and mud stains were visible on the clothes. Jim neared the garage door before Kent could completely set his feet where he wanted them, though trying to make his movements look natural.

He was just off to the side of the little red bench, crumpled clothes stacked neatly on top. Jim was now standing in front of him, holding dishes in his hand, staring at him. Kent held a black garbage bag near the neatly-stacked pile of wrinkled clothes, feeling exposed and vulnerable like he did two days ago when Jim seemed to carefully examine the damage to his car.

"Kent," Jim called out. "I see I caught you working?"

"No…just throwing away a few things." Jim spoke in a high-pitched tone. He was nervous, eyes darting to the clothes and back to Jim, as if an imaginary line were drawn between the two. Kent's body softened a little at Jim's apparent ease. He almost offered his hand to greet him, but realized that he was carrying dishes in his arms. He patted him on the back instead.

"Hi'ya, Jim, how are you? You didn't have to bring those over today. Lisa or I could have come over and got them…I think she was planning on it anyway.

"Jim let me take those dishes from you," Kent said.

"Lisa…Liisa…Liiiisa."

He called out to his wife, not wanting to walk to the door. Not wanting to leave the clothes on the bench unattended left for Jim's scrutinizing eyes. He waited for a moment. When the door didn't open, he yelled again, "Liiiiisa…Liiiiiiisa."

After a moment of dead silence, he looked up and noticed Jim was eyeing him with a look of curiosity. He thought about it for a second and flashed a grin back, realizing how silly he looked feet frozen in one spot yelling at the top of his lungs, appearing as if he couldn't move.

He didn't want to move from there though. Finally, he relented, turned and walked slowly toward the door, every inch of him pulling his feet forward, not wanting to leave the clothes laying unattended for Jim's inquisitive eyes.

Before he could reach the door handle, it turned and the door opened. There stood Lisa, her hair gathered on top of her head, wrapped in a white towel. She wore an above-the-knee-length pink terrycloth robe, bare footed, one hand on her towel, the other waving timidly at Jim. She was visibly irritated at first with Kent hollering, but when she saw Jim standing there, her scowl changed to a reserved smile.

"Oh, Jim, I didn't know you were out here."

She looked at the dishes in Kent's hands. "You didn't need to bring those. I was going to come and get them this evening and bring you all over a chocolate pie."

Kent looked over his shoulder at Jim as he brushed past Lisa. "Lucky…you," he said. He flashed a sarcastic smile, while carefully balancing the dishes in his hands.

Lisa hit him on the rearend, and snapped, "You can see why I'll never make him another one." Glancing at Jim, she shook her head and rolled her eyes. Jim shot a smile back, bemused, but with some sadness.

Seeing Lisa and Jim together reminded him of Tina; the banter, the playfulness, the simple times, the special friendship they shared. The way they looked at each other, with such familiarity. He admired it. He remembered such qualities, one fluent with the other, smooth gentleness and unspoken communication. *It is the kind of treasures in life that one takes for granted,* he thought. But now all was gone. He was left prey to the angry world, regardless of what happened.

Standing there for a moment, he had slipped away, where he had so many times before since her death. He didn't like the place where he went, because it caused such pain, but yet something always pulled him there in his unguarded moments. A shroud of sorrow would cover him, and start to suffocate him with grief. It was too full of her memories and they reminded him that she would no longer be with him anymore.

"Jim? Jim? Jim, are you all right?" Lisa asked.

"Wha…oh yeah, I'm…I'm all right. Sorry, sometimes lately I slip away a bit."

"Jim, I want you to come inside and sit down. You don't look so well. Feeling okay?"

"Oh, I'm fine, just I get a little…" Jim's eyes stared off outside, trying to not let her see the tears beginning to form in his eyes.

Lisa gave him an understanding smile and nodded her head. "I know," she said. "Hey, I just made some fresh lemonade, come in and have some. A cool drink won't solve world hunger, but it might help right now."

"No, I need to get back…you know…the kids, I don't want them to be alone for too long."

Jim clinched one of his arms at the bicep with his hand and used it to point up the street to his house. "Sunday nights Tina always played a board game with the kids, and they'll be missing that I suppose. I need to get back."

He looked at her hoping she would understand and not press him anymore to come in. He just didn't feel like being with people right now, especially a married couple, to see them do things that married couples do, that would be too much.

"Well, okay then. I understand. At least let me go get the pie for you. I'll be right back, okay?"

Kent, not wanting to leave Jim unoccupied, called to Lisa from inside the house that he would bring the pie. Lisa turned and shook her head.

"Kent, I'll be right there, I want to wrap up some of my cinnamon raison cake for him I made this morning. I'll need you to help me carry it, just wait right there."

"Lisa, you don't need to..."

Lisa interrupted Jim. "Don't argue with me now, just wait, I'll be right back with it."

"All right, that sounds fine," Jim said.

"Now that's more like it. You know not to argue with a woman." She gave him an ornery grin and then disappeared from the door.

Suddenly he stood in the garage alone. Jim followed the walls with his eyes, taking note of different items, details and small particular things that a garage has out of boredom. There was a sharp pair of grass sheers hanging on a rusty nail, old coats hanging on an even older wooden coat rack, shoes to match laying in wait for their owner underneath, and miles of shelves crammed full of things waiting for use, but more than likely nobody had any use for. His eyes wandered lazily, circling slowly around the garage, like a butterfly contemplating for the exact spot to land, until they came to rest on the little redwood bench, clothes folded neatly on top.

He looked at the suit and coat, studying them closely, finding them peculiar. They didn't look particularly old, even though they were wrinkled—almost even new. The dark blue suit appeared expensive in fact, and what looked like a knee-length tan coat—*camel hair perhaps*—had to be. Glancing back at the door for a second, he stepped closer, and gave them greater scrutiny.

He thought it a bit odd that Kent was about to throw like-new clothes away. Odder that he was putting them in a bag before he did. And odder yet, those clothes to be thrown away were in such a neat layered stack. What was the point—so the milk bottle wouldn't touch the clothes? So the clothes wouldn't touch the sides of the garbage can, in case Kent changed his mind and decided to wear them again? *Why?* He thought it strange that Lisa, as had Tina, often volunteered her time in food and clothing drives for the needy. Would she allow such earthly treasures to be simply thrown away?

The questions bothered while he waited and he grew more impatient at their desire to have a forum in his head. *This evening only*, he thought, *the debate over why Kent was throwing away his clothes.* He grinned, standing there alone, thinking he was every bit funny.

But still, he stared at them contently for a moment, intrigued. He noticed a white dress shirt sandwiched in between the pair of pants and jacket. It was perfect white, except for a small part that was crimson stained. He reached down for a moment, though he scolded himself for snooping, and thumbed through the folded clothes like a deck of cards. A pair of underwear, t-shirt, and tie were sandwiched in the middle. He felt something underneath the clothes. He pressed lightly, and then harder, something hard and bumpy lay underneath. He pulled the bottom coat back slightly from the bench not wanting them to appear disturbed. There, underneath, a muddy black pair of Florshiem wing tip shoes lay. The left one had a crimson stain on the tip of the toe, below it, the crack of the leather soul looked like it was outlined in dried red paint. Each shoe had a blue sock with cream-colored diamonds stuffed into it. They were mud caked, and when he picked one up splinters of reddish mud flaked off, dark splattering stains dotting them throughout.

*Why would Jim be throwing away one complete set of clothes right down to the tie and socks?* Something about that didn't make sense. *Even down to throwing away the shoes?* He thumbed back through the clothes again, but this time slower, carefully examining each one.

Then, as if he had just discovered that his hand had come in contact with a flea-infested rat carrying the plague, he stepped back in horror, releasing the clothes, them falling back to where they had lain. His hand remained outstretched. He stared at it as if it were ravaged by disease. He lifted it up, palm facing toward him, fingertips stretched upward, incredulous to what they had just touched, trembling as they jutted upward. Nerves on end stinging his spine, his scalp crawled.

He looked back to the stack of clothes, his mind trying to sort out what he had just seen, searching for a probable explanation of what lay before him. Listening to the footsteps that neared in the distance of the house; he heard Jim and Lisa talking, tin foil rattling as it crinkled over pie plates.

Swallowing hard, Jim looked at the door and then back, trying to alleviate the dryness in his throat, wondering what to do. A part of him wanted to believe this was just a horrible mistake, that somehow the clothes of a killer got into their garage by accident, that this was all a big mistake. But something told him down deep in his mind that it wasn't an accident, that they had been put there by design, for a purpose.

Prying his feet from the concrete, he forced them toward the redwood bench again. He grabbed the clothes frantically, fumbling them through his fingers, ears perked to ever-closer footsteps as Kent and Lisa neared close to the door. Hastily peeling the dress coat back from the rest of the clothes, he pulled it out halfway from the stack. The edges of it felt sharp in his hand. He glanced at it briefly; light tan dried flakes of mud clung to the edges of the cloth, as if it had been delicately dipped a half an inch in a bowl of it. A coat sleeve fell down onto the main body of the coat, its underside coated with dry mud. Drawing in a gasp of air, shuddering at what he might expect, he flipped the sleeve over and glared at it in panic, unable to remove his eyes from it. Soaked into the fabric were crimson stains, some larger, others small speckles splattered along the top.

He clinched the clothes tightly in his hands, incredulous to what he had seen, his mind searching for explanations. He found none. Letting the clothes fall back in place, he backed up half terrified and shaken, as if being cornered by a nefarious beast, his eyes never leaving the clothes laying on the little redwood bench.

Standing there, he felt afraid, thinking about what he had just seen. *How much did Lisa know?* he wondered. Arms dangled by his side, hands trembling, staring at the door as an elbow. He pushed it open. He watched Lisa appear at the door, and then Jim tried not to show the horror of what he had just seen, afraid that one or both of them would do him in right there in the garage. His faced was strained, brows furrowed, looking back at them startled. He was filled with terror, uncertain and unsure of what or who trust now.

"Jim! You look white as a sheet...you okay?" Lisa set her pie plate down on top of a shelf and walked over and felt his head. Her hand was cool and moist. He cringed at her touch. He didn't answer. He stared at her and then at Kent blankly, not saying a word. He only heard silence when they spoke, he saw their lips move, but he couldn't hear their words.

This was an instinctive condition he adopted early on as a child. Lying words that flirted with him at first and then cut deeply, hurting words that killed him again and again, engulfing him in audible crackling fire, were words and voices he would make still. Those content on devouring every part of him and through him, to his heart, to inflict pain and darken his mind, that licked at his soul like crackling whips of flames, trying to permanently burn it, to blacken it like a piece of flesh thrown whole in a fire. He had so perfected the art that he physically heard nothing, only sweet silence. It was a strange sensation, a dangerous one; he knew when it possessed him. It blurred his senses, stung his nose deeply and caused a deafening ring in his ears. He always feared it might become a permanent physical affliction.

His head was numb, little beads of sweat dripping down his sideburns; he felt devoured. Tears swelling up in his eyes and voices growing dim and then louder, fading in and out...in and out. Not sure of what he knew, but knowing that his instincts were often right. Something wasn't right—*south of cheese for sure*. It was the kind of feeling he always got when he was a kid, when he knew something wasn't quite right—that something was going to happen. When everything went wrong, not the way it was supposed to be. *Like when mean little Anita would come to play.*

Betrayal, fear and hatred all embraced him. They were all too familiar, but he had not felt them for a long time. Tina was the interdicting antibody for them. When those long lost feelings came to feed, she was there. But now she wasn't and there was no one to intercede.

Now feeling it, he felt comfort from his long lost memories and accompanying malaise of emotions. He recognized the intimate allure of them, missing them, perhaps addicted to their intoxicating familiarity. They brought an excited feeding frenzy in side of him. As a child, he hungered for them; the residue they left was sweet on his lips. He craved them in the pit of his stomach when it knotted. He wanted them, the wicked spirit, the by-product of anger, the resentment that could weave a wicked fire in his heart, releasing it when needed, keeping it hidden well.

In the back of his head, he thought his demons had been waiting, hidden somewhere deep inside, in some dark place. Waiting for him to return to them, for them waiting to embrace him, knowing he would eventually return, not know when, but assured just the same he would come back some day.

*"Let life take its course, you'll come...you'll come back. You taste my legion of memories on your lips and you'll come back to me, like a lost lover seeking my kiss."*

"Jim…Jim…Jim! Are you all right? You…you are pale as a ghost."

He felt his arm shaking, his eyes clearing from the blur; the words began to trickle in.

"Jim, come in the house, come in and sit down. You don't look so good."

He was oblivious to Lisa's voice, hearing her though, feeling her lightly shaking his arm, concern written on her face. Jim stared at Kent, looking deeply into him, their eyes meeting, but not knowing what to say.

Kent felt nervous. He shifted his feet toward the little red bench, wanting so much to pick up the clothes and run screaming from the garage. "*I did it...I did it...I killed her.*" The *dirty hungry guilt* began curling up its bushy tale in his throat, like it had the day at Jim Hall's house. He felt the tickle of a hideous laugh in his ear.

Finally, a concerned smile broke into Kent's face. "Why don't you come out of the garage and into the house where it's cool…you don't look so good."

*You're lying...you want me out of the garage for another reason...to kill me.*

"No, I have to go…I'm not feeling well—I have to get home." He turned and began walking down the drive, his feet heavy, pounding the concrete, the back of his head burning. He felt their eyes on him.

"Jim…Jim, take your cake and pie." Lisa raised the pie plate, tin foil crinkling under her thumbs, her voice calling after him. She walked forward a few steps. "Your pie…don't you want your pie?"

He never turned, nor said goodbye, he just kept walking toward his house, following the asphalt down the street. His legs were overly heavy, pulling them forward, his mind swimming, as he watched sweat fall to the hot black surface below. He made himself walk, feeling a mixture of uncertainty and shock, listening to Lisa call his name and then not hearing her at all.

"I wonder what got into him?" Kent asked.

"Losing Tina, this is just too hard right now…I guess," Lisa said. She looked at her husband briefly, switching away a gnat hovering about her face.

Kent watched Jim walk down the street and disappear into his house. He walked over to the right side of the garage, sitting the pie plate on top of the white freezer lid that occupied a corner in front of the garage. He took a long breath, unsure of what to do. He worked his hands together, feeling his fingers, thinking about Jim, how strangely he had behaved, uncertain why he had acted so oddly, wondering if he had poked his nose around in the clothes. *Poked it where it didn't belong*, he thought. He explained away Jim's strange behavior in his mind, owing much of it to just losing Tina. He shrugged it off as nothing more.

Yet something in the back of his mind bothered him; the very real possibility that Jim knew something. The very idea that Jim was harboring suspicions plunged an excruciating spike of fear and anxiety into his spine. The idea of it made him grimace. The thought of what Jim knew lingered dangerously close, like a pendulum swinging back and forth, he watching it advancing nearer, waiting for it to put an end to his life. *What could he do?* he thought. *"You could kill him," a little voice said.* Kent shut his eyes tightly and refused to breathe until the voice went away. Finally it did, but not without making their impression on him.

Nothing, there was nothing to do, but get rid of the clothes, to put them in them in a sack and smash them far into a garbage can as far as he could. Tomorrow was Monday, trash day. In the morning the little sack and whatever else was in the wretched garbage can would go wherever garbage goes. To some landfill somewhere, and that would be the end of that, no one could find it after that. If Jim even did suspect something, the evidence was slowly disappearing around him, and soon there would be none.

"What are your clothes doing out here, honey?"

Lisa's voice snapped Kent from his thoughts. He turned around and looked at her. She was no longer looking down the road toward Jim Hall's house; she was staring at the clothes, her face filled with extreme curiosity, eyes narrowing on them.

"Oh, uh…I was planning on giving them away." It wasn't a good explanation, but the only one he could thing of.

"Give them away?" Lisa asked. She said the question as if disbelieving what she heard. "I bought you that coat last year for your birthday, it is practically brand new…and I know you couldn't have worn that suit for over a year."

She put the dishes down that were now heavy in her hands and laid them on top of the deep freezer in the corner of the garage. She walked over shaking her head in disbelief, about to examine the stack of clothes. Jim lunged in front of her, blocking her way to the little redwood bench, frighteningly intercepting her hand, as she reached forward with her hands to touch the neatly folded pants.

Lisa looked at him, surprised for a moment, not knowing what to say. Jim searched for a rational explanation. He could tell that Lisa was becoming uneasy, feeling as if he were hiding something. Her eyes full of uncertainty, her hand stranded in front of her, Kent's hands gripping her wrists.

"I didn't want you to get mad," he blurted out. He released her wrist and took the clothes into his arms and placed the whole stack into the large sack as he spoke.

"I know you bought that coat, so I didn't want you to get mad." His mind was running with the words now, searching for a soft landing, an explanation, something, *God, something*.

"I wanted to give these clothes away…to, to Goodwill. I, I thought it might help somebody out." It was all he could think of. He ran with it, trying to make the best of his excuse, stuttering, but not giving time for Lisa to interrupt. "I know how you are always after me to do something for charity or to give…give something…uh…more of my time. Uh…I thought about that, and I do want to do that, but right now this is something that I can do right now…until…until I have more time." He hoped the reasoning was good enough and that the explanation would stick. He looked at her sincerely, holding the large bag in his arms.

Her face once tense gradually eased, relaxing into a worried smile. But it wasn't an easy smile, more forced, as if she may have accidentally stumbled onto something. She looked at him warily, but thinking, maybe he was really trying to do something nice, and maybe all those Sunday morning sermons she drug him to were now sinking in.

He smiled, and stepped toward her, freeing an arm. He wrapped it around her waist and placed a kiss on her lips. She smiled more broadly and acquiesced to his confession. Though thinking it weak, she conceded within herself that it might be true.

"That's so nice, Kent. I…I don't know what to say." She paused for a moment. "You don't have to worry about that coat…if that is what you want to do. She stood there convincing herself that this was important to him, thinking about why a charitable condition had suddenly struck her husband causing him to change.

"I think it's great, the days are getting hotter now…and, and the coat, well, you can just get a new one this winter. I'm proud of you, Kent, for thinking about the less fortunate, those that have needs." She forced the words; she didn't know why.

Maybe he was thinking about somebody else other than himself for once, but the prospects of Kent Jackson doing anything for anybody else seemed remote. But, she had long ago accepted Kent Jackson for what he was—nothing more, nothing less. Being charitable just wasn't his style. It wasn't that he was a bad guy or anything like that; he was just centered on what he thought was important. After all, he was good at other things. Not everyone had to be as altruistic as she was. She just wanted him to be a little more.

She closed her eyes and kissed Kent on the cheek and hugged him. She tilted her head, red highlighted brown hair falling back on her shoulders, and whispered, "I love you," in his ear. He kissed her back and then they held each other's hands, their fingers laced together for a moment and then they parted.

Kent opened the back of the van before she left, placing the unsavory bag of clothes in the lighted van. She took the pie plate and cake box back into the house, delicately balancing them as she walked up the unfinished wooden steps. She glanced back, and he watched her. He smiled at her, peering around the van and she looked uncertain at him again, with a less-than-convinced face, the oversize bag tightly clutched in his sweaty left hand.

As soon as she had disappeared, he jerked the bag out again, twirled and took two steps, and with his right hand opened the garbage cart and with his left, threw it in hard. The sound of the bag made a heavy *thuuuuud* splashing plastic containers and jugs, bouncing them off the sides of the cart and crunching other bags.

He took a large metal head rake and sharply plunged downward into the garbage cart over and over again, with all the exuberance of a mad man, and smashed the bag deep into the bin. With each dull plunging thud, he lost a piece of himself, thinking about what Jim had lost. Unrelenting, though, in his quest to avoid implication, he felt satisfied when he closed the garbage cart lid and slammed the door to the trunk.

*Finished. Done.*

He looked around a little, out the garage door and back to the house, sweeping areas in between. He took a few steps toward the door. Startled, he turned and looked behind him and then at the garbage cart. *What was that?* His ears perked. It almost sounded like a sweet melancholy voice, but only audible for a brief second, or was it just the hot Oklahoma wind whistling off the house, or was it in the wind? *It had been a long day, hell, it had been a long week*, he thought. His mind was fumbling under the stress of the week.

He turned and began to walk toward the door again. Suddenly, a sharp gust whipped through the garage, slapping his body violently from behind, fluffing his hair, rippling his shirt, nearly toppling him over. A warm chill ran up the back of his spine, raising the hairs, until they felt stiff on his neck. He wiggled his ears with his index fingers, trying to ease the tension in them. His eardrums felt as if they were being pulled outward with a suction cup. He was tense and nervous, walking backward until his feet found the foot of the steps. He looked hard straining his eyes, listening to every sound. He then turned abruptly, climbed the few steps as quickly as he could, and disappeared behind the door.

# Chapter 14

He slammed the door behind him and leaned against it, panting, sweat rolling under his shirt, down his body. The television was on, but he could not hear it. His head throbbed wildly, with each beat of his racing heart. He slumped slowly down the door, his moist palms bracing for his brief descent. He sat there, lifeless hands lying on the cool floor. He stared at the pictures on the wall, as his eyes pulsated. Memories of his wife captured there in them. It was now all that he had left of her. Silent photographs looking down at him, haunting him from their frames.

"Tina, my God, Tina, what happened to you?" He said the words out loud. He said them over and over, and then silently turning them in his mind. Confused and full of despair, he leaned over against the wall and shut his eyes tightly.

He dreamed of her for a moment, her standing in front of him. A flower in her hair, softly calling out his name. Running to him through a green meadow, her voice lightly whispering words that he could not understand. Her face beautiful, as he remembered it, her body tempting as it always had been. But, the vision of her faded, another took its place. It sprung like a trip wire in his mind. Tina lying muddy and lifeless on the side of Coventry Road, gasping for breath, but finding none. A man bent over her, lifting up her head, screaming for her to live. He remembered in the dream how she pleaded for him to save her life, how the man in the long tan coat stood up and walked away from her...leaving her to die.

*A long tan coat?*

He opened his eyes wide. His mouth was dry. The dream that night, had it been real? He didn't know. Maybe Tina had come to visit him the night she died, to deliver her killer to him. But even though it was hard to fathom, the probability was there. He couldn't quite believe it to be real, but there was no disputing something wasn't right.

A surge of surrealism rose about him, but he refused to believe what he was thinking. His mind searched for a reasonable explanation. But there was none.

His common sense told him that Lisa more than likely had nothing to do with this. The long tan coat that lay in the Jacksons' garage belonged to Kent, not Lisa. There was no denying that. Rubbing his forehead with his hands, as if he were trying to remove all the tension, looking up at the ceiling, studying it. He thought about Kent standing there, stooped over the neat stack of clothes, bag in hand. He was out in the garage by himself. Doing the nefarious business of bagging the bloody clothes. Kent was startled, visibly nervous when he walked up to the garage. There was no doubt he was hiding something; the way he didn't want to budge from the small bench. Probably, just not hiding from him, but probably from his wife as well.

He recalled how odd he acted the day he came over with Lisa, after Tina had died. He was jumpy, and dug at his tie, visibly uncomfortable being there. *Yes, it all made sense now.* And he remembered something else, the night he rode back from the Lakewood City Morgue, in the detectives' car. How the lights vanished as the car approached. *Maybe he had stayed, to see them come home. Maybe he couldn't sleep and didn't want them to see the lights on.*

Pushing himself up, leaning on one hand, he stumbled over to the large picture window in the living room. He stared down the street at the Jacksons' house, one hand against the window frame, the other brushing his goatee back and forth, a flurry of questions querying his mind. *Kent's wreck, was it planned? Was he trying to cover up the damage to his car that the impact of hitting her had caused? Yes, it was planned,* he whispered to himself. It was planned and it was near perfect. It would have been perfect, if he hadn't come along and seen the Toyota and what lay embedded in the body of it—tiny yellow plastic.

He could still remember how the etches in the paint felt as he ran his fingers over them. Rough and jagged, nipping at the tips of his fingers, small yellow slivers—and now he knew, *yes, it was Tina's yellow CD player, at least splinters of it anyway,* lodged into the deep rough crevasses of the paint. He pictured Kent standing by his front door, almost waving as he passed by sitting in the backseat of the detectives' car. His wife dead and he was the one responsible. Waving at his neighbor as if nothing had happened.

Yes, it was planned. He planned to get rid of the dent in the car, like he planned to now get rid of the clothes. *It was all planned.*

Jim walked haggardly to the kitchen and leaned against the sink. He pulled the silver handle up on the faucet and let the water run through his hands. Cupping them, he dipped his face in the cool puddle of water and then ran his wet hands back through his hair.

His mind flashed to the dream he had the night Tina died. The foggy image burned into his mind, of her head being laid to the ground. The man in the long tan coat walking casually back to his car, as if nothing had happened. *Was it Kent? Was it he that killed Tina?* His hands tightened forming fists, his lips pressed together firmly, jaws clinching in growing irritation. His ears began ringing, a sharp pain bit his nose. Cupping his hands under the cool water, he pressed his face in it again, trying to find comfort in it.

He recalled the light being on at the Jacksons' home when the detectives brought him back from the city morgue. How suddenly the shades closed and the light in the house was doused as they drove by. *Perhaps Kent's conscious was bothering him or perhaps he was just concerned that at any moment he might get caught. Kent may be a murdering fucking hypocrite*, he thought, *but maybe he was a hypocrite with a conscious, a conscious that wouldn't allow him to go to sleep that night.*

He pondered Kent's motives as he stared blankly at the water running though his hands. Kent was saving himself, and he was doing a good job. Was it unintentional? Vehicular manslaughter would have been tough on his career, especially if he had been drinking. Was that it—he was drinking and didn't want to get caught—was that worth his wife's life? Making the decision had to be tough, leaving her there, walking away, letting her die to save his own skin, but not knowing what to do or what course he should take. Perhaps there was none.

*Yeah, Kent was a clever one all right, a high-powered business man—that dealt in risks probably every single day—this was just one more*, he thought. *His job, being a success, it meant everything to that guy.* He considered that perhaps Kent was better than him, that he would beat him at this, that he was probably over there right now, thinking how he was rubbing his little less-than-fortunate nose in it. (*I dare you too even think that I killed your wife...I am too big to even let this complicate my life.*)

Kent's imagined loud booming voice echoed in Jim's head, like the ominous sound of a distant gunshot. His heart pounded harder, his eyes tightened down into slits. The insecurities that had been bred into him as child, they came to feed—fear, hate and hurting pain—the kind of pain that keeps on betraying you.

Perhaps he was discovering too late that he had done it all wrong—that all that he had become was not good enough—that he had lain over against all his instinct. And now what he treasured had been stolen from him by the cruel disregard in the world. It was a cruelty that feeds on its own.

He had come to believe that rewards abounded for those that played within the boundaries of morality and law, that there was heaven and it held out a special promise for those that played by the rules. But, he thought to himself, it may just be in the realm of possibility that *all that was just bull shit.*

But horrified, he now discovered that all that he was raised to believe was not true—feign beliefs at best. He thought about his disillusionment. He was ashamed. The thought of his misplaced trust on values he held sacred penetrated his very integrity, generated an angry rage turned the core of his brain into a molten epicenter that dived down through his very existence.

Perhaps he was responsible for his wife's death—perhaps by proxy. Maybe his inherited intrinsic philosophy of life had killed her—the man that actually did was just the vehicle in which he had misplaced his trust. He had been rewarded for playing by the rules with omnipotent prejudice, he thought. Perhaps heaven had shown him whose earth it really was. He pondered the likelihood of that, staring up at the splashboard.

"Well then, perhaps the rules needed changing." He heard his voice; it sounded eerie and foreboding. It almost frightened him. It was like a stranger's voice, as if a nasty parasite had attached itself to his larynx and forced him to speak the words. He sounded cold and hollow, calculating, almost clever.

*Kent's house is twice as large as mine*, Jim thought, *and everything the guy touches turns to gold. He has a wonderful family. He really doesn't seem to do anything special to deserve it—I mean, I work just as hard he does, but do put a priority on the placement of what is most important and serve those priorities. But Kent*, he thought, *served himself and in the end he has a lot to show for it and seems to make him just that much more immune to misfortune and tragedy—particularly the kind that has befallen him.*

*What has he gained from playing by the rule book? Has it mattered in the end?*

He thought that Kent was probably in his house right now grinning about it, hysterically chuckling to himself in his shadowy mind, thinking how it took a little doing, but he had got away with it and that it was nothing more than mere inconvenience. After all, it was a small penance, for being at the wrong place and at the wrong time.

He thought that Kent might succeed—that he would get away with it. In the back of his mind, Kent was getting rid of evidence, getting rid of it all piece by piece and he was just letting him do it. The thought angered him more and more. He caught a faint reflection in the water sitting at the bottom of the stainless steel sink. The water was now calm and still there, his hands dangling over it, elbows pressed hard with the weight of his body leaning on them, an occasional drop of water sending short ripples over the surface.

He looked at himself. His face resembled that of when he was a boy—scared, alone, and angry—but he felt a new element being added to the mixed bad of emotions—revenge. He struggled to look harder at his weak reflection—*am I really going to let somebody take a shit on me again?* And this was just not a normal fucking over—no! Not like the routine one that would happen when he was a kid. This was more tragic than even that; it involved the taking of a life. It involved ruining all hope in life, stolen away from him. All this time his wife's killer had been under his nose.

More short ripples rolled through the cool clear water. This time not from his hands, but from tears falling off the end of his nose. He was petrified at the thought of being alone…annoyed at thinking that Kent was going to get away with it.

He pushed himself off the sink, and without thinking a hand fumbled for the phone, another pulled his wallet out of his hip pocket laying it on the counter, pulling out a white card. He would call Detective Trower right now. He would tell him what he knew: that he thought one of his neighbors had killed Tina—that he was trying to cover up the evidence, by, by…by giving away his clothes. He would tell him how he had smashed his car into another, trying to cover up the damage that was caused to his when he hit Tina. He would also tell the detective about his dream, of the long tan coat. *It all made sense didn't it…wasn't it clear that Kent Jackson had killed my wife…wasn't it?* He thought about that question for a moment, about its implication. The answer that slowly slipped from his lips was a resounding…"no."

Listening to what he had just told himself, it almost sounded ridiculous, even absurd. *No, no…it was too late anyway…Kent had smoothed out all the sharp angles. The evidence…all the evidence, he was making it go away, to disappear, as if no one would ever know who did it.* He slowly hung up the phone, making a number of attempts to put it on the receiver. His face looked beleaguered, his head hung low, eyes tracing the floor as he walked over to the kitchen table and slumped into a chair. He drifted, thinking what to do, or rather what could he do?

His breath quickened. He was angry; a rush of blood flushed into his face. His body was tense, eyes piercing through slits. He suddenly stood enraged, making a tight fist and slammed it down on the table, over and over again, until his knuckles bloodied. In a trance he gazed at the raw meat his hand had produced, his mouth quivering with every uncontrolled breath.

He tilted his head toward the ceiling, and shouted to God, "Why did you let Tina die!"

He paused, as if waiting for an answer. None came. He continued in spurts, sobbing as he ground out his unforgiving cries for answers.

"Isn't it enough what I have been through? What more can I bear? Haven't I given my pound of flesh…haven't I given it? Haven't I? Now, now you ask me for more, for more…for goddamn fucking more. What more can I give?"

He stood there for a moment, waiting—but there was only silence—no reply. He stood there, bent over the table, arms now supporting his body, his head dangling between them, glaring at the table top. Slowly he spoke with indifference, with calm, as if something had moved over him, evoking apathy at all he once held sacred.

"No, I will not give it, no more," he said faintly.

"No punishment was good enough," he slipped the words out under his breath. He wiped his eyes with his hand, it shaking, and then put it down on the table again. Pushing his head up he stared at the wall glassy eyed, as if actually looking at something besides a white wall. His eyes were almost hollow now, filled with ungodly darkness. He spoke to it morosely, as if it were his double, in a 3$^{rd}$ dimension, a subtle reflecting understanding ghost.

"No," he said. "This time things are going to be different. Things are going to go my way."

He squeezed his lips tighter and stood tall and erect. His stare penetrated the wall.

"Kent Jackson," he pushed the name out from his mouth, like a long uninterrupted breath. The name was unpalatable now; saying it stung the back of his throat. It felt like an angry hornet was embedded somewhere deep far back beyond his tongue, penetrating the soft flesh with its poisonous quill.

After some pause and thought, the words slipped lethargically from his tongue and parsed there way between his lips, fatally unretrievable, and with finality, vibrating in the air. "I am going to unleash a heavy burden on you, Mr. Jackson. I will extol a price for what you took from me." His voice was rising now. "What you took from me, I will take from you! I will be compensated!" he screamed.

With each word his bloody fist pounded the table again, splattering speckles of blood everywhere. He ignored the withering pain, his mouth quivering erratically as if he were rabid, searching for an antidote that would ease his emotional malaise.

*There is no justice good enough*, he thought.

His voice rose again in wrath. "Kent Jackson will receive his good measure of compensation…there will be no goddamn doubt about that!" he said. "His…his merit has earned him a reward, a reward set aside in hell."

His eyes stared blankly ahead, reflecting on the horrible deep dark corners of his mind, where he was afraid to go. Finally he pushed the words up from his throat and to his mouth, and said, "I won't be able to forgive you. I will not be able to forget either. May God help me; may God help you."

He paused for a moment, thinking about the words, how they rolled over his tongue. With a long deep breath he exhaled, a boiling rage rising up from inside him. "Revenge…justice," he said. The words were thick and heavy in his throat.

He sat there deep in thought, turning the words over and over again in his head. "Revenge and justice." He whispered the words again. They felt good when he said them; they were sweet with truth. There was an inevitable integrity about them, ripped from tragedy itself. They yielded a certain power that cut through the air like a double-edged sword. The words seduced him and they would never leave his lips again.

# Chapter 15

He sat in the living room in front of the large picture window. The room was pitch black and the only sound was the steady beat of rain on the window. Occasionally, a passing car would drive by. Its headlights would shine around the room, passing over Jim's face. They illuminated a distilled scowl, one that reflected a momentous truth, a truth that waged war in his mind, his soul and his body.

His eyes were staring toward the Jacksons' house. He strained to see it between the sheets of heavy rain. He looked at his watch; it was 11:23 p.m. He waited.

* * *

Most of the neighborhood was dark now; flashes of white lightening lit it up intermittently, briefly defining the outlines of the rooftops. He had dozed for a moment; his head fell to the right. He jerked it back like it had a rubber band and looked up quickly, glancing down to the Jacksons' house, but seeing nothing, he began to drift again. His head gradually twisted to the right, like a ship being swallowed by the depths of an unforgiving ocean, sleep creeping onto its rails. He yanked his head up again, peering from half-opened eyes, expecting nothing, but more rain.

He sat up abruptly, snapping out of the drowsy condition that was persistent with casting its spell. Leaning forward, squinting his eyes, straining to see down the street, scooting himself up on the edge of his seat, he could see Kent, *finally*, like he knew he would be, wheeling the garbage cart quickly down the drive. The cart veered wildly, fishtailing as he ran. He wore a bright yellow raincoat with a hood that whipped violently around his body in the wind. He glanced at his watch; it was nearly two o'clock.

Jim stared hard at him from the window, as if he was focusing every ounce of his anger and hate on him. He watched Kent steer the cart to the end of the driveway, and then push it up onto the corner of the yard. The front wheels accidentally slipped off the curb. Kent pushing on it in a lean, slipped on the rain-soaked grass and fell down in front of it. He wrestled the cart for a moment, and at one point his coat hood fell off his head and the rain fully drenched him. Finally he pulled one wheel over the curb and then two, and then pulled the cart fully back onto the yard.

Jim smiled cruelly, watching him, a bit amused at how he struggled with it. *It couldn't have happened to a better guy*, he thought.

Kent lay against the cart for a moment, as if deciding whether it was safe to leave it or not. He dashed back toward the lighted garage apparently deciding it was. The light that shimmered on the wet driveway ebbed as the garage door slowly closed, leaving it dark again.

Jim looked up and down the street from the window. There were few lights on in the neighborhood. He walked to the closet and pulled out an olive green raincoat and a flashlight. Pulling the coat sleeve on one arm, he put the light in his hip pocket as he walked in the dark to the door stumbling at one point over the corner of a chair. He put the other sleeve on in front of the door, and straightened the coat around him, pressing it down carefully with his hands. He did so as if he were getting ready to meet a prom date, primping his clothes behind the door. Perhaps a nervous reaction to the quest he was about to undertake.

Gradually he cracked the door open, peering into the night. A cool mist blew into his hardened face. He took his hand and wiped the moisture from his eyes, straining to see the Jacksons' house.

He hesitated for a moment, glancing up and down the street again. It was quiet. The rains dancing on the pavement, pattering as they hit. The houses were dark now, most of the people in them he expected were asleep.

He saw a light disappear on the second floor of the Jacksons' house. He pushed a foot through the crack of the door, the other followed and he was outside. He stood there for a moment, closing the door quietly, and then sprinted through the sheets of rain. He held his hood firmly in one hand while he galloped through the shadows.

He ran up the street, the rain pelting his face with huge droplets, his boots smacking the wet pavement with each stride. Tiny rivers streamed down the sides of the street, the curb acting as its conduit. He splashed them running across the Jacksons' driveway collapsing on the garbage cart, nearly tackling it. He leaned over on it, gasping for air, looking at the houses as he did, searching for signs of life that might be looking back at him. He saw none.

He looked behind him, at the Jacksons' house. It was dark, as if no one were home. He reached for his flashlight and pulled it from his hip pocket, wiping the rain from his face with his free hand. Each raindrop registered an eerie high pitch *thud* as it splattered against the rubber of his raincoat. The wind whipped around him, smacking him with sheets of rain, the noise of it striking him reverberating up through his hood.

He opened the lid to the cart slightly, slipping an arm in, and switching on the flashlight and then sticking in his other arm and then his head. A soured smell rose up and stung his nose, flies buzzed against the garbage bags, taking sanctuary from the weather, and occasionally one would dart toward him and hit his face.

He imagined what he looked like—a body being eaten by a green monstrous trash can, with an unusual illuminated mouth. *A lion tamer*, he thought, *defying death in the jaws of a large garbage cart*. He chuckled at the idea.

One hand pushed and pulled and tore open garbage sacks while the other targeted them in the light. Most of them looked the same, black with yellow tie strings. He knew the clothes were there, that Kent was going to get rid of the last piece of evidence that would incriminate him—*but where?* His feet strained for leverage on the ground while he tried to reach the sacks at the bottom of the cart, finally pulling them slowly up through the others at the top as they slid down. He would tear the plastic in each sack, not bothering to untie them, spilling their contents and then moving on after determining that it wasn't it.

He lifted an overstuffed black bag from the bottom. It was somewhat heavy, but mostly soft, his heart racing now, as he tore into it. He pulled a tie through the little plastic black hole; the end of it looked as if it had been dipped in blood. He stared at it for a moment, not believing, despite seeing it there in front of him. His body began to convulse, as his hands fumbled the tie in his hands, he spewed vomit down the side of the sack, letting it fall and clutching the lip of the garbage cart as he did. It must have been a combination of rotten food smell and his dead wife's blood dried on another man's tie.

He wiped his mouth with his free hand, breathing deeply as he grabbed for the sack again. A fly stirred from the bottom and buzzed up into his face, momentarily landing on his lips. He brushed it away, with his hand. "Goddamn it," he said out loud. He wondered if it was true that if a fly landed on you they threw up 700 times and it lapped it back again in rapid order. For his own sake, he wanted to believe that was bullshit.

Jim became irritated now and pulled on the bag with all his might, and the wind now whipped the rain up in his face. "Goddamn you, fucker—come out of there," he said under his breath. Jerking the bag up quickly, it passed with some difficulty between the lip and the lid of the garbage cart and landed onto the ground with a slap. He looked around him, feeling he had made too much noise, his eyes investigating every detail and shadow of the nearby houses. But there was no one, not even a light, just the sounds of rain beating the ground around him.

Instinctively, he pulled the bag up by the top and ran with it, splashing through the miniature streams, running like a man possessed, not stopping to look back, until he slammed through his front door. He threw the bag ahead of him and collapsed on the carpet, heaving air in and out of his chest. He kicked at the door two or three times trying to shut it, finally he rolled over onto his side and kicked it completely shut.

He lay there panting on the floor, ears muffled from the hood, eyes pulsating as he stared into the dark. He pulled himself up to his hand and stretched up and turned on a light. He collapsed back down in a fit of agony. His chest rose and fell with each breath until the need came less frequent. He lay there thinking about what he had done, but most of all he thought about the contents in the sack. He tilted his head up and stared at the bag that lay behind him. He glanced away, still breathing hard. He propped himself up on one hand and leaned to his left. He ran his fingers through his hair several times, trying to wring the rain out of his hair.

Pulling himself up with one hand on an endtable and the other on a chair, he stumbled toward the bag and swooped it up in one hand, feeling his way down the dark hall. He opened the door to what had been Tina and his bedroom. Flipping on the light switch, it crackled. He stumbled into the room, the bulb above him sizzled occasionally and flickered, alternating different shades of yellow and white. He poured the contents of the bag onto the bed, then let it slip from his hand, staring at the secrets it had held. He stood there, horrified, his ears ringing, his nose stinging him. He rubbed it a little and then wiggled his ears one at a time with his index fingers, trying to get them to work.

He slumped into a chair, hypnotized by the mud and blood-stained clothes. They lay there, just as Kent had worn them that day…the day he had killed his wife—*Tina*.

The last suffering moments of her life lay evident before him. How she had pleaded with him in the dream to save her. He couldn't, no matter how hard he tried. There, before him, now lay the long tan coat that he had seen in the dream. He glared at the coat—stained and sickening—he hated it. His lips trembled now, a tear rolled down his check. He leaned his head back on the chair and he closed his eyes and he dozed.

* * *

(*...Jimmy...*)

He heard him whisper his name from the back of his mind, his voice tempting and familiar, but haunting at the same time. He could feel him move through him, like a cool fall breeze...so delicate and near, a mystery, not knowing from where he came.

(*Jimmy...*)

He lay there hearing the voice calling his name, listening to it repeat his name for a long time. At first he thought it was Aunt Mae, or maybe even the kids, *but why are they calling me Jimmy? And...and the voice is a man's voice, not a woman's or a child's.* Thinking about it, he became suddenly alarmed sitting up in the chair and open his eyes. His heart began to gallop in his chest, his eyes widening. A man, who looked very familiar, sat across from him on the bed smiling.

*What do you want?*

*(I thought it was time we had a little chat, Jimmy.)*

*What about?*

*(I think you know, Jimbo. But let's not beat around the bush, shall we? Let's get right down to it, okay? How far are you going to let this thing go, Jimmy...I mean how far are you going to let him go.)*

*Who?*

*(You know who, goddamn it, the animal, Jimmy, the filthy fucking animal that lives down the street. No, Jimmy, I'm afraid you can't let him get away with this; you'll have to have a talk with him. A voice of reason perhaps. Maybe a little more forceful than that. Maybe something, shall we say, appropriate perhaps, given the circumstances.* (The man's voice was rhythmic, raising at the tail-end of his word as if asking a question.) *Maybe some downright goddamn ugly revenge is in order. Can you say that word with me, Jimmy, just for a moment? Revenge?)*

*Rrreeevennngeee.* The word slipped thickly from his lips, the word almost uncomfortable in his mouth, yet somehow he took pleasure in saying it, but not knowing why he said it.

*(Ahhhh, yes, Jim...revenge. Now, it might just be me, Jimbo, but I think that's really what's in order here...some downright good ole goddamn ugly revenge.)*

*Yeah...I know...you're probably right. I just—*

*(Well hell yes I'm right, you should listen to this side of yourself more often...shit, Jimmy—you have to start given me some more face time, goddamn it...you know it? I mean, I don't want to be too hard on you here, God knows you've been through enough lately, but freekin-jeepers, all I am askin' here is that you just give me a chance to make a few things up to you.)*

*Yeah, uh...I know you're right and about the face time too. Some revenge, yeah...revenge...it has occurred to me. I just don't know though...I don't think Tina would've wanted me—*

*(Now don't be a schmuck, Jim, are you going to be a schmuck all your life? I mean, goddamn it, come on, give me a little help here. Admit it, Jimmy...come on now, admit it, rrreeeveeenngggeee...it sounds good, doesn't it—sexy* (the man wiggled his eyebrows)*—tasty on the old meaty tongue—right?)* The man winked at him. He sat there smiling, momentarily tapping his lips with his index finger, and finally nodding attempting to reassure him.

*(I mean it sounds right on your lips—doesn't it? I like the way you said it a while ago—REVENGE—you said it so beautifully. Say it again, try on for size,. take it for a spin around the old block,* the man said winking at him again.)

*Re...re, rreeeveenngeee.* Jim said the word with some hesitation. *I...I like it too, but I—*

*(Jimmy, it just comes down to this—to really ask yourself, how many times are you going to take a fuckin'...are you going to take one all your life? Huh?)*

*Uh...no, I can't, I can't do that anymore,* Jim said. He shifted uncomfortably in his chair.

*(Well now, that's just goddamn right, now isn't it, Jimmy, so you know what I think you need to do?)*

*Wwwhhaaat?* Jim said. He slurred the word, afraid of what the answer might be.

*(I think you need to prioritize right now and take some inventory of your life. I think it's time you start thinkin about that sick filthy fucking animal that lives down the street. And how you're going to deal with him...I mean, come on, he did kill your wife, now, didn't he? He did leave her to bleed out on the side of A GOD-FORSAKEN ROAD, DIDN'T SHE, WELL DIDN'T SHE?*

The man's face reddened and turned hard with anger for a moment as he screamed the words, but then it softened a little.

*(The mother of your children, Jim, she's dead, she's dead, goddamn it, and that filthy...fucking...animal, down the street did it.)* His face was kind now, his voice calm and soothing, even reassuring. *(Do the right thing, Jimmy, okay? Don't let me down; don't let her down.)*

Jim jerked forward in his chair for a moment gasping for air as if he had been held submerged under water on the verge of blacking out. He was sweating profusely, heaving air into his lungs, his body shaking at its very core. He looked around him frantically, but nobody was there. Sitting back in his chair, catching his breath, he looked at his watch. It was 4:29a.m.

He leaned forward, his hands on his knees propping his body up. He had awakened suddenly and violently. He never wanted to go back there ever again, to the dream, if it was a dream. He didn't like that Jim Hall who lived deep and dark down there; he was scary. But he admitted to himself that he had a point and the point was made, no matter how uncomfortable it had become.

*Don't let her down.*

The ugly clothes stared at him from the bed, mocking him, telling him that he should be used to taking whatever life's little torments had in store for him by now. *Don't let her down*. The words ran through his head, haunting him now. He thought he was worthless and cowardice and that down the street his wife's killer slept soundly, because he knew he would never have to pay for what he had done.

*No.*

He picked up the long tan coat and touched one of the crimson stains gently and slowly with his fingers. It made a sound like a match being struck against a hard rough surface, before igniting. He gripped the coat tighter in his hands, his anger raging like a brush fire burning out of control on a dry hot windy day. By the time he dropped the coat, the rage had burned deep within him and had blackened his spirit and devoured his soul. He closed his eyes finally, and drifted asleep once more. The words *don't let her down* still echoed through his head.

* * *

Knocking on the door for the fourth time, Detective Trower turned to walk away. Before he could, it opened. In the darkness stood Jim Hall, peering out at him, like some nocturnal animal awoken from its daytime slumber. It was Monday, 12:30 p.m. The sun was soaking up every raindrop the sky had given the earth the night before.

Detective Trower turned and smiled at Jim, extending his hand.

"Good afternoon, Mr. Hall."

"How are you, Detective?" Jim said. He took a step into the sunlight and squinted his eyes, shielding them from the glare. He shook Trower's hand, curious as to why the detective was there.

"Fine—you?"

"Good."

"Is it okay to talk?" Trower asked.

"Yeah, let me get my shoes. The kids just got home from their Aunt's and I...I'd rather they not hear what we say."

"Okay, we can talk in the car if you want."

"Yeah, that'll be fine," Jim said. "Just give me a minute."

Trower walked to the car and got in the back seat, sitting behind detective Flint.

Jim stumbled out of the house nearly tripping on the thick doormat. Jim pointed to the front seat as he approached the car. Detective Flint motioned for him to sit in the back. He opened the door and fell in, seemingly exhausted at the walk.

"How are you, Mr. Hall?" Flint asked.

Jim thought the question stupid given the circumstances but figured he was being polite.

"I'm okay," he replied.

But from the looks of him, the detectives both knew that he wasn't all right. He looked like a meal half eaten and whatever was doing the eating was coming back for the main course.

"Jim, we just thought we should come by and personally tell you, that we've basically come up with nothing so far. But we're still looking for witnesses to come forward and still running analysis on all the evidence we've recovered."

He listened to the detectives talk of their efforts and their prospects. The words flew off of him like a sheet of plastic. He wanted to blurt out what he knew; he wanted to run into the house and get the muddy blood-stained clothes and hold them above his head. He wanted to scream out Kent Jackson's name, that he did it, that he had killed his wife. But he didn't. He sat silent, morose, listening to the detectives, listening to what they done, thinking about what he was going to do.

"Now, it hasn't been for a lack of trying," Flint said. "We've done everything. Sometimes hit and runs are just like that. Nobody has seen anything." Flint shrugged his shoulders. "So basically it's a waiting game, until something turns up."

"But we're still trying," Trower said. "And we won't ever stop trying," Flint added.

"We just felt it necessary that you don't keep your hopes too high. Eventually we will catch him. Probably some kid, out for a joy ride. He'll talk to one of his buddies for long, and then they'll talk to us," Trower said.

Flint nodded.

The words rang hollow in Jim's ears. He stared blankly over the front seat, out the front windshield of the car, at his house. He smiled faintly. He knew finally knew what he must do. The purity, the thought of it, the elation of the fantasy, it numbed his head.

"It's okay, I understand," Jim said. "I know you both are doing the best you can."

He opened the car door abruptly and got out.

The detectives looked at each other and Flint shrugged his shoulders.

Trower got out of the car and walked Jim to the door.

"I have no right to say anything to anyone about their loss or how they deal with it," Trower said, "but I have experienced close and firsthand how it affects different people. It's strange, but tragic events often have a way of changing people, sometimes for the good, sometimes for the bad." He paused for a moment and looked at Jim with a curious eye, as if he were looking into his soul. "I hope you can understand what I just told you, Mr. Hall. It's just my experience."

Jim looked into his eyes and nodded. But Jim was already changed and he knew it…he asked himself if perhaps Trower knew it too. He probably had a good sense of people. His good sense though was a little late.

He told the detective thanks for all he had done, and then opened the front door. Trower stared at Jim, wanting to say something else, but the moment was gone.

"Well, Mr. Hall, if you ever just want to call and talk or ask a question about the case, you are more than welcome."

"I appreciate that, Detective," Jim said. He slipped a hand out from the doorway and then turned slowly closed the door. His eyes never leaving Trower's as he did.

The detective would not see Jim again for over a year.

Behind the door, he stood and slowly slid down the back of it until he came to a gentle rest on the floor, his knees bent in front of him. He hugged them and momentarily pondered the consequences of the rebirth he had taken. He felt the horrifying abyss that was in the throws and agony of conceiving him. Strangely it felt comfortable, a familiarity to its warmth. He had become a friend to the orphaned little boy he knew so well, but hated. Now he embraced him. He invited him into his soul, to share the depths that churn there, boiling and turbulent. Anger would now be his mother and Rage would be his father, conceived from a tragedy of life, hurled into the dark abyss, forging a son named revenge.

# Chapter 16

He sat on the high table, the paper protector under him rattling at each move he made. His feet dangled, not able to touch the floor. Opposite the wall from him hung a poster of the human body. To the left of it was a white plastic case with a red lid, filled with used needles. A trashcan occupied a corner of the room with a red bag poking out around its edges. On the opposite end was a sink with foot pedals on the floor. Near the sink on a counter sat a container with long cotton swabs. To the wall next to him there was a blood pressure machine and different tools for checking into the mouth, eyes and ears.

The room was cold and sterile. Being there bothered him. He pictured it in his mind as an anonymous holding pen for people with horrible diseases waiting to die. *The stories these walls could tell*, he thought, shaking his head as he imagined for a moment what they might have seen. His mind shuttered at the thought.

He hated doctors, not in particular, just in general. He hated hospitals too. He went yearly, and not hardly anymore, unless he was really sick with the occasional sinus infection or flu.

The doctor he was seeing was an old family friend of the Vances, and Tina had always insisted that he go to him for an annual checkup, though he didn't think he really needed it.

Jim was uneasy, but that was nothing unusual, he always was when he went to the doctor. He glanced at the closed sliding door a few times when someone would walk by. Each time his body tensed, anticipating the closed door opening to reveal a doctor, *with a short saw in his pocket and the words this won't hurt a bit on his lips*.

There was a light tap on the door and then it slid open, catching Jimmy unaware. In came a man easily approaching 65, gray hair whirled around his head, across the bald spots, wearing an artificial wily grin on his face.

"Hi, Jim," he said, entering the room with more youth than the age that appeared on his face.

He shook Jim's hand firmly while gripping his arm with the other.

"Doctor Boland," Jim said, nodding.

"How are you holding up?"

"Oh…well as expected, I guess, trying to hang in there, you know. How are you?"

"Oh fine, fine." Looking at Jim most sincerely, he said in a low gentle voice, "Jim, I am truly sorry to hear about Tina. I delivered that little girl and doctored her, from the time she was small. I watched her grow up, you know. Now it breaks my heart to know that she is no longer with us…just breaks my heart." Dr. Boland stood there shaking his head for a moment, and then glanced away. He turned and took a rubber hammer from the counter nearby and twirled it nervously in his hands.

"Well, what can we do for you today, Jim?" he asked. Doctor Boland looked at him with concerned serious eyes; they felt as if they might burn right through him.

"Well, Doc, I have been having some problems lately and it's kind of embarrassing to say." He looked up at the doctor for a moment, their eyes met and then he looked away again. "I…I feel as if I'm coming unglued, like I'm actually going to spin out of control." He looked at the doctor again. "I'm no longer sleeping and when I do, I wake up feeling like I have just run a marathon. I am not eating—I don't have an appetite—the pit of my stomach feels like a hard baseball. I just feel like I am losing control."

His eyes drifted off looking at the floor. He lifted his head a little, looking at Doctor Boland. "Am I losing my mind?" he asked.

Dr. Boland smiled a little, and walked over to the wall and retrieved the little light hanging there. "No, Jim," he replied, talking with his back turned. "I don't think so. It sounds pretty normal to me, given the circumstances." He turned now looking at him and raised an eyebrow. "In fact, if you didn't have some or all of these symptoms, I would seriously question if you were normal," he said.

"Did all this start after Tina died?" he asked.

"Yes, right after," Jim said.

The doctor shook his head slightly, as if to understand.

"Your mind is trying to cope with loss, Jim, and when it can't cope, it finds a release valve, and it doesn't quite operate like it should for awhile. It over compensates in some areas and under compensates in others." He stood there in front of him, now shining the light in front of his eyes and then with his steady hand carefully placing the instrument into his ears.

"Any problems swallowing, Jim, or headaches in the morning?" he asked. Jim shook his head.

"Nausea, dizziness?"

"No."

"Well, I tell you what we're going to do. I'm going to prescribe you some medicine that will help you sleep and take some of that edge off your frazzled nerves. I am sure you don't have anything physically wrong with you. Just take them for awhile and see how you feel. And, if they don't work, well then we'll go from there. Okay?"

"Okay, that sounds fine," Jim said.

He briefly smiled at Jim and turned and sat on a stool at the counter, writing out the prescriptions under Jim's watchful eyes.

"Does what I said make sense to you?" the doctor asked.

Jim nodded and said, "Yeah it does, and…and I am glad to hear that I'm not going crazy."

"No, you're not going crazy…not crazy at all, you're going to be fine. Perfectly normal in fact." He tore two sheets of green paper off the thin small tab. "Now take this one," he held one of the little green sheets up in front of him, "in the morning and take this other one," he raised the other in his hand, but not as high, "at night."

"Understand?" he asked.

Jim shook his head.

He slapped Jim's knee and said, "What else can we do for you now?"

"Well I guess that's about it," Jim said, "I will give the pills a try." He hopped off the table and walked to the door. Doctor Boland put his hand on his shoulder. "Jim, now the pills may make you drowsy, so watch yourself while driving the car. Also, stay away from alcohol. That's only going to complicate the problem."

The doctor patted him on the back and put the prescription in his hand. "You're going to be okay, Jim, I promise you. Things are just going to be rough for awhile."

"Thanks, Doc, I hope so." Jim shook his hand, opened the door and walked down the hall.

"No worries, Jim," Boland called to him.

Jim clutched the green sheets in his moist hand tightly. On his face he carried a shrewd grin. He turned the corner and headed for the door. His head was completely empty, except one thought pulsing through his mind with each heartbeat—*revenge.*

He climbed into his Chevy Tahoe, complimenting himself on a job well done. He had rehearsed the words all morning, repeating the important phrases he needed to say, even practicing them in the rearview mirror on his way to the doctor's office. He grinned.

Pulling from his parking space, he accelerated away. He looked back in the rearview mirror at the building, and then he looked at himself. He hadn't changed all that much; it had been a little over a month since Tina's death. His "priorities" were just different now, that's all. *It had to be this way*, he thought, *so the filthy fucking animal could understand what he did was wrong.*

# Chapter 17

He waited for Kent Jackson to leave his office. He looked at his watch, it was 6:15 p.m. He saw several men walk out of the nice twenty-story building, and following behind them was Kent. He tapped his wedding ring on the steering wheel with his finger. He watched him, his eyes never blinking, his teeth clinched.

*Always the last to leave, aren't you?*

*The last to get home, the last to kiss his wife.*

Jim Hall waited every day for almost a week outside of Kent's office building, waited for him to leave, so he could follow. Hoping he would stop, hoping to run into him coincidentally, hoping to offer him the proposition of a drink *and maybe something more.* He grinned—*something more indeed.* "Goddamn right there will be something more," he said softly.

He watched Jim get into the Toyota that had long since been out of the body shop, fixed to perfection. He pulled behind him as he slumbered down the street toward State Route 4. Jim occasionally dropped back, keeping just out of site from the Toyota. Hoping he would stop this time, this night, *just one time*. He could taste it on his lip.

They traveled down State Route 4 and got off on the Sperry Street exit, which crossed over to Freemont, north of Applegate. Jim expected this to be another uneventful evening, just like the others, with Kent going straight home. But that changed when he pulled into Walgreens on Sperry Street. That got Jim's attention.

His heart raced with anticipation. He could see Kent getting out of his truck as he passed by. He looked in the rearview mirror and switched to the left-hand lane and put his blinker on to turn. He turned around, and raced back to the pharmacy and parked his car, in the least conspicuous place, on the east side of the parking lot.

He lurked between the aisles, pretending to search for something that he could not find. He stalked his prey until he found it and from behind an end cap of Super Depends he saw Kent Jackson by the pharmacy "drop off" counter.

He walked toward Kent. The closer he got, the more sluggish his legs felt. Each step was an effort almost beyond means. His arm felt agonizingly heavy, as he held it up outreached almost parallel to his face. A few more steps and he would reach him. A few more steps and that is all it would take.

"Looks like you have a little wait?" He said the words, looking directly at him from the side. He was able to approach him without detection and caught Kent totally by surprise. Kent jumped like someone who had just been slapped with a wall of ice cold water. He turned his head visibly irritated, unhappy that his dream-like trance was broken by such a rude greeting, or perhaps it was an awakening.

"Where have you been hiding? Haven't seen you in a while." Jim stuck out his right hand. Kent stood there, his eyes widening and mouth dropping slightly. Jim could hear the gasps of air that he was sucking in and out at a rapid rate. It was apparent he was caught off guard. He probably thought he was done with the Halls and would never have to talk to Jim again.

"Uh, hi Jim, how have you been doing?" He reached out and weakly shook Jim's hand.

"Oh, guess I'm doing all right...it's been kind of tough, you know." Jim looked at him with the saddest eyes he could muster.

"But, I'm doing better."

"Yeah...good. I'm sure it has been tough. I've been meaning to come over and see you...to see how you've been, but you know how business is. It never goes away." His voice trailed off and looked at Jim for a minute sheepishly; knowing his explanation was weak.

Jim knew he was lying, but he said nothing, acting as if all were fine. Smiling at him, everything hunky-dory.

"We need to get together sometime, Jim, and have a drink or two." He thought the words would pacify Jim, that he would be happy with the assurance that by God, his neighbor was going to be right there by him through thick or thin—through hell or high-water. Of course, there was nothing farther from the truth. Kent had no intentions of being a good or any other kind of friend to Jim. As far as he was concerned, he couldn't care less if he ever saw the guy again—the sooner the better.

He didn't even look at his face. It reminded him of Tina, lying there on the side of the road dying that horrible death. It woke up the *dirty hungry guilt* inside of him, and he didn't like to bother it, because when it was disturbed it tried to get out. It damn near suffocated him the last time. It scared him, and so he wanted nothing to do with Jim.

"Yeah, that sounds good." Jim looked at the long line. It would be awhile before it was Jim's turn, let alone his prescriptions filled. There was a small woman standing at the front, arguing with the pharmacist about her insurance. Her baby was screaming, its chubby face turning red and hanging over her tear- and puke-drenched shoulder.

"Looks like this line's not going to be moving anytime soon," Jim said. He nodded his head toward the front of it.

"Yeah, I think you're right." Kent glanced at the long line, shaking his head in disbelief.

Jim pointed his finger to a tray over by the counter, with the words "drop off" located above it. "Tell you what, why don't you put those prescriptions in the 'drop off' over there and we go have a drink over at Shepp's Place down the street. Then you can come back after awhile and pick up your prescriptions." Jim looked at him, shaking the bait in front of his face, hoping he would bite.

"No, I really need to get home, Lisa will be—"

"I don't think that is going to happen anytime soon." Jim pointed a finger to an elderly woman who was at the counter now, holding her prescription bottle up to the light, reading every word it said to the pharmacist.

"It says here that I need to take two, three times a day, for four days, now when do I begin that, tonight or—"

"Sounds like a philosophical question that just might take all night, Kent. Come on, have a drink with me. I'll buy." Jim grabbed his arm and tugged it toward the counter, giving him a grin.

"Oh, all right, but I can't be gone long, Lisa is expecting—"

"Come on," Jim said. He pulled him toward the "drop off" tray.

Kent dropped his prescriptions in the large blue tray, turned and walked hesitantly with Jim to the door. He didn't feel right about this for some reason. He felt leery of Jim for some reason, like he was up to no good, but other than the feeling, he had been nice enough, it was just something there, lying underneath. After each step the feeling gripped him, rose up in him and told him not to go. He thought several times of just stopping and saying he couldn't go, or that he suddenly wasn't feeling well, or that he remembered something he had to do, or that he thought he needed to do. But he didn't, for some reason. His legs kept moving; he felt uneasy, looking at Jim. He was smiling.

They walked out the door for a moment. Jim looked at Kent.

"Do you want to take yours or mine?"

"Let's just take mine."

"Sure, sounds good to me," Jim said.

They both got into Jim's Toyota and drove down to the bar.

The ride was smooth and uneventful. There was little conversation, which lent an uncomfortable feeling to the car. Jim didn't mind though, he was occupied by the incessant thoughts of Tina being hit by the Toyota. His mind shuddered at the thought. He could almost feel the muffled thud of her body inside the cabin of the truck. He heard the sound of it and for a moment he went deaf, with a slight ring in his ear.

"Does this thing handle the road pretty good?" Jim asked.

"Yeah, uh, it does a pretty good job staying between the lines." Jim looked at him with a slight smirk.

"Well, I guess a lot of it's left up to the driver, isn't it?" Jim replied.

Kent looked at Jim a little nervous. Jim let a smile spread over his face.

"Yeah, I guess," he said.

Kent's palms began to sweat. He squirmed in his seat, struggling against the belt that held him snug. He wanted to turn around, to be some place else. But he didn't. He saw Shepp's Place a block ahead and tried to relax a little, telling himself to get a grip, that his paranoia was getting the best of him. That Jim Hall didn't know a thing. That he was in control here. After all, wasn't it he that made the decision to choose whether this man's wife should live or die—*for the good of all*, he thought. He was in control.

***

The bar was dark and musty smelling. The odor of beer-drenched floors and smoke-saturated walls permeated the air. It smelled like old bars smell. There were only a few patrons, most sat at the bar counter, some turned and stared when they walked in.

A dark-haired girl with a spider web tattoo on her neck came over to the table where Jim and Kent sat.

"What can I get for ya two fellas?"

"Well how about a couple of draft beers, the darker the better," Jim said.

"You got 'em."

The girl walked off with a wiggle. Kent stared at her as she walked away. Jim stared at Kent and smiled. *See something you like?*

"How are the kids?" Kent asked. He turned to him with a concerned look on his face.

Jim played along.

"Well they're doing as well as expected I suppose…they miss their mom a lot. This whole thing has been a big shock for them. You know it's tough losing a parent." Jim paused for a moment staring at the table, and then stared directly back at him. "It's tough, I had to do it, you know, living without parents."

Kent sat there looking at him, wishing he hadn't asked. He wiped his hands over his lips nervously and nodded his head as if he understood. But, he didn't and he didn't care.

The waitress came back with their drinks. Kent was tense as he drank his beer quickly. Jim motioned for another.

"No, I really shouldn't have another, I don't like to drink before I drive."

"Don't you?" Jim asked. But he quickly extinguished his knee jerk remarks to Kent's comment. "How wise…but just one more won't hurt," he said.

He motioned with his finger to the waitress, but she didn't see him.

"Just a second, I'll go get us another."

"No, Jim, wait, that's okay, I really need—"

But it was too late. Jim was already walking toward the bar. It was no use to call after him. The music from the jukebox was too loud, and the aged speakers rattled as "Momma Don't Let Your Babies Grow Up to be Cowboys," echoed from them. He just sat and watched Jim, irritated that he was there. He looked around the dreary bar, wondering when he would get to leave. He hadn't really noticed it before, but he didn't really like Jim that much. All this time he really thought he had. But, he found his morose upbeat personality very irritating now, especially when he covered his grief with smiles and small talk. He thought about just leaving for a moment, leaving him there, that was what he really wanted to do. But he didn't. He thought it was the least he could do, considering what he had done. He would stay there and take his medicine—take it for a little while at least. Then he planned never to see him again, if he could help it.

Jim purposely walked to the bar counter where no one was sitting—his back was to Kent. The closest person was an old man with a cheap red and white cap. On the front of it was an advertisement for Red Man Chewing Tobacco. He sat about four stools down. The old man smoked a cigarette, drawing the fire down clear to the butt. He never looked up. He sat there staring at the beer in front of him, probably looking for better days. Looking at him, Jim thought that it wouldn't be too long before he found them.

He asked for two frosted glasses and a pitcher of beer. The waitress brought them to him on a tray and asked if he wanted her to pour. He shook his head and handed her a ten dollar bill, and told her to keep the change.

"Thanks," she said.

"No problem," he said. Then he watched her turn, and walk down to the end of the bar toward the register.

Jim glanced around and then over to the old man. He was leaning with his head turned against his arm, the other arm bracing it up, the cigarette burning over his head, while ash dropped onto his cap.

Jim had planned to do it later, but he decided the time was right, to do it now.

He took a slip of paper from his shirt pocket and quickly poured the white powder into one of the glasses, watching it form a heap at the bottom as he did. He turned around and looked at Kent, and raised the pitcher up, indicating he was going to pour them at the bar.

Kent smiled weakly, tapping his watch, indicating he needed to go.

*Just one more freaking minute and you'll be mine, you filthy fucking animal.*

Jim shook his head and held up one finger, and mouthed the words *just one more*. He poured the beer slowly into the glass, watching the powder dissolve in the dark amber liquid, it creating a *witch's brew*, he thought, *that would tame the filthy animal.*

He walked back to the table, where Kent sat looking uncomfortable in his well-worn wooden chair. He shifted back and forth clearly agitated, forgoing some of his former politeness.

"I really don't have time for a pitcher, Jim, I told you I really got to be getting back and I—"

Jim interrupted, "No problem, we'll just have one more and be on our way."

Kent nodded his head, a little more assured that there was an ending to this nightmare.

He drank his beer quickly, while Jim deliberately drank his slow. He needed time for the *witch's brew* to work.

Jim made small talk about the neighborhood, about Tina, about anything he could think of, watching Kent as he grew more and more quiet, calm and lethargic. He poured him another beer. Kent didn't resist this time. He drank it slowly, staring into the bottom of the glass looking through the frosty head.

Kent watched his arm put the beer down. It felt as if it was not part of his body anymore, as if someone else was offering him their appendage. His eyes drifted down to the green and white checkered floor tiles, each having its own simulated marble design. He began to think how grand they were.

Jim watched him closely. His movements became over exaggerated; his head listed to the side and his speech began to slur when he talked. At one point he put his elbows on the table, with his head in his hands.

"I don't know what's wrong with me, I feel dizzy, I—"

He didn't say anymore, just stopped in mid sentence and rubbed his face with his hands, and stared at the green Formica tabletop.

"Can I get you fellas another pitcher?" the waitress said. She looked inquisitive at Kent, glassy eyed, head leaning back and to the side a bit.

"He all right?" she asked.

"Oh he's just fine—this is our third bar today—so he's doing real good." He slapped Kent on the back as hard as he could, like they were pals, and grinned. He winked at the waitress and tucked another ten into the hip pocket of her tight jeans. Jim stared into space and the waitress winked back.

"Well all right, y'all have a goodnight then."

"Will do," Jim said, nodding. She turned around wiggled back to the bar.

"Kent, it's time for us to go, old buddy," he said out loud. He helped him up from the chair by the arm. "Can you walk?"

"Yeeaaahhh, I, Ith can wwaaalllk."

He walked, but he walked slowly. The door loomed in the unforgiving distance. Once out in it, Kent stopped, and stared at the sun as it disappeared in the ground to the west. His mind wasn't right, he tried forcing it to think, but it was if there was a thick fleshy barrier growing in his skull, refusing to let through what needed to get through, yet letting him think about images that he didn't want to think about. But as soon as they would appear they disappeared, and relatively seemed unimportant, just after he thought them.

"Kent, do you want me to drive?"

"Nnnooo, Ith…I thiiiink Iiii got iiiit."

They climbed into the Toyota and pulled out into the street. Kent was all over the road, all the way to the pharmacy.

"That was real smooth driving, Kent," Jim said, "can't wait to do that again." He chuckled and gave Kent a smile and punched him in the arm. Kent nearly fell over.

"Sorth abouuuth thath, Iiii just don't know wwwhhhaaath is wwwrroooong with meee. Three beers usually doesn't affect me like this," he said. Getting out of the car, he displayed a brief smile.

"Well, sometimes it just happens to the best of us," Jim said.

He looked at Kent as he walked in front of the 4Runner. "You don't look so good, my friend."

"I feddelth very tirrred. I musth be geeeetthing the fluuu."

"Tell you what, I'm going to wait around until you come out and see if you're all right—if you're good enough to drive."

Kent leaned against the Toyota, elbows to the hood. "Ith apprrreccciate that, Jiiimm, but yooouu don't have toooo. I think I'llll—"

"Look, just go and get your medicine. I'll be here when you come out, just in case."

Kent nodded his head and walked in front of the automatic doors. They parted, as if to welcome him. He glanced hesitantly back at Jim, to see if he was still there watching, a little uneasy now. Jim gave him half of a smile, and Kent turned abruptly and walked in.

Jim got into his Tahoe and waited for Kent to return. He didn't want to be seen with him more than he had to, and he was glad that he had parked on the east side of the building where fewer people were.

Watching him come out was like watching a mime walk in slow motion. His steps were exaggerated. Each one he took was like he was stepping up a flight of stairs. Holding himself up with the wall, he fumbled for his keys. Jim's hand held the door handle, ready to spring on his prey, embolden by the lateness of the evening.

As he came around the corner, Kent fished in his pocket for his keys. He walked swaying, in a diagonal course, stumbling several times. He reached the hood of his 4Runner and leaned on it for a moment and then finally produced the set of keys.

Jim walked slowly toward him, behind a row of cars, looking left and right, and behind him to make sure he wasn't seen. Kent took a couple of steps to the door and swayed a bit, as he tried to find the right key. He fumbled them and they fell to the ground. He reached a hand down to retrieve them, but a foot pressed down on top of the keys.

Kent stared up. "Jim, Ith think...I'm havin a lille trubale with ma keeees," he said, slurring his speech badly now.

Jim picked up the keys with his hand. "Well now, Kent, let's see what I can do for you."

Jim held the keys up, and pressed the wireless remote entry pad. The door unlocked automatically. Dangling the keys up in the air, he looked at Kent and grinned. Kent tried to reach for them, but he quickly took him by the arm, carefully watching for prying eyes that might be watching. He saw none and began walking Kent around the vehicle to the passenger door.

"Listen, Kent, I don't think you're in any condition to drive home, I think I better take you home."

"Naaahhhh...ya donth neeth ta dew thaaat...I'le bee all riiight." Kent stood leaning against the Toyota, his eyelids half closed over his dilated pupils. Kent thought that something wasn't quite right, but the alarm in his body refused to go off. There was a message registering in his head, that Jim now was there for a reason and that reason may not be a good one. With a sudden urge, he knew that he should try to get away, though his body rebelled against him. He lurched forward, trying to get his body to run but only fell into Jim's arms.

"Now, Kent, I didn't know you cared." He looked deep into Kent's empty pools, those spaces that were now drawn and red, vaguely resembling the clear blue eyes he had a couple of hours ago.

"It's tough being helpless, isn't it?" Jim whispered. "It's tough being at the mercy of someone that can save your life, isn't it?" Kent stared at him blankly, then he began to struggle weakly against him, knowing now he was in trouble. But it was useless, the drugs he had gotten from Doctor Boland now took full affect on his body.

"Noooo," he moaned loudly, grabbing Jim's hair and pushing against his face with his elbows. Jim balled up his hand and punched him in the stomach. Kent crumpled to the ground. Jim glanced around him to see if anyone was looking. He saw no one, the parking lot almost empty. Jim was struggling to get up, trying to crawl away at the same time. Jim pulled him up by his collar and drove a knee hard into his back. Kent let out a sickly cry and withered once more.

Jim opened the passenger side door and shoved Kent up into the seat by his belt and collar. He glanced out the driver's side window and saw a police car pull into the parking lot on the far end of the other side. Kent, seeing it too, began to fight hard against Jim, pushing him away with his hands, trying to kick him out the door. Jim tried leveraging his feet, one foot on the ground, the other on the floor of the cab, grabbing his clothes again and again as they ripped from his hands, Kent pushing them away each time. Kent yelled loudly with all his strength, directing his voice in the general direction of the police car. Jim pushed both hands hard toward his face trying to cover his mouth. Jim glanced at the police car. The officer stared straight ahead, content trying to catch speeders, not paying attention to the parking lot.

Suddenly, Kent, with all his strength, broke free of Jim's grip, trying to lunge across the center console, reaching his hand out for the door handle. Jim caught him by the belt and yanked him backward, standing stooped in the cab thrusting a forearm against his throat, trying to crush the air from it. Kent's screams became muffled, each one taking all the air he could muster from his lungs, sounding as if a strange creature were dying in pain, screaming as he did.

Both of Kent's hands pushed up against Jim's forearm, now bearing down on his throat. He tried to let out a scream, but couldn't. Jim fumbled for something in his hip pocket, struggling to hold Kent still. He quickly jabbed a Talon stun gun into his chest, and sent a jolt into him. Kent lurched back in his seat stiff for a moment and then went limp, quivering as he stared up at the top of the Toyota's cab.

Jim pressed against him, getting down from the passenger seat and leaned against the door pushing air in and out of his lungs, staring at Kent. He lay there groaning, his head draped backward over the side of the seat, eyes fixed blankly. Thinking he had killed him, Jim gripped Kent's wrist, checking to see if he had a pulse. He found one, and slapped him on the cheek. "You'll be all right for now, it just feels like you're dying."

Jim walked around the front of the Toyota, looking at the policeman sitting in his car. He pulled out of the parking lot with his lights on and drove away down the street. He looked at Kent. "Well, I guess I don't have to pretend to be so friendly now, do I? I suppose my true intentions have been exposed at last." He spoke with a panting growl, nervous and excited at the same time, anticipating what he was about to do.

Kent tried to move from his paralyzed position, but his brain would not tell his body what to do. He spoke something unintelligible that gurgled in his throat. His eyes flickered rapidly, straining to focus, almost rolling at one point into his head. Jim put his hand behind Kent's neck and shoved him up straight in the seat.

Jim was silent, staring ahead, thinking. His dedication to what he planned to do was intensely written on his face. The old self now had spiritually departed. His new self was reunited and embraced by the long dark shadows of the child he once was. And with it disappeared any semblance of the man that Tina had loved. Now, he existed solely as an entity dedicated to exact revenge for her, his compassion surgically removed by the atrocities of life. He now was consumed by hatred built up over his years. The fire was now ignited, sparked by losing Tina. He was a vengeful wild fire burning out of control.

Kent sat there quietly, as if temporarily content to acquiesce to the predicament he was in. What he didn't know was that his life would now be changed forever and nobody would be able to stop his nightmare that was now beginning.

# Chapter 18

Driving for about an hour, they turned into a small gravel driveway that lay nearly hidden in heavy brush and trees. The driveway wound its way up a steep grade through a deluge of dense foliage, sprawling at the foot of the road. The end of it opened up to a small parcel of land covered with sparse grass, rocks, trees and vines. A cabin sat off in the distance on a bluff; a lake lay just over its edge.

Kent slept most of the way, passed out from the drugs and alcohol in his system, his head lodged between the door and the bucket seat. At each bounce it looked as if it one might separate from the other.

Jim rolled to a stop in front of the cabin. The sound of rock crushing together beneath the tires reverberated off the lake and surrounding trees. He opened the door and stretched for a minute and walked around the back of the Toyota to the passenger side. He pulled open the door and as expected, Kent tumbled out onto the rocks in a heap.

He awoke when his body fell to the rocky ground. Jim left him withering there and walked to the cabin and unlocked the door, then opened it wide. Kent began to stir on the ground. His hands dug into the rock, crawling a few inches and then collapsing. He turned his head and lay there sucking air into his lungs, dirt clinging to his face, some of it finding its way into his mouth. Jim stood there silent, as if standing in judgement, glaring at him.

Jim pulled Kent by the back of his collar, dragging him about seven or eight feet at a time and then dropping him face down to the ground. Kent groaned each time he was dropped, face and body slamming into the rocks. A flow of dark blood began to flow from his nose and splatter on the ground, painting the large sandstone pebbles below.

Jim cussed him with each pull, the words aimed at Kent, spewing from his mouth when he exhaled. The thought of having to carry such a waste of human flesh irritated him. He supposed it was the one flaw in his plan—having to drag a drugged-up sack of shit into the house.

He pulled Jim to the bottom of the stairs. His head banged into the bottom step. Kent moaned. Jim drug Kent's lifeless body up the stairs, his head catching on each step, Jim jerking the body hard, pulling it free each time. Yanking him through the doorway, Kent's body twisted, catching on the frame, then coming to rest at the center of a large room. He sat him up on the floor, blood flowing freely from his nose now over his blue suit jacket and white shirt. He pulled him up into a tall straightback kitchen chair.

Jim never said a word. To Kent, the silence was deafening. Sitting there, head hung to the side, his blank eyes drifted to a fireplace on his left, and a door lay on both sides. He heard footsteps and slowly turned his head. Jim walked passed by a kitchen door to his right.

He worked his bloody hands back and forth slowly, trying to remove the numbness. He felt his chipped fingernails with his thumbs. They were packed to the quick full of tiny rock and earth. Blood spewed from his nose, dripping off his chin to his shirt. A good-sized nick in his ear above the lobe oozed red droplets that dripped slowly one at a time onto his shoulder.

Kent tried to think, but his brain felt like a pound of worthless flesh, saggy and weak. He felt Jim staring at him. He saw his shadow in his periphery, knowing that he was in danger, but due to the drugs unable to quite come to terms with it or how much.

He heard footsteps approach behind him. A sick ripping sound filled his ears, from behind his head. Suddenly, a thick piece of tape was roped over his head and brought tight to his mouth. Jim wrapped the Duct tape around Kent's head three or four times, until the whole half of his face disappeared. Kent clawed at it weekly shaking his head back and forth like some rabid dog. Jim grabbed him by the hair and tore the tape from the roll and bent over in front of him and looked directly in his eyes that were now starting to fill with tears, as he stared up at him in terror.

He picked Kent up by the collar and ripped his shirt, accidentally dropping him. Blood flew from his face as he hit the floor. Jim pulled him up by one arm and perched him back into the chair. Another ripping sound filled the air. He pulled a long piece of tape from the roll. He stuck the end of it on Kent's shirt. He flinched, the fear tearing into him. He tried his legs, but they didn't work, they were too weak to lift him up. Jim walked around him five times, effectively sealing him to the chair.

Kent took a couple of steps around the side of the chair and kicked it over. Kent went sprawling onto the floor. He tried to get up, but before he could, Jim had quickly pressed a knee in his back and wrapped his wrists and ankles in Duct tape.

Jim retrieved another chair from the kitchen and drug it across the hardwood floor and placed it in front of Kent and sat there in it, staring into his hollow eyes. It was a stare that was unwavering, unyielding, and relentless in its attempt to study the creature he had before him.

Kent's eyes filled with fear. He realized there was a great possibility that soon he might die. Tears formed in them and streamed down his cheeks onto the tape that was now blood splattered. Not bleeding as bad now, he struggled for air, his nostrils now the only passageways for life. He thought of Lisa and his children.

He had not heard Jim speak since leaving the parking lot. He found his silence eerie. His face was filled with rage, his eyes were translucent windows, illuminated by a fire that burned inside. Something dark lurked inside of him, perhaps a revenge that grew great with hunger, he thought, wanting to devour him.

Studying him closely, Jim said, "Do you know why you're here?"

Kent shook his head, as he tried to gasp for air through the tape that tightly bound his mouth. He dare not say why he suspected he was.

"Right now, I want you to think about the reason why you're here," he said softly. "I want you to focus on that. I hope to God that you can. Do you understand what I am saying?" He was calm, reserved, words composed simply, but to the point. Jim thought him to be dedicated to the words he spoke.

Kent didn't nod. He shook his head, and tried to speak under the tape. It wasn't that the words were understandable, it was the reflection. Kent still didn't understand the gravity of the situation. His voice inflection indicated he was trying to make a deal.

Jim leaned in at him suddenly from his chair, his eyes fixed on him, like a dangerous lion stalking prey. He did not blink, searching for something, as if trying to see behind Kent's eyes.

Jim erupted, "I will rip that fucking tape off your face and stab you in the heart!" he screamed. "Do I look like a fucking Monty Hall…No I don't—do I? I look like the guy that is going to slice half your head off, just to hear you scream from both sides of your head! You got that!"

Jim slumped back in his chair, eyeing Kent, looking for a reason. Taking a deep breath, Jim spoke again more calmly, "Do you really think this is another business deal that you are simply going to put together? Do you? You better think of the reason why you're here. You're here for one reason and one reason only, that is to make amends—to give your pound of flesh. If you think this is all just going to go away, you are sadly mistaken. Do you hear me, you sonuvabitch, you're sadly mistaken!

Kent cowered in fear. He was scared to make any expression on his face. In the back of his head, he knew there would be no reasoning with Jim, that there was a a reason why he was still alive.

"Are you smirking at me behind that tape? ARE YOU? I think you are, you sonuvabitch!"

Kent drew his head back shaking it frantically, trying to indicate no, crying under the tape, his throat making distressing sounds as if being muffled deep in a canyon.

Jim sat back in his chair and took a long deep breath, looking deeply into Kent's eyes, not blinking. His head felt like a pressure cooker that was about to explode.

Jim frowned deeply at Kent. His voice was agitated, but a little calmer, yet cracking, almost weeping as he told him, "I loved her, Kent...God, I loved her and you took her away from me. Do you understand that...how much that hurts...that you took her away from me?"

Kent's eyes widened exposing the whites. He was shocked at what Jim told him. He tried to make sense of it in his mind, still unbelieving that he could know what he had done. The more he forced his brain to work, the more helpless he felt. But, he was aware of one thing, that Jim was doing this because he knew he had killed Lisa. And if he knew that, he thought, he would be killed.

Jim looked up at him for a moment. "I don't think you can understand that." He pointed a finger at him, elbow bent, becoming more perturbed. "No, I don't think you're capable." Jim got up and walked around the room appearing nervous, disturbed and bothered by the dilemma. He walked at the far end of the room and turned, leaning on the wall, his back to it. He appeared consumed with great anger, bothered by his company, each moment emotionally decomposing.

"You see," he said, "you took something from me that I never had...that was, somebody who gave a damn about me." He looked at him for a moment, pausing, searching for a reaction in Kent's eyes, but only seeing terror.

"You see this cabin, Kent? This was going to be where Lisa and I retired. We used to come up here and work on it, and then sit out on the back porch and look out over the lake, just relaxing. She loved this place. It's not much, two bedroom little hole in the wall, but she loved it."

"So I guess I thought it was appropriate to bring you here, to let you see it...to let you see what she will never see again. This place, Kent, that brought her so much pleasure, it will now become your albatross.

"No one will hear you scream," Jim said. He walked toward him, knife in hand, gleaming as it crossed a path of light. Closer he could see its sloped serrated edge, the point pentacle sharp, gripped tightly in Jim's sweaty hand. Kent struggled in his chair, thinking only of what to do, what could be done, trying to pull himself up from it, against it, screaming, his voice muffled by the tape.

He rocked the chair back and forth, trying to somehow break the bindings that held him, trying everything that could free him. Jim came closer, determination showing on his face, his footsteps louder but slow, that sound being the only one Kent could hear; all others unimportant at that moment, with the ever-growing promise of death with each slow step.

The legs of the chair rocked wildly back and forth, Jim straining his neck upward with each tug of his body, eyes bulging, his blood vessels pulsating out from his neck, trying to break free. He tried every means available to save his life.

He felt deathly sick at his stomach as Jim came toward him. His throat felt thick and tight, sweat streaming down his forehead into his eyes. Kent started to gag. He leaned his head over reflexively as if to vomit and then began choking. He lunged forward, full of terror, throwing his head high up in the air, strangling on his vomit. His face reddened, as gurgling sounds rose up from under the tape covering his mouth. He convulsed, leaning his head forward, and then slinging it side to side trying to breathe. He couldn't. His eyes were now embraced by fear, knowing that he would die.

Jim watched the spectacle through drawn slits, his body tensing at the sight. He thought that for a moment he would let him die—that he would let him die the kind of death that Tina did, undignified, one that had left her with little respect. He watched Kent turn a bluish color. He felt even within himself the struggle for life that he was going through, his body almost joining in Kent's tense struggle for life.

"You're not going to die on me yet, you sonuvabitch," Jim yelled. He rushed the rest of the way toward him with the knife. Kent's head withdrew in fear, bobbing back and forth strangling—spew drizzling now from his nostrils. Jim grabbed hold of Kent by the hair. He slipped the knife under the tape and cut through it in one swift cut, and the point of it pierced into his cheek. "You'll die when I want you to," Jim screamed.

Jim pulled the tape off his lips. It ripped at Kent's convulsing face as he did. Kent leaned over, choking out vomit, spewing it onto the floor, some of it oozing out his nose. Jim took two fingers and pressed them deep into Kent's throat and pulled out the contents, flinging it away. He leaned the chair over letting Kent's head dangle forward, letting the vile drain from him as he slumped against the tape at an angle.

Jim let the chair fall back. Kent's head whipped back and then forward. Hacking the strangling spew up, Kent spit repeatedly, and made concerted attempts at clearing his throat. His hair was sweaty, his face soiled with his own stomach contents, tape flapping from both sides of his face. He sat there gasping, struggling for air, panic now surrendering to some relief.

Jim turned Kent's chair around slowly as he gasped for air, exposing a nearly empty room, with large French doors located near the center of the back wall, light shining through them, illuminated from a lamp on the back porch. In the center lay a thick brown rug; on it the design of a large tree, with birds on its branches and animals surrounding its trunk, lying on light brown earth. Located near one of the left walls were a piano and a couple of old white armless chairs, set near the fireplace.

Jim walked over and pulled the rug back, exposing a door underneath. He unbolted a latch and lifted it up with some strain. The door, thick and old, creaked back on its hinges, then he let if fall with a muffled bang.

Kent walked over to him and grabbed his chair. He tilted it up on its hind legs, scooting it to the door like a wheelbarrow; it screeching all the way. Jim took out his knife again, directly in front Kent, and he stared at him while he unfolded. He stared directly into his eyes.

"Please no," Kent cried.

"Change of plans," Jim said, ignoring him. "I think there is a good possibility if I leave the tape over your mouth tonight you will strangle to death, so welcome to your new home."

"What do you mean?" Kent asked.

Jim sliced through the tape in silence. When he finished he slapped him on the back of the head. "Get up," he said.

Jim stood from the chair, his legs weakened, and he fell down.

"Get down into the cellar," Jim said.

"Why do I have to get down into the cellar?" Kent asked. He lay there in a heap trying to move, to get up to his knees. "What are you going to do with me?"

"All the answers to your questions will come to you in time. Look on this as a life-changing experience, Kent. But for now, don't piss me off anymore than I already am, just get your ass down in that cellar."

Kent lowered his body down into the dark abyss, looking up at Jim as he did, hoping that he would somehow have a change of heart. He didn't. Kent's searching eyes disappeared in the dark.

Jim lifted the heavy door standing it up on its hinges. He peered into the dark hole, hesitating for a moment, and then let it slam shut. He covered it back with the rug, straightened it, and moved the chairs back to the table. He drug both chairs back to the kitchen and placed them around the table, and took the sticky tape and balled it up into his hands and threw it away. Thinking for a moment, he went to a closet and got out a mop and broom. After removing all the distresses of the evening from the floor, he washed the mop and broom thoroughly in the old porcelain sink. "Done," he said, after examining the room for any testaments of the evening. He walked to the door, turned, and with a final look he turned out the lights, closed the door and left.

# Chapter 19

Lights rolled by as Jim peered at them through the windshield, the darkness swallowing them up in the rearview mirror. He drove carefully, afraid to be pulled over by the police in a car that belonged to Kent Jackson. He knew he couldn't survive the roadside cross-examination by the police. He was tired and if suspicious, eventually they would find Kent down in the cellar before he died.

He drove the speed limit and made sure he kept the wheels perfectly in between the lines. He was relieved that things had gone so well. Except for Kent nearly dying, his plan had been picture perfect. He faintly smiled at the thought of it for a moment, cruel as it was.

He thought about the dank pitch-black cellar that Jim would stay in that night. He thought about the confusion and desperation he probably felt. He tried to imagine himself there, and the prospects that he may die. He shook his head. The thoughts disturbed him. He pushed them from his mind.

* * *

The cab's vinyl seat felt cool as he touched them with his warm hands. He spread his fingers out over the seat, absorbing every inch of comfort they had to offer. It was another hot dry dusty night in Oklahoma, when the air was still and the heat suffocated you in it if you stood or sat in one place too long. The taxi began to pick up speed, and a hot wind forcefully parted Jim's sweaty brow through the cab's window. The passing fumes of cars and buses irritated his nose.

"Where to?" the cab driver asked.

"102 East Sperry Street. It's an apartment building near Shepps Place, do you know where that is?" Jim had memorized the building number, seeing it when he had driven by with Kent.

"I know where it is."

The drive was a pleasant one. Jim kept the window down and let the air blow into his face. It was sobering and he welcomed it. After about twenty minutes they turned onto Sperry Street. He looked at Shepp's Place when they drove by, wondering what other horrors the bar or its parking lot might have seen during its long years in business.

"This is it, right here," Jim said. The taxi rolled to a stop in front of the Deer Wood apartment building.

"Will right here be okay?" the cab driver said.

"This will be fine," Jim answered.

Jim lumbered and got out of the cab lethargically, his legs and back stiff and all the tell-tale signs of exhaustion begging to appear in his face. He struggled with his stiff legs as he pulled himself out the door. It had been a long day, he thought, but he was almost done.

"How much?" Jim asked.

"Fourteen dollars," the cab driver replied.

Jim handed him twenty and told him to keep the change.

"Thanks, man, appreciate it, you have a good night," the cab driver said.

"Sure," Jim said. He walked toward the apartment buildings watching the cab driver pull away, waiting for his taillights to disappear in the distance. He stopped and turned around when they did, and began to walk toward Walgreens that was about five blocks away.

The old cement sidewalk battered his feet through his Timberland boots. His legs felt heavy and his shins ached with each step. Tonight was typical of Oklahoma in the latter parts of July. The darkness gave no relief from the hot wind flowing up from the southwest. And when it mixed with the humidity, from the dew on the early morning grass it produced a hot stifling air that sometimes felt suffocating, making it difficult to breathe and not letting up until early morning.

Jim's hair began to feel damp from the moisture in the air. He could see the parking lot now in front of Walgreens, his Chevy Tahoe sitting alone at the corner of the parking lot. The sweat began to bead up on his forehead and roll into his brow. The pavement felt like it now tried to swallow his feet, his legs sticky, clinging to his pants, his feet like hot fire pokers burning inside his boots.

Pulling the truck door open he lifted himself in, relieved that he was sitting and that he was there and that he had done it. He leaned his head against the steering wheel and turned the key. The engine came to life instantly, and he fumbled for the fan knob on the air conditioner and turned it up to high. The hot air blew into his moist dark hair, which was waving back and forth. Then it slowly turned cool and comforted him, while his thoughts turned to Kent down in the dark cellar, underneath the cabin. He wondered again what he would feel like if he were Kent, alone, deep in the bottom of an abyss, in pitch black dark. Out of his element, out of his environment, staring alone, his pupils wide trying to sense what was in the darkness. An ugly feeling of hopelessness spread across him, the fear of being trapped, of contemplating being killed. The fear of not knowing.

He dropped the gear into drive and pulled from the parking lot and pointed the car toward home. He smiled faintly as he thought about Kent, and what horror he felt at that. But, he wanted to make sure that nothing spun out of control though, but was in the confines of control. That there were calculated boundaries, that governed humane actions against those that were not humane, that this was justice, no matter how uncommon it was and that it had to be carried out with extreme integrity to himself.

He passed a neighborhood church as he neared Winding Creek Drive and thought about the purity of his actions, how it had to be. To allow himself to be devoured like those that devoured him when he was child was not acceptable. Their actions were undeniably free of self-restraint. They took revenge on the helpless victim that had nothing to do with the pain against them, like *mean little Anita*. He, on the other hand, was different, though they were the catalysts for his burning rage that had glowed helpless like coals for so many years buried under ash, giving all appearance and all pretense of emotional composure. No one realized what lay dormant within him, he thought, it not being stirred, awaken for years. Tina charmed it, perhaps tricking it to go to sleep, convincing it to believe it was no longer needed.

But now it was. Tina was gone. And Kent had stoked the coals and sparked the flame. He took pleasure over the hatred that now consumed him; he was intoxicated by it. Tina was no longer there, lifting him above the debris of memories that threaten to trample him. Now, the only thing he knew was the familiarity of hatred and rage; they made him secure, they embraced him. Now he would strike with a vengeance, a certainty. But controlled.

*Yes, the control was necessary.* If he didn't have it that would make him just like the ones that had soiled his life. They had no control, no jurisdiction over their emotions; they succumbed to their beastly desires at any given moment. They were unmerciful and without reasoning. No, he would have control. He would take the rage by the tail and tame it and make it his slave.

He turned the key and the motor died. He sat in his driveway looking at his house, its shadows contrasting slightly with the darkness from the streetlight. His mind drifted from the weariness that now was on him. He began to fall back through time, to a place unreal. To when he was a boy, longing for a family to love him, for a home to care for him.

When he was ten, he had lived with a man and woman for nine months, before a social worker took him away. They lived in the country in a white farmhouse and managed a chicken farm. He loved it at first. He dreamed of it becoming his home. Jerry and Barbara were in their mid-forties and had always dreamed of having a child, but they couldn't on their own.

They were both nice enough at first. Jerry was a tall skinny man with a slender face and a hook-nose. Barbara was plump and always wore a well-worn apron over a simple dress, and usually cackled loudly when she laughed. They were country folk.

But Jerry changed. It wasn't changing though; he probably had always been that way. He had come to learn about people—they didn't change, that was just the way they were. They would remove the mask from their face and there they were, exposed in their true light. Sometimes good, sometimes bad, but there they would be.

In Jerry's case the mask came off early. He became mean and abusive. Barbara never did, but still she was guilty enough, always turning a blind eye to her husband's violent fits that often ended in some sort of beating of him, though sometimes her too. Perhaps she was happy that he was there, a release valve of some sort that could be vented toward him, taking the pressure off her at the same time. She did try to comfort him after Jerry's ugly spells, but when they were frequent, she would retreat somewhere back into a deep recess, withdrawing, not wanting to feel his anger her body already bore the scars of.

Jerry was a difficult man to live with. Often he talked about how a young man should work, like his father had made him work. He would dribble on about how he needed to learn that life was not about a free ride, and according to him, that was exactly what he was now getting. He should be very grateful that they had taken him in. "No-ont and noboty," he remembered him saying, "wanna a no-good kid liken to you'in of ypur'in age." He would tell him that he was too old to make a woman happy about a child and too young to help a man properly with a hard day's work.

Regardless of his occasional fits of obscene anger that were often filled with violent threats and ridicule from being such a bastard child, from motherless stock. He tried to please him, eager and wanting to. Always wanting to show him he could be a real man, a man that Jerry's father had been. Or that he claimed he had been. However, each attempt at proving himself worthy to be that man was beaten back and beaten down into his head like a hard metal spike, as he was a "nowd-good" that would "neva mount'ta nothin'." The verbal harangue would often precede a beating, and with it, each lash a condemnation of his worthlessness, each fist, a culmination of years of hatred built up in Jerry. The hatred was probably the result of his father's rash of injustice against him. The circle continued.

He shuddered at the times when Jerry would cruelly chase him in the woods with a fishing pole, pissed at whatever had gone wrong in his day, taking the blame out on him. How he would hunt him for hours, the day would give way to evening, as he would call for him, his face in a torrent of sweltering anger, to come out and take his beating like a man. He closed his eyes, and still could hear his voice: "Ya bedder come out'yere boy, com'on get your'in woopin you lil'le worthless sack-a-shit. Colm'ere ya wortless bastard of a boy, colm'ere out and take yer beatin'." Maybe five times out of ten he would find him, his long lean body suited well to running him down. Those great strides would thump behind him, as he chased him, coming closer and closer slashing out with the pole until he would catch him and stand over him with God-like prominence and say, "This fer-ya ow'in good."

He supposed the faces changed but the results of his beatings never did. Perhaps it was a reaction that Daddy Jerry couldn't control; but then again, he may not have wanted to.

This was just one of Jim's childhood memories, a sad experience that was more than plentiful but like many others that lined the well-stocked shelves built up in his mind.

He was that from which he came. The cruelties he learned as a child were now but a tool he controlled, to do with it what he will. While no one deserved it without merit, Kent had earned an unforgiving punishment that he had learned all too well. He would dole out a fitting measurement of grief to him, that Kent had done to him. *Wasn't this justice? Wasn't this right?* He thought it was, and now he was beyond the rapids. He now had committed himself to the end.

As he opened the door to his truck he looked at the Jacksons' house. The house was full of lights, the porch light on. She was waiting for Kent's return. He walked across the corner of the yard to the sidewalk. The grass covered his boot with witness of the dew. He wondered how long Lisa would wait before she called the police, or had she already? Did Kent look at his house, the same way he now looked at the Jacksons'? He stopped for a moment and thought about Lisa. He felt sorry for her; he knew the worry she must be going through.

# Chapter 20

John Nickels had been a Blackwell real estate agent serving the Lakewood City area for a little over ten years. He was now branching out to market Majestic Lake properties after a recent retirement left a vacancy in the local Blackwell Real Estate office. Patty Nichels, John's wife, was elated at the idea. She had long wanted to move to the lake area, thinking it would be a great place for their three kids. While the Lake City had good schools, she wanted their kids to live in a more rural environment as she and her husband had as children. Now they had their chance and were hoping to find a house and move to the Majestic area by September.

John thought Majestic Lake was beautiful and so did Patty. They often drove down on the weekends and rented a condo on the water. The cherished memories they had there on Majestic Lake filled them with the anticipation of living there.

* * *

John squinted in the sun as he drove his van down the long winding roads and hills that surrounded Majestic Lake. This was his third week showing properties. He had already made one sale since working the area, and today was promising to be another. The only bad part was the hour commute, but for now, he would have to grin and bear it. Soon, he and Patty hoped to find a lakefront property affordable enough that they could purchase. But, until then, the double lane highway between Lake Majestic and Lakewood City would be his friend.

Although Majestic Lake was beautiful, it was also confusing finding your way around. John had been lost nearly a dozen times since he began working the area. To compound problems, small driveways were nearly hidden, jutting back into small holes cut out of the thick woods and foliage. Signs didn't deliver much help considering there were hardly any and often mailboxes were covered in vines that only a mail carrier could know exactly where they were. Majestic properties were easy enough to sell all right. It was just getting around and finding properties that was the hard part. Often times he would search in vain for a Blackwell Real Estate sign for hours, only to find that another agent had mistakenly put a sign on the wrong property.

This particular afternoon he was having the same problem. He had scheduled an appointment with a customer for 5:30 in the evening. It was five o'clock and he still had not located it. He looked at his scrawl on some notebook paper. It told him the property was located near Shooter's Creek, five miles west of the old brick schoolhouse on Lake Road 2. "Drive three miles north to the Lake Access Road and then look for a large oak tree on the left-hand side, with a Blackwell Real Estate sign on your right next to driveway." Such were the directions given in the listing book that was nestled on the passenger seat in Jim's Chrysler Minivan. Locations at Majestic, he thought, were literally a 911 nightmare. If the police or an ambulance actually had to come and find you—one might as well kiss your ass goodbye.

John slowed at the access road and then turned left heading west glancing at his odometer, each time a mile would click off. But, there was no large oak tree at this location on the left-hand side of the road. He rubbed his earlobe a little and looked around. There was an oak tree about a half a mile back, with a small driveway, but he didn't see a Blackwell Real Estate sign.

John drove up the road another mile and finally he saw a Blackwell Real Estate sign, but no oak tree on the right hand side. The sign read: "Blackwell Real Estate Agency: The people you trust to find you a home." He turned in anyway to a short driveway. He thought about how moronic the slogan sounded as he drove the snaky path. He looked at his watch; it was 5:28 p.m. *Perfect timing,* he thought.

There were kids playing on an old fallen log near the edge of the woods. A small white house sat right off the water to the left of a clearing with a walkway leading down to a dock. Smooth sandstone rocks made up the driveway and a few trees jutted throughout the clearing.

He slowed the vehicle looking at the house and then stopped, got out of the cool van, and looked at it for a moment. The heat seared down on him and fogged his glasses. Wiping them with his handkerchief, he held them up and peered up through them toward the sky. Satisfied, he placed them back on his face and pushed them into place with a single chubby finger. Folding the handkerchief several times he wiped his forehead and then the back of his neck.

He strained to breathe. The surrounding dense canopy and flowering trees trapped the hot moist air and forced it down into his lungs. He was a heavy man and didn't take to the heat well. Each breath was a struggle. Each step he took was a strain. It was the third straight day the temperatures had been over the one hundred degree mark. He often felt that on days like these, the sun could actually melt the pounds off his overweight body. But, the same body would stare him back in the mirror each day.

When the children saw him, they stopped playing on their makeshift toy, an old log, and ran towards him, racing and jumping over stumps. Their feet crunched in the smooth sandstone pebbles. There were two boys, about seven and nine, and one girl around eleven.

"Beat ya pollywogs, didn't I," she said. She was panting and out of breath.

"No ya didn't and I'm tellin' Momma you tried to trip us," the older boy said.

"Did no such thing, liar liar pants on fire," she quipped.

She looked up at John and smiled. Her smile indicated that the words that rolled freely off her tongue were just business as usual.

"What's your name, mister?" she asked. Her voice was thick with an Oklahoma draw.

"My name is John, little lady."

"Hi John," she said.

"These are my brothers Danny and Tobie. We're going to go fishin' with our daddy today, you wanna come?"

John stood there smiling as a man in shorts with a crew cut shirt opened the door and walked out on the porch of the small house.

"You all go on, leave that man alone. Tobie, get away from his van."

The kids slowly walked away back to the old tree trunk laying on its side, ready to resume its role as a grand ship in the high seas.

The little boy called Tobie was slow in going, had a bur haircut and curious eyes, wearing only a pair of shorts.

He turned to John.

"Can I ride in your car, mister."

"Go on now, Tobie," the man on the porch said.

John patted the little boy on the head as he walked over to the porch and stuck out his hand.

"Hi, John Nichels, how are you doing today?"

"Good, name Larry Parker, you?"

"I'm doin' good," John said.

"I'm hoping I'm at the right place. I work for Blackwell Real Estate. I am supposed to meet someone here to show a house."

"Well that's the first I've heard about," Larry said. "We got our place up for sale, but nobody has called about an appointment today."

"Well I guess I got the wrong place."

"It's not hard to do around here. What address is it?"

"82455 Rural Route 3."

"Well, that's your problem, this here is 82451. You came down too far."

John looked at his watch—5:38 p.m.—and then looked up at Larry. "Thanks, I have to go and see if I can find this place and try to keep my appointment."

"Sure thing, man…and if they don't want to buy that place, maybe they would be interested in this one," he said.

John smiled over his shoulder as he walked back to the van. "Okay," he said.

He pulled out of the driveway and waved to the kids. They waved back to him as he drove up the narrow lane to the road. Seeing them made him miss his own children. He thought about just heading home, thinking he would never find it in time. But he had come this far, and he would at least try one more time to find it.

The driveway by the oak tree was his best hunch. It was the only oak tree he remembered seeing and there was a narrow driveway nearby. He decided to see if that was it.

The van drifted close to the sides of the road, nearly running off it several times. Its motor whined as it strained up the steep hills and then down them, wind shuddering against the sides of the van, feeling as if the vehicle would break apart anytime. Finally, he came to the oak tree, which had a faded advertisement plastered on the side that read: "Reelect Sheriff Richard Bower: a name you have come to trust in law enforcement." And above it was another sign, except this one was written crudely on a thin white board. It simply read: "Dock repair, Call 918-257-5552."

The mouth of the driveway in front of the oak tree was sharply carved into thick underbrush and trees. Slowly he turned the van into it and followed the narrow path up a winding lane. On each side lay a thick wall of trees, stringing vines and underbrush. He navigated the narrow winding lane with great care, as the natural walls on both sides of him surrounded the van. He had a slight prick of apprehension, but dismissed it almost as quickly as it came. He owed much of it to the unfamiliarity of the place, but still a scent of it lingered with him.

The end of the lane opened wide into a good-sized clearing. At the far end sat a handsome cabin with a large porch; a blue Chevy truck sat in front. *This has to be it*, he thought. But if it wasn't, somebody here may know where the house he was looking for was. He got out of the air-conditioned van, and the immediate weight of the heat once again pressed down on him. He breathed the thick moist warm air and pushed it out. A great effort accompanied each attempt to inhale and exhale. He nearly tripped over the uneven-sized sandstone rocks, stumbling, straining to see through his cold fog-filled glasses. At the step he began the arduous climb to the porch, his body resisting his effort, as gravity struggled to drag him back to the ground.

The house had been fixed up somewhat and in his salesman-like mind. He began to think of potential clients. *If this wasn't on the market*, he thought, *it should be*. Though it was a little rough, it would have no trouble selling. Fishing a key out of his pocket, he tried it in the lock of the front door. He frowned when it wouldn't go but half way into the keyhole.

A large red curtain hung in front of the door window. Pressing his face against it, he curled his hands around his eyes, trying to look in, but couldn't see anything. Slowly he walked around to the side of the cabin, following the wraparound porch. He tried looking into each window, but they were all tightly closed. He neared the back of the cabin and did a few shuffling side steps looking around the corner as if he didn't want to startle anyone, just to let them know gradually he was there. But nobody was there.

The back of the porch was opened up over a long bluff, overlooking Majestic Lake. A long slender walkway meandered around the bluff to the water. A fishing dock bobbed gently as short little waves lapped against it. *How peaceful*, he thought.

Turning around, two large French doors stood in front of him. The glass etched with intricate leaf cuts near the top and at the bottom. A curtain covered the doors, but just partially. Stepping in front of the right door, he cupped his hands around his eyes and peered in through the glass. It was then that he noticed them in the darkness. It took him a moment to register something wasn't quite right. It took him another moment to realize that something was terribly wrong.

Backing away from the window in terror, John turned and fell with a sick thud tripping over an uneven board on the porch. His hands pushed his large body upward very quickly, unnaturally for a man his size. He was frightened and it showed on his face. He turned his head behind him, watching the doors, while he stumbled to his feet. His body felt weightless, adrenaline pumped through his veins. He ran down the back of the porch, nearly falling on each step. As he turned the corner from the stairwell, one of his feet clumsily caught on a clay pot. It fell over breaking into pieces making a small clink as it hit the ground. He stumbled and fell, skidding into the grass. He looked as he got back up to his feet at the French doors again. He saw the shadowy figure of a man looking at him from the door.

The hair raised on John's neck. It felt like bristles rubbing against his shirt, and every inch of his skin crawled in panic as he broke into a full run around the back of the house and then to the side of it. His gigantic body shook in jiggles with each earth-pounding step he took. As he passed the front porch, he saw a door open. A man ran from the front door and down the porch almost twenty yards away, racing him to his destination—the van. Sweat began to fling from his face as his chubby body jarred with each sluggish stride.

Fear filled his eyes as he watched the thinner quicker man race ahead of him to his van and run around to the side of it. John slowed as he saw the man pull the keys from the ignition and hold them up in his hand. He looked at John for a moment, his face not showing any emotion, but only determination.

Seeing that he was beaten to the van, John sharply turned and ran away from the house and van into the woods as fast as his little stubby legs could carry him. He dodged trees and jagged rocks that were strewn on the ground, turning occasionally looking behind him, but seeing nothing. He began to feel somewhat relieved thinking he would run deep into the woods and hide. *Hide till dark*, he thought. Then run to the road.

But then he heard the footsteps thumping behind him, mixing with his own sounds of heavy panting as he struggled to suck in the thick air. He strained at every gallop to make his body go faster. He feared what was behind him. Every inch of his brain told him not to look behind him, that it would just slow him down. But he had to look...he had to see. How close...how close was the man behind him? He didn't know.

He turned and looked behind him in full stride. He caught a glimpse of the man behind him. It was just a snapshot, but it electrified his head. The man wasn't running full out, rather he was following, waiting, knowing that the fat man would soon tire. John ducked his head and ran with all his might.

"Oh God no," he cried.

The trees blocked his immediate view as he dodged each one, his thick arms brushing their sides. Behind him he heard crunching leaves and twigs, and they were lighter, quicker than his own. He began to cry under his breath. He could feel him now, closer, almost upon him.

"God help…God help me! Help me! Help me!" John screamed. But there was no one to listen to his cries, only the trees, rocks and the determined man that was chasing behind him. John sucked air in and out of his lungs with each breath, with each pleading word. His ears were ringing at each jar of his body. "God no, please no!" he screamed.

He felt a hand grabbing at his shoulder, trying to pull him down. John stumbled, off balance, but kept running like he was falling forward. Another hand now dug into his shoulder and then a push overcame his feet and his big body went slamming to the ground.

The man put a knee on John's neck as he lay sprawled out on the ground underneath him. Dirt-stained hands flailed in front of his body swishing through leaves that littered the ground. His head was buried in them, bunched up in front of him, as he had impacted the ground.

John felt the man on top of him, a knee burrowing into the back of his neck as he heaved air in and out of his body underneath him. The man's body moved with him as he struggled for air. John gasped out words between each breath. "Please…let me…go! Please…Please…oh God…help me!"

John reared up suddenly, knocking the man off, lunging on his hands and knees, trying to stand. The man tackled him and pulled him down back into the leaves, the upper half of his body now bent over an old tree trunk that had fallen on its side. He lay there gasping, sucking in the heavy humid air that was slow in coming.

"Goddamn it, what are you doing here?" the man said.

"Please…I didn't see anything…let me go," John pleaded. "I won't tell…I won't tell…no one." He said the words in rapid pants.

"See what…what are you talking about?" the man asked.

"Please, I won't say anything—"

"What in the hell are you doing here?" the man asked. He leaned on John with all his weight, shaking his head, not sure what to do, but sure what he couldn't do.

"Look…I'm a real estate agent…John Nichels is my name."

"Why the hell did you ever come here?"

"I'm…I'm sorry, I'll go away and never come back…I thought this house was my appointment…I was supposed to show a house today and I thought this place was it," John said.

"I can't let you go now," the man said. He looked at John's desperate face, his sweaty hair mopped on top, leaves sticking to it, his lips curled, his nose bleeding and his eyes filled with tears.

"Please don't...please...let me go...I've got kids...I've got a wife at home...they will be expecting me," he pleaded.

Jim stood up, looking down at him now, looking grim. "I'm sorry," he said.

The man rolled over. "Look! Look!" John fumbled for his wallet and showed him a picture of his wife and two children. He held it up in front of him with a shaking hand. "Please, please don't, they need me...look at them...don't—"

The man looked at the picture. He felt sorry for him and he felt sorry for his wife and kids too. He looked at John, sympathetically and shook his head. "God, why did you come here? I wish you hadn't...I'm sorry."

The man snatched a large rock from the ground that was lying by the log. He quickly grabbed it and lifted it up over his head. John pulled himself over the log and started to claw through the ground, fingernails pulling up leaves and earth as he strained to get up and away. "Don't...please don't...don't kill me," he pleaded. He tried to get to his feet, turning as he did. He stumbled at first, and then stood and turned again to run.

The man didn't want to, but he had gone too far now and he couldn't let him go now.

He hurled the large rock through the air, just as John turned and it glanced off his back. John began to run now, but Jim quickly fell on him again.

"No! No!" he cried. John said the words over and over again, but they had no affect.

The man was now determined, no longer doubting what to do, and no longer hearing John's pleas nor cries for help. His ears now filled with a slight high pitch whine, his nose stung. He saw John cowering on the ground before him like an animal, looking for shelter in a hale storm, but not finding it. John's lips were moving, but no sounds were heard.

The man wrapped John's thick neck in his arms and began to squeeze, turning and pulling his head at the same time. At one point his arms slipped off around John's sweaty neck and head. The man reestablished his hold and twisted as hard as he could, his shoulder pressing down on John's head, the crook of his elbow tightly against his throat, like a boa constrictor slowly killing its prey. His left hand was full of John's hair. He pulled it, and pressed his head down more, bucking with each last attempt John made to lurch upward from the ground. John resisted against the man's attempt to break his neck. He leveraged his hands, clawing in the dirt, but the man gained leverage and bear down on him hard.

"I'm…sorry…but, you…saw…too much…back…there." Each word accompanied a jerk of John's neck, an exertion of all his strength. The man reassured him, as he slowly killed him, that it would be over soon. John's head turned red, then blue, his hands helpless to do nothing but scratch at the leaves and dirt in front of him. His legs flailed back and forth behind him. With one final excruciating yank, the man heard a hideous crack, and John's body lay still, his lungs emptying of the last breath, a rattle rasping from his chest. *It was done*, the man thought.

The man turned John's limp carcass face up to make sure he was dead, then released him and fell back against the ground, breathing hard, pulling the moist hot sticky air in and out of his lungs. He looked at him, panting. "May God have mercy on both of our souls," he said in a whispered breath. John lay there in a heap, his face still distorted from the agonizing pain, dirt and leaves smudged over much of it, eyes blankly staring at the sky.

The man got up and reached down and tied John's shoes together and drug him back through the woods from which they had come, not but ten minutes before. He thought of the man's wife and children as he did; how they would miss the man he had just killed. He thought of him as a victim of circumstance, an unfortunate and unintended victim of an uncommon justice. A few tears dripped from his face as he drug him from the woods.

# Chapter 21

Lisa pulled the blinds back and looked down the street. She tapped her fingernails on the window impatiently and glanced at her watch. It was 7:48 p.m. and she was worried about Kent, expecting him home by now. She had talked to him a little over two hours ago and he was getting ready to come home. He mentioned to her that he was going by Walgreens to pick up a couple of prescriptions.

"When is Dad coming home?" David asked.

"Well, I don't know; he is supposed to be home," Lisa replied. She glanced at him. Her face was filled with worry. She looked out the window again, pulling the blinds wider apart as if the problem was she couldn't see through them.

"Mom, I'm hungry, can we go ahead and eat?" Samantha said.

"You show so much concern," Lisa said.

"You're really worried, aren't you," Samantha said. "I'm sorry, I guess I just never thought that there was something wrong."

"I know he's been late before, but he hasn't been this late in a long time...and...and usually he calls."

David and Samantha stared at her puzzled for a moment, as if it finally dawned on them that something might be wrong. Lisa turned toward them for a moment and put her hand lightly on a chair and leaned her forehead against it, looking at the floor thinking. After a moment she said, "Well, let's go ahead and eat."

She waited until her children left the room, pretending to follow them to the dining room. Instead she picked up the phone and dialed Kent's cell phone for about the sixth time. There was no answer. Then she dialed his office number, it rang three times and then a voice said, "Hi this is Kent Jackson, I'm not—"

Lisa hung up the phone before his voice mail message finished. She called Kent's dad, Stan Jackson, who lived in the country, but Kent was not there. She brushed her fingers over the dial pad for a moment, then called the operator for the number for Walgreens, then called them.

"Is there a pharmacist on duty?"

"There is, ma'am, but she is getting ready to leave."

"I need to speak with her please…it's urgent."

"Okay, hold on for a minute."

Lisa heard the phone shuffle briefly and then a few clicks and then a woman answered it.

"Yes, this is Shelia, how may I help you?" The woman said the words politely, but her voice indicated she was in a hurry.

"Hi, my husband was supposed to pick up a couple of prescriptions, but he has never came home with them…could you tell me if he has been there?" In the back of her mind, she could imagine what the pharmacist was thinking. *It wasn't her problem that her husband wasn't coming home.* But instead the pharmacist asked, "Were the prescriptions in his name?"

"Yes."

"What is his name?"

"Kent Jackson." Lisa's voice was now filled with anticipation of the answer.

Nearly a minute ticked by, when the pharmacist returned to the phone.

"Yes, he picked two prescriptions up a little before seven thirty."

"Oh, okay…thank you." Lisa's voice trailed off to nothing.

"Well thank you for calling—"

Lisa hung up the phone before the woman had time to finish. She was clearly puzzled where he had been for over for two hours before he picked up the medication and where he was now. But, she was just glad that everything was all right and he would probably be home soon.

Ten minutes later she walked slowly to the dining room. David and Samantha watched her as she came in. They could tell she was worried. Her face was tight, and her lips were locked in a frown. She sat down and picked at her salad while the two of them ate. *He should have been home from the pharmacy by now*, she thought.

After a few moments she stood up from the table, letting her napkin fall from her lap. She walked hurriedly to the kitchen and picked up the phone and dialed it. At that moment Lisa Jackson made a determination that something was wrong, terribly wrong. She spat out the words in sporadic clumps on the phone to the desk sergeant, her mind trying to engage her tongue. Despite his reassurances that everything was probably okay, Lisa insisted it wasn't. Finally the sergeant relented and let her talk to a detective.

Again her words were erratic as they fell fragmented from her mouth. If Kent did not show up that night, the detective promised that he or someone else would talk to her in the morning. Lisa sat the phone down on the receiver, trying to reassure herself that everything would be all right, that what the police had told was true, not to worry. But as the night turned to morning, she was worried. Kent had stayed out at night before, but not without calling, but this time she felt that something was very wrong.

At 6:00 a.m. the next morning, Lisa called continuously, leaving nearly a half dozen messages for the detective. By the time 8:30 rolled around, Lisa was getting ready to go down to the police station herself when the phone rang. It was Detective Randy Trower.

Within fifteen minutes she had him convinced that they didn't have a fight, that he hadn't left her for another woman and that she would have remembered if he told her he was going to be this late. Though secretly, she could not be certain of the second thing. *Had he left her and the kids...for someone else?* She didn't know, but thought it doubtful. Kent wasn't perfect, but she didn't think he would do that.

After an hour, Detective Trower sat with Lisa at her dining room table asking her questions.

"Did he say that he would be home late last night?" Trower asked.

"No," Lisa replied, her voice quivering. "He said he was coming home."

"Is he ever late?"

"No, he just told me that he was going to pick up some prescriptions at Walgreens." Lisa dodged the question. She didn't want him to think he was just out drinking or something with another woman.

"Did he?"

"Yes, I called. He had picked them up around 7:30 last night, but never showed up."

"Was he late up until he picked up the prescriptions?"

"Yes." That was probably the most telling piece of evidence. He was late, but he picked up his prescriptions. *Apparently not too much wrong with him if he was able to do that,* she secretly thought.

Trower gave her one of those looks like, *I'm wasting my time here*, but continued to play along. If she wasn't so sincere, he would have left before this, but he stayed.

"What about relatives, a friend, anybody he would stay with?"

"No, I have called everybody."

"What was he driving?"

"He was driving a gold Toyota 4Runner."

"Do you have his license plate number?" he asked.

"Yes, I should have it in a drawer over here somewhere."

Detective Trower sat there looking at her intently and then dialed a number into his cell phone.

"Yeah, this is Trower, put out a missing person on a Kent Jackson. He's driving a Toyota 4Runner, license plate number," he looked over at Lisa, who called off the numbers and he repeated them, "XQL 1091. Okay…thanks." Trower stood up.

"Mrs. Jackson, I'm going to run a check of all the hospitals, airports and bus stations to see if anything turns up. I will call you in a couple of hours. In the meantime, sit tight and I'll let you know what we turn up, if anything." He smiled at her and she faintly smiled back. She saw him to the door and watched him drive off.

She walked slowly back into the living room and quietly sat on the couch where her children were, but she didn't notice them, not a first. Suddenly, she became aware of them and realized they were there, watching her, trying to see what her face would tell. She looked up and saw their examining eyes. They were on the verge of tears, sitting on the couch close to one another in the living room. She stood up and walked over to them, feeling guilty that she hadn't thought of what they were feeling before. She hugged them and they hugged her back.

"Is Dad going to be all right?" Samantha asked.

Lisa didn't know what to say. Finally she smiled and said, "I think so," though that is not what she meant to say. She meant to say *yes, sure, your father is fine*, but somewhere deep inside herself, she knew something had happened, something terrible.

Lisa didn't expect to hear from detective Trower for another hour, and was surprised to see him when she glanced through her window and saw him pulling in her driveway. Her heart felt heavy, and she didn't know what to think. It could be good or bad news. Suddenly, her head felt light, not knowing what to think, not knowing whether she wanted to even open the door. Her hand lay on the doorknob, unable to move, to turn it, but finally, and slowly, she did.

"Good afternoon, Mrs. Jackson," Trower said. He stood at the door and gave her a brief smile, but through it she could see that there was going to be something she didn't like. Lisa pointed to a couch in the living room. "Please sit down," she said. "Sam, David, why don't you two go upstairs for awhile." After some resistance to their mother's request, they did.

Trower sat down and seemed pained to begin, and then abruptly said, "We found your husband's vehicle." There was a pause. He looked directly at her, she now bending her knees slowly to sit, shock written on her face.

"Was he—"

"No, he wasn't in it."

It was in the long-term parking at the airport. We checked with the airlines and it appears he bought a ticket to Jacksonville, Florida.

"But…why?" Lisa asked. She said the words without thinking, unable to think at least, to think about the worst, maybe something worse than his own death. The unimaginable was now starting to form in her head, but she refused to accept it and dismissed it, refusing to believe.

"I know this has been tough on you, Mrs. Jackson, and this is a hard thing to face, but at this point we're going to seriously have to start looking at the possibility he may have left of his own free will for some reason or another."

Lisa didn't answer. She sat there and thought about the possibility of it. *Sure they had problems, but nothing serious*, she thought. But maybe it was serious to him. But maybe it wasn't about problems, but something else.

There was a long period of silence after Trower spoke, his words seeping into her head causing realities unimaginable to her only a day ago. "Well, Mrs. Jackson, I just wanted to come by and tell you in person what I found out. If you think of anything that might help us in finding him or hear from him, please let me know." He stood up and walked toward the door. Lisa stood with him and followed, but said nothing.

"We will continue to look for him, and I will let you know if we come across anything. But I just want to let you know that sometimes people don't want to be found, and often that is the case." Lisa stared at him for a moment, the words digging into her ears and penetrating down into her heart.

She opened the door for him, still saying nothing. To Trower, it was quite apparent in his face that he thought Kent had likely had an affair with another woman and left with her, or left. It was also apparent to him that Lisa was now starting to think about this possibility too.

"I'll let you know if we hear anything, you do the same," he said, then carefully smiled at her.

She faintly smiled back, and said in a whisper, "Goodbye." Then she closed the door.

Detective Trower walked back to his car convinced no foul play had come to Kent Jackson. He had seen it a thousand times before—a man leaves a woman, a woman leaves a man—without a single word, for whatever reason.

He told himself as he put the key into the ignition, *that he would like to have a fresh dollar bill for every missing person that turned out that way*. He pulled out of the driveway looking at the house and thinking about the wife and kids that live inside and shook his head. *What a shame*, he thought, *what makes a man leave all this?* He shook his head and drove away.

* * *

She looked at the envelope and turned it over in her hands and looked on the back and then turned it over again. It had no return address. Its postmark was from Florida. She ran her fingers over the ink that spelled out her address. *It is Kent's handwriting*, she thought. She slowed her feet and drug them and then finally stopped. She tore away the end of the envelope. *Why am I getting a letter from my husband, shouldn't he be dead or something?* she thought.

In her mind she had denied what was so reasonable to believe. The only explanation was his inability to be with her in life. His disappearance, to her, mostly likely was his death. It had been nearly two weeks since he had disappeared and she loved and missed him. She forced her mind to restrain from thinking about betrayal. But never did she think this could be an affair or that he could just leave her and the children. But yet, what was the letter doing here, in her hands? She was surprised and shocked to see his handwriting, so familiar, so haunting.

She didn't want to open it. She knew it might change everything. She tugged the letter from its envelope and unfolded the pages slowly. She glanced over it and noticed it was not long. She began to read, intently, gulping up every word. She began to walk back to the house, her legs like iron. She drug one foot in front of the other, hoping she would make it. Her legs were heavier now. She was reading, thinking as she walked. The words cut into her deeply. She felt faint. The sun glared off the white paper, temporarily blinding her, blocking her attempt to read it all over again.

She fell down to the concrete on her knees and her body collapsed over them. The letter seesawed back and forth in the air and finally landed beside her on the ground. She wept. Her hands and forearms baked on the hot pavement, but she could not feel the pain. There was a greater pain she couldn't ignore. It tore at her heart. It screamed at her for being such a fool.

She fell over sideways in the yard and lay there, her hair spilling around her on the grass. The sun beat down on her body as she lay beaten. Her life was over as she knew it, her truth and trust crushed by the letter that now lay silent beside her. She lay there, her body sunken into the ground, broken. At that moment, for her, it was the end.

* * *

Detective Trower read the letter first and then tore open the brown paper package. As he sifted through its contents, he held up two black pair of dried mud-caked Florsheim shoes, one in each hand. He stood there looking at them with astonishment and then poked through the rest of the clothes. They all had some form of stain on them. A few were light brown in color and others were a dark crimson. He reached over and immediately picked up the phone, glancing at the letter again as he dialed.

"Yeah, it's Trower, you remember Tina Hall…I think we have our man."

"Who?" Detective Flint asked, from the other end of the phone.

"You will never believe this. I just got an anonymous package naming Kent Jackson as Tina Hall's killer. It looks like another woman is not the only reason Kent Jackson left town. I'll let you know if forensics check out."

# Chapter 22

He ate an early dinner with Janie and Kevin. They talked about the usual things: school, friends, life. They hardly spoke of Tina: to admit she was no longer there with them would be too unbearable, the loss of a mother and wife too unthinkable. The finality of her death too painful to think of, to talk of.

Kevin would speak of his mother, but only in generalities, of how he missed her, how he couldn't believe that she was gone. He was like her in a way, careful with other's emotions, but unselfish with his youthful passion. He often held her picture in bed at night, looking at her, remembering her voice: the sound of it sweet and soft. It called to him until he slept. His mother was security, sanctuary and stability. She exhaled life into him and the warm breath of reassurance. She was a catalyst for change when things seemed unbearably bad, but most of all she was a pivotal figure when difficulties arose. Kevin's candid remarks about his mother often drew long stares, no one knowing what to say, and no one knowing how to say it if they did.

Janie had shut down emotionally, a trait she had learned from her father. She spoke little of her mother, often her voice was distant, but carried the heavy weight of her mother's death inside. The thought of not having her there was too painful to talk about, to say it out loud perhaps. Losing a mother at this important point in her life was devastating, but when is losing a mother not?

Sometimes Jim would stand at the door of her bedroom and listen to her cry late at night, helpless, and at a loss for what to do. He wanted to go to her, to comfort her, to heal what hurt inside, but he knew that nothing could, not even him. He was incapable of remedy, what was once there now was too empty to fill. He himself fell mortally slain at her persistent haunting memory. He could not heal her deep agony; it was a wound that no one of this earth could mend. He could not heal his own. The sorrow inside was just as great and its relentless assault just as unbearable.

For all of them, she was mother, wife and best friend. They missed her dearly, but each in their own way. She was loved even more so in death.

Finishing, they began collecting dishes and taking them to the kitchen. The kids groaned over the mundane task as usual.

"Aunt Mae is here, Dad," Janie said.

Aunt Mae knocked briefly and came in, as she always did.

Jim poked his head around the corner of the kitchen into the living room.

"Have you eaten yet?" Jim asked. "There's plenty."

"Oh, I ate such a large lunch, I'm not really hungry."

"Well, you know where the refrigerator is, if you want something."

"Yes I do."

"Jack is going to be gone for a couple of days with his fishing buddies, or so he says, so I thought I would come over and keep the kids company for awhile, that is if you all can put up with me."

"Oh, they'll like that, stay as long as you want," Jim said from the kitchen. He grinned at Janie and Kevin, and they silently laughed back.

Aunt Mae was like a second mother to the kids, especially now. She was made of different stuff than what her sister was made of. Perhaps the kids could sense that. They loved their Aunt Mae, her eccentricities and all. She would knit while watching old reruns of Hawaii Five-O on the oldies cable channel, and drink sweet tea and smoke long dark brown Moor cigarettes. It was comical to watch the smoke curl over her head, and even more so when she would suspend her frantic knitting and stare engrossed in the nefarious mayhem on the big tropical island. She was a good woman and they all cared about her, including Jim.

"I won't be home until late," Jim said. He walked from the kitchen to the dining room, buckling his watch back to his wrist and then sitting down in the chair to put on his boots. "I have some errands to run, so if I am not back by late, don't wait up."

"Okay," Aunt Mae said.

Jim stepped back into the kitchen. "Does anybody have a kiss for me before I go?"

Janie gave him a hug around the neck and kissed his cheek.

"Daddy, do you have to go?" Kevin said.

"Just for a little while, but I'll tell you what, Daddy will cook you a big breakfast in the morning…okay?" Jim smiled at him. Kevin smiled back and gave him a hug. Jim picked him up and carried him to the door and then put him down.

"I'll see you, buddy." He opened up the front door and walked to the truck.

"See you, Dad," Kevin called to him.

Jim drove slowly down Winding Creek, looking at the Jacksons' house. He recognized the blue Crown Victoria as he passed by. It was Trower and Flint. *What comes around goes around,* he thought. He knew the horrible worry and anxiety Lisa and her kids were going through, but quickly turned his thoughts away from it. He couldn't allow himself to be persuaded by external factors. He had to be vigilant against those elements that would distort the purity of his anger, compromise his integrity of what he had to do and might prevent Kent Jackson from meeting the sword of justice. Admittedly, though, he knew revenge was the bearer of that sword, and misguided or not, it would be swung decisively and for a reason.

* * *

Jim made the hour drive in forty-five minutes. He was curious in what he would find there in the basement. There was a good possibility he supposed Kent could be dead, that he may have succumbed to dehydration or fright or worse. After all he had spent nearly twenty-four hours in a dark hot cellar. But, in the back of his mind, he knew he was still alive. He did have air, and it would take longer to die of dehydration, though he was no expert at the subject.

He opened the door to the cabin cautiously, knowing there was no way Kent could have escaped, but cautious just the same. He stuck his head in gradually and glanced along the walls and back to the kitchen. As he stepped into the dark room, he shut the door behind him and walked slowly to the kitchen. He pulled a table out to the center of the living room floor and then sat two chairs at it.

Scooting the table and chairs, he heard Kent faintly yelling from the cellar, his voice strong, but heavily muffled by the wood floor and thick rug. Taking a pitcher from the kitchen cabinet, he filled it and put it on the table along with a plastic glass. Returning back to the kitchen, he opened a drawer and put on a pair of long black thick gloves. He glanced out the kitchen window for a moment, looking between the curtains. He opened another drawer and took out a small bundle of paper, envelopes, strands of smooth rope and a pen, all still wrapped in packaging. He gathered it all in his gloved hands and carried it to the table, neatly placing all of it on the side of the table near the fireplace.

Jim walked back toward the back of the living room and then stooped and pulled back the heavy rug and then walked over to the French doors. He flipped the third light switch to the left and opened the door to one of the bedrooms near the fireplace. On his return, he pulled the dull black Ruger 9mm semi-automatic pistol that had been resting in his hip pocket. He held it tightly in his gloved hand and aimed it forward with his arm outstretched, with the other hand he bent and slowly pulled open the cellar door in the floor.

"Get back," Jim said.

Kent was standing at the bottom of the stairway, one foot pulled forward to the next step, the other supporting his body. His back was slightly bent to accommodate his head nudged against the cellar door. He looked like a desperate animal ready to spring.

"You move, Kent, and I'm going to kill you where you stand," Jim said.

"Okay, okay, I'm not going to do anything," Kent said. "Please, just let me out of here. I need water."

He looked haggard and dejected. His eyes were drawn and he was unsteady as he walked up the stairs. His body swayed back and forth as he stood at the top of them. His eyes danced and darted around the room and then back to Jim.

Jim motioned with the point of the gun for him to sit down in the chair to the left of the table. Kent looked at the table, then walked over and slowly sat down, steadying himself with his hands pressed on the table. He watched Jim walk to the kitchen and fill a pitcher of water and bring it and a glass to the table. He didn't take his eyes from it, licking his lips as if he could already taste its wet substance.

Jim sat the pitcher and glass down on the table and then walked behind Kent. Kent reached out for the glass and pitcher, but before he reached them, Jim stepped up quickly behind him and slipped a smooth rope over his neck and jerked it tight. Kent's head snapped back and he lurched forward in his seat. Jim took the other end of the rope and held him until his body relented for a moment, then he pulled the rope taunt, pulling Kent's head back, then tying it to the back of the chair. Kent began to wheeze as the tension of the rope cut into his throat.

"Give me your left hand," Jim said.

Kent slowly moved his left hand behind him. Jim grabbed it hard and put a noose around his wrist and tied it snugly to the back of the chair.

He walked around and took the chair opposite of him and poured a glass full of water and then sat back and stared at Kent for a moment.

"I need some water," Kent pleaded. "Please, I'm not feeling well...water...please?"

“I want you to do something for me first.” Jim shoved a piece of paper and a pen in front of him. “I need you to write something for me.”

“What?” Kent asked.

“I want you to write a letter to your wife saying that you have left her, and that you have left her because you’re in love with somebody else. I want you to tell her how sorry you are, and that you will not be coming back.”

Kent sat there stunned. He began shaking his head back and forth. “No! I won’t do it.”

“This is the beginning of what you earned…what you earned when you killed my wife.”

“Jim, I…I don’t know what you’re talking about, you’re mistaken—”

“I want you to stop right there before you go any further, Kent. I will not listen to you deny what we both know is true…it is an insult to me and it is an insult to Tina. If you deny it again, I will put a nice well-formed round hole in your head. I will gladly watch while you flop around on the floor dying.”

Kent became erratic, his mouth quivering in fear and his jaws moving without many words. “But, I didn’t—”

Jim raised the gun in front of Kent’s face. “Is that what you want to tell me? I need to know, because if it is, we can dispense with all this. You won’t need to write any letters and I can go home early tonight.”

Jim paused, furrowed his brows and stared intensely at him, showing he had every intention of following through with the words he said. Then his voice became quiet and methodic as he stood straight up, shoving the chair out from behind him with a screech and pulling the gun up to Kent’s forehead.

“I want you to picture yourself for a moment in this cabin about a couple of minutes from now. You’re lying sprawled out on the floor with a smoking black hole in the top of your head. The embrace of death is on your face, and the silent grip of terror on your lips, and nowhere, I promise you, will you resemble your former self. Now, let me give you one better. Picture yourself one hour from now, you’re at room temperature, wrapped up in a plastic sheet, in a shallow grave, with me shoveling dirt onto your waste of flesh body.” Jim raised his eyebrows and nodded his head and then chambered a round in the barrel. The mechanisms inside the pistol pushed backward on the spring and made two loud snapping sounds, the second louder than the first.

“Let’s get this over with then.”

“No, no…no don’t, no…” Kent jerked his head away, bracing for the bullet.

"Pick up the pen and write. This is your last opportunity to do the right thing," Jim said.

Kent began sobbing, tears rolling down his cheeks. He brushed the side of his face on his shoulder, and stared red eyed up at Jim.

"Each moment you hesitate, it's just that much closer you come to room temperature." Jim walked around the table and pressed the cold thick metal barrel to Kent's head and nudged him. "Do the right thing," he whispered. "Do…the…right…thing."

"Okay, okay, please don't kill me." Kent broke down into a new round of sobbing, and he slowly picked up the pen.

"Shut up," Jim shouted. He put his hand over Kent's mouth, turning his head—listening closely for a moment. Kent's eyes looked up at him in horror not knowing what he was doing.

Abruptly Jim spun around and looked at the French doors behind him. Through them he saw the outline of a man staring through them. He just stood there for what seemed an eternity, looking at him—the man at the door looking back at him, while he held the gun to Kent's head, his hand covering his mouth. Kent turned and saw the man staring at them. He shook his head violently away from Jim's hand and screamed for help.

Jim noticed the expression change on the man staring through the doors, as if he now was coming to grips with what he was seeing, now understanding he was a witness to something he shouldn't be. Jim stood there frozen, gun now heavy in his hand. He looked back at Kent, who was screaming his head off at the man to help him. He looked back at the man looking at him, thinking rapidly, a million thoughts flooding his head as the man began backing away slowly from the door, as if he couldn't take his eyes away from the horror he was seeing.

Jim ran toward the door, but he only caught a glimpse of the man running away. Jim's mind began swimming, calculating, thinking of what to do, but knowing in the back of his head what he must do. He ran passed Kent who was still screaming in his chair for help, trying to pull himself free from the ropes, choking himself as he did. Jim ignored him. Reaching the door he opened it and saw a fat man with black hair dressed in a suit running past the side of the cabin to a minivan parked about twenty yards away. Jim ran toward the van, hoping to head him off before he could get there and leave. From the corner of his eye he watched the man stumble and fall on the ground. Jim rounded the front of the van and ran to the driver's window and ripped the keys from the ignition. When the man stood up, Jim held the keys up in front of him. He could tell the man knew he was in trouble. His well-rounded face changed expression from one of hope to one of fear. Jim quickly ran around to the back of the van. He could see the fat man had already turned and that he was heading toward the woods. He thought about shooting him right there before he disappeared into the dense foliage, but wouldn't risk the noise being heard across the lake.

He began to run after him. From the looks of him, he knew the fat man would tire soon or turn on him. He knew it wouldn't be long. He could hear him gasp for air. A sick heaving sound accompanied by grunts lingered in the dense void behind him as he entered the thickness of the woods. His fleshy body scraped tree bark as he tried to dodge past them, his suit tearing at the upper arms and about the elbows. His feet crushed into last fall's dead leaves and the layer of twigs that lay underneath, fallen from the trees above.

Getting closer to the man, Jim could feel his fear, the desperation, watching him as he turned his head, trying to catch a glimpse of him in his vision, wanting to know how close Jim was, how near. Jim was almost upon him now. He jutted a hand forward and pushed him. The man stumbled and then Jim slapped another rigid hand down on his shoulders pulling the man down to the leaf-strewn earth. The man slid to a stop on his belly, pushing the underbrush forward in front of his head, leaving the cool dark moist soil exposed underneath. He tried to get up and run again, but Jim was on him.

The man lay there on his belly pleading with him, begging him not to kill him between gasps of breath. Jim put the gun in the back of his pants. The man struggled and grabbed his wallet out of his hip pocket and showed him a picture of his wife and kids, pleading with him to let him live.

Jim felt sorry for him as he watched the fat man plead for his life. But he knew that he could not spare him. He had seen too much; it was too late.

Jim got off of him and found a large rock and hoisted it over his head while the man squirmed breathless beneath, his eyes full of fear. He hurled the rock down at him. The fat man lurched up and it grazed him on his backside. Before he could get up all the way Jim leapt on the man's back, bringing him down again on top of an old laid-over tree trunk. He thought about Tina as he choked him. The man's hands clawed the ground in front of him as he did. Jim watched them as they dug frantically into the mud, but he felt little compassion, only the feelings of necessity—all for Tina. He had come too far now. The man screamed for his life, but Jim only heard Tina's voice. He twisted the man's pudgy neck harder and harder. It took every ounce of his strength to kill him. Finally he heard a sickening snap of his neck. The fat man's body went lifeless in his arms, his spirited breath now still.

Jim fell back away from the man, breathless, staring at him, not sure what he had done, but knowing why he had done it. He felt bad for him and for his family, but knew he couldn't change it, nor would he if he had things to do over. It was done.

He looked at the fat man laying there, staring up past the canopy of the trees into the dimming blue sky. He heard a rattle rise up from his chest and then watched his eyes glaze to gray.

Jim turned him over, tied his shoelaces together and drug his heavy body out of the woods, pulling him by the laces. The man's head bounced back and forth following his body, seemingly to nod at each dip or branch on the ground. Jim pulled him out of the woods and up to the van and looked at the man's clothes. They were covered in dirt and grass stains.

Jim searched through the van and produced two suits and a number of dress shirts. He took a blue suit and a dress shirt and hung them on the outside of the van. Jim pulled the body onto a plastic sheet and undressed him, then washed his muddy hands. His body looked like a white-beached whale, lying in a sea of plastic. Jim hurriedly dressed him, washed his socks and shoes and placed them back on his feet. Jim sat up the dead man's body and leaned it forward over his legs and then heaved him off the ground. He was heavy, and he strained to get him to the van. He laid his limp body down in the back of the van and then collapsed against the door of the van after he shut it. He looked down at his watch as sweat filled brow. It was nearly eight o'clock.

Jim walked into the house. Kent was lying on the floor, wheezing heavily, struggling for air, the chair with him in it leaning over to the side. He pulled him up from the floor, Kent's neck bore heavy on the rope. He gagged. His body rocked back and forth as Jim sat him up in the chair.

"Please...I need some...water," Kent said. His voice strained to get the word out.

Jim put the gloves on that were lying on the table and pushed the paper and pen toward Kent again. He walked to the other side of the table and collapsed in his seat, laying his head back on the chair.

He looked at Kent after a moment. "Pick up the goddamn pen and write," he yelled.

Kent quickly picked up the pen, terrified of what Jim might do now. He seemed different, unsavory, removed from the world.

"Write the letter to Lisa in your own words. Do it now!" Jim screamed.

Kent jumped in his seat and began to write. Jim held the single sheet of paper with his gloved hand.

Minutes passed and Jim leaned forward and read from the paper, his eyes intensely scrutinizing it.

> *Lisa,*
>
> *I didn't want to do this, but I have to. I can't be with you anymore. I can't see the kids either. I am going away and won't be coming back, but I will always love you and the kids very much. I'm sorry—*

Jim ripped the paper from under Kent's hand and glared at him while he crumpled it between his hands. "I don't think I have to tell you that I'm in no mood to put up with this. No one is going to believe that bullshit you wrote. Either you are going to write the letter right or you're going to join the friendly, but quite ex-real estate agent out there."

"Did you kill him?" Kent sheepishly asked.

"You're not here for me to answer your questions," Jim snapped angrily. "You're here because you're going to make amends for what you have done."

Jim fished his gun out of the back of his pants and placed it on the table.

"Now do it again. This time I hope you do it right." Jim's words were sharp, biting. There was no mistaking his irritation.

Kent picked up the pen and began to whimper in a small voice, "I don't want to write this…I don't want to leave my wife—I love her."

"Yeah, I didn't want to lose mine either, but it happened. You made it happen. At least you won't lose her to a terrible death, one in which she will lay broken and dead beside a desolate road, abandoned by a drunken irresponsible fool. But that is what I got and it is what you gave me…isn't it?" He pointed his finger straight in his direction, his voice beginning to rise. Kent hid his eyes, scared and trying his best to hide his shame. He said timidly, "I'm, I'm sorry, but I, really it wasn't my fault it was—"

Jim slammed his fist down hard on the table, sending tiny ripples over the surface of the water in the pitcher. The contents of the table all took a hop at the concussion. "It was no accident, Kent, that you made a decision to leave her bleeding to death, was it? Was it, Kent? Answer me, you sonuvabitch!"

"I…I don't," Kent looked away for a moment, "I…I didn't—"

"You didn't want to get into trouble…well it looks like you are in trouble now, aren't you…aren't you?" Kent didn't answer. He just sat there crying, his lips curled in a sorrowful snarl, his chest heaving in jerks. Still, he couldn't admit what he had done. He couldn't say that he killed her and Jim knew it.

"I can guarantee you, Kent, that you are more upset that you're in this mess than you are at killing my wife. It is, my friend, a behavior you will atone for...believe me, you will atone for it. Do you understand me? To you, somewhere in that thick mess of gray flesh, you think this was an accident, but I assure you, there will come a day when you will beg me to confess what you have done. You will know that it was no accident." Jim stood there for a moment; his hands now clinched into fists, his eyes full of angry tears. He was a man possessed with all the hatred one could possibly bear. It burned brightly in him, like an insatiable fire licking at the sky on a hot summer day.

"Don't make another mistake that might cost you your life. Write the letter again, but I hope to God you do it right this time."

Kent picked up the pen and began to write. Tears fell from his eyes on to the parchment mixing with the black ink. Jim looked on and thought it added an element of credibility. Kent wrote off and on for nearly an hour, though he wrote little, but reflected deeply on the words he did write. It took every ounce of him to craft the cruel unforgiving task. It was a letter he let him finish at his own pace. He let him have that at least. When Kent sat back, Jim snatched the single sheet of paper in his gloved hand and read it.

*Dearest Lisa,*

*I know you must be worried about me by now. You have no reason to. I'm fine. This letter may cause you even more pain than my absence has. I won't be coming home. I found someone and we are very much in love. I wanted nothing from you, so I am leaving with nothing. I have no excuses for what I have done. You have done nothing to cause this. I am the one to blame. I am sorry, Lisa. I love you and I love the kids, but this is what's best for me right now.*

*Love,*<br>*Kent*

Jim looked up at Kent. "Good," he said.

"Seal it now," Jim said gruffly. Kent licked the narrowed glued ends and sealed it.

"Put a stamp on it," Jim barked again. Kent took a stamp and licked it on the glued back and pressed it firmly to the envelope.

He held the letter in his hands, staring softly at it, looking dejected. He knew it contained his future. His eyes were now sunken into their sockets, a morose appearance showing drably on his face. It was despair.

"You're going to destroy me," Kent said weakly.

"You're missing the point," Jim replied.

"What is the point?" Kent asked in a hoarse whisper.

"The point is—what I'm going to do is punish you, to let justice be served my way, to make you feel my pain, to let you taste the whip of my revenge. I suppose you think this is uncommon, but my wrath is born in the resentment I have for you." Jim sneered at him with the words and then continued. "Your inability to find empathy in others, and ignore the weight of your own accountability, has built a heavy debt that you must now repay. What it boils down to, Kent, is this. I'm going to take from you what you took from me."

Kent looked up at him horrified, unwilling to confront the ominous proposition the words secretly contained, and, not daring to ask their specific implications.

"Now you can drink," Jim said. He shoved the glass in front of him. Kent took the glass in his shaking hands and held it to his quivering lips and drank the water in gulps.

"Another?" Jim asked. Kent nodded.

Jim poured another glass. Kent quickly grabbed it and drank it down and asked for another. Jim poured another.

"What did you do?" Kent asked.

Jim didn't answer.

"Did you kill him?"

"Shut up," Jim said.

Jim stood slowly. Kent watched him as he did, not taking his eyes off him, as if he was a rabid animal, afraid to turn his back on him.

"You don't need to worry about that…it doesn't concern you," Jim said. He eyed him back, aware of the new perception that Kent now had of him—a killer. He knew he was different now; no longer the mild-mannered neighbor Kent once knew, but now a man hell-bent for revenge, a cold-blooded killer.

Jim got up abruptly, pulling the gun off the table, and stuffing it under his belt. His thoughts troubled him. The word "killer" jabbed his head. He had trouble relating it to who he was, but he guessed that's what he had done—*kill*.

He walked to the kitchen and retrieved two bags from the refrigerator and carried them down into the cellar. Kent watched him disappear through the hole in the floor. About a half a minute later, he emerged and went and retrieved two more bags from the pantry that was off to the right of the kitchen. He carried it down to the cellar also.

Kent watched as he came out of the hole in the floor once more, and then Jim walked toward him and then veered behind him. He heard a flicking sound that sounded like a knife. Before he could protest, his ropes were cut free from his neck and hand. Kent immediately rubbed his wrist with his other hand. A deep red mark that circled it matched the one on his neck.

"Get up," Jim barked.

Kent moved slowly. His neck and wrist still felt a ghostly noose.

"Undress," Jim said.

"What?" Kent asked, his voice filled with alarm.

"Undress now!" Jim snapped.

Kent did it. He felt nervous about removing his clothes. It scared him. He fumbled for the buttons on his dress shirt and then took it off as well as his pants and socks. He stood there in a t-shirt and underwear.

"I said to get your clothes off…now!"

Kent hesitated for a moment not wanting to remove the rest of his clothes, but finally he did what he was told. He stood there in front of Jim, his hands covering his genitals, looking humiliated.

"Get down in the hole," Jim said.

Kent seemed uncertain at first—hesitant.

Jim began to look harder at him. He wondered what he would do if Kent ran. Half of him just wanted to kill him right there with his gun, but that would be too easy; it wouldn't serve his cause, he thought. If he killed him out right, he would be conceding to the child within him. That lack of control would make him like his old foster daddy, Jerry, and he didn't want to be like Jerry—impetuous, impulsive and prone to fits of violent anger. He hated the thought of him and the other restless spirits that angrily waited in his memories. There, in the darkness of his soul, those ghosts stood vigilant. Those remnants of unbridled stirrings waited restless inside him. They were produced by something churning inward—something deep, sick, and foul. If seeded, he knew that internal rot would lay waste to his soul.

The malaise stalked him from his childhood; he knew that. It waited for him to yield to its seduction—unforgiving, it demanded total possession. To succumb to it was slow death—the rage—*goddamn it*. He was always scared the boy behind the man would snatch him and keep him. He had to resist.

Jim pulled the gun from his belt and raised it. "Get down in the hole now!" he yelled.

Kent scurried over to the cellar hole and scrambled down it. More nervous now than ever, more afraid, thinking seriously that Jim might snap.

Kent thought about the man that Jim had killed, if he had killed him. The thought of it made him shudder. It made him feel nauseous.

Dampness stuck to him as he walked in the cellar. The musty smell of it wrinkled his nose. He looked around, and saw it for the first time in the light. In the right hand corner, about six feet off the ground, was a white PVC pipe hanging down from the unfinished rafters. It had a small thin chain attached to a spring valve and a large drain hole lay directly underneath, at the end of slightly-sloped concrete.

"You will get your water from here," Jim said. He pointed toward the pipe. The end of it was crude and unfinished. As he neared the bottom of the stairs, he motioned at a small table to Kent. "In one of those you will find clothing. In the others you will find food and toiletries," Jim said.

Kent stood there naked, looking around the room. It was of meager size, not much to it—a square room, with a small table, a chair, and a cot with a folded blanket on it, a trashcan and a small refrigerator.

"How long are you going to keep me here?"

"All that in due time, but not now," Jim said. Jim looked at his watch—it read 10:15. "I won't be back for several days, but you will find that you have all you need."

Jim began to walk up the steps.

"Hey! How long are you going to keep me here?" Kent yelled.

Jim ignored him and kept climbing the stairs.

"Listen to me…I've got a right to know!"

"No you don't," Jim said faintly as his legs and then shoes disappeared from the top of the stairway.

Kent jumped as the cellar door slammed down on the floor. He heard the scuffling of feet. He visualized Jim pulling the heavy rug back over the door. It made him claustrophobic. He felt trapped, like a rat in a snake's lair. When he heard the muffled sound of the front door close, his anxiety built. He felt like scratching a hole through the side of the concrete wall of the cellar, and burrowing through the earth to the surface of the ground, but he knew that it would do him no good. He was helpless and at the mercy of Jim Hall—a captive of his intentions.

Kent rummaged through the sacks, and found the one which contained the clothes. In it were two large sweat pants, two pairs of socks, two pairs of shorts and two sweatshirts and two short sleeve t-shirts, all gray in color, except the socks which were white. All were of thick material, but of the anonymous cheap discount store variety. At the bottom of the bag was a pair of thin brown house slippers. They lay on top of two towels and two wash cloths.

Two of the other bags were filled to the top with food—mostly canned; though there were two loaves of bread and some oranges and grapefruits. The other bag contained items such as a toothbrush and toothpaste, shampoo, as well as other toiletries. It even contained one medium-sized plastic plate and a large hard plastic fork. A can opener was found as well, along with two plastic bowls with covers.

He slowly rubbed the side of the fork with his thumb feeling its rough texture. The plastic scraped his skin as he brushed it harder and harder. He stared up at the closed door in the ceiling and began to sweat profusely. His left shoulder twitched uncontrollably. The sweat rolled into his eyes, the salt burned them. For all anyone knew, he was dead to the world. He thought about Lisa and his children, how they must be anguishing over his disappearance. He glanced away from the door and looked at the bags, their contents sprawled out on the small table. Looking at it all, it dawned on him that perhaps he would be there for a long time.

* * *

Jim propped John Nichels up in the passenger seat. He was cold, his skin pasty in the humid night. His lids were half-open, exposing glassy blue marbles, blank and expressionless, devoid of life. His lips were blue. His face itself testified to bewilderment. It seemed to question the very reason he had died that day. He didn't like that and covered his face with a small cloth that laid in the back seat.

Jim eased the van onto the main road from the driveway. He drove five miles up the black top road toward a steep high bend curve. It was called Devil's Point because it jutted out from a small cliff over boulders and water. The roads either way were on steep hills and led down to it. It had been fatal to those, unfortunate enough to navigate the steep curve in the past, and Jim figured it would not be suspicious if one more appeared to meet their death there again.

Jim drove slowly toward Devil's Point, and each bump or pothole caused John Nichels to bounce aimlessly in his seat. Twice he fell sideways on Jim and he had to shove him over. Another time he fell face forward on the dash and Jim sat him up by pulling on the back of his collar. The cloth fell from him and exposed his face once again. Jim began to stiff-arm him to keep him steady. A car met them about half way there and the headlights illuminated the front seats of the van. Jim looked over at John. His face was a hideous ghostly white, his lips blue and he almost appeared to be now grinning, almost as if he had heard something funny.

*But there was nothing funny about this business*, Jim thought. He regretted having killed John Nichels. He regretted the fact that his family would now be without a husband and a father. He could still see the man's wife and children. The images haunted him.

Jim pulled the van to a stop about thirty yards from Devil's Point. He stepped outside the door, leveraged his foot on the floor and pulled hard on John, trying to drag his huge body across to the other seat. Finally, he had him propped up in the seat. He put John's cold hands around the steering wheel, trying to lock the wheels into the position.

Jim knew that he would only get one shot at this, so it had to count. He leveraged John's leg toward the accelerator, though the momentum of the downhill slope would have broken the steel rails on the bend. He wanted to make sure that there was sufficient force to do so.

The engine began to whine louder as Jim pressed John's lumber leg on the pedal. He pushed his right leg a few times to adjust the speed to where he wanted it and waited to see if any cars were coming over the hill. He looked behind him and ahead of him as far as he could see. There was nothing.

Jim looked at John one final time. John was staring forward, his eyes almost now fully open, his arms entangled in the wheel. He looked as if he were prepared to meet his fate at Devil's Point.

Jim slammed the door and reached over and slipped the gearshift into drive. It lurched violently forward with a squeal of its tires. The van maintained a near perfect straight line as he sped toward the guardrail. The headlights lit up the railing and it seemed odd to Jim how the van never slowed. He knew it wouldn't, but it was odd just the same.

The van smashed through the railing, its rear tires jumping a little off the ground on impact. The vehicle shifted a little sideways and it appeared at first that the railing would verily hold it on the highway, but it didn't. The railing was strong enough and the van plowed nearly sideways, taking most of the railing with it. Jim couldn't see John, just headlights, but he imagined what he looked like after impact.

Seconds seemed like an eternity, until Jim heard a distant crash. Jim ran down the steep hill toward the van, but before he got there a huge fireball erupted into the air. He immediately thought of a dragon belching fire and expected to see one climbing up the side of the cliff when he got there. But there wasn't one. Just the minivan, engulfed in flames, lying mortally wounded on its side.

Jim walked back from the fire and turned around. He felt stunned over what he had just done. He almost felt ashamed. The feelings quickly disappeared as he heard a car come up on the backside of the oncoming hill. Jim turned and ran into the woods. He watched the car as it slowed around the curve, its headlights beaming out into the dark where the guardrail was. Apparently the driver never noticed what lay down below, the initial explosion now just short leaping flames, not seen from the curve. The car drove on.

Jim turned and made the five-mile hike through the woods. He stayed close to the road, ducking further into the brush when a car would come along. But that was seldom. He felt better when he reached the cabin, though he knew the memories of John Nichels would haunt him for the rest of his life.

* * *

The next afternoon, Jim Hall boarded a flight for Jacksonville, Florida, under the name of Kent Jackson. He had with him only a single carry-on bag. In it were two letters, the first addressed to Lisa Jackson from Kent Jackson, the second sent anonymously to Detective Trower, Lakewood City Police Department. The last letter was attached to a package with Kent Jackson's bloody shoes and clothes. It contained all the forensic evidence to prove Kent Jackson was Tina Hall's killer.

Jim returned on a red-eye flight that night to Lakewood City. When he departed the plane, no bag was in his hand, nor did he have the letters. All were now en route to their appropriate destinations. Part of the plot born out, the fate of Kent Jackson was now beginning to be sealed in a silent tomb.

# Chapter 23

Kent watched the light bulb flicker. He stood near it, naked, bathed in a chick yellow glow. He looked up at the long inch-wide white water pipe poking down from the ceiling. He walked over and pulled the chain that operated a spring valve. A forceful stream of cold water surged out of the pipe. He let the chain relax and then pulled it again and stuck his head under it. The water sent a chill straight down his spine, making it rigid. It felt cold, but good. He lifted his hand and rubbed his hair and face as the water doused him, washing some of the filth away. He let the chain go, and the handle attached to the end snapped up in the air, then fell down again. It dangled over his head as water dripped from his wet hair.

Two days had passed since he had eaten, since this nightmare had begun. Since Jim had kidnapped him and brought him to this horrible abyss. Hunger pangs exploded in his stomach, engulfed him, and food was all he thought of. He walked over to the table and rifled through the bags, looking for the easiest food he could eat. He found one of the oranges and he tore the skin from it, clawing it like a wild animal. He bit into an exposed part and squeezed the orange ball, sucking out the juice into his mouth. *Nothing had tasted better*, he thought. The flavor of it mixed with the haunting flashes of Jim Hall, drinking with him, killing that man, making him write the letters. He quickly devoured the orange, eating some of the peeling with it. His mind was as much of a mess as his culinary sloppiness.

He took a can opener in his shaky hands and cut off the top of a can of pork and beans, the juice spilling from the lid as he did. He ate them from the can at first with his fingers, until he remembered the oversized spoon. Light brown bean juice ran down his unshaven face. He shoveled the beans into his mouth, the can not but an inch from his face as he did. He worked the spoon, shoveling back and forth with methodical precision. When he was done the can sat empty, and his face looked like that of a toddler who had just had a puree snack.

He fished through the bags again and found a bar of soap, a washcloth and a towel. In the back of his mind he didn't want to use these things, nor did he want to eat the food. To him, that would be accepting his current situation, admitting to Jim Hall that he acquiesced to it. A part of him wanted to stay just as he was—to be standing there hungry, soiled and naked the next time he came. But, he knew he had to survive.

It was clear that Jim planned to keep him there for quite some time. *But why?* he thought. Perhaps he just wanted to keep him there forever. The thought of being in this damp dungeon for the rest of his life horrified him. He thought of the words that he had said, about taking from him what he had took from Jim. It sent a sliver of glass through his stomach that seemed to cut every nerve. The thought of it: *forever*.

The word scared him. He thought of several things he could have meant—taking his life from him, as he had taken it from him? *Lisa...could he mean something about Lisa?* he asked himself. *Oh god no*, he thought. *Don't kill Lisa*. But he didn't know. All he knew was that he was in a damp, poorly-lit room, with meager furnishings. It was the only thing that was tangible in this never-ending nightmare.

Jim walked over and stuck his head under the pipe again and pulled the chain. A cold stream of water jetted out again, splashing on the back of his neck. Jim wet the washcloth and washed vigorously the dried blood and vomit from his face, neck and hands. When he had finished he yanked the chain again and rinsed the soap from his body.

He dried with a towel in front of the table where the bags lay. Water droplets made crisp crinkling sounds as they fell off his hair and arms onto the plastic bags as he searched for clothes. He pulled a t-shirt and shorts from the bag and crammed them under his arm while he looked for underwear, but there was none.

He put the clothes on and sat down in the old chair in front of the table. It creaked when he moved in it. Leaning his head down, he closed his eyes and thought of nothing but Lisa, Samantha and David. At that moment their images were clear and crisp in his mind. He could see their faces perfectly. He thought of how much he loved them and wished he could tell them so. Surprised at his thoughts, he managed to smile slightly and wipe a tear from his eye as he did.

He seemed to now notice their importance in his life. *A time of crisis*, he thought, *makes one rather intuitive*. For the first time, there was nothing before them, nothing that crowded them out, and nothing that competed for his thoughts. He was alone with them, in his mind, only interrupted by the creak of the chair he was sitting on and the occasional moan from the cabin that settled on its foundations. It felt good, despite his predicament. Perhaps he had found what was true, locked in the desolate bowels of the dark abyss.

# Chapter 24

She had identified the clothes as belonging to Kent, and she was shocked when Detective Trower informed her of the anonymous letter. He had shown her the package full of clothes and had asked her if she had sent it. She knew nothing of it, but the detectives believed she sent the letter and the package, because her husband left her. But after a search of her house and a lie detector test produced nothing, the police cleared her of all suspicions.

It had been hard to understand why her husband had done such a thing. Leaving her and the children as he did, combined with the news he had been involved in Tina Hall's death was devastating. It was hard coming to grips with the shame her husband and their father had placed on the family. None of them truly understood it, but learned to live with their hurt, feeling it at times, like a piece of glass entombed in a callus of flesh.

After months passed, she was done with humiliation, so she freed herself from the stench of it, but still the wound it caused lay gaping open within her, infected from insecurities and festering with emotional affliction. Two months after her husband's disappearance, Lisa divorced him for abandonment, unwilling to live with the malaise any longer, but yet unable to heal the scars he left deep inside of her.

* * *

Kent Jackson had lost everything he ever dreamed of or worked for. He lost himself, his job, all he had cherished in life and soon he would lose his very reason to live. He knew little of this at the time. He had not considered it, not even once. He just assumed that once this unthinkable nightmare was over, there would still be all that once was.

The only thing he did know was he was imprisoned by a madman's vengeful fury. His former life was all that kept him breathing now. It sustained him in the darkest hours of captivity and through the hidden terror of his nights. All that once existed now only existed in memory. He was no more, as he knew himself. The man he loved so well before was now deceased, yet he did not know it.

* * *

He saw her from a distance. She was sifting through sweet potatoes on a vegetable counter, inspecting each one for blemishes. As he came closer he noticed her. She was proportional in build and taller than Tina was and more ample, but not by much in her hips. In his mind she was lovely. At one point she looked up as he approached, but failed to recognize him.

"Choices," Jim said. He picked up a potato and held it up and eyeballed it, and then turned his head and smiled at her.

Lisa turned toward him. "Jim…how are you?" she said. Her voice was full of surprise. She threw one arm around him, while still clutching a potato in her hand.

"I haven't seen you in so long."

"I'm well," he replied.

"How's your kids?"

"They're doing great…you know they miss their mom, but that is to be expected."

"I know…it must be devastating for them." She stared hard at the floor for a moment and then held her head up, trying to blink a tear out of her eye.

Jim looked at her intently and reached out a hand and lightly touched her arm. He knew what she was thinking. "It must be tough on you as well."

There was an uncomfortable silence for a moment. Jim thought he had stepped over a forbidden boundary. He thought she was embarrassed by what they both knew, it was evident that she hadn't talked about it before. She looked at him. Her eyes pleaded with his not to broach the subject.

"I'm sorry, Lisa," Jim said, "I know it's been hard…what Kent did has nothing to do with you and I know this has probably been just as painful on you as it has me."

"I'm sorry, Jim, I…I just don't know what to say…what Kent did was so terrible, so…so unbelievable and then to just leave me and the kids like that and…and not face up to his responsibilities, it…it…"

She buried her head in her hands and broke down in light sobs. She felt ashamed of what Kent had done or at least what the detective had told her he had done. She still couldn't believe it. How could he just leave her lying there like that, and then come home and act as if nothing was wrong, when everything was? This wasn't the Kent she knew, but all the evidence was there that this really was.

She thought of Detective Trower, and the sick feeling she got when he told her the evidence was conclusive, that Kent had been at the scene of the accident and the tests on his clothes had shown the blood was Tina's. To seal Kent's fate, Lisa had confirmed the clothes belonged to Kent. He was now a wanted fugitive in the killing of Tina Hall.

Lisa thought that maybe he couldn't live with it, the guilt of killing her. What he had done might have become too heavy to carry, too heavy of a burden. Although, she thought it awful to think that way. It was easier living with that explanation than the alternative. It was more palatable and less hurtful leaving her for another woman. But either way she felt betrayed.

Lisa looked at Jim through pained eyes. "I'm sorry," she whispered. She turned to leave.

"Lisa...please...don't leave," Jim said. "You're not to blame."

She turned toward him again and said, "I feel so ashamed. I feel ashamed for not knowing...what Kent did." The words were cumbersome for her. They lay heavy on her tongue like molasses. She hung her head and couldn't say anymore. She choked back tears that wanted so desperately to come.

"It's okay," Jim said, "it's not your fault. You're a victim in this just like me." They stood silent, Jim looking at her, Lisa staring blankly at the sweet potatoes, not wanting to look at him.

"Hey, let me buy you a cup of coffee or a cold drink or something," Jim said.

Lisa glanced up at him and shook her head. "No...I've got to get home. The kids will be expecting me."

"Are you sure?" he asked.

Lisa hesitated. "Yes...I'm...I'm already late. I just stopped to pick some things for dinner."

"Well, okay then...I understand," Jim said. He hung his head, as if he were sad, even his voice reflected it.

Lisa looked at him and thought that she might have been too hasty in answering, that perhaps he needed someone to talk to—after all, what would a cup of coffee between neighbors hurt? *Nothing...nothing at all.* But still, she needed to get home...the kids were alone and they hadn't been doing too good since Kent's disappearance.

"I tell you what, why don't you and the kids come over tonight for a good home-cooked meal."

Jim smiled. "That is real kind of you, Lisa, but I don't want to put you out," he said.

"Jim, you won't be putting me out…how about, oh, around six?"

"Well okay, if you're sure?"

She grinned at him and nodded her head and said, "Yes, I'm sure."

"Okay then, but I warn you, I'll come hungry."

Lisa broadened her smile. "All right, around six then."

"It's a date," Jim said. And with that, he grabbed his cart and headed off back down a grocery aisle.

Lisa stared at him, her smile fading. *A date*, she thought, *is that what it is?* Even the words made her feel guilty. They made her feel as if she was doing something wrong. *It's just dinner*, she thought, *and the kids will be there*. She assured herself that it was okay and threw several more sweet potatoes in the bag for that night's dinner. She even selected an extra large potato for Jim.

* * *

The evening went well. The dinner was excellent. The aroma of the food diffused the tension that was first present. The smell of grilled chicken breasts and baked sweet potatoes with melting butter and light brown sugar mingled in the air and swirled around them, combining with the sweet odor of a just-baked chocolate pie, all of it tempting their palates. The aroma lured them to the dining room and it surrounded them defiantly, forcing them to think of nothing more important than the food that lay before them. They acquiesced to their hunger and fed till they could eat no more.

It was perfect, as Lisa somehow wanted it to be, for a reason that she herself did not know. Their children were school friends and they were kind to each other, sensitive to the awkward circumstances in which they were bonded to. Jim and Lisa's eyes met several times over the dinner table that night. They went unnoticed by the children, but to each other there was a connection and it was not ignored. It was a subtle unseen attraction.

Jim had planned all along for them to be together. It was his blueprint for revenge, his design of hatred. But he even admitted to himself that he was attracted to her. Lisa, unsure, scared, insecure and brittle, fell powerless to the spell that promised to ease her loneliness, her emotional loss, her pain and uncertainty. She was cautious, but at the same time enamored with Jim's presence, unable to resist him. Her perception of him being vulnerable made her feel comfortable too. It eased her apprehensions.

In Jim's mind, he knew his apparent vulnerability was a valuable tool to render her defenseless. But, also he knew the shame she felt for Kent was just as potent. It was important to his conquest of her. He could leverage it, to manipulate her, to snap her emotions rapidly like a whip cutting crisply across the air, if she became too inflexible. He would have her, through her own sense of guilt and indebtedness to him, until she could cling to nothing else.

He would replace Kent as the desire of her affection. He would become all she clung to, all she thought was real. He would take from Kent what he had taken from him. He would have Lisa, and Kent would enter the world again someday like a newborn infant, naked unto the world and with nothing. He smiled at the thought of it.

"This was a nice evening, Lisa," Jim said. "I had a wonderful time." As they stood just inside the door—it ajar—they watched his kids begin the short walk toward their house down the street. The crisp breeze nipped at their faces as they watched. It was late February.

"Are you sure you wouldn't like to take some chocolate pie home?"

Jim looked at her with eager eyes. "I tell you what, why don't you meet me tomorrow at the Riverside Park, and we'll make it a picnic."

Lisa looked at him for a moment and hesitated. Everything inside of her told her to say no, that it was too strange for her to be involved with the man whose wife was killed by her husband. The idea of it seemed ludicrous, but still, it was true. She resisted what opposed her seeing him, and said, "Yes." She was unsure why she had done so, but felt that it partly was a desire for something good to be born of something so tragic.

"Good," he said with a smile and turned to leave. "I will pick you up at twelve."

"Oh, I can meet you there...Jim, Jim I can meet—" She called after him. But, he pretended not to hear her.

"See you at noon," he called over his shoulder.

Lisa opened her mouth to protest again, but nothing came out. She just stood there and watched him disappear into the long shadows of the evening. She turned and walked slowly back into the house and looked for a moment behind her. She thought he might appear once more in the darkness, but he didn't. He wasn't there. Perhaps she wanted him to be. She didn't know. She just stared into the pitch black, her eyes not leaving the darkness. Only as she closed the door did she lose sight of the void that held promise of producing him once again.

* * *

As April ensued March, the relationship between Lisa and Jim matured. Partly by design, and partly by desire, they created a refuge from the storm that had so recently devastated their lives. They grew dependent on each other, but for different reasons.

For Lisa, she had come to respect and silently love the man that once was only a neighbor. She adored him for his strict devotion to her. He cared for her openly, expressing it with soft words, gentle touches and a kindness and understanding that made her feel secure.

To her, Jim was exactly everything that Kent wasn't, though, she hated to think of it that way. What had been devoid in her life—dead, really—for so long, she now almost took for granted. Jim had a passion for life that was infectious, and she inhaled him and took all of him in that she could. He had persevered through so much and yet he was able to retain a benevolent charm. It cultivated her own spirit, and gained her a new found appreciation for each day that replaced bad ones in the past.

She thought as a father, no one rivaled Jim. He had done a great job compensating for the children's loss of their mother—at least the best he could under the circumstances—but also displayed a great concern and interest in her own children. Never a disparaging word crossed his lips about Kent. To her, he stayed entrenched on the moral high ground, above the self-strangling noose of resentment, cynicism and pity. Lisa knew she had fallen deeply in love with him.

For Jim, it was a time for continence. He covered with ash the hot embers of hatred that wanted to burn out of control and consume him. Ironically, he did find in her what existed in Tina and was absent in himself, and her comforting spirit filled the pangs of his wounded soul. She was a comforting sanctuary from the ebullient storm that meshed with the pain of his past. The two emotions, that of love and of hatred and revenge, often collided. He found that his love for Lisa was often at odds with his obsession for revenge, the growing passion he found for Lisa and the budding of what might be threatened that dark beast within him. This passion, it threatened the very essence of who he had become, or in his mind, who Kent and others that littered his past had made him become. The essence of it justified his actions. It was the framework, fundamental to what made him breathe. Yet it was Lisa who made him forget, who made the demons recede far back into his mind.

Often he would find himself taking solace in her, though he often resisted, but failed in doing so.

As spring awoke the earth, so were the nearly forgotten emotions that Jim had buried less than a year before, when Tina had passed. But, he often found himself in his spare time thinking of Lisa, loving her in his mind. He wished the circumstance of it to go away, of why they were together. After all it was him that had manipulated the situation to make it so. Without that he knew that he and Lisa would never have been. Through his careful scheme and direction he had ultimately created their relationship. Without it, Kent would still have what was his. But now he had nothing, and that was to Jim's liking.

But he knew that down in that deep dark decrepit cellar he was losing more than just Lisa—Kent was slowly losing his mind and who he had once been. And that was to Jim's liking too.

Often he thought about switching off the lights, leaving him down there condemned to eternal darkness, never returning, letting him feel his way around, lost in an unforgiving pitch black, much the way he was lost after Tina's death. Sometimes he simply wanted him to die; sometimes he wanted to kill him.

As the skies tore with lightning and the heavens let loose their torrential rains, it announced the beginning of a violent Oklahoma spring. Jim was torn against himself, much as the elements were in turmoil. His growing love for Lisa and the agony and guilt of his wavering revenge gnawed at him. This is what he struggled with during these days. What once was so festered in his mind had been tempered by the presence of Lisa's growing love for him. But, what to do was unclear. Still he considered Kent must endure certain punishment for his transgression. He didn't feed off this idea as he once had, like a sow to the slop, but he did feel that he needed to fulfill the justice that still slowly burned within him, despite it being dampened by the cool liquid words that dripped off Lisa's altruistic tongue. He needed to end what he had begun.

He was incomplete until that happened, but perhaps he had always been incomplete and had never known it. Those thoughts frightened and tortured him at times and just perhaps being incomplete was his true self. The idea unnerved his very existence, and he put those thoughts away in a dark place, one that he would visit as little as possible.

# Chapter 25

They lay there clutching each other. Jim brushed Lisa's hair, looking deep into her eyes. He hungrily fed on them, soaking his gaze into her. They pressed their bodies tightly, holding them in place close to each other. Jim caressed her.

They rolled together, she laying on her back, he laying on top of her. He kissed her neck, and squeezed her nipples gently with his hands. She moaned. He gently eased himself in her. She moaned again and lifted and parted her legs more, wrapping them around him. She pressed against him, her legs pushing him deeper into her. They clung to each other, moving rhythmically, rapidly, and naturally, as if they had always been.

Then quickly, Lisa seized Jim in her arms and legs, tightening her face, her grip on his arms. He grasped her shoulders and moved rapidly in her, his eyes never leaving hers, until they lay silently entwined. His warmth seeped from her, her body pressed firmly against his. The hungry storm that once raged in their loins now rested. They had become one.

"I love you," Jim said softly. The words surprised him. He fixed his eyes upon her.

"I love you too," Lisa whispered back. A joy washed through her voice.

Right away he wished he hadn't said it. It was an admission of what he did not want to happen. He had not planned to fall in love with her, but it was unavoidable. In the back of his mind though, he was still determined to have his revenge. He supposed the love for her and his vengeful hatred of her ex-husband could coexist inside the same human shell. But it was hard to entertain the two.

"I've waited so long for you to say that," Lisa said. She had so badly wanted to say it herself for some time, but had held the words back, afraid, not wanting him to feel obligated to her feelings for him.

"I have wanted to say if for a long time too," he said.

She ran her fingers through his hair. "I don't want you to go tonight," she said.

"I don't want to," he said. He looked at her apologetically.

"I know you have to. Your kids are expecting you and you should go spend time with them tonight. But, that does not mean I'm not going to miss you," she said. Her lips formed a smile as she teased his chest with her fingers.

"I know," Jim said.

He sat up in bed. "You will call tonight if you need anything..." Jim paused, "in fact, why don't you just come over with me to my house."

"Oh, I don't know...I think you need some time with your kids...they have been through a lot and I don't want our relationship to infringe on their time too much—not that I don't want to be with you."

He leaned over to her and kissed her lips gently, softly. They felt like butterflies on her lips. "You're sweet, you know," he said.

"I know." She winked at him and then smiled.

Jim dressed, while Lisa threw on a robe and saw him down to the front door. He hugged her before opening the door. He pushed her hair back from her face and stared intently at her for a moment, locking on to her light blue pools.

She pressed her face against his hand. "Come back to me soon."

"Dinner tomorrow?" he said.

"You know the answer to that—what time?"

"I'll call you."

"You better."

Jim kissed her gently and then opened the door and walked out to his truck and then made the short drive up the street home.

Lisa watched him as he went. There was silence except for the gusts of wind that rattled the windows as it blew against the house. She thought about Jim as the house creaked on its foundation. She already missed him. Curling up in a large overstuffed chair, her legs folded up beside her, she lay her head down on them.

For some reason subtle memories of Kent slipped into her mind. She found those memories and the image of Kent now surprisingly foreign. The memory of him faded somewhat. But, it wasn't just faded, it was tainted with disdain that she had reserved for him, who he had been and what he had done, not just to Tina, but really to all of them. Most of the time she chose just not to think of him.

Once, she had given all the love she could to Kent in the hope that one day he would return it. He never did. She had always felt he was in love with his work, not her, or at least he never indicated otherwise. Not only had she suffered from his apathy, but also he largely ignored their children as well. Often, she thought, they were treated as mere byproducts of their marriage, nothing more.

Jim was different. He was a role model that shined brightly, illuminating not only his children's lives but her children as well. He listened. He asked questions when he misunderstood. And when he was misunderstood, he went to great lengths to correct what he wanted them to know, to feel and to believe. He was intuitive to what her and the children felt, and when they felt it. He was a man of great empathy, she thought, and she never knew him to succumb to quick anger. She felt that he had always been meant for her and now God or fate, one had brought them methodically together. She lifted her head and turned it toward where he stood just minutes ago and sat there, tears coming from her eyes, a smile gripping her lips, she empty of him, but full of joy.

* * *

Jim sat there drumming his fingers on the chair. He watched Aunt Mae as she started to slightly lean to her left, eyes closed, the knitting needles growing idle in her hands. He looked at the kids and they were in a trance, watching an old western on television—*Shane*.

His thoughts were erratic. They darted from Lisa to Tina in his blackened burnt-out mind. He was torn between the ghostly feelings he had for his dead wife and the birth of feelings that queried his heart for Lisa. He felt guilty, even dirty and adulterous, that he was succumbing to much more than he had planned for with Lisa. To exchange one for another was troubling for him. It was different when Lisa was just a tool for revenge against Kent. But she had the power to cut into him and see his inner man, much the way Tina had.

*Damn that Kent*, he thought. It was he that put him in this unsavory emotional condition—torn between her that was faithful unto death—and the oasis that Lisa presented, protecting him much the same way Tina had against the swells of a lecherous dark sea that wanted to devour him. What he had now was her and she was tangible, he could touch her. She offered all the promise that once was, and all that could be.

He glanced at the television and watched the flicker of the screen as Shane used his fist to make his point with the cattlemen in the saloon. Each hammer he threw sent a lightning bolt burning through him. At that moment, he was enraged at what Kent took from him, enraged with guilt and haunted by his dead wife. Stricken almost numb with anger at his very core, he watched the fists land, each one of them he could feel, as Shane stood their facing down the epitome of evil. His frustration was ebullient; it brought on an uncontrollable desire to taste the sweet satisfaction of revenge at that very moment.

His heart pounded wildly in his chest and his mind proposed dark propositions as he thought of Kent. *He is the one who put me in this predicament*, he thought. *He is the one who caused me so much pain.* His fettered emotional constitution irritated him. Kent's narcissism that Lisa often described in icy graphic detail pounded his head like a fighter walloping a punching bag. His head hurt acutely at the center of it. He couldn't think anymore or he would go mad.

His fingers drummed the couch louder. Quickly his eyes darted around the room, first to Aunt Mae, who now snored wildly, slumped over to one side in the chair. Then to the television—"Shane...Shane...Shane," the little boy called. And then to the clock on the wall, where his eyes came to rest. It read seven forty-eight. The clock ticked loudly, as if it struggled to be heard.

Jim could stand no more. He rose from his chair and walked to the door. His hands tightened into fists by his sides, his demeanor unsettled, inwardly perturbed. His eyes, cheeks and lips inflamed with pure hatred and burning rage.

*A bridle right ta'yer mouth boy, right ta'yer mouth.*

"Daddy, where are you going?" Janie said. She was only half awake now.

"I have something I need to do. I'll be back in a couple of hours. He tried to smile, but only could make a half-hearted effort. "I love you, Janie...Kevie. You guys take care of Aunt Mae...okay."

"I love you too," Janie said.

"I love you, Daddy," Kevin said.

"See you both in a little while." Jim opened the door looking at them for a moment and then he closed it slowly behind him.

* * *

The long drive had done nothing to cool his burning rage. Kent, the whipping boy of his predicament, would face a fury that knew no boundaries.

When Jim arrived at the cabin, he tore the rug off the floor. He pulled back the cellar door and rushed down the stairs and leaped in front of the cot, where a startled Kent Jackson was now waking. Jim stood there, his chest heaving, his shoulder bowed. He was nearly grunting like a wild animal looking to kill as he glared down at him. Kent scooted himself backward on his cot, away from Jim.

"You…you," he yelled at him. He pointed his finger in condemnation at him at him. "You, you goddamn sonuvabitch."

"What?" Kent whispered sheepishly.

Jim's hands formed clinched fists, his jaws locked, and he flinched the muscle that wrapped around them. He snarled like a wild rabid dog, and his behavior was as unpredictable. "Can't you see what you've done? What you made me do? You fucker! You fucker!" he yelled. Then, through clinched teeth, he asked him again, quieter now, more restrained: "Can't you see what you did…to me…to my wife?"

Kent stared at him, afraid to answer, but the silence was too revealing. It prompted him to speak. "I'm sorry, I—"

"No, you're only sorry you got caught…you self-centered asshole," Jim said hatefully. "You shit ass fucker, you better know what you've done…maybe I'll beat your ass right now until you're dead…then you'll know."

Jim lunged at him like the rabid dog that Kent thought he was. Kent struggled to keep his composure. He tried to swallow but couldn't. Fear gripped him and he thought that in the next couple of moments he would die as he fought to keep Jim's fists from his face. But eventually they found their way. One fist slammed into their target after another, until Kent's face turned into a bloody pulp.

Kent screamed for mercy, trying to save his life, but Jim would have none of it—he was enraged. Jim stood up and grabbed Kent by the hair and kicked him in the stomach and then kneed him in the face. Kent's nose exploded in blood as he collapsed to the floor in front of him, his hair ripping from his scalp, still in Jim's hand.

Kent lay over his knees, face on the ground, hands holding his stomach. Blood oozed from his nostrils and flowed freely over his lips and down his chin.

Jim stumbled back to the cold concrete wall, exhausted and horrified by his own wake of destruction. His mouth was gaping, his lungs gasped for air, and he leaned forward hand on his knees panting and sweating. He watched with curious contempt the bloody sprawl before him. "Look…look what you made me do," Jim screamed. "See what you have done?" He spoke in spurts as he struggled to catch his breath. "Why did you have to do it?" he whispered. "Why don't you understand my pain?" He looked at him with disgust. "You understand nothing, but your own pain."

Jim lifted his face off the floor and fell to his side. "Just kill me," Kent mumbled in a montra. "I can't take this...I can't take this anymore...just kill me."

"No...no, you narcissistic sonuvabitch. Don't you know there is a fate worse than death?" Jim yelled. "There is. There is," he said. "And you will see what is worse than death."

Kent watched him as he slowly walked up the stairs and then disappeared through the hole. He lifted himself upon his knees and leaned against the meager cot, blood dripping from his nose onto a single white sheet that covered it. "What do you mean?" he said hoarsely. "What do you mean?" "What do you mean there is a fate worse than death...tell me...tell me?"

And as Jim had done, so many times before in his captivity, he heard the door slam shut and the sound of the rug being drug over it.

He lay there exhausted at his own words. "Answer me," Kent whispered. "Answer me." His question went unanswered, but he repeated it. His bloody lips mouthed the words long after Jim had left.

* * *

Jim and Lisa were married the following September. Neither one of them had known such happiness. It was a marriage with roots that fed on horrid deception, but it was hidden from Lisa, as was the darker part of Jim Hall.

It was decided he would sell his house and he and his children would move into Lisa's house, because it was larger. To Jim it was the trophy of what he had accomplished. Even though he now knew he loved Lisa deeply, he also knew he had exacted a crushing revenge on Kent. He would lay in his bed with his wife and listen to her breath—her body next to his, only a touch away.

# Chapter 26

The marks etched in the concrete wall counted one hundred and seventeen days. He stared at the marks, and brushed them with his hands. He figured it was around the end of November, probably close to Thanksgiving. He didn't think Thanksgiving had come yet.

He worked his hands together, and counted them again, this time saying the number under his breath. "No, no, this time it is not one hundred and seventeen days, this time I count one hundred and twenty days," he said out loud. He counted again. "Yes, yes, it is one hundred and seventeen—see you were mistaken," he told himself. "You were mistaken." He smiled as he felt the marks again.

He talked often to himself and to Jesus. He prayed for forgiveness almost hourly in detail about those sins that had brought him here. He would recite Bible verses his parents had forced down his throat as a kid. He hated learning them, but now they were one of the very few things that were real down in the small depressing cellar. Reality didn't exist down there, only time did—lost time that clicked away in his head.

Every so often Kent would fling himself down to the floor and beg God for forgiveness. Sometimes he would do so speaking in the King's English, just like in the King James version of the Bible: "Oh, I beseech you, oh merciful God; oh have mercy on my soul. Wilt thou deliver me from my bondage like you delivered the children of Israel. Wilt thou lead me out of the wilderness Lord...please show me the land of milk and honey...please show me Canaan." But there was no Canaan, no sanctuary, only confinement and isolation that answered him back.

He thought of his mother and father as he groveled on the floor. How they tried to ingrain in him the Lord's Word and moral implications for not adhering to the Word. He was the son of a preacher, but a son that wouldn't listen: *why couldn't I have listened?* he thought. Now he was paying a penance for his rebellious nature, for his abandonment of God. He didn't want to hear it right now; his own conscience was doing a good enough job of cannibalizing him. He tried to extinguish the guilt rising up in him, but couldn't. His father's accusing voice whispered faintly in his ear.

He thought of the moral boundaries that squeezed him tight as an adolescent. The invisible hand of righteousness had remained wrapped around his throat choking him ever since. His dad had planted in him the seeds of salvation. Then he poured a steady stream of self-condemning religion on the fertile soil of his brain to make it grow. But Kent had fought a hard fight against it, not to let it grow wild in his brain. He hated it, and sometimes he hated his father for planting in him the fear of everlasting judgment.

But there was no doubt the guilt always found a way to seep into him, no doubt at all, no matter how hard he tried, especially when he had crossed forbidden boundaries his parents had taught him would damn his soul. His old man's voice echoed back into his ears and sent a stream of fire into his head of shame and remorse for those things that had not lived up to the moral expectations of his father.

At night he would have unforgiving nightmares about his unsavory past. In them, his father's presence stood over him in judgment, bellowing condemnation. It sent a chill into him as he was devoured by his shadow. His soul would scream for redemption, but he found nothing worth redeeming in himself.

He would see Tina Hall's face, the color of it washing away like rain on wet paint, her breath quickening, trying to catch up with what her lungs required, her heart not being able to sustain the pace. He felt her soul as it slipped from the world, her crying as she died, not for herself but for her children. And he felt the pain too, for at those moments when he thought of her they were one.

He would see the face of his old high school girlfriend, the one he had gotten pregnant. Her face would appear from time to time through a great dark mist. She was always cradling a baby in her hands and shadows of long curtains enveloped her. He would walk slowly toward her, the baby cloaked from his view, coddled in a light blue blanket, lying in her lily-white arms. The smile on his face disappears as he sees what she holds in her hands. There in the shadows, he can just make out the baby's features, but there is something wrong. He pulls back the cottony blanket to reveal a shriveled fetus lying outstretched in her arms. He looks at her questioningly, and she looks back at him with a blank unadulterated stare and whispers softly to him in a ghostly voice, "Look what you have done to our baby, Kent, look what you've done."

At that moment a single tear runs down her cheek and falls from her face. It seems like it falls forever, the tear tumbling straight down, striking the baby on its pruned face, the moisture penetrating the wrinkled skin. The tear begins to stir the waters of life in the child, hydrating the shrunken infant, until it fills her mother's arms. And then Kent looks into the face of his own child. It is the face of a God-forsaken nightmare, Rosemary's baby, a sick biological anomaly whose memory would haunt him for the rest of his life; even though it was a dream.

From its forehead grew tusk-like nodules, thin and sharp at the ends. It bellowed a horrid high-pitched cry that echoed through the room. Its body became engulfed in an inferno of red tint. Its chubby hands pawed the blankets incessantly it was wrapped in. And when its eyes fixed on his, they penetrated him, and it spoke in an unnatural throaty whisper. The words it hissed were thick with condemnation and judgment, its lips moved with precision, accusing him of vile acts he thought were secret. It hurt his ears to hear its strange slithering rasp.

"I am waiting for you here in hell," it cooed. The words sent a chill into his spine, feeling like his back was being split open with a scythe. The dream so real, the voice so sure, the ungodly face so close, he could feel its hot vengeful breath. But he could not run from it. It was there with him, inside of him, never to leave, and the image would replay over and over in his head.

And at other times, other ghostly figures would come to call. But one in particular would disturb him. Kent's mind drifted back to a warm July summer night. A night he wished he could take back forever. It was the summer between his college freshman and sophomore year; a summer of maddening humidity and demoralizing heat, but quite typical as summers go in Oklahoma.

Kent drove his old Chevy Monte Carlo fast through the wet downtown streets of Lakewood City. He shifted hard in the turns, and squealed the tires, fishtailing over the rain-drenched asphalt. In the passenger seat sat Chester Findlay, gripping the dashboard hard as the car bounced across one street to the next. In the back seat, with his fingers tethered to the seat in front of him, was Norman Fletcher.

"This bitch can run," Kent said.

"Damn straight it can," Chester said. His chinless face looked over at him, flashing the thumbs up sign. "Fuckin' eh," Norman shouted over the stereo. "She'll run till hell freezes over."

"This mother's gonna run tonight," Kent said.

"Yeah, stand on it—let's get crazy!" Norman yelled. He slapped Kent on the shoulder, as "Somebody Get Me a Doctor" by Van Halen blared out of the speakers.

They drove for hours, just for shits and grins, drinking Mickey's and Little King Ale and smoking homegrown weed—the usual entertainment for a Saturday night. And then, something happened, something that none of them would forget for the rest of their lives.

Nicole Freeman and Kent had been quite an item the year before, but she had broken up with him during their senior year in high school. Nicole had become infatuated around mid-term with a local college football player and dumped Kent rather hastily. It had been hard on him; he had been in love with her deeply and it took him some time to get over it, and the humiliation she had caused him. It seemed about everyone in school knew they were broken up before he did. Kent had never forgiven the indiscretion.

His eyes glassed over when she slipped her long tan arms around his neck. She was too drunk to notice his apathy. Her breath reeked of alcohol and cigarettes, and the smell of her mouth irritated him. And after a period of heavy flirtation she passed out in his arms. He held her for a moment as if he were holding a piece of rotted flesh, but smiled as he did, for appearances. He assured her friends he would take her home, and when he looked at her, he told himself that was all it would be. But in the back of his mind he knew better.

He put Nicole in the back seat of the Monte Carlo, leaning her up against Norman, who was sitting on the right side of the seat. When he slid in behind the wheel, he put his hands on the keys in the ignition, but before turning the motor over, he looked at Nicole with contempt in the rearview mirror. His lips pressed together tightly as he turned the key. The motor made a thunderous sound as he sped away from the curb and into the night.

The man staggered, tittering on the curb of a street, trying to keep his precarious balance. He swayed back and forth in the sticky humid air. The man was probably younger than he looked, maybe even in his early forties. You could see some glimpse of youth hidden deep in his dark filthy eyes, but much of it was covered by spider web cracks surrounding the features of his face.

His long straggly salt-and-pepper hair was greasy, as was his untrimmed beard. He looked kind of like Charlton Heston in the *Ten Commandments*, but with far less dignity. Uncombed hair floated about his face. In the meshed strands were sticky deposits of dead scalp and debris, trapped like cotton balls to a greasy mop. It made you wonder if they were lice eggs or just clumps of dandruff. The appearance of his nasty head broke all concentration when looking at him. It almost rendered a conversation useless, as one could not concentrate on the subject at hand, because his hair was so menacing.

He wore a wrinkled long sleeve red and black plaid shirt stained at the elbows and at the cuffs with a tan dust color. Despite the heavy shirt, he did not sweat; though, it was near eighty degrees that night. His shirt lay open at the collar, and about three buttons down, black hair jutted from his chest and seemed to make a continuous flow of hair to his face.

His hands were blackened as if he had shoved them into motor oil and let them dry. When he worked his hands, the black skin opened up to expose flesh tone crevasses. At the end of his hands jutted long fingers, his nails chipped, their ends packed full of dark filth.

He wore an old pair of corduroy pants, so old the ribs were worn smooth. They were tan and about two inches too short, exposing his filthy ankles. The flap over his fly was pulled taunt, the zipper broken, the gaps exposing pubic hair. His jeans were worn and faded, nearly white on the knees, thighs and buttocks. He wore a cheap pair of off-brand slip-on deck shoes. A gaping hole in one shoe exposed his big toe. Its nail was greenish and porous and looking as if it was being expeditiously devoured by a potent fungus at that very moment. The thick and once white rubber soles of the shoes that surrounded the frayed canvas were scuffed and caked with oily hot-patch. In his total being, the derelict was disgusting from head to toe, and in Kent's mind there was nothing like him on the face of the earth. He was awed by his unsightliness.

Norman Fletcher and Chester Findlay were two oddball guys that followed Kent Jackson around like lost pups. They were the Barneys or Nortons or guys like them, sidekicks without too much upstairs, but they held out the promise that a little intuitive insight would rub off from their fearless leader.

Everyone knew Kent was going to make something of himself, somewhere after college. He would be the man all others wished they could be at the ten- and twenty-year class reunions. He reeked of success, even at a young age. He had been the senior high school class president, school valedictorian, a starting forward on the Lakewood City University Basketball Team, president of the Young Entrepreneurs Business Club and yet he was totally, incomprehensibly and intractably bored to death.

Norman, whose dad was a rancher, and Chester, whose dad wasn't much of anything at all, liked hanging around Kent for really one main reason, especially on Saturday night. They officially classified him as the "fuck magnet." They were more than happy to get what strange came their way by just hanging around him, waiting for what fell off the old pussy tree. Usually it was friends of the good-looking one, which weren't so good looking. Or if they had run the gambit that night and come up empty they would begin with what they so fondly called "hoggin'," which was merely a euphemism for a last ditch effort at getting laid by fat chicks who were desperate. And, usually Kent would get the better-looking hog, but sometimes it was hard to tell.

Every once in a while Norman would reach over and grab one of Nicole's tits and squeeze, while he yelled out "HONK." The whole car would erupt in laughter at the adolescent behavior. Nicole just lay there slumped over on him, passed out, not aware of anything, or where she was.

Kent looked at Nicole through the rearview mirror. He thought about how good her body once felt against his, how the sounds of her voice used to sound when her body seized her. But he also felt the pain that she had caused him, the humiliation, and he was filled with anger as he looked upon her sleeping face. She deserved something, he thought, something more than what he could ever do to her.

Tonight Kent would not settle for a greasy roll in the back seat with a beer-soaked cigarette mouth. Tonight he would seek his gratification another way; he would settle the score. The thick opaque evil muck was present even then with him, perhaps just a speck on his brain, nascent, immature, but present just the same, concentrated in its raw form. It would spread that night through him, spread its evil web deep into his brain.

Nicole was a beautiful girl. Her brownish blonde hair highlighted her nice soft summer tan that adorned her toned firm body shaved. She was from old money. A daddy's girl who got whatever she wanted. A girl who lived in an unreal world where nothing was her fault. Pure with assured confidence that whatever the world had to offer she would be able to buy at retail, and that money would be able to smooth the hurt if life became too rough.

In the years following she would find out how wrong she had been about that, about everything, that money couldn't douse the burning pain of memories. No amount of money in the world could erase the deep scar that would affect her from it. The memories would be cut gruesomely in her soft gray matter. It would lie inherent in her, like when she lay sleepless at night for years to come. Like the half-life of a nuclear waste dump that couldn't be removed, the memory seeped its toxic poison into the fertile ground around her, deep into her brain. She was wrong, dead wrong. No, she wouldn't be able to forget this night, not until they pulled her out of a bloody bathtub ten years later. Only death could make the pain of this night go away.

The Monte Carlo idled on the dimly-lit street. The derelict stood wavering beside it. Kent had a thin veiled smile on his face. The bum stumbled in front of them, nearly falling on the car hood. He steadied himself with one arm against it, swaying back and forth. He held out a thin skintight hand.

"Sparth me a quather? I'm thussta livel shorth."

Chester turned to Kent. "What the fuck did he say?"

Kent ignored him and leaned his head out of the car. "Sure, no problem, but wouldn't you much rather have an Andrew Jackson?"

"Whoth And Jackthsss—"

"Look, never mind, I got a twenty spot for you if you get in and go for a ride with us."

The wino looked into the car with glassy eyes. Norman was in the back seat eating Cheetos, Nicole slumped against his shoulder. Kent looked up at him and grinned. Chester looked nervously at the wino and then back at Kent, not sure what he was doing.

"Jesus H. Christ, look at the dirt on this sunvabitch," Chester said.

The wino walked back to the car seat and wiggled the handle of the back door. "I guess that means a yes." He winked at Chester and with a cool calm voice said, "Let Romeo in, Norman."

Norman opened the door and the bum climbed across Nicole. "What the fuck," Norman said. "He smells like shit. He smells like Chester's shorts."

"Bite my shit pipe, you filthy homo," Chester said.

"Cut it out you guys. Hey, Romeo, what's your name?"

"My name is Se Baaaxtiiin."

"What? What did he say," Chester said. "I can't understand a fucking thing this guy is saying."

"All right if we just call you Romeo?" Kent asked.

The wino nodded.

"Good," Kent said.

"Goddamn it, he reeks," Norman shouted from the back seat. "He smells worse than a heaping high dungel-berry sandwich."

The car was hot and dank, and the odor started radiating from Romeo's skin. Kent's nostrils filled with the wretched smell. He pictured the pores in Romeo's skin puffing out green putrid gas.

"For the love of Christ, get him out," yelled Norman.

Kent began to laugh. It sounded wicked and non-human, as if he were really getting off on this form of sick torture. It was like playing the hot game when you were a kid, and rolling up the windows in the dead of the summer in your father's car with your friends and turning on the heater. Waiting silently, sweat pouring from your face, waiting for the last one to finally cry out and give. And you got to scream pussy at them. It reminded him of this.

"Give him some Cheetos," Kent said. "He looks like he needs to eat." Norman handed the bag to Romeo. Romeo thrust a grimy paw down into the plastic bag with an ear-shattering crunch.

"Its all yours now," Norman said. He rolled his eyes. "There's no way in hell I'm eating out of there again."

The air was stagnant with a thick stench creeping through the car, wrinkling everyone's noses. Even Nicole stirred momentarily from her drunken stupor, only to pass out again, this time leaning her head on Romeo's shoulder.

It was like having a spoiled raw piece of fish that had been in an unplugged refrigerator too long, about a month too long. The odor unfurled under their noses, rancid, tempting the throat to gag with repulsion.

"You're one stinky mother fucker," Norman said, using all the tactfulness he could muster. "A bungus hole times ten," said Chester. They laughed hysterically, until they thought their sides would burst. It was contagious, even Romeo laughed.

Kent pushed his foot on the accelerator. Air began to flow through the car, carrying away much of the putrid smell. But at each stop light and stop sign, the fleshy smell of rotted meat would return, torturing their nostrils, the smell corkscrewing into their nose and down into their lungs, their heads finally driven out of the window for a quick gulp of fresh air.

Kent pulled up to the barn in a deserted pasture. Norman's dad owned the place and used it for his cattle. The pasture smelled of sweet honeysuckle mixed with the pungent odor of cow shit and the early morning scent of fresh dewed grass. It was nearly 1:00 in the morning.

"Get her out of the car," Kent said to Norman. His voice was sharp and demanding. "Get Romeo out too, Chester. Take them both to the barn."

"What are we doing here?" Chester asked. He had a questioning bewildered look on his face.

"Yeah, Kent, look, if my old man finds out we were here, I'm going to be in deep shit," Norman said.

"Look, everything is going to be all right, just do what I say." He shot them both a look like platoon sergeants do in old World War II movies—a look like he meant business.

Chester stood beside the car, unsure of what Kent was up to. Romeo was still sitting in the back of the seat, Nicole's head on his shoulder, she unaware where she made her pillow. He poked his head back into the window, peering into the back seat of the car.

The funky reek began pushing up in the car in the hot still air. Chester was looking at Romeo, and Romeo was hungrily looking at Nicole. Looking at her like someone looking at a cool glass of water, who had been in the desert without a drink for a very long time.

Chester opened the back door and helped Romeo out, who was reluctant at first. Chester told him it would be all right. Romeo got out. "Jesus Christ, brother, you need some Lava scrubbed on your ass," Chester said. Romeo smiled faintly.

"Wheth myth twwwenth dollarthsss," Romeo said.

"I've got it," Kent snapped, "but you'll have to earn it first." Kent's eyes looked dark as the full moon shone brightly on his face, highlighting all but what appeared to be hollow holes on both sides of his face, making him look like a ghostly sight standing in front of the barn.

Norman stooped into the rear passenger seat and pulled Nicole from the doorway and lifted her up and laid her on the trunk, she moaning, her body limp. Norman gave a sickening cackle as he stared at her lying there. Her legs spread eagle, she sprawled in every direction, and Norman stood above her pointing his finger at her chest, uncontrollable laughter bursting from his lungs. "Look, look at this," he yelled.

Kent came running around to his side from the front of the car and Chester walked back to the trunk. Kent and Chester stood there, mouths gaping open, not sure what they were seeing at first and then it registered. They looked at each other and then at Norman and began to laugh.

It was her white blouse they were laughing at, and it would become the butt of their personal jokes for the next school year. On her blouse were big sets of orange hand-prints, where her neatly rounded breasts pushed through her shirt. Romeo had felt up the girl in the back seat while he was eating Cheetos. It looked like someone had dipped their hands into orange paint and pressed them all over her shirt.

Kent winked at the bum that was grinning now, looking back at them. The grin was unnerving, but it soon disappeared. His eyes narrowed and a ravenous look appeared in them. Perhaps he understood better than what Norman and Chester had, why he was there, what he would be required to do.

Kent handed Romeo the twenty. "Don't do anything I wouldn't do," he said. He turned toward Norman and Chester, and said, "Take her to the barn."

Norman had hold of her legs and Chester laced his arms in hers. They carried her to the barn and laid her in the soft bedding of the hay that lay strewn all over the floor.

Kent turned on the headlights and they lit her body, laying there, waiting. Kent turned toward Romeo, who seemed to be a little steadier, a little more lucid. "Now is your chance to be a star," he whispered, so the others couldn't hear. His tongue was tight as his lips formed the inviting words. "She wants to fuck you. She told me."

Romeo walked with a staggered limp in front of the headlights, almost dragging one foot behind him, the one that had the shoe with the gaping worn hole that exposed the infectious big toe. He moved lethargically over the wet grass, his shadow casting an appalling monster-like figure over Nicole, who lay there still on the ground.

Romeo stood in front of her, his rancid odor preceding him. Kent, Norman and Chester watched from the shadows of the barn. He knelt before the girl. His grimy hand touched her soft cheek, and he poked it with a blackened nail. He lay on top of her abruptly and kissed her roughly, his thickly-coated white tongue slithering out from its sheath on her lips, probing her mouth. His dirty hair and beard fell on her face and neck. He began to devour her savagely, sweat gathered on his musty body and smudged onto her chest and belly that were now exposed and dripped off his face on to hers. Their bodies glowed in the car's headlights.

Nicole began to moan, her head rocked back and forth and sometimes to the side, as if she were nodding in agreement at what he was doing to her. She moaned again, this time calling out Kent's name. Her motionless arms came to life as she put her hands on Romeo's shoulder, believing he was Kent, her eyes still closed. She felt his greasy hair. She wrinkled her nose and then as if a gentle breeze had awoken her, she opened her eyes. Then wider, like they were being pulled apart by a train of horses.

Kent looked on in horror, his hands clenched tightly, his face locked in a grimace as if it were too painful to watch what he was seeing. But, he did watch. He watched her young quivering legs being spread apart by the beast. She just lay there for a moment, frozen, incredulous, feeling sure her eyes were betraying her mind, her body. Her nose furled at his stench. The smell, oh God, the smell seemed to suffocate her while he was inside her. Her head tossed from side to side in agony. She realized in one quick sharp moment she was being rocked back and forth and that an animal, a greasy animal was on top of her, inside of her, pawing her. Then she began to scream.

Kent tried to block the foggy memory out. What he did was cruel. He had never thought of it in such brutal terms, until he had time to think—a lot of time. There had been lots of time to think about it deep in the dark abyss—the cellar. He put his hand over his eyes and rubbed them, hoping the image would go away. But in the self-induced darkness, the memory gathered its strength and burned again.

The headlights illuminated the bodies in the barn, Nicole flailing, screaming, reaching toward the retreating car. Romeo, entrenched, holding her, his filthy body on hers. They drove off, Chester and Norman scared. Kent was scared too—scared he might get caught. But he didn't get caught, and that was probably to his disservice.

Someone picked up Nicole that night as she walked down a country road, partially undressed, torn. She said nothing about it. She would not live through the humiliation. She would not have people talking about her or her family. But that night, she died. Her soul became dormant. She left all she knew to be real, and was departed from the life she knew.

The cloudy fog slightly thinned. He came back to the dank room. He was glad to be loose of the memory, at least for awhile. He welcomed the reality of his unkind surroundings. The memory had dug into him tightly. It had severed him from what was real. *It was the fever*, he thought. *It was the fever.*

He had always avoided blame at all cost throughout his life, able to deflect it when accusations struck near. He was able to wear the Teflon suit well. But now, he was the one to blame. He had been assigned an accuser. Tina Hall had died because of him. Her husband would make sure that he would pay for every ounce of her flesh.

He had a dark blackness that hungered for his brain that caused him to do those things. He now owed for all his transgressions and was confined in the belly of the beast to pay the debt. Jim Hall had made sure of that.

No longer was he incarcerated physically, but through the stress of his internment, he was now incarcerated in his own mind. He thought Kent a tool that the Lord was using to punish him. But that tool was a devil. He would walk around the cellar, thinking of himself as Job from the Bible. But instead of being punished for no good reason, he had every reason to believe he was being punished for a variety of transgressions. He was not a son that sought

God's heart. He was not the husband that spiritually led his family. In retrospect, he had been a failure on all accounts, to his parents and to his wife. Ultimately, he reduced his thinking in terms of religious analogies and connotations. He had not loved his family. He had loved himself. It was this he must pay for. Jim Hall was the angry devil bent on carrying out his sentence. At his darkest moments, he often thought he heard the Devil begging God to destroy him and God granting the permission to do so.

*God was testing him*, he thought. *Waiting to see if he would deny him...like he had tested Job.* In his tortured state, he imagined that God sent insects into the room to spy on him, to see if he sought redemption. Once Kent saw a cockroach crawling on the cellar wall. He felt that God had sent it surreptitiously, but as it crawled along the wall in zigzagging patterns, he began to think that God was having it write out a secret message. He studied it for hours, trying to interpret the correspondence, but eventually drifted into troubled sleep.

Sometimes he looked directly at the knothole in the low-hanging wood rafters in the ceiling and think he was staring into God's furled angry eye—he also saw his mom and dad's eyes in smaller knot holes. They all cast a disapproving glance upon when he entertained their presence. He would plead to the God, raising his hands to the knothole, like a boy in Sunday school saying a prayer, to deliver him from the Devil—Jim Hall. He never did.

Sometimes when Jim came to the cabin and opened the cellar door to provision him, he would speak (which mostly he did not), and his voice to Kent sounded like the Devil. He even looked like the Devil, Kent thought. The same one he had feared as a child. He feared Jim. He knew he held the keys to his end or his freedom. He just wasn't sure which it might be.

He thought Christmas was near, but wasn't sure, though he didn't think it had passed. A terrible fever ravaged his body for six days. His throat burned each time he swallowed. At times he felt as if it would close up and suffocate him, and leave him writhing on the floor, deprived of oxygen. He figured it to be pneumonia, though he wasn't sure. The fear of dying preyed on his already tortured mind, day and night in the dark cellar. Hypochondria and paranoia set its hooks deeply into his soft gray matter. He was sick, confused, and without bearings to right himself, a ship listless without sail on an aimless sea.

He thought Jim Hall might have poisoned him. He could picture him mixing up a brackish concoction of deadly poisons and slowly feeding it to him in tiny amounts, masked by his food so that he couldn't taste it. He imagined Jim, the Devil, stirring the lethal potion, evilly smiling as he did so.

Other times his mind went wild with uncontrollable hypochondria, thinking that a dreaded disease was ravaging his body, laying waste to his eternal organs like the plague. He could feel it eating him, inside, the disease, its appetite never being quenched. He became fearful of mouse droppings, thinking them deadly little packages carried and left by tiny hairy bodies. The mice frequented the cellar often, and even when they didn't he still imagined them running near him in the night. He often thought he could hear their little toenails tapping on the concrete as they ran. He smelled their musty odorous bodies and saw the evidence of their invasion every morning. He shuddered at what disease they carried. *Probably*, he thought, *the Devil had finally sent them to kill him.*

Five days ago he had begged Jim to take him to a doctor and not let him die, that he thought he had the plague. And then just as quick, accused Jim of slowly poisoning him. Jim Hall just looked at him with a devious grin, enjoying the sight. Kent Jackson, a one time Oklahoma businessman of the year, now reduced to a babbling pathetic piece of shit of a man, standing before him in cheap gray sweat pants and shirt, ranting about mouse droppings. *You've come a long way, shithead...a long way*, he thought.

# Chapter 27

Jim opened the cellar door and carried down the life-sustaining bags of food. When Jim brought groceries, it was a big deal to Kent. It was all he had to look forward to, little else changed. When he came with those plastic grocery bags, Kent's eyes widened almost to the size of shiny silver dollars. He not only was excited by the new culinary additions, some begging intrigue, as they lay wrapped in various fashions in colorful waxy paper, but by what was written on the labels. He had become expert at memorizing the extensive names of chemicals that preserved potted meats, as well as other nutritious artifacts found under their tin covers.

But this time was different. Kent was morose when Jim came in. He didn't even raise his head off the cot. Jim didn't say anything to him as usual and put the plastic bags down on the table. He turned to walk back up the stairs, but a voice caught his ear before he reached the first step. A voice lost, depressed and dripping with uncertainty.

"Is it Christmas?" the voice asked timidly. "Has Christmas come?"

Jim stood there in front of the stairs, poised to climb up the short distance, listening to Kent's voice, debating about whether to answer him. Finally he said, "No, not yet, but it's close."

"How close?" Kent asked.

"Two days," Jim answered.

"I want to be with my family for Christmas...please turn me loose and let me be with them." Kent drew a long pause and said, "I promise I will tell no one about this."

"You don't need to worry about your family anymore," Jim said ominously. His eyes were hollow and empty, vacant of any perceivable empathy.

"Wha...what do you mean...tell me...is there something wrong?"

"Nothing wrong that I know of."

Kent stirred from his fetal position on the bed and sat up.

"There's something you're not telling me...I want to know what it is."

"I have nothing to tell you...only that you're here for a reason, and that reason is of your own doing."

Kent sat up on the edge of his cot, like a cornered scared cat that was about to bolt.

His body was rigid as he leaned forward, pulling up clumps of white sheet in his clinched hands. He looked like a man that had just been sentenced to an eternal world of darkness where fear of the unknown would possess him until his last days. Until his last dying breath uttered the words of his confession—a confession he had struggled for so long to keep.

"Please, please," he said. Kent paused, the dirty hungry guilt now crawling up in his throat, thick and salty with fear. He couldn't appease its ferocious appetite anymore. It wanted him. It hungered for him, wanting him to say the sick words, the words that only his tortured sole possessed. He paused, seriously considering what he would say, or if he would say anything at all. But his haunting memory betrayed him and the dirty hungry guilt cut through his mouth, wielding a razor sharp double-edged sword, exposing the ugly truth with every swath it cut.

"I...I killed...I killed her," Kent said in a low whisper.

"What did you say?" Jim said.

"I'm, I'm sorry, I didn't mean to. I know it's no excuse. I was drunk...I didn't see her in the road, Jesus, she was just running on the side of the road, in the rain and...and I hit her...God, I hit her."

"But that's not all, is it, is it...you stupid fuck," Jim said. He stared at him with a snarl on his face, his eyes filled with contempt.

"No," Kent said sheepishly. "She, she was...alive." He broke down and began to weep. His arms covered his face, now bent over on his legs. Then after a moment, he spoke. "When I got to her, she was badly hurt."

"She was dying," Jim said sharply, pointing his finger at him.

"Yes...yes she was."

"Why in God's name didn't you get my wife some help, you...you self-centered sonuvabitch."

"I...I didn't want to get in trouble. I know, I should have. I was scared though, I didn't know what else to do. I thought she might die anyway, even if I did get her help. So, so, I fig—"

"So you figured you would leave her, didn't you, leave her and save your own skin." Jim looked at him accusingly and spoke with pointed precision. "You probably thought that since Tina would die anyway, it wouldn't change a goddamn thing if you went for help or not." Jim stared at him hard now. Kent felt his terminal gaze, though he wasn't looking at him. But still he felt it just the same. It was the kind of look that burned holes through your skin. Hot penetrating pools devouring his dignity until it was gone, like human skin melted away by a hot intense explosion.

"So...you didn't tell anybody, you just drove off and left her there...left her to die. That's pretty much the way it was, wasn't it?"

Kent nodded his head, his eyes staring up at him. "I'm sorry," he said in a soft low whisper of a voice. "I'm sorry for all the pain I've cause you, Jim."

Jim didn't answer, he just watched him.

The expression now on Kent's face exposed the raw fear that he felt tugging inside him. The knot in his throat now felt large as a apple. His chest was tight and his breath quick. He wanted to jump up and run. He was scared now, not sure how Jim would react to such a naked disturbing confession. His admission seemed to just hang in time, exposed and rotten, laying there for all to see, like the proverbial turd floating in a punch bowl.

Jim turned to leave, as if he couldn't stand the sight of him any longer, afraid that he might kill him if he looked at him for one second more. He hated him. He thought to himself how he would savor the meaty flesh of his revenge.

"Please, please don't leave me down here. Turn me loose and I won't tell anyone."

Jim took a step forward up the stairs.

"Please...please don't leave me here...don't leave me here again. I can't take it...I can't take being here by myself." Kent walked toward him as he talked frantically. All the paranoia gathered up in him, the desperation and anxiety, telling him that he would surely go mad this time if he was left alone again, walking closer and closer toward Jim, eyes now fixed to the hole above, the way out.

Jim squared up his body. "Look, you better just back—"

But before he could get out the last word Kent had lunged forward with a gallop and then leaped past him. Kent screamed in terror, "I need to see...my family, goddamn it." But before he could bolt clear, Jim grabbed him by the shirt and tried to drag him down the stairs, but it ripped. "Shit," Jim yelled as Kent broke free and ran up the stairs, but as he cleared the opening to the floor of the cabin he tripped. Jim was behind him, grabbing and clawing his legs, trying to clinch his legs together. Kent was nearly to his feet, kicking and stumbling forward, struggling away from Jim's clutching hands. Kent reached the front door to the cabin, fumbling the handle in his hands, trying to figure out the lock before it was too late.

But it was too late. Jim hurled his body into Kent's like a locomotive out of control, knocking his head against the wall and then they fell to the floor. Kent felt a sharp pain ignite in his back as he lay face down on the hard wood. It was Jim slamming his knee into his lower back. The pain was excruciating, it temporarily paralyzed him and he felt sure he would never walk again. Jim got off of him and watched him coldly, his chest heaving air in and out. He waited for him to bolt again, so he might finish his handy work. But he didn't.

Kent rolled to his side and lay there like a heap on the floor. His eyes were fixed upward almost in a trance-like quality. For a moment Jim thought he was dead. But he noticed that he wasn't dead, he was staring out the front door window. And then it dawned on him, Kent hadn't been outside of the cellar for five months; he hadn't seen the outside once.

"The sky…the sky," Kent mumbled. The mantra grew in his voice. "The sky, the sky."

Jim drug him by his legs toward the cellar. Kent did not struggle, he just stared at the window, repeating the words, "The sky…the sky," until he could see it no more.

"You can either go down the hard way or the easy way," Jim said. He stood in front of the cellar door with Kent in tow. He expected him to move on his own down the stairs, but he didn't. He just lay there and mumbled, "I saw the sky…the sky…I saw it." *The sky, the sky…*

"Well I'm real happy for you, but like I said, if you don't get your ass down those stairs, I'm going to do it for you." Jim gave him a look that said he meant business.

Kent slowly got to his hands and knees and sort of inched his way over the cabin floor down through the cellar door and then down the stairs, almost in slow motion. It reminded Jim of watching some slow moving sloth on *Wild Kingdom* or something when he was a kid. Jim slammed the heavy cellar door down on the floor, thoroughly pissed as hell with Kent. He pulled the thick rug back over the door and stomped on it for good measure.

He felt a growing satisfaction inside him as he walked to the front door of the cabin. Finally Kent had confessed to hitting and killing Tina, and leaving her to die. He had admitted it. It took him five months, but he had finally done it—coughed up the confession like a smoker's dry hack. He had killed Tina all right. Kent's tear-soaked words confirmed what Jim already knew, and what he felt, that his brand of justice was forged from the hands of righteousness. It was true. The seeds of his vengeance had now yielded fruit.

He let a simple smile creep over his face as he stepped outside the cabin and onto the porch, locking the door behind him. His thoughts lingered in the cellar below the cabin, where Kent lay, a man finally beaten, crumpled, and brutally defeated. He was unforgiven by the unforgiving. He knew Kent would soon meet his destiny eye to eye and he would be the messenger to deliver it. Fate had settled that long ago.

# Chapter 28

Kent Jackson had moments of clarity that peaked through the dark abyss. He had been in the cabin's cellar for a little over a year now and he and his captor had recognized his mind had slipped to a great extent. He often struggled for lucid thoughts, but just as often he succumbed to the long shadows of his parents, his past, or some phobia. It all haunted him now, sometimes in tandem.

The southern Baptist doctrine his parents constantly heaped like burning coals on his head as a child, and as a teenager, now rose up in his isolation like a phoenix escaping from a darkened hulk of a soul. A soul he had adopted as an adult in exchange for the one his parents had tainted. The fear-based scourge was on him, and it tormented him day and night.

His routine consisted of waking at different periods of the day and night, he never knew which, until he looked at his wristwatch. If it weren't for the watch, he would lose all track of time. He feared that, but he feared many things now, most of them associated with the unknown. He paid close attention to the time. It gave him somewhat of an anchor on reality, but a slim one.

Regardless, he had lost a part of himself. He began talking to himself in his head, but after a while, he babbled, muttering as if he were a senile old man. He would ask himself questions and then offer an answer. And sometimes...he was afraid of his answers. They were often dark and muddy.

During the day and late at night Kent would walk around the cellar, hugging the walls of the 10x15 foot room. He would look at each feature of the concrete walls as he passed by them, memorizing each nook and cranny, every crack. Each time he passed his cot, he would count off a number out loud. "One, two, three." Sometimes the numbers would climb in the thousands. Once he had walked almost the entire day in a circle, just to see if he could do it. He did.

As days drifted into weeks and weeks into months, and the months slipped into a year, he drifted into a deeper slippery slope of unbridled mental darkness. The only sustaining hope that kept him from being digested in the stomach of the dark abyss was his love for his wife and children. He imagined them missing him and waiting eagerly for his return. Like an overdue ship out to sea, he imagined his family worried and eagerly awaiting his return.

He chose not to think about the letters that Jim had forced him to write. Mainly because he knew that he couldn't really be sure if Lisa would believe them. Every ounce of him wanted to presume that she doubted the letters from the first and that she had convinced the police that something wasn't right. But he couldn't be for sure, he knew that he had not planted the solid pillars in the ground the relationship required to sustain and survive it through his absence.

That was his fault, he would give anything now for the time he had thrown away playing golf or staying late at night, when he could be home. Now those things were not as important. Nothing was. He would trade it all in a heartbeat just to see his family again. Just to have a minute that he could tell them that he loved them. He had never said that word before. The word love. It was foreign. He had not loved anything but himself and he knew that.

Still, he liked to think of his family missing him. He imagined them looking out the big front green door of his house or the living room window, waiting patiently for his return. And someday he would walk up the perfect sidewalk and into the lush green yard and they would see him and he would see them and they would come spilling out the door, running toward him, he running toward them, like in some cheesy movie. They would all embrace each other holding tightly, never wanting to let go. Kissing, hugging, all of them falling down in the yard, and he telling them his awful tale and then they go back into the house to live a life that would be filled with happiness, and absent would be those unsavory times that made life interesting. That was the way he liked to think of it, to think of them.

These thoughts of family were his hope. It was all that stood between him and the rising black waters of despair, a thin veil from the dark devouring muck that threatened to fill his nostrils. This suffocating substance came after him at every unguarded moment trying to swallow his mind up with less than lucid sane thoughts, like a wildfire excited by brittle dry brush burning incessantly devouring all that stands in its way. Darkening all that it touches, leaving what's left, charred, crumpled and shattered in its wake. It was a gluttonous monster. It preyed on him in the abyss, in pursuit of his fleeting sanity.

When his defenses lowered, he let go for only a moment, then came the desperation, the ravaging grip on his mind. The suffocating muck would rise in the black waters, hidden there, grinning, nefarious, casting its long enveloping shadows. It would tug at him, trying to pull him under, to creep up into his nostrils, each breath, inhaled the life-taking ink of the abyss.

He would open his mouth to catch a breath, but instead, the thick baneful pitch would invade, oozing hot into his mouth and down his throat, filling his stomach and lungs up to the top of his sinus cavities with utter horrifying affect. And with each moment, he would struggle and claw, trying to escape its grip. He would use all the power he could muster to climb free of it and away.

Each time he would pull himself from the undertow of the gapping ink pit, trying to escape immersion into darkness. The seduction of the depths of insanity called him to acquiesce, to its persistent proposition. To surrender would be to take leave of the world and what he had made in it, his family, they would be no more as he once knew them. His mind, goddamn it, his mind. He must keep it intact.

# Chapter 29

He no longer talked to Jim when he came. He no longer tried to argue his case for setting him free. He no longer tried to escape, and he no longer cared what happened to him. He was resigned to die alone in this pit called a cellar, in this deep abyss that had become a tightening noose around his neck.

Often he thought of what Jim had said when he was brought to the cabin. *I will take from you what you took from me.* He had rolled those words over in his brain, about every day he had been there. Trying to see into them, to find something hidden, to read between the lines. He finally came to realize what Jim had meant. He would stay down in the belly of this beast forever, this God-forsaken cellar. His final tired breath would be drawn here. He figured what it meant was a life for a life. His life as he knew it for Jim's.

But something else happened to Kent in the dank basement. He was not only altered by the present circumstances, thanks to Jim, but he was also left to his past. His lecherous life had been so repugnant, it had been let loose down there in the unknown, searching him out in the darkness both day and night, wanting to feed on what was left of his mental abilities.

His past iniquities gripped him hard and galloped unbridled through his brain. He couldn't be redeemed. He would not be restored, unlike Job who found favor again in God's eyes, his past was so full of wretched improprieties he was convinced that God had sent Jim Hall to exact his revenge. He thought his parents probably begged from their graves to spare him, but it was too late. He had cursed them when he was a youth and cursed God, and it was God that would have his pound of flesh too. And it was this malignant constitution that had surrendered him up to his fate. What was merely an inky speck on his brain as a youth had now progressed. The black ghost of mental malaise had pulled open the floodgates. His footing was lost. The ravenous rip tide grabbed him and pulled him under. He thought about Lisa as he suffocated. Her face, her voice, her touch, gone in the twilight of the murky abyss.

# Chapter 30

He opened the cellar door. The light was off. It sent a foreboding feeling through him, as if something terrible lurched beneath the darkness. He stood there for a moment and decided something terrible did—his name was Kent Jackson.

Kent would unscrew the light bulb when he wanted to sleep. Night and day had merely become spaces in time that the world measured. Down in the dank cellar, time had no division: there was either light or dark at Kent's choosing, and all by a twist of a light bulb.

Jim thought that maybe Kent was dead. A little tinge of regretful panic began to fondle him. He thought he had come too far for him to be simply dead. He had spent too long constructing this coup de grace to be cheated now.

He climbed down the creaking stairs slowly and saw something stirring in the darkness. Black on dark mingled together, stirring like the spine of a black bass on opaque pond water. He said nothing, waiting for what would reveal itself. Then slowly from the pitch black, he heard something move and stop, then move again and then stop. Screeching sounds began filling Jim's ears. It sounded like mice loudly chattering. But then a flicker bounced off the walls of the room and then light.

In the middle of the room stood a gaunt Kent Jackson, skin a sickly powder pale, straggly brown hair long to his shoulders. A thick uneven reddish beard swallowed his cheeks, jaw line and traced his lips. *Subhuman*, Jim thought. The screeching began again as he finished screwing in the light bulb. It flickered in his hand, illuminating a ghostly appearance.

Looking at him, Jim didn't like what he had created. He wanted to kill the ugliness that stood before him. Seeing Kent now strangely reminded him of himself when he was a kid. The look in his eyes, beaten, scared, flinched at every arm movement. A hurt hung around his neck for all to see. Forever marked with inward pain. Yes, it made him sick. He wanted to kill it. He did not want to be reminded of what he was capable of.

Kent stared at him with red-rimmed eyes. They looked like nocturnal eyes of a barn rat, the kind he remembered that ran rampant on the chicken farm his foster dad Jerry managed—just a hint of glowing eyes and then vanishing into the night. But this rat did not vanish. He stood slumped, with all the essence of his crimes born on his face.

Jim walked over to the table and sat down on a green duffel bag. He opened it and pulled a pair of scissors from his bag, a pair of clippers, a razor, shaving cream, a comb, a mirror, a pair of tan slacks, a dark brown button-up shirt, white tube socks, simulated leather shoes that buckled. The clothes and shoes were far from new. *Second hand at best*, Kent thought. But it had been a long time since he had worn shoes and he eyed them wantonly.

Jim sat the small oval mirror in the center of the table. It stood there reflecting the bare white concrete wall it faced. Kent stared at it, afraid to move, afraid the mirror might capture his reflection. Scared he would see himself, see how horrid he had really become. He didn't want to look into the eyes of a monster, and have those eyes belong to him. He looked away.

Jim motioned for him to sit. Kent walked slowly, his eyes sinking down like lead fishing weights in water, his feet scooting in small steps, his wild locks of hair bouncing on his head and about his face. He wilted in the chair, obedient, unsure, eyes darting, but not meeting the image now staring back at him in the mirror.

"Look," Jim said. He pushed the mirror in front of him. "Look at yourself...look at what you've become." Jim adjusted the mirror for the most accurate view of the image before him. "Look, goddamn it...look at who you are!"

Kent's eyes lifted reluctantly to the reflection of the mirror. The reflection turned back an incredulous stare. His face chalky white, his cheeks drawn, his shoulders slumped. His brows furrowed, his eyes squinted, he touched the ends of his shoulder length hair. He ran a finger down his pasty white cheek. He grimaced, his face instantly doused in turmoil. His diminished appearance sickened him, as it did Jim, though for different reasons. He jerked his hands up in front of his face, not wanting to see anymore, horrified at who he had become. He prayed at that moment he would be struck with blindness. He no longer knew the haggard aged man in the small mirror, but the image he saw was him.

Jim slapped the back of Kent's head. "Now you see yourself, Kent Jackson, now you see yourself for what you really are...a filthy fucking animal." Jim paused and asked him again, as he raised his chin to the mirror, "Do you see him?"

"You did this to me!" Kent screamed suddenly. "I'm not him." He strained his body forward, in an uncontrolled motion, tears streaming down his ghostly white cheeks. His mouth wrinkled as he spat out the words. He looked up accusingly, gripping the mirror in his hands, and said with a more controlled but shacky voice, "You did this to me."

"No," Jim shot back. "You did this to yourself." Jim pulled him by the beard directly in front of the mirror. "This…this." Jim pointed toward the mirror. "This is of your own doing. You made that man reflected there…you!" Jim paused for a moment, thinking, then spoke again. "When you decided to leave my wife to die on that wretched God-forsaken road, you made your deal with the devil, you…you fucking ass. And now you must lay with him, in his nasty diseased bed for the rest of your goddamn life."

Kent was taken aback by Jim's torrent of anger. Rarely had he talked when he came, nor stayed long. His mind was numb, and though he tried to focus, he couldn't think of why he was there, and what he was doing. He could barely think at all. But one thing did come to his mind very clearly: *surely, tonight he would die*. His heart sank at the prospect.

For a moment he thought about the man who he was sure Jim had killed. He could still see his rounded face peering in through the French doors. Their eyes met as he sat tied to the chair. He recognized the changed expression. Something wasn't quite right and then he knew and started backing away slowly, not sure at first, but then knowing what he saw. He faded from his view, never seeing him again.

That was probably the last time anyone saw him alive, except for Kent, he thought. Nauseated at this line of thinking, and a little worried, he tried to engage Jim in conversation. "What is this for? Why…"

"Cut your hair and that shit growing on your face!" Jim screamed.

Kent finally looked up at Jim from the mirror and nodded his head.

An hour later, Kent sat looking as if he was of the world again. Around him small piles of hair lay clumped. His face was shaved smooth and his hair was neatly cropped into short locks. Not as neat as a bought haircut, but tidy just the same.

Kent looked into the mirror. He almost looked liked the person he nearly was fourteen months before. But, he knew he wasn't. He had changed. And if he ever left this solemn pit, he would be changed for the rest of his life. No matter what aesthetic appearance he might possess now or later, no amount could erase or hide what lay beneath the surface, hidden. He had walked in the valley of the shadow of death, and lived, but barely. But it had a price. Inside him lay the wasted remnants of a life that had walked through a long dark forest of horrors, but would never forget what he saw there, that is if he lived.

Jim thrust the clothes and shoes toward him. "Put them on," he said.

"Why? What's happening?" Kent said. His voice now agitated, his mind confused, not sure what the near future held in store for him. Frightened...very frightened, frightened that soon he would be dead.

"Just put them on," Jim said again, more angry this time. "My patience is wearing thin."

Kent did what he said. And after about ten minutes, he stood fully dressed in front of him.

"You clean up real pretty," Jim said. Then pulled out a black hood from the green bag and a roll of Duct tape.

Kent stared at it, face filling with distress, all the uneasiness and reservation swelling up inside him, bulging at his throat, until he thought he could take it no more, and his throat would just explode from the knot in it. *So this is the way it's going to end, with a hood over my head, in complete utter darkness. Suffocating, as each inhaling breath sucks in the cloth of the hood into my mouth. Waiting, my breath quicker, my body no longer satisfied with the inadequate amount of oxygen. Waiting in the dark shadow, for what could come, for perhaps a bullet to smash my temple, or a quick hastily prepared noose to be slung around my neck and jerked up to the top of some oak beam. Or maybe a long sharp knife, unexpectedly thrust into my chest.*

*Maybe in just a few short seconds I will be sprawled out on the ground, somewhere, who knows where, dying. Dying an awful death, a death that has no boundaries of pain. Muffled screams will be escaping from behind my indignant death hood. The last thing I will see is the horror of eternal darkness as I open my eyes. And then nothing. I won't exist.*

His thoughts nauseated him to the point of nearly vomiting. And now more than anything he wanted to live. He figured that he probably wanted to live more than anyone else in the world.

"No, I will not do it...I will not put the hood on," Kent said. "I will not die this way."

"You will," Jim shot back.

Before Kent had time to respond, Jim grabbed him by his newly-cropped hair and thrust him down to the concrete floor bouncing his nose off the floor. Not enough to break it, but just enough to send a message—don't say a word again. Kent had saw a blinding light when his head hit the floor, and now it was full of fog and confusion. Almost a split second after, he felt an agonizing pain in his back, but not an ordinary pain, a lightning bolt perhaps. It plowed through his back, cutting up his spine. His muscles tensed and his body twitched and then grew numb. *The stun gun*, Kent thought, as he lay there paralyzed.

He watched helplessly as the black hood descended over his head. He felt his arms being pulled behind his back and then the sick ripping sounds of Duct tape being pulled off the roll and wound tightly around his wrists. "Don't kill me," Kent said, his voice reduced to a raspy whisper. His breath was quick now, in short bursts, as he felt the hood press tightly against his face. It was almost enough to be suffocating, but not enough to kill him.

"I'm sorry I killed her, I'm sorry…please don't kill me. I've—"

"Shut your rat hole up, you lying sack of shit. You know good and goddamn well you're just worried about your worthless skin! Listen, damn you, if you're going to die, then you're going to die. You have no choice in the matter, so shut the fuck up."

Jim lifted him up on his feet, anger dripping from his terse face. Kent stood there whimpering, and he felt like fainting. He could barely suck enough air down into his lungs. His arms were drawn tightly back, causing excruciating pain with each breath. The pain was pointed in his back, where the bolt of electricity had discharged and his head was confused, foggy, everything now around him viewed in dream-like quality. A cold sweat broke out on his back and forehead. Then he fell face forward, headfirst onto the hard cold concrete floor. All thoughts disappeared, all worry gone; there was nothing for a few moments but darkness.

# Chapter 31

Kent woke up to a throbbing head. He pried his eyes open, but saw nothing. For a moment he believed that he had awoken in the cellar and the light was off. But he remembered the hood, it now rubbing gently on his face. His body vibrated, and then he heard the drone of a motor. He felt with his hands, which were still taped behind him. Cloth, thin cloth, like that found in an automobile, any automobile. *Yes*, he thought, *he was in a car*. He wondered if Jim was driving, but he dared not speak.

About a half hour later the vehicle came to a stop on a deserted dirt road. The fingernail moon hung overhead in the sky. Jim got out of the truck and walked around to Jim's side and opened the door and pulled Kent out. Jim yanked the hood off Kent's head and they faced each other.

Jim pulled out his Old Timer pocketknife. And with the long blade, flat and sloped on the end, what in this part of the world, farmers called a "nutter." They called it that because it is perfect for slicing into testicles, any kind of testicles, swine or cattle. Jim supposed it could even do humans if need be, the balls or the throat. *If need be.* Kent looked at the blade and grimaced, and braced himself for the sudden thrash that would come piercing through the darkness across his neck or would it be worse. Would he leave him bleeding slowly to death between his legs on a deserted country road?

Kent had seen the blade in his hand, and had little doubt of its intended purpose. Already his throat began to ache. He could feel the cold steel making a sickening slice across his skin, opening up a swollen artery. He could imagine the gush of blood that would soak his shirt.

Jim spun him around violently and gripped the knife firmly in his hand. He pressed it suddenly against Kent's throat and paused. Then spoke with slow cruel precision.

"I told you one time that there was a fate worse than death. Well now, you will soon see what that is." Jim smiled. "Fourteen months in purgatory may seem like a long time, perhaps a tall price to pay. But, I guarantee you will look back on it and see that it was nothing compared to the price you will pay now." Kent flinched with fear as Jim swung the knife around with his arms. "You may ask yourself why, why all of this trouble for one man. But, to me you are you are not a man, but a devil, a demon that put your evil dirty finger on my family, on my wife, ripping all that we knew apart—my family goddamn it. And you thought you would get away with it too. If left to the police you probably would have. Oh yes, you would have. But my conscience wouldn't stand for it, wouldn't allow it."

Jim pressed the knife hard against Kent's throat. His other hand pulled his head backward by the hair. His eye twitched as the cool wind of fall whipped around his rigid body. Kent stood limp against him. He had to cough but held it back, afraid that the sudden surge would be just enough to penetrate his skin. Jim leaned into his ear and began to speak again. "You took from me the only thin veil that stood between me and humanity. You awoke me from my slumber…and now you have to deal with it. With a vengeance, it snatched you up from the comfort of the earth and buried you in her belly. All the hatred of my tortured youth, bulging at the seams, tearing when you killed her, is now concentrated on you. You are the whipping boy for my past and my present. It is you that will know my form of justice. No matter how uncommon, it is a monument to the truth, for the love I have for the one you so carelessly took from me. Believe me, believe me and hear me well. You, Kent Jackson, have only sampled my vengeance. Now you will fully taste it. It will be crammed into your mouth. You will scream for mercy. Do you hear me? Scream for it. The final taste I will savor, it will be sweet like honey to me, but sour, spoiled and pungent like vinegar to you and I hope you choke on it."

Jim jerked his head back hard, pressed the tip of the knife to the jugular on the side of his neck. "Now we will act out the final scene of this play." Then he released his hair and pulled the knife from his throat. And then with one quick thrust he slashed the knife upward between Kent's bound hands, slicing the tape between them and shoved Kent into the gravel on the side of the road. After a moment, Kent looked up in time to see Jim's feet disappear into the truck. He heard the door slam and then he drove off. He watched his taillights until they disappeared in the distance.

Kent sat up and looked around him. He bunched gravel and rocks in his hands and squeezed them tightly and then released his clenched fists, the contents flowing between his fingers and palm. He was thinking. Thinking about Jim's words.

He pulled some long strands of grass from the side of the road. Such simple things defied reality, his reality. Could he really be free? He stood up and looked around, unbelieving. The air smelled sweet, the dew was on the grass. He began walking down a dirt road. Crop fields surrounded it on both sides. He looked at his watch but couldn't read it. It was too dark.

He walked in the near moonless night. The gentle sweet wind on his face. This was all surreal, yet it reminded him of simpler times. A time when he was a boy, his mother a homemaker and his dad a preacher at the First Lakewood City Baptist Church and they all lived in the country or what then was the country, now it was full of subdivisions. *But that was a better time*, he thought, *and a simple life, but gone now*.

His mom was dead, almost four years now, from breast cancer. His dad, a hollow seventy-one-year-old man, lived alone, beaten by this old world and ready to find another. He had a stroke soon after his mother had passed, and he got around with the help of a walker now, but he still could live by himself, though he was a little cloudy in the head. Thank God for his youngest sister, who had taken care of him so diligently all this time. *What she must think of me*, he wondered. It probably was not good, whatever she thought.

He had become estranged from his parents since he graduated from college. They just didn't see life the same. But now, Kent saw it differently. He did now see some of it like they did. They weren't as strange as he had once thought, backward and full of bullshit. Friends, family and church—those were what was real. He had been so sure at one time, so sure, but now he was unsure of everything. His perspective had changed...*a year of seclusion will do that*, he thought. He hung his head for a long while as he walked, images of his mom and dad running through his head. Every once in a while he would display a smile or a frown, maybe stop for a moment and shake his head, but then he would start walking again. The dirt road dead-ended at a paved road that ran left and right of it. He turned left and walked, not coming across one car.

His thoughts turned to Lisa and his children: Samantha and David. Thinking about them made his heart leap in his chest. He couldn't wait to see them. His pace quickened, as he said to himself in a whisper, "Yes, home, I've got to get home."

The green sign hung by a single bolt. It waffled back and forth in the light cool breeze. Shotgun pellets had peppered it pretty good, but he could put together enough letters to make out the town names. Clever, with an arrow pointed ahead and the word Republic pointed back from which he had come.

The towns meant little to him. He had no idea where he was and no idea how long it had taken him to get there.

About twenty minutes later a small gas station appeared in the distance. It was an old kind that didn't come with a delicatessen selling Krispy Cremes or foot longs roasting. No, this gas station probably did two things: fix cars and sell gas. And there was some doubt in his head that it probably did this anymore. The archaic building seemed to be near ruined, but still there were fresh signs of oil as he passed the pumps and the electric was still on.

As he came closer to the part of the building where you went in to pay, he could see through its slanted hut style windows it was closed. He inspected the door and window facing the pump and noticed advertisements. He glanced over one taped loosely to the door, Aurora Assembly of God Chili Cookoff, October 29th it read. He thought that it was probably close to that date now. He looked up and saw the faded Seven-Up clock on the wall; it read two forty-seven. He ran a finger down more advertisements, and there next to the one that talked about a turkey shoot being held at Nixa was the word Missouri. He was in Missouri.

There was a payphone nearby and Kent tried calling Lisa collect, but the operator said the number had been disconnected. That puzzled him, but he didn't think too much about it. After all, she could have had it disconnected for about anything. A crank caller or who knows what.

Kent kept on walking, heading west. He had been in Missouri before and knew something about it. He would take Route 60, through Aurora, Monette and Neosho, Missouri and then into Oklahoma, past Fairland, to old Route 66 at Afton and then to Vinita, and then south down through Muskogee and then southwest to home, Lakewood City.

# Chapter 32

It took him nearly three days to find his way back to Lakewood City, Oklahoma. He had hitched and walked and ate what he could find in trash cans at fast food restaurants. He had been tempted several times to run to the police and tell them everything, but he decided he needed time to put things together, to do it right, if he did it at all. The more he thought about turning in Jim Hall, the more he thought Jim would raise suspicions about him killing Tina Hall and he didn't want to get in trouble for that. *Yeah, Jim had this figured out all right*, he thought, *down to a tee, to a science. It was a catch 22, tell on me and I'll tell on you.*

More than anything, though, he just wanted to put things behind him. After all, what he had been through was pretty incredible. To be kidnapped by your neighbor for a year—that just doesn't happen every day. Right now, he just wanted to get back to his family, to see Lisa, to feel her warm body, to hug his kids and tell them that everything will be all right now...that Daddy is home for good, he was really home.

Kent felt good about being back. He had grown up around Lakewood City, and had lived near or in it most of his life. He knew this city like the back of his hand. His pace picked up and he began to smile just on the outskirts. It was almost dawn.

From the highway he followed Grande Avenue, which ran the length of the city parallel to State Route 4. He followed it for nearly an hour and a half on foot until he reached Coventry Road. He didn't want to take Coventry, but it was the quickest way home.

Pressing one foot in front of the other, he stared ahead at the spot where it all began—that event that seemed like an eternity ago—where he killed Tina Hall. It was a cool early morning, almost 7:45 a.m. His clothes thin let the stiff breeze pass through. It chilled him to the bone, but it felt good to be outside. His eyes looked into the inky horizon ahead of him as the sun began to rise up over his shoulder, casting a red glare highlighting the sky around him. It was a beautiful Oklahoma morning, and he never felt so much alive.

He thought about the Kent Jackson who had driven down this road that fateful evening. That man was a confident, selfish, self-serving asshole, but now he was a thin shell of that man. *A different man*, he thought, *a man given a second chance.*

He walked up Winding Creek Drive. He could see his house now. His heart began to pick up. He could feel it pounding away inside of his chest. He broke into a jog and then a dead heat run, his voice almost audible now with each breath, calling their names: "Lisa, Samantha, David…Lisa, Samantha, David…Lisa, Samantha, David."

The mantra continued until he reached the sidewalk in front of his house. He stepped into the front yard and eased a single word out of his mouth as he looked up past the green front door with the big brass knocker to the bedroom windows. "Home," he said. The word was sweet and he had said it loud. He was home and everything would be all right.

In his mind he replayed what he thought of as the coming home scene, over and over. This was one of his favorite fantasies when he was locked in the cellar. Getting to come home, to see his family, to sleep with his wife, to hear their warm kind words of affection. He pictured her in his mind, how he remembered her. *Would she look the same? No, she would look better?*

He took a deep breath and tried the door, but it was locked. He took the brass knocker in his hand and knocked it against the door. But there was no answer. He knocked again, this time harder.

*Come on. Come on. Come on.*

He felt a small acorn begin to form in his throat, waiting there in anticipation. Finally the door slowly opened and there behind it stood Lisa, in a pink floral print bathrobe and slippers. Her eyes were wide and unbelieving as she stared at him. She squinted thinking she was seeing somebody that looked a lot like her ex-husband. But, surely it wasn't him, she thought. *Maybe it is just somebody lost, asking for directions, somebody selling something that just looks like him, anybody…anybody at all, but God, don't let it be him.* But it was, she knew it by the way he stood there looking at her, it was Kent.

"Lisa…Lisa," he said. Tears streamed down his eyes. "Oh God, Lisa, I missed you." He stepped inside the door and took her into his arms and hugged her tightly. His eyes shut, his hands pressed her limp body against his. Tears swelled up in his eyes and landed on her shoulder. "I missed you so much. I love you," he whispered, "I love you."

He loved her more now than anything he had ever loved anything, more than life itself. A thousand thoughts of a new life with her and the kids passed through his head. A smile began spreading across his face. *Home,* he thought, *I've made it home.* He hugged her more tightly and began to realize that Lisa's body was totally lax and she had not said a word.

Slowly he opened his eyes to tell her again that he loved her that he missed her, how things would be different now and what happened to him and where he had been. His chin nested between her neck and shoulder. His eyes opened fully now, as he began to speak to her, but they caught on something and stilled his tongue. It took a long time for it to register, to focus, for this important piece of information to his brain. Despite seeing, he couldn't believe. He looked up and there before him, standing near the stairway, was Jim Hall. His mind screamed in disbelief, but he uttered not a word. His tongue had swelled over the horror of the image. The image of him had killed the sweet serenity of the moment, that serenity he realized, though, must only be taking place in his mind. Something was wrong.

His face grimaced. A sharp pain gripped him around the head like a spiked metal clamp. He felt a torrid heartbeat in his eyes. They pulsated wildly in their sockets flashing images of Jim, his children standing nearby, with Samantha and David next to him.

He wondered what Jim was doing in his house with pajamas on, and why his kids were there. And that is when he noticed a stinging in his shoulders, like angry bees. It was Lisa, pushing against him, her long nails embedded in his shoulders. Finally he released her and she broke free of his embrace and stepped back away from him filled with shock and surprise. Kent saw her face fill with contempt and disgust as she looked at him. "How dare you," she said. "How dare you come back here after what you've done."

He didn't hear anything she said, her mouth moved in surreal fashion, but nothing came to life in his ears. A burning pit exploded in his stomach. Confusion began filling his mind, much like a chemical reaction gone out of control. He felt like fainting, but fought off the urge to. He looked at Jim. Jim smirked at him.

"Samantha! David!" He cried their names out. "I'm home," he yelled. They looked at him blankly, not rushing forward into his warm and waiting arms that he had spread open.

This was not at all like he had imagined or dreamed of so many times. No, this was far from fantasy, they stood unmoving, no smiles crept over their faces, no happiness filled their eyes. Only the mild creep of contempt crossed their faces—a look of disgust filled their eyes full, as they stared at him gangly holding open his arms in his filthy secondhand clothing.

Kent's eyes shifted back to Lisa. Her lips were pressed tightly together, eyes cast in hard stone. Now he saw it, or rather the lack of it. No love showed in her, there was no recognition that she missed him, nothing.

"What's wrong with you?" he screamed. "What's wrong with all of you?" He paused for a moment.

No one answered. They just stared at him.

"What is he doing here?" He pointed a dirty finger toward Jim, while looking at Lisa, raving feverishly at her. He waited for them to answer, his chest heaving, waiting for the reason, waiting to hear the words he feared.

"Are you fucking him now, is that the deal? Is that it?" His eyes searched Lisa for an answer, but none was offered.

"Well that's the pot calling the kettle black," Lisa said.

"Yeah right, let me tell you what your sleep-over-fuck-friend has been up to, you goddamn whore. While you two have been playing house, Jim boy here has had me locked down in a dirty ass cellar. You know that?" Kent clinched his fist while he talked and most of his words came through clinched teeth. He was determined to tell everything he could, no matter how ridiculous it might sound, how so very improbable, maybe even impossible. "Don't you know what this sick bastard has done," he said. The words were sharp but quieter now, slippery and pointed like a dangerous snake. But still, Jim stood there with a "what are you talking about" poker face.

"He kidnapped me and put me in a cellar. And you...and you know what else he did, he killed a guy...yeah, killed him in cold blood right outside of his house on the lake while I was tied to a chair."

The entire time Kent made large wild exaggerated hand gestures, pointing at Jim and smiling as if he was telling a little known secret that everyone was eagerly waiting to hear.

"Then he locked me down in that goddamn cellar for a year, for a whole freakin' year. And, and—"

He stopped and began to look into each one of their eyes, Lisa, his son, his daughter. They were blank, as if listening but unbelieving.

Finally Lisa spoke. "Kent, how could you do all this, I...I can't believe I was married to you...you're nothing but a liar and a killer." She shook her head and turned her face from him.

"What do you mean?" He was shocked by her words. *How did she know?*

"You know very well what I mean…you killed his wife." Lisa pointed at Jim.

Kent felt small now, miniature even, in front of her and the kids. He didn't know what to say. He had nothing to hide behind. He wondered how she knew and what she knew. But still, he gathered himself, hoping to work a miracle.

"Did he tell you that…are you going to believe this liar?" Kent pointed accusingly at Jim. "This is what he wants you to believe, what he wants you to think, so he can have you for himself…for God's sake, Lisa, open your eyes."

She looked at him grimly, and he was unaware she possessed the smoking gun. She watched him intently as he shifted his feet back and forth, waiting for the verdict. And then she spoke.

"It was not Jim who told me about you killing his wife."

"No, well then who? Please tell who could convince you that your husband of sixteen years killed our neighbor."

"Detective Trower, that's who."

The words she spoke cut through the air like a knife, and he felt his stomach and heart and the rest of his hidden internal organs deflated. It felt like the end of the road, the end of his life. He knew to the full extent at what lengths Jim Hall had gone to in order to exact his revenge. He knew at this very moment, that he would never be free again.

"I identified your bloody clothes and all the forensic tests came back positive…you…you're a monster, why did you have to leave her? Why couldn't you have done something for her at least?"

Kent looked at her, seemingly bewildered. *Yes, why didn't he?* He knew all too damn well why he didn't—to save his skin. But now he needed Lisa, he couldn't face another incarceration without her.

Kent ran to her, kneeling in front of her. "Lisa, Lisa, look at me." He tried to get her to look at him, but she refused. "Don't you see, don't you see what's going on?" His eyes pleaded with her to believe him.

"It's me, Lisa, Kent…Kent!" He looked for some previous recognition of her love for him, but found none. But still he tried to speak some magic that would undo the nightmare that was unfolding. "I love you. You can believe me…please…please believe me…I will be here for you now."

David, his twelve-year-old son stared at him and said, "Dad, did you kill Mrs. Hall down the street like they say?"

The words from his son stopped him forcefully, like a fly in honey and silence pursued his lips—a deafening silence, the kind that screams guilt. He didn't know quite what to say. He was sure now he looked quite like every bit the heap of disappointment he felt for his own self. He wanted to run now, run like a coward out the door. In a way this was worse than being in the cellar, at least there he didn't have real accusers. No, those in the cellar were just ghosts in his head. But, he knew he finally had to give it up and just come clean with it, to *own up to your shortcomings* as his father liked to say.

"I, ahh…I didn't mean to, David. It was an accident, well, an accident at first. But, your dad made a wrong decision and Mrs. Hall died as a consequence. I—" Jim couldn't really say anymore—couldn't go on. He broke down crying. It was a devastating omission.

His answer was soaked with guilt. He turned to Jim, not realizing how pathetic he looked, how quite insane they all thought he was. A look from Lisa and he could tell that she probably wondered if he hadn't always been. Suddenly he had a craving to have a gun in his hand. He wished he had one. If only he had a gun right now, he would shoot that devil Jim Hall in the head and then end it right here, right here in front of them all. It would be cure to his gnawing inward flailing pain.

There was a long period of silence. And finally, Kent said to Jim. "What are you doing here in my house…what's going on?"

"I live here," Jim said.

"Jim and I were married this year," Lisa said. "He and his children live here now."

"How could you do that, Lisa, goddamn it, how could you do that…after all I've been through, I'm your husband. I thought you would be here for me. Can't you see that he's a criminal, damn it, a criminal!" Kent screamed.

"How can you stand there and lie and tell these wild stories…you're the only criminal I see. You're wanted by the police! Don't you understand that!" Lisa screamed back. She jabbed her finger in the air punctuating each word she spoke. Kent felt it as if she were actually stabbing his chest with it. "You're pathetic, you're sick…you sick bastard, after you left here with some slut and then we find all this out about Tina. We never knew you, no…we never knew you at all…you cruel bastard."

"Honey, please, haven't you heard what I have told you," he said.

"Don't you call me that, don't you say anything else…just get out!"

"He killed somebody for God's sake, Lisa. Lisa. Listen to me." Kent pointed accusingly toward Jim. "He drugged me and made me write that letter to you. He locked me up for a year. And then—"

"Daddy, stop it, stop it," Samantha screamed, "you're scaring me... please, Dad."

He fell silent and looked at her and at them. They weren't listening and they didn't believe him. He began to wonder at that very moment if anyone would.

*That crazy fuck Jim Hall had them right where he wanted them. He has me right where he wants me. He has manipulated this whole fucking thing.*

The urge now to kill that devil in front of him was stronger than ever. Looking at him he could visually see his head explode, as he pulled the trigger.

"Don't you see?" He abruptly turned to his kids and then to Lisa again, hoping they would begin to believe him. "Don't you see what kind of game he's played here...don't you see?"

Janie began crying out loud and ran into her father's arms for comfort. She spoke in sobs. "I don't want to see him anymore, Daddy, I don't...he killed my mom...please, Daddy, make him leave."

"It's okay, babe, it's okay," Jim told his daughter trying to reassure her, "he's very confused."

"Confused...confused!" Kent shouted. "Goddamn it if I'm confused. You're the confused one! You're the one with serious problems I can assure you."

They all stared at him, like he was some sort of pitiful lumbering wounded giant, breathing its last breath, and they were waiting for him to fall in an untidy heap.

Lisa had heard about all she could take. "Kent, I want you to get out, get out now! I'm calling the police, so you better—"

Kent grabbed a hold of her arms and held her close, while Jim let the scene unfold, reserved, poised ready to pounce. He waited for the death blow. This was better than anything he could have ever imagined.

"Honey, please listen," he said, pulling her toward him, "it will be better this time. I will forget about all this. You and me, the kids, we'll take a long vacation, we'll take time to clear our heads and start new. I've been—"

Lisa stared up at him, like he was some sort of robot that wouldn't shut off, like a bad dream that wouldn't end. She put her hands over her ear, thinking that if she heard one more word out of his mouth she would go mad.

"Get your hands off me!" she yelled. Kent braced her more tightly. "You know you still love me, you know it, say it, say it. His voice was tight with desperation. He groped her as if at this very minute she would come to realize she wanted him, that he was the only husband she could possibly have. He stared at her with ominous ravaging eyes and shook her. Her head whipped back and forth. He yelled into her face, "This is my house, I belong here! You are my wife and these are my kids and you will stay with me."

She tried to pull free from him, but he jerked her back close, and before he could put his arms around her, she slipped and fell to the ground.

"Mooooom," David screamed and ran to her.

Jim now came to life. *The final act*, he thought. He grabbed Kent by his neck, and put him in a chokehold and forced him out the door.

Lisa winced in pain as she got up and ran to the kitchen for the phone. Janie and Samantha ran after her. Kevie looked on in horror through his young eyes. It was a scene he thought for sure he would never forget. David watched as Jim took his dad outside and closed the door behind them.

He held Kent tightly around the throat, the crook of his forearm and bicep choking off his air. Kent's arms flailed in the air, but it did no good. Jim held him tight. He pulled his head back forcefully, his ear now less than an inch away. Jim turned and looked at the front door to make sure that nobody had opened it. He leaned his face forward into Kent's ear and whispered, as if telling him a secret that he wanted no one to know. "Now you see, don't you?" Jim waited for a response, but knew he wouldn't get one. "You feel it…don't you…it hurts deep, doesn't it? So deep that no one…no one thing can remove it."

Jim's voice was soft, smooth, melodic, surreal. It felt like a butterfly gently fluttering in Kent's ear, brushing bitter poison into his skin, he absorbing it, and it spreading throughout his body carried by the red rivers. Every callous word slowly poisoned, the paralysis it caused eternal.

The words were penetrating, the kind that you heard only once in a lifetime, the kind that rang right up there with, "Your wife's been killed in an automobile accident" or "I'm sorry, you only have one month to live." The words settled in deep and festered, intransigent to all forces that would try to remove them.

"Listen now," Jim spoke quietly. His voice was dry and it crackled. "I told you, how many times did I tell you…that I would take from you, what you took from me. Didn't I?" Jim tightened his grip around his throat. "Didn't I?" he said again. Kent moaned, then gagged and tried to cough. He couldn't. Jim had him clinched tight. He felt dizzy and his breath became struggled gasps.

"And now I have it," Jim said, his voice growing ever so more quietly, still even. "I have Lisa. I sleep with her." Kent tried to lunge from his grasp, but

Jim held him tightly, then drew him closer and put his mouth in Kent's ear again and whispered, "She carries my baby. She carries a son."

The words leaped down through Kent's head. They burned his throat, his stomach, and through the flesh of his feet. He tried not to believe, but what Jim said, he had reason to say it. Jim was too pure with hate for it not to be true. *And with that*, he thought, *the final nail had been driven.*

They both heard sirens far off in the distance and the mechanical pieces of the door behind them began to work.

"This is my justice," Jim quickly whispered. "Accept it. No matter how uncommon, it is what you have earned, what you deserve. It's done. I took what you took from me. I've killed your life." And with those words he released him, and Kent fell to the ground trying to catch his breath.

Lisa opened the door behind them. "The police are on their way," she said, trying to catch her breath.

Kent rose up on his feet, looking in the direction he heard the distant sirens, but saw nothing. He turned for a moment and looked at Lisa and mouthed the words *I love you*, then fled from the yard and down the street toward the woods that began at the cul-de-sac at the end of Winding Creek Drive. And then, he was gone.

# Chapter 33

Detective Trower drummed his fingers on the kitchen table nervously. Jim and Lisa stared at him, waiting for what he was about to say. Finally, with a strained voice he said, "We've looked for him for three days straight now…it's been tough going, back in some of the low land areas where its soggy. We lost his trail about two days ago. We think he made it to his dad's house, we're not for sure, the old man can't talk very well."

Jim looked at Lisa. She gave him a worried look back.

"Do you think you'll catch him?" Lisa asked.

"Oh we'll get him, it's just a matter of when, but we'll get him."

"Do you think he'll try to come back here?"

"No, I don't expect that. In fact, I think he is probably a long ways away from here by now. Maybe even Texas, trying to cross the border." Trower smiled and displayed a reassuring look. Lisa stared back, unsure. "Don't worry," Trower said as he stood up from the table, "we'll get him. I'll let you know."

Jim walked the detective to the door. And they shook hands. He watched him drive away, while standing in the doorway thinking. He wanted to believe that they would catch him. But he wasn't sure. Lisa came up behind him and gave him a hug. He felt her round tummy on his back. He smiled. He turned to her and kissed.

"I love you," he said.

"I love you too."

"Quit worrying, it'll work out."

"Yeah, I suppose you're right. You always make me feel better, you always have the right words," he said. She smiled. He hugged her and patted her back gently, his eyes never leaving the open door. And with a hand, as if swatting a fly, he shut it.

# Chapter 34

Kent crawled in through the window, his muddy shoes staining the white walls. His old room looked the same after all these years. Tiny trophies from little league on the dresser, a high school diploma, yellowed now, in a frame hanging on the wall, in front of the baseball glove, ball and bat wallpaper. His old basketball lay quietly in a chair. Above him, Bruce Lee struck an ominous pose on the wall, fingers jutting out in a martial arts stance, red abrasions across his taunt cheeks. Old tattered comic books piled on his old desk. On top was *Iron Man* and beneath it *Sgt. Rock* and *The Avengers*. A big plus sign with his initials was carved into the desk. In the top spaces were his initials and his old high school girlfriend's initials were etched in the bottom spaces.

The memories of the room flooded him like the deep rich aroma of coffee. He just sat there looking at everything that he used to be, thinking about how different he had become. He wanted to be the boy again he saw in the group baseball picture that was sitting on the dresser, that innocence, that naiveté, the world before him to discover.

He walked past his bedroom door and down the hall. He could hear the Channel 7 KOTE News. He walked slowly, cautiously, not knowing if the police had been here or were there. His dad sat in a chair, hearing aids in both ears, eating a bowl of chili with crackers, in front of him an old copper-colored TV tray. The TV volume was so loud it rattled Kent's own eardrums from where he stood. As he watched his dad eat, memories poured through him like water in a strainer. He'd missed him. He felt a tear trickle out of his eye. What he wouldn't give right now for somehow to go back and play catch with his dad out in the backyard by the old oak tree. He could still hear him say, "Watch out, Kenny, here comes a fast one." And then he would fake a tremendous wind up that would seem like it took an eternity, then release an underhanded slow ball. Dad would just laugh.

The memories faded as his dad went into a coughing spell. Kent watched, afraid he would witness his father's death then and there. But finally he caught his breath and his breathing settled back down into a normal rhythm, dullness in his chest a fading.

Kent said, "I love you," out loud, knowing that he couldn't hear him, but wanting to say it just the same, wanting to feel the words pass through his lips and touch his father. For all to be just like it was when he was kid. No worries, *just Mom's fried chicken, Dad's silly windup and lazy summer days and going down to the creek to fish with his old dog Champ.*

Kent walked back down the hall, wiping tears from his eyes. He opened the closet door and felt around on the shelf above the coats. He noticed his mom's coat was still there waiting for her. He could almost see her round the corner of kitchen on Sunday morning in the wintertime, and opening the door to get her Sunday dress coat.

He felt it. The cold steel, this ancient mechanism that could deliver what he longed for. It was heavy in his hand as he pulled it from the closet. The metal now tarnished, a dull gray and black, but still showing hints of light oil in places. He gripped it in his hand, the barrel thick and long, the handle, carved from bone by his Uncle Cecil, given to his dad an eternity ago. He flipped open the revolver and six empty chambers showed. He reached up and felt around under the hats and gloves and found a box of .38 cartridges and stuffed them in his pocket along with the gun.

He walked to the edge of the living room where his dad was, almost standing in it. He was intently watching an old rerun of *Matlock*. Kent mouthed the words "goodbye." The old man just stared at the box that spit out vivid colors and sounds, not knowing his son was there. But for a brief moment, he'd turned to look at where his son had been standing, feeling as if someone had been watching him, but nobody was there. Kent was gone forever.

# Chapter 35

His thin body slipped effortlessly through the window. There had been a time when it would have not been so easy. But that was a long ago. *Echoes*, he thought, *just echoes of time past, floating like ghosts in my head.*

He crawled quietly, past the Chevy Tahoe and Ford Windstar, to the back door of the house. Suddenly he saw it open. He froze in terror, his heart bolting in his chest. But no one appeared. He slid around to the side of the van and waited, listening, wondering who was there, and if they would find him. The moments inched by.

It was his son David, taking out the trash to the large green dumpster at the end of the garage. He watched him through the tinted windows of the van. *He made a fine boy*, he thought. He felt proud at that moment for some reason—perhaps because he was his father. He wanted to call out to him, to tell him how much he missed him or something like that. But he didn't. Holding his silence like a breath under water, he let the emotion dissipate inside of him, and David went back inside.

It had been nearly three months since he had last seen him. *Already taller*, he thought. That had been the day he found out that Lisa was now Kent's wife, the day he found out he had no more family, the day his life slipped through layers of rock and found a new all-time low in the pit of the earth.

He looked down at his watch; it was nearly 8:00 p.m. He slumped next to the van. It was cold and the smooth concrete floor of the garage was as well. He was used to it though by now. He supposed that living outdoors in the elements had made him like a wild animal. His reflection in the van's dark glass had told him he looked like one.

He had cut a square piece out of an old faded truck trailer tarp and cut a jagged diamond shape in the middle for his head. It served as his coat. He found some old irregular olive green fatigues in a dumpster behind an Army surplus store. He wore them over the pants that Jim had given him in the cellar.

His hair had grown some and was matted together. Under his banes his eyes wielded paranoia at every look. They were now empty without hope, eerily a dull gray—the color of winter sky. His crows' feet around his eyes and lines around his mouth were covered in a light greasy dust, his hands were darkened, jagged long nails outlined in black, packed with filth to their edges. He was no more what he once was.

His hands shook uncontrollably and overwhelming compulsions and paranoia continuously attacked his mind. He anticipated everything with nervous reaction. Rational thoughts ebbed to and from his consciousness like the tide on a sandy shore.

He wondered what his business partners at the firm would think if they could see him now. "They would probably talk about how handsome I was," he said quietly to himself and grinned. He looked around and thought about how good his voice sounded in the garage. He hadn't used it for quite some time and it felt good to hear it, to sound human.

Another hour ticked by. He drifted in and out of dreamless sleep, slumped up against the van. His backside and legs numb from the cold concrete floor. He rubbed his stiff legs and moved them back and forth. He knew soon they would have to work, that his haggard body would need to come to life one last time. He needed them just one more time.

The metal resting now in his hand felt heavy, the bone handle cold. He thought about how impersonal it was as he held it, how pure. It didn't discriminate. It didn't care who used it, whom it was used on or what it was used for. It only obeyed the master's need. He looked at it and thought it beautiful. He drifted again, his last thoughts on how it would serve him.

He awoke with a jerk of his muscles and lurched forward. He looked at his watch, thinking he had slept all night, but it was only ten o'clock. He stood up. His body ached from the cold, his clothes were stiff with frozen dried mud. He walked to the back door and listened. He heard nothing. He took a key from under the mat where he knew it would be and unlocked the door and opened it slowly. One dirty hand gripped the bone-handled .38 tighter as he entered into the kitchen. His eyes were almost dark now, hollow, devoid of future and full of his dead past.

The bottom stairs were dark. He walked softly. His taped mud-caked shoes made dark tracks on the plush cream carpet. He found his way by the soft nightlights sprinkled throughout the house, like little lighthouses directing those who seek food or drink, or the relief of a bathroom in the night.

He heard them upstairs. His breath quickened. Lisa called out to Jim, asking if he had seen her slippers. He answered that they were beside the edge of the bed.

*The devil…the devil's voice knew what to say. He was unyielding in his power and pursuit of him, he was close and he would kill the devil.*

He imagined him, as he had seen him so many times, coming down the cellar stairs.

*The ugly devil, his head upright, his voice bathed in self-righteousness, absolute, cunning, full of contempt. He breathed in life and turned it into hatred,* he thought. *And he was there, upstairs, he could smell the beast—hear him. His black tongue filling the thin air with lies.*

He stood watching the stairway clinching the cold metal in his hand, its weight in his hand reminding him of its importance, its impartiality. He walked to the back of the living room, thinking he would let them go to sleep. He leaned for a moment on the wall, one long index fingernail pecked at the wallpaper gently, with precision.

*No need to hide*, he said to himself, *gonna kill the devil soon.*

A light abruptly flickered on in the stairway, illuminating half the living room. He heard the soft mashing of carpet as pink slippers climbed down the stairs slowly, her body moving effortlessly in a nightgown, her hand gliding along the rail.

For a moment he was caught off guard. He stood there stoically, watching her, she surreal. Her face beautiful, her mouth, her lips. He closed his eyes for a moment, pretending he was still part of her life, and she was still in love with him.

He knew this was the only unselfish act of his whole entire life. He would kill for her now, to save her from the devil that had put her under this hideous spell. He was determined to rescue her from this beast that was born in hell and took the shape of a man. Tonight, Jim Hall would die.

The thought of killing him made him tremble with intoxicating desire. He could already smell the burning gun powder, see the short burst of flame, watch him fall, mortally wounded, *dead, dead, dead. It would be best for Lisa, for the children, for him. Tonight he would send him back to that lake of fire from where he came.*

Lisa switched on the foyer light, half way illuminating him standing there. For a moment she didn't notice him as she turned to walk back to the kitchen. Then their eyes locked onto each other. At first she didn't recognize him, his appearance almost grotesque. He was thinner, face drawn, filthy. His demeanor was morose and dark, though he did not speak.

"What are you—"

"SHHHHHHH." He put a finger to his lips and whispered softly to her. "I need you to stay down here, Lisa…it's the devil I'm after."

He stepped toward her from the shadows. His eyes danced wildly, agitated but empty. He smiled faintly, then it disappeared from his lips. Her eyes fell to the gun clutched in his hand.

"Jim!" she screamed.

"Shut up!" Kent yelled.

Jim leaped from the bed, a copy of Harley's *His Needs, Her Needs* fell into the floor. He could tell by the sound of her voice that something was wrong. The kids already stood in the upstairs hallway as he sprinted past them and down the stairs.

"What's wrong?" he asked, "what is it?" He stood looking at her puzzled for a moment at the bottom of the stairs. Then he stopped talking, like he just saw a rattlesnake ready to strike. Kent stood there, gripping the bone-handled .38. His hand trembled, the gun unsteady as he held it tight, pointing it directly at him.

"Look! Look!" Kent yelled. "Look who's in control now." He pounded his free hand at his chest wildly. "Me, me…now it's me that going to do the telling, you fucker, do you hear me…it's gonna be me!"

Samantha heard her dad downstairs. She ran to Lisa and Jim's bedroom and rummaged through the drawer of her mother's night stand looking for Detective Trower's card that she had told her a number of times was there. She found it and frantically dialed the phone.

Jim held his hands in front of him, showing Kent there was nothing in them, trying to calm him down.

"Kent…pleeeease, just let it go," Lisa pleaded, "don't make this worse than it already is."

Kent ignored her and glared at Jim, as if he was the first man he had seen in a hundred years. "You're going to tell her what you did to me…how very sick you are." His voice trembled as he said the words. Then he erupted abruptly. "Tell her! Tell her!" He screamed the words out spewing them from his mouth. He gripped the gun tighter.

"There's nothing to tell, Kent, you know that and I know that. For some reason you want to hold me accountable for your past mistakes…I don't think that's fair, do you?"

"Don't ask me questions, goddamn it. Do you think I'm here to answer your goddamn fucking questions! You're sadly mistaken, my fucking friend, if you believe that! Sadly mistaken!" Kent's voice grew louder and louder as he swung his arms wildly. With each moment he became more agitated.

Jim took a step forward with arms outstretched, palms up, his milk chocolate pajamas with cream piping brushed coarsely against his skin, every nerve in his body standing on end.

"I can understand why you're upset," Jim said cautiously. He eased one foot in front of the other in small steps. "I suppose I would be upset too if I were in your situation, but—"

"Shut up!" Kent screamed. "Shut up, shut up, shut up. You move one more fucking muscle and I swear, I swear, I will blow a new fucking shithole in you a goddamn foot wide. Now shut your lying devil tongue!"

He held the gun tightly. It shook wildly. Jim watched the end of the barrel. It seemed a foot wide looking down its black throat.

"Now you tell her, you tell her, you sick sadistic fuck, tell her what you did to me!"

Lisa gave Jim a frightened look now and eased herself toward him, despite Kent's warnings not to.

"Please, Kent," Lisa said, "please…I'm the one you're angry at, I'm the one. He didn't do anything. Can't you see that, Kent, can't you see you're confused?"

"Shut up and get away from him, Lisa," Kent screamed. "The devil has taken a holy shit in your mind…get away now!" Kent screamed unintelligibly, the sound of it filled with frustration, like a wild animal with a paw caught in a hunter's trap, screaming at what it would have to do. For a moment he looked down at the floor, thinking, tears streaming from his face, then he suddenly pulled his eyes up from the carpet. "You're dead, Jim Hall, you're dead," he said softly. He took a step forward and pulled back the hammer on the gun. His teeth were clenched, his eyelids turned to slits, his hand now shaking uncontrollably.

Jim shut his eyes and thought of Tina. he saw her waiting for him, standing beautiful floating on a marvelous cloud. She called his name. He heard the loud bark of the gun and waited for a split second, expecting to feel the burning pain in his body and then to pass from this life into death. But he felt nothing, and opened his eyes to see Lisa fall in front of him and land at his feet. He watched her as blood began to spread from under her body turning the color of the cream carpet a bright red. Her mouth opened and closed sporadically, as she gasped for air and choked on the blood that filled her lungs. A haunting hand clinched his ankle for a moment and then it went limp.

Jim dropped down to his knees beside her and turned her over. Her eyes were fixed, her mouth now still. Jim clutched her in his arms and blood gushed from the wound in her chest onto his pajamas as he yelled out her name. She didn't move. Her head fell listlessly to the side. Her eyes stared off blankly at the ceiling. She was dead.

Jim glanced up at Kent. He still held the bone-handled .38. It dangled down from his hand lifelessly by his side. Kent looked at him with horror.

"Lisa," Kent screamed. He wanted to run to her. He took a couple of steps. He waved the gun in the air, motioning for Jim to get away from her. "Why, why…I didn't mean to," he said, "I didn't mean to." He looked at her body, as if he were willing her to get up. Finally he looked at Jim.

"For you? For you? She gave her life for you?" He sobbed uncontrollably for a moment, then raised the gun.

Jim saw Kent's finger press against the trigger. Squinting his eye, forming a slit, Kent took careful aim. Jim stood, and Kent followed him with the gun, its black hole promising to belt out another volley of smoke and fire that would slay him too. He heard the ear-shattering bellow of the gun, this time louder than before. He flinched, ducking his head, expecting to surely fall dead on his wife Lisa that lay mortally wounded before him. Instead, he watched Kent's head jerk back and then forward, as blood splattered the white wall and curtains in front of him. His eyes fluttered briefly as he fell, his mouth gaped apart. His upper body crumpled over his knees, his body lay mangled, violently distorted and then slumped on its side. The bone-handled .38 rested quietly beside him.

Jim watched as Detective Trower walked from the back of the kitchen that adjoined the living room from both ends. He rushed to Lisa's side and took her pulse as uniformed police broke down the front door, their pistols raised. He heard screams fill his ears in this cruel surreal moment, as Lisa's children drifted down the stairs. He held Lisa's hand and patted it gently. He bent down and kissed her cheek and wished as he brushed the hair from her eyes…that he could die too.

# Chapter 36

He sat alone, observing the stirring of winter. The soft gray sky let loose its blankets of snow, the purity of it untouched as it lay on the ground unspoiled. He marveled at its simplicity. The drifts like large white ocean waves, frozen solid before they crest.

He took a long deep breath. Life was different now. He was alone today, left to himself. *That was not particularly good*, he thought, *to be left alone.*

*But the children would be home soon.*

He leaned forward and looked down Winding Creek Drive at his old house. Tina was playing in the yard with Janie and Kevin. They were making a snowman and throwing snowballs. A smile appeared briefly on his face, but faded. He laced the fingers of his hands together and brought them up and leaned on them with his nose. He peered gingerly over them, his vision blurred, the image gone. Nothing there, he breathed uneasily as his eyes cast an icy gaze.

It had ravaged him and left him with nothing. It had pursued him and fed on his soul. He had nothing more to give it, yet it yearned unyielding for him to come, to look upon the undefeated.

He took slow steady breaths, sitting there, his hands now folded resting in his lap, but clinched stiffly to each other. Afraid now perhaps, afraid it would come back for him.

His vengeance now was like a dying ember, laying quietly, restlessly with nothing else to burn, yet seeking everything to devour.

His justice empty, the belly of it ached. The stomach bottomless, it not satisfied. He felt the hunger form in its mouth. Its jaws gaped from its grotesque head, the blood of revenge splattered across its lips and mouth. It matted in its hair and stained its teeth.

He couldn't look at it. He created it and it horrified him. He now realized it would not be satisfied, no matter what he did. It would consume all that it possessed if allowed. For hours it would beg and plead with him not to send it away. Its hunger pangs were loud. It desired for the fires to be stoked and it to be fed.

Jim stared out the window a little while longer and listened to the subtle falling snow. He began to hum a simple tune through his tightly closed lips. It brought him comfort as the late evening began to drift into night.

He picked up the gun he had laying in his lap and let his thoughts turn to Tina.

Printed in the United States
31900LVS00002B/85

9 781591 293682